Rastor

Lawton Rastor, Book 2

SABRINA STARK

CHAPTER 1

I had two guys in the trunk of the sedan and my brother tailing us in a vintage muscle car. The muscle car was mine. The sedan wasn't. Some might call it stealing. Me? I called it justice.

From the sedan's driver's seat, I reached out to crank up the music. The song was alright, but that wasn't the reason for cranking it. The thumping – it was annoying the piss out of me – because it wasn't coming from the speakers.

I glanced over my shoulder. Dumb-asses. What were they planning to do? Jump out at the next stop sign?

Yeah, good luck with that.

In this neighborhood, they wouldn't last five minutes.

It was after midnight and cold as hell. A few hours earlier, those two trunk-buddies had shown up in dark clothes and matching ski masks. They'd tried to kidnap the girl I loved. They'd scared her. They'd hurt her – not bad, but bad enough, because even a little was too damned much.

At the memory, I felt my hands tighten on the steering wheel. They deserved more than a good ass-beating and whatever embarrassment was coming next.

Something in my gut twisted. Tonight, those guys weren't the only ones who'd hurt her. *I'd* hurt her, too. I hadn't meant to. But I had.

I was a monster.

An image of Chloe flashed in my brain. She was nearly naked

and cuffed to a chair. She was shivering with cold and slumped in defeat. *I'd* put her there. *I'd* kept her there. For hours.

I blinked long and hard. Somehow, I'd make it up to her. I just needed the chance. I didn't deserve it. But I'd get it. Or die trying.

Ahead in the deserted street, I spotted a crumpled shopping cart, lying sideways across the pitted pavement. I eased the car around it and kept on going. We were deep in the city now, downtown Detroit, and not the nice part, assuming there was such a thing.

Home sweet home.

Inside my pocket, my cell phone buzzed. I pulled it out and glanced at the display. It was my brother, calling from the car behind me. I turned down the music and answered with a half-hearted, "Hey."

"Pull over," Bishop said.

"Why?"

"Because the dipshits are trying to get out."

I felt a slow, cold smile spread across my face. "Yeah?"

"That's not *good* news," he said.

It was good news to me. But hey, I had my reasons.

Up ahead, I spotted yet another burned-out building. An old neighborhood store? Hard to tell with the place mostly gutted, just like the building beside it, along with dozens of others that we'd passed along the way.

Next to this nearest building was an alley that it shared with the death-trap next door. I took a right turn and pulled deep into the darkened space. In the rear-view mirror, I saw Bishop pulling in behind me. Knowing him, he wouldn't be too happy about it.

I could see why.

An alley wouldn't have been my first choice for whatever was coming next. But hey, at this point, did it matter? If things went to shit, it would serve me right. And as far as Bishop, he could handle himself just fine.

A minute later, he and I were standing outside the sedan's trunk. It was still shut. Looking down, I saw what Bishop meant. They'd been working at a taillight, trying to shove it out. And then what? Signal someone?

I glanced around. No one – and I mean *no one* – in this neighborhood would be coming to their rescue, unless the rescue involved putting them out of their misery. And hey, if that happened, who was I to complain?

At the thought, I almost smiled. Instead, I held out the remote and popped the trunk.

And there they were – two player wannabees wearing a lot less than they'd been wearing earlier. One wore striped boxer shorts. The other wore plain black briefs that looked a few sizes too small. Probably, the guy was hoping to make his package look bigger. Somehow, he seemed the type.

Neither had a shirt. Or shoes. Or their phones. They'd surrendered them an hour earlier, thanks to some not-so-friendly persuasion from me and my brother. But we'd let them keep the other stuff – the gold chains around their necks, the fancy gold watches flashing on their wrists, the rings that glittered on multiple fingers.

What a couple of douchebags.

Lying there, the guys looked up, looking shell-shocked and maybe a little afraid.

Okay, a lot afraid.

Good.

Their hands were tied, but their feet weren't. Probably, they'd been using those feet to kick at the tail lights.

I gave them a good long look. "So, you want out?" I made a show of stepping back. "Be my guest."

The two guys exchanged a glance. Slowly, they sat up and looked around, taking in the destruction around us. After a long moment, the guy in the boxers spoke up. "Is this a trick or something?"

"No trick." I flicked my head toward the darkened street. "Go ahead. Start walking."

He looked toward the street and swallowed. "Walking?" He hesitated. "But, uh, I've got the car, so…"

I gave a small laugh. The sedan? *He* didn't have it. *I* did. And I wasn't giving it up. Not yet.

"No car," I told him. "You want out? You'll be going on foot."

The guy's face was smeared with thin streaks of dried blood, but not as much as there could've been. My fingers flexed. Not as much as there *should* have been.

Fucking Bishop. And here, he claimed to be the voice of reason. Maybe.

But I was in no mood to be reasonable.

Smiling, I pulled the blade from my back pocket and flicked it open. I recalled the knife at Chloe's throat, held there a few hours earlier by the idiot in front of me. *His* knife hadn't been real. But at the time, I didn't know that. And neither did Chloe.

I recalled the sounds of her fear, and the sight of her lying there, helpless while some stranger in black held her down. Even now, the memory of it tore through my heart. I could still hear her whimpers, fake knife or not.

Standing at the trunk, I lifted my own blade. Now *this* thing? It was real. And sharp.

In my old neighborhood, we lived by a code. If someone hit you, you hit them back – the harder the better. I held the blade higher. It glittered in the moonlight, and I felt my smile widen.

Bishop's voice cut across the shadows. "Don't."

I didn't bother to look. "Don't what?"

"Whatever you're thinking. We don't have time for this shit."

Hey, I'd make time.

In the trunk, the guy in the boxers had scrambled backward. When he tried to move further, he bumped his head on the trunk's open lid. "Son-of-a-bitch," he muttered.

Yeah. He was.

Again, I flicked my gaze toward the street. "Go ahead," I told him. "Run."

The guy's gaze shifted to Bishop.

"Don't look at me," Bishop said. "I'm not gonna save you."

It was a lie. If I went too far, he'd be pulling me back, just as he'd done earlier. Not for their sakes, for mine – or at least, that's he'd told me when the dust had settled.

So who was Bishop saving, anyway? Me? I made a scoffing sound. I didn't want to be saved. For one thing, I didn't deserve it.

And for another, I didn't need it.

I leaned toward the guy and said it again, lower, quieter. "Run."

But the guy didn't run. And neither did his friend.

Too bad.

Apparently, they were smarter than they looked. Between the trunk or freedom here, in *this* neighborhood, they were choosing the trunk.

Smart for them. Disappointing for me.

The way it looked, we were back to Plan A.

I gave the guys a hard look. "Alright, here's the deal. You wanna run, this is your chance. It's your *only* chance."

The guys exchanged another glance. Funny, they were awful quiet compared to earlier, when they'd been yelling loud enough to wake the dead. I knew the reason for their new and improved silence.

I glanced around. It was this place. Even idiots like them knew better than to attract the wrong kind of attention in a neighborhood this shitty.

The guy in the black briefs gave a small shudder. From the cold? Or fear? Who knew? Who cared? Maybe he should've worn long johns.

Not my problem.

Brief-guy spoke up. "What if we don't? What then?"

"If you don't run?" I leaned back. "Well, then I've got an offer. And you'd be smart to take it."

In a few short sentences, I laid it out. We were taking them someplace else, someplace safer, but a lot more public. They'd have to explain themselves, probably to a crowd, and later, likely to the cops.

If they so much as whispered Chloe's name – or mine, or Bishop's – well, in that case, they'd be going on another trunk-ride. But this time, I'd be dropping them here, whether they liked it or not.

"So," I told them, "your story had better be good." I made a show of looking around. "Or else."

Soon, I was back behind the wheel. This time, there was no

thumping. I'd used the knife, but not in the way I'd wanted. Instead, I'd cut their ropes and slammed the trunk shut again, leaving them to come up with a decent story for when we stopped next.

Forty minutes later, we were there.

And twenty minutes after that, so was she – Chloe.

The girl I loved, the girl I'd lost.

CHAPTER 2

Hidden in a horde of gawkers, I soaked up the sight of her. She was standing on the opposite side of the crowd, near its outer edges. She was talking to some shaggy-haired guy while the rest of the crowd watched and waited.

In the center of the action was the sedan, along with a couple of cops, who were studying the car's trunk in obvious confusion. The trunk was locked, and the sedan was familiar – to me, anyway.

It was the same car I'd been driving earlier. Now, it was parked between two large tour busses, massive silver things that had provided the perfect cover for the initial setup. None of this was an accident. The busses, along with the sedan, were there by design.

My design.

The sedan was covered in graffiti and thumping like crazy. The thumping – and yeah, some yelling – was coming from the trunk. And that was fine by me.

At this point, they could thump and yell all they wanted. But if they said the wrong thing to the wrong person, there'd be hell to pay. And they damn well knew it. At the thought, I almost smiled. Part of me hoped they *would* talk.

Who knows? It might be fun. Well, not for them, but hey, that wasn't my problem either.

No. My problems were different.

My girl – I needed to win her back.

Hidden in the crowd, I stood there like an idiot, trying like hell not to plow through the mass of bodies and carry her back to my *own* car, and then back to my place, where we could talk, *really* talk. I'd tell her everything, starting from the beginning and ending with the fact that I couldn't live without her.

If I had to, I'd beg. Shit, I'd already begged – not that it had done any good.

The crowd shifted, and I muttered a curse. I couldn't see her. Not anymore.

Something like panic gnawed at my heart. Chloe shouldn't even be here, standing outside in that thin coat of hers and a skimpy uniform that covered nearly nothing. The night was freezing, and I knew firsthand that she'd had a hellish night.

She should be at home under the covers, or better yet, at my place – *not* at work, where even inside the restaurant, she'd be running around taking care of other people, instead of letting *me* take care of *her*.

Still, I was insanely happy to see her here, because it told me something that I'd desperately needed to know.

She was okay.

Thank God.

Scanning the crowd, I pulled the dark hoodie lower over my face and tried like hell to blend. I wanted to see, but didn't want to be seen – not by Chloe, not yet, and not by anyone else who might recognize my face.

Yeah, right.

Wherever I went, almost everyone recognized me. As far as I was concerned, that wasn't a good thing. I turned and looked toward the restaurant. The place was packed. Against the long bank of front windows, I saw faces pressed against the glass, watching the spectacle in the parking lot.

I made a scoffing sound. If they thought this was a spectacle now, they'd be in for a real treat when the trunk was popped.

When I turned back toward the car, I saw something that made me pause. It was Chloe. But this time, she wasn't lost in the crowd. She was well above it, wobbling on the shoulders of the same shaggy-haired guy that she'd been talking to earlier.

Watching, I could hardly breathe. She was so damn close.

To him.

What the hell was she doing?

I stared across the crowd, feeling my muscles tense as I took in the scene. The guy was big, but soft and doughy. Chloe's thighs were wrapped around his naked neck, and his meaty hands were gripping her bare knees, holding her unsteadily as she looked out toward the sedan.

Innocent or not, I didn't like it.

I shifted, trying for a better look. Her crotch *had* to be grinding against the back of his neck. Was that her skirt pressed up against it? Or her panties?

From that stupid-ass smile on his face, I didn't want to speculate.

That fucker.

I shoved the hoodie from my head, trying to get a better sense of what was going on. Did she know that guy? She *had* to. Either that, or she was getting way too friendly with a stranger. What the hell was she thinking?

I looked to Chloe's face, and suddenly, my anger evaporated. Her gaze was locked on the sedan. Her eyes were wide and filled with worry. She lifted a trembling hand and touched her throat. I knew why. She recognized the car. And, from the look in her eyes, she remembered the knife.

Real or not, it had left an impression.

The worry on her face brought everything back home – how scared she must've been and worse, how I'd made things a million times harder by freaking out afterward.

Freaking out – the phrase was too nice for what I'd done.

Desperately, I searched her face, looking for clues on how she was holding up. Was she really okay? With all that makeup, I couldn't be sure. I wanted to wipe it all way and see the face underneath – the *real* face, the face I loved, the face that haunted me, even now.

Something squeezed at my heart. What if after tonight, I never saw that face again?

No. I couldn't let that happen. I *wouldn't* let that happen.

The Shaggy guy called up to her, saying something that I couldn't make out. Chloe looked down and exchanged a few quick words with him, along with an older guy standing nearby. When she looked forward again, I spotted something in her hands that I hadn't noticed before – an unfamiliar cell phone.

Perched on the guy's shoulders, she held out the phone and started taking photos – or maybe video – of the vandalized sedan. For herself? Or for someone else?

Did it matter?

No.

Watching her, I was powerless to move. Not too long ago, I'd held her. She'd been mine – the girl I'd been wanting for years. But like a dumb-ass, I'd lost her in the space of a few short hours.

I'd taken punches that didn't hurt half as bad.

I was still watching when something else caught my eye – movement just behind Shaggy. It was the older guy, edging backward until he stood a couple of paces behind Chloe. After a quick glance around, the guy looked up, zooming in on Chloe's backside.

He gave a sly grin and craned his neck for a closer look. What the hell? Was he looking at her ass? And just how *good* of a look was he getting, anyway?

Before I knew it, I was on the move, jostling my way forward until something made me freeze in my tracks. It was the sight of Chloe, motionless now, looking straight at me.

Our eyes met across the distance. Her lips parted, and she lowered the phone. Around me, the noise of the crowd faded to nothing. Their faces blurred, and time stood still. She looked straight into my eyes.

And then, a split-second later, she was gone.

Son-of-a-bitch.

That idiot had dropped her.

CHAPTER 3

Frantically, I scanned the crowd, looking for any sign of her. One minute she'd been there. And then, she'd been tumbling forward out of sight.

The pavement was hard. The crowd was massive. She was small and underdressed, with bare legs and a thin, short coat that would do nothing to cushion her fall.

I could hardly breathe. Was she okay?

A split-second later, I was on the move, dodging bodies and vehicles as I took the only route not blocked by police tape. Unfortunately, it was the *long* way, around the nearest tour bus. I was halfway past it when a male voice called out from somewhere behind me, "Hey! Aren't you–"

"No!" I called back, and kept on going.

Because right now, I wasn't Lawton Rastor, the guy everyone thought they knew. I was something else, a maniac man on a mission. I *had* to find her. Now.

But when I reached the area where I'd seen her last, there was no sign of her – or of the asshole who'd dropped her. Near the spot where she'd been standing, I spotted the pervert who'd been ogling her ass. I shouldered my way toward him and said, "The girl who fell – where is she?"

At something in my expression, he backed up, hard and fast, bumping into the side of a nearby Chevy. "Where's who?"

"The girl who's *ass* you were looking at." I gave him a hard look.

"My girlfriend. That's who."

The guy swallowed. "Your girlfriend?" He glanced around as if looking for a quick escape.

In this crowd? It wasn't gonna happen. I leaned closer. "Where *is* she?" At this point, his earlier ass-ogling was the least of my concerns. "Tell me," I demanded. "Was she hurt?"

"I, uh, don't think so."

"You don't *think* so?" It wasn't good enough. I *had* to see for myself. "Where'd she go?"

"Uh, the car, I think."

"*Her* car?"

"Yeah. Maybe." He glanced around. "I don't know. The guy's phone got busted up, so…"

Screw the phone. Those things were replaceable. Chloe wasn't. I was already on the move. From our history, I knew exactly where Chloe parked. Unfortunately, it was on the other side of the building, in the employee parking lot.

Shit. While I'd been making my way here, she'd been going in the opposite direction, probably around that other tour bus.

I was just circling the building when I saw what I'd been expecting for a while now – a tow truck, rumbling into the parking lot. Obviously, it had been called to open the sedan's trunk. I didn't even pause. Screw the truck. Screw everything. I *had* to find her.

There was only one problem. When I reached Chloe's car, she wasn't there. I stood, peering through her car-windows, looking for some sign of where she might be.

I saw nothing.

Cursing, I pushed away from her car and looked around. A few car-lengths away, I spotted movement in the back seat of a Lincoln Town Car. A moment later, a rear-window slid down, and a female voice called out from the shadows, "Hey! Lawton!"

Damn it. I couldn't see the face, but I recognized the voice, and it sure as hell wasn't Chloe's.

Sure enough, when the car door swung open, Brittney stepped out, looking like she'd just returned from clubbing. With a sultry smile, she sauntered over and asked, "So, what are *you* doing here?"

In my whole life, I'd never hit a girl. I'd never even come close, not even with my mom, who some might say sorely deserved it for what she'd done to my little sister.

But so help me, I wanted to grab Brittney by that blonde hair of hers and slam her into the nearest car-window until the glass shattered and she stopped moving.

She'd been the one who'd set up that kidnapping. *She'd* been the one who'd given those guys the twisted story that had set me off. *She'd* been the one giving Chloe a hard time from day-one.

If it weren't for Brittney, Chloe would be fine right now. None of this would have happened. And – my heart clenched – Chloe and I would still be together.

Trying to get a grip, I shoved my hands deep into the pockets of my hoodie and tried like hell to keep myself from lunging at her.

The skank was still smiling. "So, did Bishop get ahold of you?"

I gave her a what-the-hell look, but said nothing.

"I mean," she continued, "I talked to him earlier." She gave a small laugh. "He was totally rude, by the way. Like, seriously, the guy has no sense of humor."

I glared down at her. "You're kidding, right?"

She paused. "Hey, are you mad at me or something?"

Through clenched teeth, I said, "You might say that."

"Really?" Her forehead wrinkled. "Why?"

Brittney wasn't dumb. And if she thought that faking it was gonna get her off the hook, she had another thing coming. "Go ahead," I told her. "Play dumb all you want. I don't have time for this shit." I turned to go.

She lunged for my elbow. "Wait! Is this about the prank?"

A prank? *That's* what she was calling it? My muscles were tight, and my breathing was shallow. I shook off her hand and whirled to face her. "You bitch."

She gave a little gasp. "What?"

I leaned closer, and my fingers flexed. "You hurt her."

She drew back. "Who? Chloe? I did not!" She gave a nervous laugh. "I mean, if that's what happened, it wasn't *my* fault. I told those guys to keep it friendly."

An image of that whole kidnapping scene flashed in my brain. Chloe was on the ground, and that guy was on top of her. Any "friendlier," and I would've murdered him with my bare hands.

"Oh come on!" Brittney was saying. "Don't look at me like that. You wanted us to be friends, right?"

Who? Brittney and Chloe? That wasn't gonna happen. For one thing, Chloe had better taste.

Brittney gave me a pleading look. "So I thought I'd include her in one of our sorority things, you know? I mean, we do it all the time." Her voice picked up steam. "We thought she'd like it. Honest."

Earlier tonight, she'd fed Bishop the same line of bull, which he'd passed along to me. I didn't buy it then, and I wasn't buying it now. For one thing, the whole sorority bit was a crock. Brittney and Amber might *claim* to be sorority sisters, but only one of them went to college – and it sure as hell wasn't Brittney.

I made a sound of disgust. "Nice story."

"If you don't believe me, ask Amber. She'll tell you."

I'd been trying to reach Amber for hours. For once, she wasn't answering, and she wasn't calling me back. None of this made sense. I'd known Amber for years, and I couldn't see her wanting to hurt anyone. But the way it looked, she had.

Either I didn't know Amber as well as I thought, or there was a grain of truth to Brittney's story. I shoved a hand through my hair and tried to think. A prank? If so, it was the worst fucking prank I'd ever seen.

Brittney leaned forward. "Would it help if I apologized?"

For some reason, that made me pause. Would it?

I thought of Chloe. I'd give anything to win her back. Already, *I'd* apologized. I'd begged. I'd delivered some justice to the guys who'd attacked her. And the justice wasn't done yet. Soon, they'd be standing outside in their underwear while a crowd of strangers laughed at them.

It was the same thing they'd been planning for Chloe. Those fuckers.

I tried to focus on the big picture. Chloe deserved an apology, and not only from me. And if Brittney *did* apologize, would that help?

As if sensing weakness, Brittney tried again. "Just give me a chance, okay? I can make this right."

She was wrong. Nothing was gonna make this right. But would it help? In the end, it all came down to one thing – Chloe. If nothing else, she *deserved* that apology. And she needed to know she was safe, and that nothing like that was gonna happen to her ever again.

So for Chloe's sake, I finally nodded.

Brittney smiled.

I didn't. Instead, I leaned close and said, "And let's get one thing straight. You'd better do a damn good job, or you're out."

"Out?" She blinked up at me. "What do you mean?"

"You mess this up, and all those parties you love going to? All the people you like to hang with? All the stupid shit that means so much to you? Well, you'll be giving it up, because I'll make damn sure you're on no one's guest list."

It was a stupid threat. Normal people wouldn't give a rat's ass about parties with people they barely knew. But Brittney, she wasn't normal. She was a bigtime star-fucker, and she ate that shit up.

I had a lot of friends. And a lot of people owed me favors. The threat might be stupid, but that didn't mean it was idle. I meant every word.

Brittney was frowning now. "You don't have to be so mean about it. I mean, I'm trying to help, you know."

"Yeah, right." I glanced around. There was still no sign of Chloe. I *had* to find her. I gave Brittney one last look. "When I call, you'd better answer. Because that apology? You don't get to put it off."

I left her there, sulking in the parking lot. Why she was there at all, I had no idea. Probably, I didn't want to know.

Besides, I had something more important to think about – Chloe. Where *was* she?

Ten minutes later, I had the answer, and it wasn't one I liked. The way it sounded, she was arguing with some guy in the parking lot. And – damn it – that guy was my brother.

CHAPTER 4

She was standing outside my car, glaring down at Bishop, who sat in the driver's seat with the window open. I couldn't hear what he was saying, but Chloe's response was loud and clear. "Oh for God's sake!" she yelled. "Will you just stop already!"

What the hell?

I strode toward them, hollering out to Bishop. "Hey! What the hell are you doing to her?"

Already, I was at Chloe's side. She whirled to face me, and our eyes met. Her lips parted, but whatever she was planning to say, the words died on her lips.

She was so damned close, but not nearly close enough. I wanted to wrap her in my arms and make everything better. But she wouldn't want that. She might *never* want that. So I held my ground and devoured the sight of her, not liking what I saw.

Under the makeup, her face was too pale, and her eyes were too hollow. The night was freezing, and she was standing out here in a uniform that was too small, under a coat that was too thin, no matter how fashionable it might be.

And now, Bishop was giving her grief, too? I yanked my gaze from Chloe and turned to face him. "Answer me!" I said.

He didn't. Instead, he opened the car door and slowly got out, shutting the door behind him. He tossed me the car-keys, and I caught them on instinct. Without a word, he turned toward the restaurant and started walking.

"Hey!" I called after him. "Where do you think *you're* going?"

He didn't turn around, but his voice carried across the short distance. "To get a burger, beer – hell, a cab, I dunno. You guys work it out. I'll catch you later."

Next to me, Chloe hollered after him. "Hey! There's nothing to work out, dipshit!"

There was no reaction. But then again, I hadn't expected any. I turned to Chloe and felt a reluctant smile tug at my lips. "Did you just call him a dipshit?"

She whirled to face me. "You think it's funny?"

"Nope." I raised my hands, palms out. "Not me."

"Then why are you smiling?" she said. "God, you are such a–" She shook her head. "I don't even know what to call you."

I felt my smile fade. She didn't have to call me anything. I knew exactly what I was. A bastard. An asshole. A stupid dumb-shit who'd driven away the only girl I'd ever loved. I swallowed. And I'd hurt her.

I recalled the handcuffs, and what they'd done to her wrists. The sleeves of her jacket covered them now, but I knew what was underneath – red, raw skin where the cuffs had been.

She'd been tugging so damned hard. I should've known that was happening. I should've let her go. Or better yet, I should've never cuffed her in the first place.

What the hell was wrong with me?

And just few minutes ago, that other idiot had dropped her on the pavement. What the hell was wrong with *him*?

Was Chloe hurt? I took a good long, look, starting at her face and working my way down. "You're okay?" My voice caught. "You look okay." I reached for her hand. "But what are you doing here? Shouldn't you be home?" I hesitated. "In bed or something?"

"Oh." She yanked her hand away. "Because some psycho locked me in his basement?" She gave a humorless laugh. "No big deal. Happens to me all the time. Life goes on, right?"

She was losing it, and I couldn't blame her. This was all my fault. "Baby–"

"I already told you, don't call me that." She pointed toward the restaurant where she worked. "So why'd you do this *here*? You *want* me to lose my job? Is that it?"

I shook my head. "No. I get it. You love this job. I know that."

"Oh yeah. *That's* why I'm working here." She rolled her eyes. "Because I love it soooo much."

If she didn't love it, that was news to me. "You don't?"

"Hell no," she said. "But I still don't want to get fired." She reached up to rub her temples. "I can only imagine what those two guys from the trunk are saying right about now." She closed her eyes like it hurt to think. "God, what a nightmare."

Obviously, she was hurting, and not just physically. My arms ached to hold her. My hands longed to stroke her face until her features relaxed into a sleepy smile. My whole body wanted to move forward, to shield her from everything in the world that was troubling her.

But she wouldn't want that, because the main thing troubling her was me. So I kept my distance and offered up one small detail that might make her feel better. It was about the guys in the trunk. "They're not saying anything."

She opened her eyes to look at me. "What are you? Some kind of mind-reader? Admit it, you don't know squat."

"I know one thing. They won't talk."

"Why?" she said. "Because they're too afraid that I'll talk too? Yeah, like that's gonna happen."

I didn't get it. "What do you mean?"

"I mean that I don't want to get dragged into some police station." Her voice rose. "I don't want to be sitting there all night, telling my pathetic story of how they tried to drag me into a car and…" She let the sentence trail off, as if unable to continue.

It hurt to see her like this. I kept my voice low, soothing. "Hey, don't worry. Nobody's dragging you anywhere. They won't talk. And you won't have to either."

She made a scoffing sound. "How can you be sure?"

"Because they know better. They're not gonna say one word about you."

She glared up at me. "Yeah? How do you know?"

I knew, because I'd kill them if I had to. But that would hardly reassure her. So I focused on something easier. "Because if they do, they'll find themselves dropped off someplace worse the next time."

Her gaze narrowed. "What next time?"

I shrugged. "Depends on them."

She glanced around the parking lot, and I could tell exactly what she was thinking. Tonight, they'd been dropped off in a public place. There'd been police, a crowd, and even a tow truck. They'd had no clothes, except for their underwear and enough bling to make them look like the shallow assholes they were.

Yeah, it was fucking embarrassing. It was meant to be. But it could've been worse. My jaw tightened. It *should* have been worse.

Chloe looked to the crowd, still milling around near the busses. "What could possibly be worse than this?"

That was an easy answer. "My old neighborhood."

I imagined those guys wandering around down there, with no car, no shoes, no phone – and just enough bling to draw the worst kind of attention. If they were lucky, they'd *only* be mugged and have the shit kicked out of them. If they were unlucky, well, they wouldn't need to worry about the next time, now would they?

"So answer me this," Chloe said. "Why, of all places, did you bring them here, where I work?"

"You wanna know why?" I said. "Because this is exactly where they were gonna drop you."

Her forehead wrinkled. "What?"

"Yeah," I said, feeling an edge creep into my voice. "They were gonna strip you down to your bra and panties and dump you right here. In this parking lot." My jaw tensed. "Want to know what they called it? A prank. Just a fucking prank."

She gave a small shake of her head. "Seriously? That's all they were gonna do?"

"All?" I said. "Isn't that enough?" I recalled Chloe on her lawn, with that guy on top of her. And then, I imagined her nearly naked out here in the cold, with hundreds of eyes devouring the sight of her, where she worked, no less.

At the thought, I wanted to hit something. Trying to keep it together, I said, "God, Chloe. They hurt you. They scared you."

"Yeah." She gave me a hard look. "And they weren't the only ones, now were they?"

She was right. "No." My voice grew quieter. "They weren't."

"So what *was* all this?" she asked. "Your idea of justice?"

"Something like that." I met her gaze, trying to make her understand. "We did exactly to them what they were gonna do to you. Seemed fair enough."

"Fair?" She made a scoffing sound. "Yeah, but you didn't stop there, did you?"

"What do you mean?"

She eyed me with obvious disgust. "I mean, you also beat the crap out of them. And, you ruined their car." She crossed her arms. "So it wasn't exactly an eye for an eye, was it?"

Tonight, I'd done a lot of things that I sorely regretted. But none of them involved those two guys. If anything, they'd gotten off light. Chloe, of all people, should understand that.

I stared down at her. "You're sticking up for them?"

She shrugged, letting the disgust in her eyes speak for itself.

I loved her, and I'd hurt her. But there was no way I could let this slide. "You're serious. Aren't you?"

My voice rose. "After what they did to you? You think that's alright?" I turned to glare across the parking lot. "Because I'm not gonna lie to you, Chloe. I'd do it again in a heartbeat. And if they ever pull that crap again, especially with you, they're not gonna get off so light."

She gave me a smirk. "So they got off light, huh? Well, what about *you?*"

I didn't get it. "What about me?"

"You got off lightest of all, didn't you? Look." She poked a finger toward my chest. "*You're* fine. Not a scratch on you, is there?" She turned and pointed toward my car. "And look. Your car's fine too. Seriously, what has any of this cost you?"

She was wrong.

"Chloe. It's cost me everything."

"Yeah." She rolled her eyes. "Right."

"Everything that matters."

"You know what?" she said. "That's real easy for you to say." Her voice rose. "Me? I'm an inch away from losing my job. Those guys, they got their car trashed. But you? This has cost you nothing." She took a step closer. "Nothing!"

Her eyes were wet, and her body was trembling. I couldn't stop myself. I reached out for her.

She slapped my arms aside. "So who's gonna kick *your* ass? Who's gonna get *you* fired?" Her voice broke. "Who's gonna trash *your* car?"

"You want someone to kick my ass?" I spread my arms. "Go ahead. I'd welcome it."

"Sure you would."

"Think I'm lying? You think I don't know that I deserve it?"

"Yeah? Well, words are cheap." She turned away.

"Wait."

She stopped. "For what?"

I met her gaze and said one simple word. "Proof." ☐

CHAPTER 5

While Chloe watched, I strode toward the back of my car. I popped the trunk and rummaged around until I found the thing I was looking for. I pulled it out, slammed the trunk, and returned to Chloe.

I showed her the tire iron. It was big and heavy, solid metal. I held it out in my open palms. "Here."

She glanced down. "What would I want with that?"

"Take it." I looked into her eyes. "And hit me."

She didn't move. "Oh shut up. I don't want to hit you."

"Alright," I said. "Get someone else. Have *them* do it."

She looked at me like I'd lost my mind. Had I? Probably. But that didn't mean the offer wasn't real.

"Go ahead," I urged, "find someone. I'll wait."

She shook her head. "Oh c'mon, you can't be serious."

She was wrong. I was deadly serious. At the memory of what I'd done to her, I could hardly choke out the words. "Why not? I deserve it. Just like you said."

She was still shaking her head. "You are seriously messed up. You know that, right?"

"Hell yes, I know it! You think I'm liking myself right now? You think I don't *know* that I deserve an ass-beating? You think I don't *wish* it was me 'suffering,' as you say?"

With a little shiver, she wrapped her arms tight around her torso. For warmth? Or comfort? Either way, it was killing me to not take her in my arms and hold her until she wasn't cold, or upset, or afraid of anything, including me.

But instead, I held my breath and waited, desperate for some sign that it wasn't over, and praying that she'd take me up on my offer – because then, at least, we might have a chance.

As I watched, something in her eyes softened, giving me the barest glimpse of the girl I loved. I felt a shred of hope. Maybe, just maybe, there was a chance after all.

But then her gaze hardened, and she said, "Alright, here's the deal. You–" She pointed to my chest "–need to stay the hell away from me. Stay away from where I work. Stay away from where I'm living. And stay away from anywhere else you think I might be."

Her words, no matter how justified, sliced through me. "Chloe–"

"You already said that."

"Please." I was drowning in despair, and from the look in her eyes, so was she. I hated to see her hurting. I wanted to comfort her. Hell, I wanted to comfort both of us. Slowly, I moved toward her.

Her gaze narrowed. "I mean it."

It took all my control, but I managed to stop. My muscles were tight, and my heart was racing. "Chloe, please. Hit me. Yell at me. Do something." My voice caught. "Anything but this."

She stared at me for a long moment, and just when I thought I'd broken through, she said, "You heard me," and turned away.

I could hardly speak. "Chloe. Wait. Please."

She turned back. "For what?"

"I know what you're thinking."

She crossed her arms. "I seriously doubt that."

"I can see it all over your face." And I could. She didn't believe a word I was saying. She didn't know – she *couldn't* know – that I'd do anything to win her back, that nothing in my whole world meant anything compared to her. I met her gaze. "You're thinking talk is cheap."

"So?"

"So you don't want someone to beat my ass? I get that. But you want me to pay, am I right?"

She shrugged.

"Believe me, Chloe. I *want* to pay."

She looked insulted. "I don't want your money."

"I know." And I did. Chloe didn't need money. She obviously had plenty of her own. What she really needed was to see me pay, to see me lose something that wasn't replaceable. Fortunately, such a thing was here, within arm's reach.

Chloe was shaking her head. "You don't know anything."

But I did know, and I was ready to prove it. "I know you want something else."

"Oh yeah?" she said. "What's that?"

"This." I shifted my grip on the tire iron. I took one long stride toward my car – the one that I'd restored with my own two hands, the one that couldn't be replaced by writing a check, the one that I'd poured so much of myself into, transforming it from a battered heap into a turbo-charged thing of beauty.

And now, I had to destroy it.

For Chloe.

CHAPTER 6

I lifted the tire iron and bashed it against the windshield, leaving a huge spider-webbed crack on the formerly smooth glass.

Chloe's voice rang out behind me. "What the hell are you doing?"

I was paying. That's what I was doing. And I wasn't done yet. Not by a longshot. I raised the iron again. This time, I smashed it against the side view mirror. The mirror held, so I hit it again. It hit the pavement and broke on impact.

Chloe grabbed at my elbow. "Don't!"

I turned to face her. "Why?"

"Because it's stupid!" She was trembling now, eyeing the destruction with wide-eyed horror.

Obviously, it was making an impression.

Good.

I hated that it was upsetting her, but I had to finish this. She had to know I was paying. She had to know I'd keep paying, that there was nothing that mattered as much as her. Justice, that's what she wanted, right? Well, that made two of us.

I tried to keep my voice level. "Isn't this the kind of justice you wanted? My car trashed? That's what you said, wasn't it?"

"No!" She tightened her grip. "This isn't what I wanted."

Maybe not. But at this point, it was the only thing I could do to prove my point, to make her see that I was deadly serious.

I looked into her eyes and softened my tone. "Well, I do."

Gently, I removed her hand from my elbow. "Because, Chloe, let me tell you something. Compared to you, this car means nothing to me."

I turned and strode to the passenger's side. I raised the iron high in my hand. "Compared to you, it means *less* than nothing." I bashed off the other mirror, and then walked to the front, where I destroyed both headlights, leaving shattered glass on the dark pavement.

She was yelling now. "Stop it!"

No. Not yet.

I raised the iron higher and slammed it down on the hood, leaving a huge dent in the glossy finish. And then, I did it again. And again. I kept at it, watching as the sleek lines were pounded into an ugly, mangled mess.

I didn't stop until the sound of a new voice, this one male, broke my focus. I turned to see Chloe arguing with the same guy who she'd been talking to earlier – the shaggy-haired idiot who'd dropped her on the pavement.

Whatever he was saying, Chloe didn't like it. So neither did I.

I dropped the iron and strode toward them. "You," I said, giving the guy a hard look. "Get away from her. Now."

With a shrug, he stepped away and turned toward my car. "Oh man." He smiled. "That is so messed up." He held out his cell phone, camera style. "Total viral." He stepped closer, zooming in on the hood.

I spared the phone half a glance, recalling what the older guy had told me earlier, about Shaggy's phone getting busted up. The way it looked, he'd found a replacement. Big deal.

He could take all the video he wanted. On my list of problems, this was too low to register. Or at least, that's how I felt until Chloe lunged toward the guy and said, "Stop that!"

He shook his head. "No way."

She turned and gave me a pleading look. "Are you just gonna stand there and let him take video of–" She gave a vague of her hands. "–this?"

The guy spoke up. "It's called freedom of the press, baby."

I felt my fingers flex. Baby?

Shaggy turned to call over his shoulder. "Am I right, or what?"

"Got that right," said a voice in the crowd. Yeah, people were watching. Maybe a dozen or so. Some were taking pictures – or whatever – with their phones. So what? I was long past caring.

But the way it looked, Chloe cared enough for both of us. She looked down and covered her face with both hands. "Oh my God," she groaned, looking way too unsteady for my liking. "This isn't happening."

Instantly, I was at her side. I placed a hand on her elbow. "Chloe? You okay?"

She gave a bark of laughter that kept on going. It grew into a crazed, foreign sound that tore at my heart. She was losing it. This, like everything else, was all my fault.

And then it got worse.

Because she started crying.

Suddenly, I couldn't stop myself. I gathered her in my arms, holding her tight against my chest, shielding her as best I could from everything around us.

I murmured into her hair, "God, this is all my fault. I'm so, so sorry. Baby, c'mon, don't cry."

Nearby, a camera flashed. I looked up and saw Shaggy too damn close for comfort. His phone was aimed straight at Chloe. I wanted to rip that thing of his hands and shoved it up his ass.

Instead, I gritted my teeth and told him, "You take one more shot of her, and you're gonna be out more than just another phone."

I turned away, holding Chloe tighter and shielding her from the guy's view. But he shifted along with us and zoomed in on Chloe's face, which was still buried against my chest. What the hell? Did the guy have a death wish or something?

I gave him a murderous glare. "Get the fuck away from her!"

The guy shrugged and took a half-step backward. He raised his phone again, looking too stupid to be afraid until a new voice – this one female – rang out across the parking lot. "Chester! You son-of-a-bitch!"

CHAPTER 7

Shaggy whirled toward the sound of her voice. I looked over and spotted a crazy-eyed redhead marching toward us. Her face was flushed, and her hair was wild. She stopped on the opposite side of my car and glared at Shaggy. "I knew it!" she hollered.

Holding Chloe tighter, I looked to see his reaction. His eyes were huge, and his mouth was open. He took a couple of steps backward and glanced around, as if looking for the best escape route.

"You bolt now," the redhead warned, "and you're walking home." Her voice rose. "And when you get there, guess what? You're gonna find the locks changed, because I've just about had it with this crap!"

Shaggy gave her a shaky smile. "Heeeey Jen. So what are you doing out here?"

"Me?" she shrieked. "What am *I* doing out here? You're kidding, right?"

"Yeah. I mean no," he stammered. "I thought you were gonna wait for me."

"You mean in the fucking restaurant?" she yelled. "Where do you think I've been the last hour?"

"An hour?" Shaggy gave her a nervous look. "Oh c'mon, it hasn't been that long."

She reached into her big red purse and pulled out a foil-wrapped container. "Still want that romantic dinner?"

Shaggy took a step backward. "No, I'm good, but uh, thanks."

Jen laughed. "Oh, you haven't been good for a long time. And you wanna know why? Because of you and your stupid Web site!"

She dug through the foil container. "You know how many times you've left me sitting alone while you chased some stupid story?" Her hand emerged from the container with — what the hell? Was that a jumbo shrimp?

Shaggy was still backing away.

But Jen was moving forward. "And you know how many places?" She raised her arm, and the shrimp went flying.

Shaggy ducked to the side. "Aw c'mon Jen! Not again!"

She reached into the container a second time. "At my sister's wedding!" She hurled another shrimp. It hit Shaggy's chest and bounced to the pavement.

Somewhere nearby, a camera flashed. Shaggy whirled toward it and yelled, "Hey! No pictures! C'mon, dude!"

But the dude — as Shaggy had called him — wasn't backing down. He took a couple more shots and then studied his phone, as if checking to see what he'd captured. Standing next him was a tall woman in a plain black jacket. She had her phone out, too. She aimed it straight at Shaggy, but I saw no flash. Was she taking video? Probably.

Funny, I'd been in Shaggy's shoes more times than I could count. For the past five years, I'd starred in thousands of amateur videos. Some were normal — me getting into my car, me eating dinner at some public place, me walking down the damn street, just trying to grab a sub or whatever.

And then, there were the other shots — me getting a blowjob from some chick in a parking garage, me beating the crap out of two guys who jumped me in some club, me at some urinal, taking a piss, for God's sake. It was the reason that these days, I skipped urinals and went straight for the stalls.

Sometimes, it felt like every private moment was right out there in the public eye. Some guys got off on that stuff. Not me. Not anymore.

The way it looked, Shaggy wasn't liking it any more than I had.

Good.

I thought of his phone, aimed at Chloe's face while she cried against me. What kind of assholes does that? Maybe I should make *him* cry. It wouldn't be hard. One quick punch, and he'd be sobbing on the sidewalk like the pussy he was.

And then, I could take a picture of *him* – see if *that* cheered Chloe up.

Probably lucky for him – and who knows, maybe lucky for me – that his girlfriend had come along when she did.

From the other side of my car, she was still screaming at him. "At my class reunion! At my uncle's funeral!" She reached into the shrimp container and pulled out a whole fistful. She flung the mess in Shaggy's direction and cursed like a truck-driver when none hit home.

I glanced around, taking in the crowd. At least they weren't watching Chloe anymore. I looked toward my car, wondering if I could rush Chloe into it and drive off, leaving Shaggy and the redhead to fight it out while the crowd gawked at them instead of us.

No. I couldn't. Because like a dumb-ass, I'd already destroyed my headlights, along with the windshield and mirrors. I wouldn't be driving Chloe anywhere, at least not safely.

Damn it.

Besides, the argument was winding down. Jen was practically on him now. As I watched with the rest of the crowd, she ripped the phone from Shaggy's hand and hurled it to the pavement. It hit hard and shattered into broken bits.

"My phone!" Shaggy yelled.

Jen gave a bark of laughter. "Your phone? *Your* phone?"

"Hey, you gave it to me."

"No. I let you use it," she said, "It's *my* phone! And what did you promise?"

"Uh–"

"You promised to leave it home tonight. But *did* you?" She turned toward the crowd. "Did he?"

A few people shook their heads. Someone near the back was still taking pictures, lighting the scene with random flashes.

Shaggy turned toward the flashing. "Dude, c'mon! Cut that out! Give us some privacy, will ya?"

I heard a laugh. It was Chloe, laughing against my chest. And just like before, the laughter sounded wrong – sharp and half-crazed. She pulled herself away and stumbled toward the shattered phone, lying a few feet away. She looked down at the thing and choked, out, "It doesn't look okay anymore."

Shaggy gave her an annoyed look. "What's so damn funny?"

Chloe was still laughing. "Do you really have to ask?" She turned to the redhead. "Sorry, I know it's not funny. I just–" She looked to the phone. "Oh my God. I *so* wanted to do that."

The redhead gave Chloe an odd look. "Weren't you our waitress?"

A new male voice rang out somewhere behind us. "She's not gonna be anyone's waitress if she doesn't get her butt back to work, pronto."

CHAPTER 8

Turns out, the guy was her boss – some pencil-necked twerp with an attitude. He'd been giving Chloe a hard time for five minutes now, and I wasn't liking it.

My hands were loose, but twitchy at my side. I was aching to hit someone. Whether the guy knew it or not, he was skating on thin ice.

The only thing that kept me from striding forward to give him a taste of his own medicine was the sure knowledge that Chloe wouldn't like it. So I stood a few feet away, watching him with open hostility until he stopped short when he noticed me standing there.

His eyes widened. "Hey, aren't you–"

"Yeah," I said, flicking my head toward Chloe. "Chloe's boyfriend."

She whirled to face me. "You are not."

Everyone was looking. I didn't care. If I had to, I'd beg her right here, right now. I reached for her hand. She blinked hard and pulled her hand away. But she didn't leave. That was a start, right?

Somewhere near my car, I heard Shaggy ask someone, "Hey Dude, can I borrow your phone?"

"Screw you," the guy said.

"Aw c'mon," Shaggy said. "Be a sport, will ya?"

"You touch that phone," the redhead said, "and you're a dead man."

Shaggy groaned theatrically. "Aw c'mon, Jen!"

I ignored it all and gave Chloe a pleading look. All I needed was a chance. "Please," I whispered.

Something in her eyes warmed, and for the briefest moment, I was almost sure I'd get it – another shot at being the guy she deserved.

But then, her dipshit of a boss cleared his throat, and she turned to look.

"Chloe," he said through clenched teeth, "might I speak with you a moment?"

He'd *already* been speaking to her. And not very nicely either. If he treated her like garbage in front of a crowd, I couldn't help but wonder – and not in a good way – how he treated her when no one was looking.

Before Chloe could answer, the guy turned and gave the crowd a long, irritated look. "In private."

With a heavy sigh, Chloe turned back to me and said, "You should go."

I shook my head. "Not before we talk."

"I can't. I've gotta go."

"Then come by later," I said. "Promise me."

With a look filled with regret, she shook her head.

It was that regretful look that made me dig in. I crossed my arms. "Alright." I flicked my gaze to my car. "I'll wait here."

"You can't wait here," she said. "It might be all night."

I shrugged. "I don't care."

She looked around as if weighing her options. Yeah, I was being pushy. I knew that. But I'd make it up to her. I just needed a chance.

Finally, she said, "Alright, fine. I'll stop by. But it might be morning before I get off work."

I felt my shoulders ease. "I'll be waiting."

Nearby, Chloe's boss muttered, "Yeah. Waiting. I know how *that* feels."

"Alright," Chloe told him, "I'm coming!" She turned back to me and said, "Go, alright? Please?"

I gave her something like a nod. I'd be going, but only *after* she was safely inside. The night was too crazy already, and there were too many people in the parking lot who didn't have Chloe's best interests at heart – the pervert who'd been looking at her ass, the shaggy guy with the phone fetish, and shit, even Brittney, lurking in the back of some Lincoln Town Car.

What the hell was that about?

Looking to keep an eye out, I sauntered back to my own car and stood, watching as Chloe and her boss walked a few car-lengths away and began talking too low for me to hear.

The way it looked, he was still giving her a hard time. I knew it wasn't any of my business, but I still didn't like it. I'd seen his type before – a big fish in a little pond, the kind of fish that got his rocks off by throwing his weight around.

I leaned against the battered hood of my car and crossed my arms. Didn't the guy know? There was always a bigger fish.

Finally, they finished talking, and together, they turned toward the restaurant. Halfway there, Chloe glanced over her shoulder, and our eyes met across the distance.

She might not know it, but she was still my girl. And somehow, I was going to win her back.

CHAPTER 9

Brittney was pouting again. "I still don't see why it has to be tonight."

Technically, it wasn't night. It was morning, nearly four o'clock, just a couple of hours after I'd seen Chloe in the restaurant parking lot.

I still didn't know what time she got off work, but I wasn't taking any chances. When she stopped by, I'd be ready.

So would Brittney, because Chloe was going to get that apology, even if I had to sit here for hours, listening to Brittney gripe about it.

We were sitting in a side-room just off the front entryway, near the front door for when Chloe showed up. I had a plan. Get Brittney's apology out of the way and then send her packing, pronto. I even had a driver at the ready just to make it nice and easy.

In the chair opposite me, Brittney gave another loud sigh. "Can't we turn on some music or something?"

"No."

"How about the TV?"

"No."

She made a sound of annoyance. "Why not?"

"Because this isn't a social call."

"What the hell is a social call?"

I shrugged. Shit, I didn't know. But I did know one thing, I was *not* going to give Chloe the impression that Brittney and I were hanging out for fun.

I glanced around. Even this room wasn't one I normally spent any time in. It was a small sitting area with slim, delicate furniture that my decorator had picked out, not for comfort, but for looks.

My chair was too small and uncomfortable as hell. When all this was over, I decided, I'd throw everything out and start over.

Maybe, I'd get lucky, and Chloe and I could shop together, see what *she* liked. If I got really lucky, this might be her house, too, someday. At the thought, I almost smiled.

"Got anything to drink?" Brittney asked.

"Yeah. Water."

"Oh come on." She slouched down in her chair. "Now you're just being rude."

"Yeah? Well, I *am* rude. So get over it."

"Oh fine," she muttered. "I guess I'll just die of thirst."

I glanced toward the front door. Come on, Chloe. You're still showing, right?

We'd been sitting for almost another hour when I finally heard a car pulling into the drive. I shot out of my chair and flung open the front door.

It was only Bishop, getting out of a cab. I waited, watching as he paid the driver and began sauntering toward me while the cab backed out of the drive.

Bishop eyed me, standing in the doorway. "Nice of you to wait up for me."

He wasn't stupid. We both knew I wasn't waiting up for *him*. I glanced toward the street, hoping to see that little red Fiesta pulling in where the cab had just left.

I saw nothing.

Bishop's voice cut into my thoughts. "She's still at work."

"What?"

"Yeah," he said. "Probably for a couple more hours."

"And you know this, how?"

He shrugged. "Caught a bus-boy at the dumpster."

I didn't ask for details. His information was always good. With a quick glance behind me, I stepped outside and shut the door.

"Someone's here."

"Yeah?" His eyebrows lifted. "This should be good."

"It's Brittney."

He paused. "Brittney?"

"She's here to apologize."

"Tonight? How'd that happen?"

I gave him a brief run-down, explaining how, after my last conversation with Chloe, I'd found Brittney exactly where I'd seen her earlier, in the back of that Lincoln Town Car. I'd practically dragged her over here, determined to get that apology done and over with – for Chloe's sake.

"But why tonight?" Bishop asked.

"Because Chloe deserves that. Don't you think?"

He was shaking his head. "Bad idea."

"Oh yeah?" I crossed my arms. "Why?"

"Let me ask you this. Do you trust her?"

"Brittney? Hell no. That's why I'm making her apologize tonight, before she tries to slide out of it." My voice grew quieter. "And, I don't want Chloe to worry."

He looked at me like I was nuts. "About some apology?"

I felt my jaw tighten. "It's more than that, and you know it." From where I was standing, I couldn't see Chloe's house, but I could envision it well enough. Earlier tonight, she'd been attacked right there in her own front yard. She'd been dragged to the ground and held against her will.

I couldn't stand the thought of Chloe being afraid, not just earlier, but every time she pulled into her own driveway or went outside to walk her dog. She needed to know, once and for all, that it wasn't going to happen again.

If nothing else, I owed her that.

She wasn't like me. She hadn't grown up in a shitty neighborhood where looking over your shoulder was an everyday thing. She wasn't used to it. And the way I saw it, she shouldn't have to *get* used to it.

I felt my fingers flex. Fucking Brittney.

I was still stewing about it when I heard the front door fly open behind me. I turned to see Brittney standing in the open space. When her gaze landed on Bishop, she smiled. "Hey, Bish."

Bishop gave her a long, cold look. "Britt."

Her smile faltered. "You coming inside? We could have drinks or something." Her gaze slid to me, and her eyes narrowed. "And I don't mean water."

CHAPTER 10

A minute later, we were all inside, sitting in the same area as before. Brittney, clutching a glass of tap-water, was sulking again. She frowned at Bishop. "Why is everyone in such a bad mood tonight?"

Bishop ignored her and turned toward me. "Check this out. I learned what they told the cops."

"Who?" Brittney asked. "Joey and Paul?"

Bishop gave her a cold look. "I wasn't talking to you."

Her mouth tightened. "You know, I thought Lawton was rude, but you're like rude times a million."

"Good to know." Bishop turned back to me and said, "The way I heard it, their story wasn't half-bad. You saw how it played out, right?"

I shook my head. I hadn't seen. When those guys had been freed from the trunk, I'd been on the other side of the building, searching for Chloe.

"Get this." Bishop grinned. "So, some tow-truck driver shows up to pop the trunk, with like a hundred people watching, and those guys jump out, wearing what?"

As the person who'd put them in the trunk, I knew the answer firsthand. "Their underwear."

"And?" Bishop said.

I shrugged. "Their jewelry."

Brittney leaned forward. "Yeah, Joey and Paul, they're like total bling-masters." She nodded like this was a good thing. "They have awesome taste."

I gave her a look, but said nothing. Yeah, they had taste alright, like disco kings from the '70s.

Bishop was still grinning. "I'm not talking about the jewelry. I'm talking about the masks."

I shook my head. "What masks?"

"The ski-masks."

I frowned. They'd been wearing those masks when they'd jumped Chloe. Even without them, she would've been terrified. But those stupid masks of theirs, thick, knitted things with only slits for eyes, made the two guys wearing them look more like executioners than idiots on a fake-kidnapping mission.

At the time, what did Chloe think? Did she think she was going to die? My fingers gripped the side of my chair. Those assholes. I knew where their masks belonged, and it sure as hell wasn't on their heads.

"You listening?" Bishop asked.

I looked up. "What?"

"I *said* they were wearing the damn things when they popped out of the trunk. You should've seen 'em." He shook his head. "Underwear, bling, and ski masks. They looked like idiots."

They *were* idiots, because they'd messed with the wrong girl. I heard myself say, "I didn't realize they still had them."

"The masks?" Bishop said. "Eh, we must've left them in the trunk. Anyway, the way it looks, they put on the masks, hoping to hide their faces."

Brittney spoke up. "But you got them back, right?"

Bishop and I turned to look. It was Bishop who asked, "Got what back?"

"The masks," she said.

I stared at her. "What?"

"They were mine," she said. "I need them back."

Suddenly, I heard a snap. I looked down to see a crack in the right-arm of my chair. My knuckles were white, and the wood was splintered on both sides.

Brittney was still talking. "I paid good money for those things. I mean, they weren't like generic ski-masks. They were designer."

Was she fucking kidding me?

Bishop cleared his throat. "Anyway, what they end up telling the cops is the whole thing was part of some prank gone wrong."

Prank. There was that word again. I said it out loud. "A prank?"

It was the same word that Brittney had used to describe what they'd done to Chloe. If I never heard that word again, it would be too damn soon.

"Yeah," Bishop said. "They tell the cops it's part of some fraternity thing, claim they were supposed to end up at this sorority bash, but got dropped at the wrong place."

"So what?" I said. "That doesn't explain the masks."

"Which," Brittney said, "I still need back, by the way."

Together, Bishop and I turned to look. Under our silent gazes, she shifted in her seat. "Well, I do. I mean, I didn't *give* them to Joey and Paul. It was just a loan. They were supposed to give them back when they were done."

I heard another snap. I looked down to see a matching crack on the other chair arm.

Bishop glanced at the chair. "You wanna hear the rest later?" The corners of his mouth lifted. "Like when you're sitting on a couch or something."

"Oh, fuck off," I muttered.

With a longer look at the chair, he continued, "So they tell the cops they're wearing the masks because they were supposed to do some panty-raid, burglar skit at this sorority house – Amber's actually. But because of some mix-up, they end up at the restaurant instead."

"And you learned all of this how?" I asked.

He shrugged. "I've got a friend on the force."

"And he believed that bullshit story?"

"The guy's not stupid," Bishop said. "He knows a load of bull when he hears it, but who's complaining? The only 'victims' were the guys in the trunk." Bishop hesitated. "Well, them and the poor saps who had to look at them."

I recalled the one guy's underwear, tiny black briefs a few sizes too small. No doubt, the crowd had gotten a good eye-full.

"Besides," Bishop added, "someone backed up their story, so there you have it."

"Who?" I asked.

"Amber," he said. "I got ahold of her, walked her through it."

I sat back in the chair. During the last two hours, he'd gotten a lot done. As for me, I'd been sitting here, listening to Brittney whine about crap that didn't matter.

And now, she was frowning again. She turned to Bishop. "Wait a minute," she said. "How'd *you* get ahold of Amber? I've been calling her all night. It's like she's avoiding me or something."

"Yeah?" Bishop said. "Maybe it's a hint, and you should take it."

Brittney scowled. "What's *that* supposed to mean?"

Bishop stood. "You wanna know? Ask her." He glanced toward the stairway. "Anyway, I'm heading to bed."

Brittney was suddenly all smiles. "Want some company?"

"From you?" he said. "Hell no."

Brittney drew back. "God, what's your problem?"

He glanced toward me. "Sloppy seconds aren't my thing."

"Hey!" she said. "I'm not sloppy." Her gaze narrowed as she looked in my direction. "And besides, all I ever did was blow him. And that was for like two whole seconds before he flipped out because of 'dog girl.'"

Dog girl? I stood. "For the last time, her name is Chloe."

"See?" Brittney said, turning to Bishop. "He's flipping out. Just like I said."

I shoved a hand through my hair. What the hell had I been thinking? The way it sounded, Chloe was still at least two hours from showing up. For all I knew, she might not show up at all, considering how late she'd be working.

And, with every hour, Brittney was getting more difficult. As for myself, I could take her crap just fine, but what if she gave that same attitude to Chloe?

I gave Brittney a hard look. "You wanna see flipping out?" I raised my index finger. "You say *one* thing to upset Chloe, and you're gonna regret it, just like I told you in the parking lot."

Again, she turned to Bishop. "See what I mean?"

Bishop's gaze shifted from Brittney to me. "Want me to get rid of her?" he asked.

"Hey!" Brittney said, turning to glare at *him* now. "No one 'gets rid' of Brittney Adams." She eyed the door. "That's it. I'm outta here."

"Go ahead," I told her. "No one's stopping you."

It was true. Even before Bishop had showed up, it wasn't like I'd been holding Brittney by force. Yeah, I wanted her to apologize. And yeah, sooner was better than later. But with every hour, the odds of her doing a decent job of it were falling fast.

If she wanted to storm out now, maybe that wasn't such a bad thing.

I waited.

She didn't storm out. Instead, she glanced toward the front door. "But I don't have a ride."

"Wrong," I told her. "I've got a driver waiting. You wanna go? He'll be here in thirty seconds." I pulled out my phone and started tapping out a text.

"Wait!" Brittney said.

I looked up and waited, not bothering to hide my impatience.

"But where would he take me?"

"Home, Amber's, wherever. Not my problem."

She bit her lip. "But..." She hesitated. "I might be locked out."

"Again, not my problem."

"Oh, well *that's* nice." Her bottom lip quivered, and her eyes began to water. "This whole night has totally sucked. You know, I'm only here because you *asked* me to be here."

She looked to Bishop and choked back a sob. "It's like the middle of the night, and I'm just really tired, you know?" With a long sigh, she plopped back onto her chair and gazed up at the ceiling. "And your brother's being mean to me."

Bishop and I exchanged a look.

Well, someone had to ask it. Apparently, that someone was me. "Which brother?" I said. "Me? Or him?"

In truth, we'd both been "mean" to her. But it wasn't like she didn't deserve it. So what if she'd had a shitty night? She'd put Chloe through worse.

She never answered my question. Instead, she gave another loud sniffle and said, "Maybe I could just nap or something?"

"Or maybe," I said, "you could just leave."

Yeah, I was being a dick. But she didn't deserve anything better, not after what she'd done to Chloe.

"But if I leave, I can't apologize." Her voice became earnest. "And I really want to. Honest. I mean, I might as well get it over with, right?" She wiped at her eyes. "You know, I've been up for twenty hours?"

I *didn't* know. And I didn't care all that much either. I wasn't even sure I believed her. But it *was* after four o'clock in the morning, so her story wasn't that far-fetched.

Thinking of Chloe, I weighed the benefits of having Brittney stick around, if only to put Chloe's mind at ease.

As if sensing my doubts, Brittney spoke up. "Aw, come on. I really do want to make it right, honest." She gave another pathetic sniffle. "I just need to lay down for a few minutes, that's all."

The way it looked, I had three choices – give up on the apology, show her to a guest room, or sit here, watching her cry and whine until Chloe showed up.

I looked toward the stairway. "Second room on the left."

A minute later, she was safely upstairs and out of my sight. As for Bishop, he stuck around only long enough to say, "You're gonna regret that."

And sure enough, he was right, because when Chloe finally showed up a couple of hours later, I learned the hard way what a dumb-ass I'd been to let Brittney stick around. □

CHAPTER 11

It was nearly dawn when I heard footsteps on the front walkway. I didn't wait for the doorbell. Instead, I made for the door and flung it open.

And there she was – Chloe.

My breath caught. She was here. Finally. She'd scrubbed her face clean of all that heavy work-makeup, and now wore jeans and pale pink hoodie.

I wanted her in my arms, and then in my bed. I wanted to hold her tight and never let go. I let out a long, unsteady breath, and her name fell from my lips. "Chloe."

She gave me a cold smile. "Lawton." From the look on her face, she wasn't nearly as happy to see me as I was to see her.

Somehow, I'd change that. I didn't care what it took. I'd make things right between us. "You came," I said.

"You wanted to talk? Well, here I am."

Yeah. She was here. And she was obviously still angry, not that I blamed her. But the fact that she'd come at all meant something more. There was hope. And for now, I was clinging to it like the life-raft it was.

Unable to stop myself, I moved toward her.

She held up a hand. "Not that kind of talk."

I stopped and tried to get past the loathing in her eyes. Yeah, I deserved it, but it still hurt to see. I swallowed the pain and asked, "Wanna come inside?"

"Uh, no." Her gaze narrowed. "That didn't work out so well for me last time, now did it?"

I couldn't blame her. The last time she'd been here, I'd handcuffed her in my basement. I'd held her there for hours. At the memory of what I'd done, I looked down at her wrists. They were covered by the sleeves of her hoodie, but I knew what was underneath – raw, angry skin from where the cuffs had been.

That was how long ago? Nine, maybe ten hours?

I looked up, meeting Chloe's eyes. What could I say?

An icy breeze whipped at her hair, and she gave a small shiver. Hoodie or not, she wasn't dressed for this kind of cold.

Me neither. I wore jeans and a basic gray T-shirt. No jacket. It was below freezing, but I barely noticed.

But the way it looked, Chloe *was* feeling it. She wrapped her arms tighter around her torso and gave another shiver. The gesture, small as it was, hurt to watch – because not too long ago, she'd been shivering in my basement, and I'd *let* her. She hated to be cold, and I'd known that.

If I had my way, she'd never be cold again.

I looked down at her thin hoodie and felt myself frown. In this weather, she needed a winter coat, not some glorified sweatshirt. Or better yet, she needed to be inside.

I gave her a pleading look. "But it's freezing out." My door was still open. I flicked my head toward the interior of my house. "C'mon. Please?"

She didn't move. "Afraid of a little cold, are you?"

I wasn't afraid of the cold. But I *was* afraid of watching her shiver again. I'd seen a lot of shit in my days, but for some reason, this small thing, I didn't think I could stomach it, not after that whole basement scene.

I shook my head. "It wasn't me I'm thinking about. Cold, hot, I don't care." I met her gaze. "I'm just glad you're here."

She rolled her eyes. "Oh please. Save it for someone who believes that sort of thing, okay?"

"Baby–"

"Stop." She gave me a hard look. "Listen, whatever reason you seem to think I'm here, that's not it." She dropped her hands and squared her shoulders. "I'm here because you didn't give me any other choice, remember?"

I looked out toward the driveway. "Where's your car?"

"At work."

"Why?"

"Because the stupid thing wouldn't start." She glanced away. "And I had to beg the busboy for a ride home."

If this were yesterday, she would've called *me* for a ride. She wouldn't need to beg anyone. And whether we were together or not, she *still* didn't need to beg anyone. "You should've called me," I said.

"Yeah? Well, maybe I didn't want to owe you a favor."

"You wouldn't have *owed* me anything."

"Yeah, right."

I looked toward the street. "So you walked here? Alone?" Yeah, it was a stupid question. I didn't see anyone else here, did I?

"Why not?" she said. "I've done it before. Besides, I'm just on the other side of your fence."

Except she didn't come the short way, did she? Yeah, there was a narrow gate out back, but the thing was locked. And as far as the fence, it was double Chloe's height, with sharp metal spires all along the top.

I gave her a look. "So you climbed it. That's what you're saying?" I knew she hadn't, but I was trying to make a point.

"No. Of course not."

"So you took the long way." I crossed my arms. "By sidewalk."

"Well, I didn't fly here, if that's what you're wondering."

Did I need to point out the obvious? "It's a fifteen-minute walk."

"So?"

I glanced around. It was pitch-black and cold as hell. She'd been alone and under-dressed. I gave her a serious look. "So it's the middle of the night."

"No. It's early morning."

Maybe. But she knew damn well what I meant. I didn't want her to be afraid. But I didn't want her to take stupid chances either.

Yeah, this was a nice neighborhood, but in some ways, that just made it a juicier target.

I had to say it. "So you *want* something bad to happen to you? Is that it?"

She gave a bitter laugh. "What do you consider bad? Because it seems to me that something bad can happen just about anywhere, anytime. Driveways, parking lots–" Her mouth twisted. "Basements."

Ouch.

What could I say? It was true. Lamely, I said, "You should've called me."

She gave something like a shrug.

"Chloe, I'm serious. Don't do that again, alright?"

She made a sound of impatience. "Look, you were the one who forced me to come here."

Like what? At gunpoint? Was that how she really felt? I heard myself say, "Forced you?"

"Cornered me. Whatever." She sighed. "So here I am. And how I got here isn't all that important."

"It is to me."

"Yeah? Well, from now on, that's your problem, not mine."

I don't know what I expected, but not this. A full-blown temper-tantrum would've been easier to handle. The way it looked, she hated me, *really* hated me.

And I loved her.

Desperate to say something, *anything*, that would make a difference, I tried to think. What could I say? What could I do?

It was Chloe who broke the silence. "Listen, I've had a long night, so can we skip the part where we debate why I wouldn't be calling you for favors?"

I looked into her eyes, searching for some sign that it wasn't over. All I got was an icy stare.

My heart sank. What was the old saying? Live to fight another day? The way it looked, I wasn't going to make any headway tonight. And probably, if I pushed too hard, I'd only be pushing her further away.

But there was *something* I could do — not for me, for her. I could make damned sure she got that apology from Brittney. And if I had to drag Brittney's bony ass out of a nap or whatever to make that happen, I sure as hell wasn't going to hesitate.

"Alright," I said. "But there's something you deserve to hear. At least come inside, alright?"

"No. I don't think so." Her gaze drifted downward and settled on my wrists. Her eyebrows furrowed.

Shit.

My arms were bare, but my wrists were wrapped in white athletic tape. The tape was for Chloe's sake, not mine. She didn't need to know that those two kidnapper-wannabees weren't the *only* people I'd punished.

Under Chloe's gaze, my wrists burned with the memory of what I'd done. I could still feel the friction from the rope slicing into my skin as I wrapped the rope tighter and pulled it harder, until the rope was red, and my skin was dripping.

I didn't regret it. I deserved it.

Chloe — apparently concluding that I'd been working out or something — looked up. Her gaze drifted to the open door behind me. "Aren't you gonna close the door?"

Why? Because cold air was flooding into the house? I didn't care. All I cared about was the girl in front of me. I wanted to gather her in my arms and make sure she was never cold again.

My thoughts were churning, but my voice was quiet. "Screw the door."

She stared up at me, and something in her eyes warmed, just a fraction. For a long moment, I had this crazy idea that somehow, it would all work out, that by some miracle, she'd fall into my arms and let me make everything better.

Silently, I begged her. *Chloe, please.*

But then, a different female voice drifted out my doorway. The voice sounded sleepy with a hint of sex. "Lawton," she called, "who's at the door?"

I froze, feeling the color drain from my face.

Fucking Brittney.

Reluctantly, I glanced behind me. And there she was, standing on the darkened staircase.

Naked.

CHAPTER 12

Desperately, I turned back to Chloe. The look on her face was everything I feared. And from where she was standing, she hadn't even *seen* Brittney yet. I shifted in the doorway, hoping like hell to block her view.

I knew exactly how this would look. Bad, just like it sounded. "Chloe," I said, "it's not what you think. I swear."

I heard movement behind me and stifled a curse. Chloe's gaze shifted to somewhere past my shoulder, and her jaw dropped. I didn't turn around, because I already knew what she had spotted – a certain naked blonde who, at this rate, I'd be strangling any minute.

I tried again. "Chloe—"

Whether she heard me or not, I'll never know, because another voice, sounding sly and possessive, drifted out the open doorway. "Oh," Brittney said. "It's you."

I turned to look, and there she was, standing within arm's reach. Yeah, it was bad, but not quite as bad as I'd originally feared.

From the distant shadows, all I had seen was bare skin. Now, up close, I saw tiny sheer panties and a matching bra. The bra was so thin, I could see the pink of her nipples poking through the nearly transparent fabric.

Knowing Brittney, I was supposed to be aroused.

I wasn't.

Instead, I was royally pissed off. I glared down at her. "You were supposed to wait upstairs."

She blinked up at me. "Oh. Was I?"

"And where the hell are your clothes?"

She raised her arms in a slow, seductive stretch. "Mmm…I dunno. Upstairs?" The way it sounded, she didn't mean upstairs in the guest room. She meant upstairs in *my* room, like we'd just been screwing or something.

A low, strangled sound broke into my thoughts. I turned to see Chloe turning away, like she was making a break for it.

Desperately, I grabbed her elbow. "Chloe, wait! Please?"

She whirled back to face me. Her face was flushed, and her breathing was ragged. "So *this* is why you invited me here? To throw *this* in my face?"

I gave her a pleading look. "There's no *this*."

If *this* was anything, it was a fucking nightmare. I had to make it go away. Now. Before I lost Chloe for good.

I turned to Brittney. "Go on. Tell her. Right now."

Brittney gave me a slow, sleepy smile. "Tell her what?"

My fists were tight, and my muscles were bunched into hard, angry knots. So help me, I wanted to hit her. Through clenched teeth, I said, "You tell her right now why you're here, or the deal's off. Got it?"

She lifted a bare shoulder. "Whatever you say."

"And for God's sake," I said, "put on some fucking clothes, will ya?"

Her lips formed a pout. "But they're dirty. And besides, it took her *forever* to get here."

I was still holding Chloe's elbow. Her body was trembling. And somehow, I knew that this time, it wasn't because of the cold.

I turned back to Brittney. Through gritted teeth, I said, "You've got five seconds."

"Oh alright. Fine." Brittney looked to the ceiling and mumbled, "I'm here to apologize."

As an apology, it sucked. Still, I looked to Chloe, hoping that if nothing else, it had bought me some time.

Chloe's gaze was still locked on Brittney. I knew what she was seeing – the long tousled hair, the sleepy smile, the see-through panties that hid nothing – and I mean *nothing* considering that Brittney wasn't a fan of pubic hair.

Brittney's half-hearted apology hung in the air, unanswered until Chloe said, "In your underwear?" She made a sound of disgust. "Yeah. Nice story."

I turned to give Brittney a warning look. "Brittney, you can do better than that."

But it was Chloe who spoke next. "Don't bother."

She jerked away from my grasp, and fearful of hurting her, I let go without a struggle. Too soon, she was turning away with a muttered, "I don't want your apology."

"Wait!" Brittney said.

Chloe stopped and turned around. She eyed Brittney with obvious impatience.

Brittney turned to me and said, "If she doesn't *want* me to apologize, our deal still counts, right? I mean, because I tried. And she said 'no.' You saw that, right?"

Was she kidding me? What *I* saw was a giant cluster-fuck that was going to cost me the girl I loved.

Before I could say so, Chloe's voice cut across the short distance. "On second thought, I'd just love an apology." She pushed past me and stormed into the house. She stopped in front of Brittney and crossed her arms. "And I sure hope it's a good one, because unlike some people, I've got standards."

Brittney pursed her lips. "Hey, I've got standards, too."

"Yeah," Chloe said, "except yours are too low to measure." She turned to me. "A few hours ago, wanna know what I caught her doing?" Chloe's voice rose. "Boning my boss in the back seat of his car."

I gave Brittney a sideways glance. I recalled the Lincoln Town car, the one she'd crawled out of earlier. Was *that* what she'd been doing in there? Screwing Chloe's boss? Talk about messed up.

Brittney was glaring at Chloe now. "Hey!" Brittney said. "We weren't boning. We were doing other stuff."

"Whatever," Chloe said, turning back to me. "So for your sake, I hope you wore a damn condom." She made a hard, scoffing sound.

"You know what? On second thought, I hope you didn't. Because you deserve whatever this skank gives you."

What the hell?

Was *that* what Chloe thought of me? That I'd go straight from her to Brittney, in what? A few hours? I glanced toward Brittney, standing nearly naked in my own house. Shit. Of course Chloe would think that. The way it looked, she'd be stupid not to. But it *wasn't* like that. Somehow, I had to fix this.

"Baby." I moved toward her and reached for her hand. "I didn't wear anything."

She jerked her hand away. "How nice for you."

"Because," I explained, "I didn't have to. She's only here for one thing."

Chloe eyed me with disgust. "Exactly."

"Not that." I turned toward Brittney. "She's here," I said, speaking very slowly and clearly, "to tell you how very, *very* sorry she is."

"In her underpants?" Chloe said. "Do I look stupid to you?"

With a muttered curse, I strode to the front closet. I reached to the top shelf and pulled out a navy stadium blanket. I hurled it at Brittney. She made no move to catch it. The blanket hit her chest and slid to the floor.

I glanced at Chloe. She looked ready to bolt, not that I'd blame her. I gave Brittney a long, cold look. "Cover up. Or get out. Your choice."

Brittney looked down at the blanket, still lying on the floor. Finally, acting more like a stripper than anything else, she slowly bent over and picked it up, giving me a good, long show in the process. She finished by draping the blanket loosely over her shoulders, so it covered almost nothing – not her nipples, not her stomach, and not any part of her bushless bush.

Chloe pointed at Brittney's pelvis. "I think you missed a spot."

With a huff, Brittney wrapped the blanket around herself, leaving only her bare legs exposed. She gave Chloe a smirk. "Prude."

Chloe smiled. "Squid-fucker."

Brittney drew back with a gasp. The way it looked, the name

meant something to her. Who was the squid? Chloe's boss?

Brittney whirled toward me and said, "Did you hear what she called me?"

"Like I care," I said. "Now, go on. Apologize. Chloe's waiting."

Brittney sighed. "Oh alright." She looked vaguely in Chloe's direction. In a bored monotone, she said, "I'm sorry about that little joke."

Little joke? What the hell? Maybe I should hold Brittney at knife-point, see if the joke was so funny then.

Chloe was staring at Brittney. "A joke?" Chloe said.

Brittney rolled her eyes. "You know. The prank. With Joey and Paul."

I gave Brittney a warning look. "That was no prank."

"Aw c'mon," Brittney said. "Yes, it was. Just a little joke. No big deal." She turned to Chloe. "Go on, tell him. You thought it was funny. Right?"

"Funny?" Chloe said. "So let me get this straight." Her voice rose. "Two masked men try to throw me in a trunk, and you call that a fucking joke?"

Brittney shrugged. "At least *I* have a sense of humor. Unlike *some* people."

"Gee," Chloe said, "maybe *some* people don't like getting dragged away in the middle of the night. Maybe *some* people are funny like that. Maybe *some* people aren't totally fucking nuts!"

"Hey, you're the one who's crazy," Brittney said. "It wasn't the middle of the night. It was like, what, nine?" She turned to me. "See? She's making it sound ten times worse than it was."

My hands were fisted, and my shoulders were tight. The more Brittney talked, the harder it was to keep my cool.

At something in my face, Brittney took a small step backward, but then recovered just as fast. She gave a toss of her hair and said, "So like I told you, it's no big deal."

My blood was boiling. "And like I told *you*," I said, "it *is* a big deal. A very big deal. And if you were some guy, you'd be getting a lot worse than the chance to beg Chloe for forgiveness."

"Hey," Brittney said. "No one said anything about begging." She threw back her shoulders. "Brittney Adams doesn't beg for anything."

Chloe gave a hard laugh. "Not even car nookie?"

Brittney gave Chloe an annoyed look. "It wasn't nookie." She turned to me. "You believe me, right?"

"What I believe," I said, "is that you're supposed to be apologizing."

She pursed her lips and turned back to Chloe. "Alright. I *guess* I'm sorry. But seriously, it's no big deal. In my sorority, we do that sort of thing all the time."

What a load of bull.

The way it looked, Chloe wasn't buying it either. She was still staring at Brittney. "Your sorority kidnaps people? Seriously?"

With a little huff, Brittney turned to me and said, "See? She's doing it again. She's making it sound worse on purpose, just to make me look bad."

I wanted to throttle her. "You want to do a shitty job at this, fine." I pointed toward the door. "Get the fuck out. Now."

Brittney gave me a pleading look. "But I'm trying to explain. She won't let me."

I crossed his arms and spoke very slowly. "Try harder."

With an eye roll, she turned back to Chloe. "What we do," Brittney said, "is steal their mascots. Swipe 'em for a day or two." She turned toward me and finished by saying, "But we always return them. It's no big deal. See?"

"No," I said. "I don't see."

And I didn't. For one thing, Brittney wasn't even *in* a sorority. For another, it *was* a big deal. A very big deal.

Brittney made a sound of annoyance. "But it was just a joke. I don't get why everyone's freaking out about it." She adjusted the blanket and gave a dramatic sigh. Looking to me, she said, "But just because you asked, I apologized anyway. So are we good now or what?"

Good? Not by a longshot.

But before I could say so, Chloe turned to me and said, "So this was *your* idea?"

CHAPTER 13

Chloe was looking at me like I'd lost my mind. Had I? Probably.

I shoved a hand through my hair. "Yeah, but–" I gave Brittney a hard look. "It was supposed to go a lot better."

For one thing, it wasn't supposed to include naked nipples and shaved privates.

Brittney threw back the blanket, and tapped her bare foot against the tile floor. The tapping made her boobs jiggle like jelly-filled balloons on a bumpy carnival ride. One bearded lady, and the freak show would be complete.

I glanced down at Brittney's crotch. No beard. Even my freak show was too freaky to be normal. Damn it.

Brittney stopped tapping long enough to give Chloe a half-hearted look. "So you do accept my apology or what?"

"Hell no," Chloe said. "That was the worst apology, ever."

"Hey, it was my first one," Brittney said. "I thought I did pretty good." She turned to me and asked, "Didn't I?"

I crossed my arms. "No."

Chloe was staring Brittney with narrowed eyes. "Just how long have you been here, anyway?"

Brittney turned to give me a long look, filled with sin and sex. "Hard to say," she purred. "We kind of lost track."

My fingers flexed. I wanted to choke the truth out of her and then toss her out on her nearly naked ass. "That's it," I told her. "Get out."

She shrank back. "But I'm not dressed!"

Like I cared. "Whatever. Keep the blanket. Just get out."

"But I don't have my car," she whined.

I reached into the pocket of my jeans and pulled out my cell phone. I texted the driver, who'd been on standby for hours now. Almost instantly, there was a knock at the door. I flung it open. And there he was, the driver, dressed in his company uniform.

"Take her wherever," I said.

The driver glanced to Chloe and said, "Yes sir."

I stifled a curse. "Not *her*." I pointed to Brittney. "*Her*."

It's not like I blamed the guy. Brittney, was, after all, mostly naked, and it wasn't exactly normal to send a naked girl packing.

The driver looked to Brittney. "Of course."

Brittney was sputtering now. "But I'm not even dressed!"

"Not my problem," I said.

She turned pleading eyes on the driver. "Can you believe this?"

I'd paid the guy in advance, along with a generous tip. With what I was paying him, he'd believe exactly what I wanted him to believe.

Sure enough, he stepped aside and held open the front door. "Right this way, ma'am."

Brittney was glaring at him. "Ma'am? Did you just seriously call me 'ma'am'?"

"Yes ma'am." He held open the door wider. "Right this way, please."

Brittney tossed back her hair. "Oh," she said, in a voice dripping with sarcasm, "well aren't *you* just so polite?"

I stepped toward her and said, "Listen, gripe all you want. But you *are* leaving. By car, or by foot. Your choice."

She gave me a pleading look. "You can't be serious."

I lowered my voice. "I can be a lot of things. And trust me, you don't want to find out."

She jerked back. "What's that supposed to mean?"

"It means you've got one minute. Go with him. Or walk."

"Oh, fine," she muttered, clutching the blanket tighter. "But I'm keeping the blanket."

I glanced down at the thing. "Like I'd want it back."

Finally, complaining all the way, Brittney stalked barefoot out the front door, and finally allowed the driver to guide her into the waiting SUV. A moment later, they were gone.

I turned to Chloe. Finally, we were alone.

Or not – because damn it, Bishop called out from somewhere upstairs. "Well, that went good."

I looked up. Sure enough, there he was, lounging against the bannister in sweatpants and no shirt. His look said it all. *I told you so.*

Yeah, whatever. I turned back to Chloe.

She was glaring up at Bishop. "Eavesdropping again?" she said.

"No," he said. "Trying to sleep. For all the good it did."

Chloe rolled her eyes. "Oh, I'm soooo sorry if we ruined your beauty sleep."

I hollered up to him. "This is a private conversation."

"Private, your ass," Bishop said. "Bet half the neighborhood heard."

Like I cared. The only neighbor I cared about was the girl standing next to me. "Oh, fuck off," I told him, and then, remembering Chloe, I gave her an apologetic look. "Sorry."

She said nothing and looked toward the front door. It was shut. I wanted it to stay shut. I wanted Chloe to stay here with me, not just tonight, but forever.

Looking at her now, my heart ached. She looked small and tired, and I knew the reasons why. She'd had a shitty night, mostly thanks to me. Somehow, I'd make it up to her. I'd make everything up to her. I just needed the chance.

Bishop's voice cut into my thoughts. "Told you that was a bad idea. But women, what do you expect?"

What the hell? Was he *trying* to be a dick about it?

Chloe made a sound of annoyance. "That's it. I'm outta here."

"Hey," Bishop said, "don't leave on my account. I'm heading back to bed."

I turned to glare at him. "Yeah, you do that." Struggling to keep my cool, I reached up to rub the back of my neck. Everything felt too tight. A lot was riding on the next few minutes, and so far, it wasn't going great.

Next to me, Chloe hollered up to Bishop. "I hope you sleep like crap!"

Any other time, I would've laughed. But I couldn't. Because I was losing her. Or maybe I already had. Sure enough, she turned toward the door.

Something like panic seized my heart. "Chloe." I reached out for her. "Don't leave."

She ignored me and flung the door wide open.

"You're not walking," I said.

She turned to glare at me. "We already had this discussion."

Okay, so maybe I couldn't keep her here. But I *could* make sure she got home safely. "At least let me drive you."

"No."

"Alright, then I'm walking with you."

"No, you're not." She strode through the open door and didn't look back.

So I did the only thing I could.

I followed after her.

CHAPTER 14

I was maybe five steps behind her when she reached the front gate. And then, as if sensing someone following her, she turned around. When she spotted me, she stopped.

Trying not to crowd her, I stopped, too.

Her eyebrows furrowed. "What are you doing?"

"Making sure you get home okay."

With a huff, she turned back around and started walking again. Again, I followed after her. It was still dark, and there was no way I was letting her walk home alone

After a block or so, she stopped and turned around again. Her gaze narrowed. "You don't need to do this."

The hell I didn't. "Yes. I do."

There was a lot of weirdness going on. And the thing with Brittney had me thinking. If she had the nerve to apologize naked, what else did she have planned? Did she have another pair of guys waiting in the wings to jump Chloe a second time?

The odds were slim, but not so slim that I'd risk it.

Chloe was still standing there, watching me. "But it's creeping me out."

"Why?" I asked.

"Because I don't like someone walking behind me."

"Then I'll walk with you. But you're not walking back alone."

Chloe glanced around, as trying to make a point. Yeah, I got it. It was a nice neighborhood, with street lights and everything. But the trees were tall, and the sidewalk was cast in shadows.

Chloe could be pissed all she wanted, but it wasn't going to change my mind. Yeah, I wanted her to forgive me for what I'd done. And yeah, I wanted her to take me back. But more than anything, I wanted her to be safe – because I'd rather lose her honestly than see anything bad happen to her.

"Fine," Chloe muttered. "Whatever. But it doesn't change anything."

I strode forward, joining her on the quiet sidewalk. For a couple of minutes, we walked in silence. The wind picked up, and she gave a shiver. Just like before, I hated to see it.

If I were wearing a jacket, I would've gladly handed it over. But I wasn't. And the way it looked, she sure as hell didn't want me warming her with my own body.

I glanced toward her house. In ten minutes, we'd be at her front door. If I were smart, I'd make those minutes count. I spoke up. "I want to tell you something."

She didn't even look. "What?"

"I know you don't want to hear it, but I do love you, and I'm so fucking sorry."

Her steps faltered, and she blinked hard. Was that bad? Or good?

Either way, I took a deep breath and kept on talking. "Which is why you deserve to know why I flipped out on you."

She was still walking, faster now. But she deserved to hear this, for her own peace-of-mind, if nothing else.

Whether she and I worked things out or not, she lived on just the other side of my fence. We were neighbors, and I didn't want her to be afraid of me. I didn't want her to be worried that I'd jump the fence and drag her away like the animal she thought I was.

So I took a deep breath and continued. "A few years ago, right after that first fight video went viral, I met this girl. It was before that reality series."

Chloe, like anyone else in the world, knew which series I meant. It was the one that had made me a household name. I felt a bitter smile cross my lips. Well, that and the sex tape.

I ignored the bitterness and kept on going. "But I was starting to make a name for myself. Then there was the money. Growing up, I never had any, you know? But it was starting to roll in. Lots of it. At least compared to what I had before."

It was a massive understatement. Growing up, I'd been dirt poor. I'd known hunger and fear firsthand. These days, I ate at the best restaurants whenever I wanted. I had a housekeeper, a gourmet kitchen, and a private chef any time I wanted, which come to think of it, was pretty much never.

About the fear, well, that was a funny thing, too. I'd outgrown it years ago. Or more likely, any fear had been beat out of me by kids who were twice my size and ten times as vicious. By the time I hit thirteen, I was taking them on every day – and winning.

And now, only one thing scared me – really scared me – and that was the thought of losing the only girl I'd ever loved.

And because I loved her, I had to share the ugly story of a different girl, a girl I *didn't* love – and that was putting it mildly.

I fucking hated her.

I shook off the anger and kept on talking. "But this girl, she worked as a cocktail waitress at this club I used to go to. She seemed nice. You know, working her way through college and all that. I don't remember what her major was supposed to be, but she was studying all the time, brought her books to the bar, always talked about what she was gonna do when she graduated."

I blew out a breath. "Wait. I remember. A veterinarian." I thought of Brandy, with her stacks of books that were mostly for show. "Yeah. An animal doctor. She was gonna take care of puppies and kittens, and nurse them back to health and all that shit."

Chloe gave me a sideways glance. "Shit?"

Chloe loved animals. I did, too. But that had nothing to do with this. "You know what I mean."

"Actually," she said, not sounding too happy about it, "I don't."

Maybe she didn't get it *now*. But she would by the time I finished. So I kept on going. "Anyway, I used to hang out at the club sometimes. And we got friendly."

Chloe snorted. "Yeah, I just bet."

I felt my jaw tense. Yeah, I had a bad reputation. And yeah, I'd done a lot to earn that reputation. But the thing with Brandy was different, because it was the thing that got me started on the road to quick fucks with girls whose names I couldn't remember, mostly because I didn't care enough to make the effort.

But Chloe didn't know this. Not yet. But she would. So I shoved aside the irritation and went on. "Not that way. Not at first."

"Why not?" she asked.

"Because I liked her." I thought of Brandy, remembering the girl she'd pretended to be. "In some ways, she was a lot like you. Or at least, I thought she was. Which is why I didn't want us to... you know."

For some reason, I didn't want to say it. But it was true. I'd kept Brandy out of my bed for two reasons. One was simple, and one was a lot more complicated.

"So let me get this straight," Chloe said. "You *didn't* want to have sex with her, and somehow she reminds you of me." Her voice grew sarcastic. "Gee, thanks."

I tried again. "It's not that I didn't *want* to. I mean, she was—" Looking back, it wasn't funny, but I had to laugh. "I mean, like I said, she was a lot like you. One minute, she'd be sweet and funny. And then the next minute? She'd be cussing like a truck driver, surprised the crap out of me. And she was—" I cleared my throat "—attractive."

And she *was* attractive. I recalled her sun-kissed hair and wide blue eyes. And her body, well, there was nothing to complain about there.

Next to me, Chloe muttered, "How nice for you."

Nice? No. There was nothing nice about this story. I plowed forward, eager to get it over with. "But things were so crazy back then. I had girls throwing themselves at me everywhere I went."

"Like *that's* changed," Chloe said.

"Maybe," I said. "I dunno. But back then, it was all so new, I didn't handle it that good." I shoved a hand through my hair. "I dunno. But this girl I liked. We were friends, maybe something more someday. I didn't know. But I wasn't gonna mess it up."

In my life, I'd messed up a lot of things. Even before Brandy, it wasn't like I'd been a saint. But there was something about Brandy, and now, I knew exactly what that something was.

She'd reminded me of Chloe, not that I knew Chloe's name at the time.

"I get it," Chloe said. "You liked her. So?"

"So you know who I'm talking about, right?"

She shrugged.

"Brandy Blue." Just the name set my teeth on edge. "The girl from, you know, that video."

Chloe gave me a sideways glance. "I didn't know Brandy went to college."

"That's because she didn't."

Chloe stopped walking, and so did I. She turned to face me. "What do you mean?"

"I mean," I said, "it was all a sham. Everything. The nice girl act, the college thing, the books. It was just one big crock."

CHAPTER 15

I thought of Brandy, wondering how I'd been so stupid to fall for her act. But I *knew* how. She'd been a damn good actress, even if Hollywood didn't see it that way. Who knows? Maybe she was a lot more convincing in person.

"A crock?" Chloe was saying. "I don't get it. Why?"

"That's the best part," I said. "This guy – someone I thought was a friend – he gets this idea that I should make a sex tape." I gave a bitter laugh. "Everyone was doing 'em. Quick fame, right? That could be me. Famous for being famous. All I needed was a willing partner."

But Chloe was shaking her head.

I knew why. The girl I'd been describing sounded nothing like Brandy. Brandy had never gone to college. Brandy hated animals. Brandy cared about one thing, and one thing only – getting famous, no matter what it took.

Well, she got her wish, didn't she? After that sex tape, she'd moved on to horror flicks. She played the same role in all of them – the nearly naked co-ed who gets slashed, stabbed, or in the case of the last movie, possessed by a sex-starved demon who literally screws her to death. Then there was that doctor drama, where she played a nympho brain surgeon of all things. .

Chloe was looking at me, like I'd lived down to her lowest expectations. "So you did it?" she said.

"That's what you think?" I couldn't keep the edge out of my

voice. "That I filmed that thing on purpose? That I wanted the world to see me fucking some chick for five minutes of fame?"

Chloe looked down, refusing to meet my eyes. So she *had* believed it? I was used to people thinking the worst of me, but for some reason, this stung.

It was time to set her straight. "You want the truth?"

She looked up and gave a small nod.

"That kind of fame?" I said. "Don't want it, don't need it. But Brandy, she wants it *and* needs it, because she's gonna be a fuckin' star someday."

"So what happened?" Chloe asked.

"So she hooks up with this friend of mine. And this so-called friend tells her everything she needs to know – where I hang out, things I like, things that piss me off. And they agree to this split."

"Of the money?"

"No. He gets the money. She gets the exposure."

Yeah, she'd been exposed alright. For a few crazy months, the only thing more famous than her pussy was my cock.

"Exposed?" Chloe said. "Literally or figuratively?"

"You saw the footage. What do *you* think?"

Chloe shook her head. "I don't know. I never watched it."

If she was trying to spare my feelings, it was too late for that.

"I saw the disk," I said. "Remember?"

I didn't bother spelling out which disk. I'd seen it sitting right there on her kitchen table. The label on the case, written in big, black letters, was a dead giveaway. Rastor Sex Tape.

When I'd first spotted the thing, I'd assumed it was something worse – footage of me and Chloe. Now that I knew it wasn't, I should've been relieved. Hell, I *was* relieved. But I still wasn't loving the idea of Chloe and her best friend watching me screw another girl.

The way it looked, they'd even had popcorn. It was nice to know I was so entertaining.

But Chloe was shaking her head. Her voice grew quiet. "Erika brought it over. You know, for my birthday. She didn't know that you and I were together. She thought it would be funny. You know, because we're neighbors."

She blew out a shaky breath. "But you and I *were* together." She glanced away and whispered, "At least I thought we were."

She was so close, and something in her voice warmed my heart. I could hear it, the same longing for me that I felt for her. I said her name. "Chloe."

She looked up, hitting me with those eyes of hers, and I felt myself swallow as everything else faded to nothing. I leaned closer. "We were. I still wanna be."

Her eyes grew warmer, and she said, "Anyway, it just seemed wrong to watch it." Her lips formed the barest hint of a smile. "Plus, well, I guess I didn't really *want* to watch you doing that with anyone else."

I had to smile. "Yeah?"

She stood, still and silent on the darkened street. The air was frigid, and the wind had picked up. I should've been freezing, but the warmth in her eyes was warming me to the bone.

I hadn't lost her. Not completely.

She gave a small shiver, and I almost smiled, because this one, I knew, wasn't from the cold.

"So with Brandy," she said, "you two ended up having sex anyway, and she taped it?"

Oh yeah. Brandy. My smile faded. "Not exactly. This one night, outside the club, I was supposed to meet her there at closing time. Get a coffee or something. So I pull up to the back entrance, and she's already there." At the memory, I felt my muscles tense. "And she's crying."

"Why?" Chloe asked.

"Well at first, it was hard to get the story out of her. But from what I *did* get, a couple of guys jumped her in the parking lot. Tore at her uniform, and tried to–" I paused. "Well, you know."

"Oh my God," Chloe said. "Did they ever find them?"

At this, I had to laugh. It was a bitter sound in the quiet night. "No. And you wanna know why?"

"Why?"

"Because they didn't exist."

CHAPTER 16

Chloe was shaking her head. "What do you mean they didn't exist?"

"It was all a big show," I explained. "The torn clothes, the fake tears. By then, she knows me pretty good. Especially with this friend of mine feeding her information. And she knows I can get a little intense when people I love are hurt..."

I couldn't finish the sentence. There was only one girl I loved, and she *had* been hurt tonight. By me. I had some serious making up to do.

Chloe's voice was quiet. "So you loved her?"

"I dunno. Not like that." An image of Brandy flashed in my brain. "It's not that she was unattractive–"

"You already said that."

And there it was again. The spark of something. She still had feelings for me, whether she'd admit it or not.

"Alright," I said, "you want the truth? I didn't see her like that."

"Why not?" Chloe asked.

I didn't answer, not right away. The reason was complicated, and it involved Chloe. When all this went down, I didn't even know Chloe's name. But she'd been there – in my head and in my heart.

I could tell Chloe that now. And then what? Would she think I'd been stalking her? Would she wonder what else I was hiding?

She was still waiting for an answer. And stupid or not, I wanted to tell her everything. "The truth?" I said. "There was this *other* girl, someone I'd met maybe a few months earlier, before everything started to hit. And I couldn't get this girl out of my head."

Chloe was frowning again. From jealousy? It would be nice to think so. But what if it was something else? Like disgust that I'd been wanting one girl while screwing another?

Tonight, I'd messed up in every way. I'd misjudged everything. I'd done things that I shouldn't. I'd said things that would haunt me forever. Now, more than anything, I didn't want to mess this up.

Chloe made a sound of frustration. "You're changing the subject. What about Brandy?"

I didn't want to talk about Brandy. I wanted to talk about Chloe. I wanted to tell her that she'd been haunting my thoughts for years. I wanted to explain that even while I'd been screwing Brandy senseless for the whole world to see, another girl had been on my mind. And that girl had been Chloe.

I felt myself frown. Right, because nothing says "I love you," like fucking one girl while thinking of another.

It was too messed up, and the risk was too high. I pushed away the distractions and focused on Chloe's real question. The night of that sex tape, what really happened?

I let out an long breath. "So that night, after this so-called attack, she wouldn't let me do a damn thing about it."

"Like what?" Chloe asked. "What'd you want to do?"

"Find those guys, take care of it."

"How?"

I shrugged. "I had a few ideas."

I thought of the two guys who'd attacked Chloe. I had some good ideas for them, too. Someday, I might thank my brother for talking some sense into me. But right now, I wasn't feeling particularly thankful.

Chloe's voice broke into my thoughts. "So what happened?"

It was a sore subject. But I'd brought it up – because Chloe deserved an explanation for what I'd done. "So we go back to her place," I said, "and I should've known something was up. The place looked like—"

How the hell did I explain it? There were flowers next to her bed, roses and carnations in a tall white vase. The lighting was soft, and her bedroom was warm. The comforter on her king-size bed was pink satin. She had matching pillows with lots of lace.

It was like Valentine's Day on steroids. I recalled being surprised, thinking, "Man, she really likes the girly stuff." Looking back, it wasn't so much a bedroom as a porn set. God, I'd been such a dumb-ass.

I made a sound of disgust. "Well, let's just say it looked like she was expecting company."

"Romantic company?" Chloe asked.

"Yeah. And she asks me to hold her, and starts kissing on me, and one thing leads to another."

Chloe snorted. "Yeah. I bet."

My jaw tightened. "Go ahead, joke about it. You and everyone else." I tried to laugh. "I should be used to it, right?"

Yeah, I was pissed. Chloe deserved an explanation. I got that. But I was sick to death of the whole fucking thing. That night with Brandy had changed everything.

Okay, some of it was for the better. I mean, it made me famous, right? But a lot of it, it wasn't so good, because in the end, Brandy became the first in a long line of girls who meant nothing to me when all was said and done. I didn't trust them, and I didn't love them. They were a blur of bodies without any faces that I cared enough to remember.

They'd used me. I'd used them. But somehow, it didn't feel like a win-win.

And then there were the punch lines, starring me, Brandy, and, in the words of one Web site, my giant cock. It was every guy's dream, right? To get rich, famous, *and* known for being well hung?

Hey, at least I knew how to use it. That had to count for something, right?

Chloe's voice drifted over my dark thoughts. "I'm sorry." She paused. "Really."

I shook my head. "It's alright."

But it wasn't. All this time, Chloe had been different, untouched by all of that ugliness. She'd been kind to me when I was a nobody.

There I'd been, lying on the sidewalk, half-dead and headed for a crash. She'd picked me up, maybe not physically, but close enough. And then, she'd pulled me from the darkness.

And for years afterward, she'd been the thing that kept me going when a different kind of darkness crept around the edges. It was a funny thing. Thanks to Chloe, I knew there was sweetness to offset the sour, goodness to offset the bad, and somewhere in the world, a girl who liked me for all the right reasons.

Or so I thought.

"No," she said, her voice softer now. "It's not alright. I don't want to be like everyone else. At least, not about this."

At the regret in her voice, my anger evaporated. "That's the thing," I told her. "You're *not* like anyone else." I reached for her hand. "Not about anything."

Her hand was small and soft, and this time, she didn't pull away. Instead, she leaned closer and asked, "So what happened then?"

She knew. Everyone knew. But I said it anyway. "So we had sex. Obviously."

And not just once. The tape was what, three hours long? Longer than most Hollywood productions.

When Chloe said nothing, I kept on talking. "So a few days later, the footage of it hits all these Web sites, and Brandy's gone." I made a scoffing sound. "To Hollywood, L.A., whatever. Big surprise, huh?"

"What about your friend?" Chloe asked.

Oh yeah. Glenn. My so-called friend. Turns out, he orchestrated the whole thing, right down to the bed itself, which he'd bought on credit. But hey, he got his investment back, didn't he? And then some.

"The next time I see him," I said, "he's driving a Jag."

"Did you confront him about it?" she asked.

I'd done more than confront him. But that was a different story. So all I said was, "You might say that."

"So what about Brandy?" she asked.

"What about her?"

"You ever see her again? I mean, I read about that thing in

Beverly Hills."

Oh yeah. That. I'd seen how it played in the media. It wasn't good, especially because the real story played out a whole lot differently.

CHAPTER 17

The story, according to the tabloids and all those Web sites, had me screwing Brandy in the men's room and then going on an ass-beating rampage afterwards. Only half of that was true, and it wasn't the screwing part.

"Yeah. About that," I said. "Her acting career? It wasn't exactly taking off."

"It seemed like it was going alright," Chloe said.

"Yeah. She had a few parts. But she wanted something bigger. So I'm at this dinner – some promo thing for a celebrity endorsement. And she corners me in the men's room."

"Seriously?"

In my mind, I could see it. I'd come out from a bathroom stall, and there she'd been, sitting on the restroom counter, with her skirt hiked up and her blouse unbuttoned. There was no bra, no panties, and no hesitation to flaunt it.

Her thighs were spread and her back was arched. She wore red high heels and matching lipstick. She was the perfect picture of a centerfold, but all I felt was disgust.

"Yeah," I said to Chloe. "And the way it looks, she's ready for a sequel."

Apparently, the sequel involved me nailing her next to the bathroom sink, or letting it play out a different way – the way it *did* play out. Either way, Brandy got what she wanted, plenty of attention.

"A sequel? Chloe said. "You're kidding,"

"Only half," I said. "Because Brandy's not stupid. She knows damn well I'm not gonna fall for some secret camera thing again. But she still could use the publicity, right? So she gets half-naked and corners me."

Chloe shook her head. "You *did* say this was in the *men's* room, right?"

"Yeah. And as soon as I see her, I take off. But she follows after me, making this big scene. And from what she's yelling, it sounds like we just did it right there in the stall."

In my mind, I could still hear Brandy screaming as the crowd grew thick around us. "You asshole! What do you think I am? Your personal cum dumpster? Well next time you want a quickie, call someone else, because I'm not your plaything!"

Her skirt was crooked, and one of her boobs was hanging out of her open blouse. Her lipstick was smudged, and her eyes were filled with big, fake tears.

As for me, I'd been fully clothed, which, the way the tabloids saw it, just made me a bigger asshole. Like I'd unzipped my fly and stuck it to her fast and hard.

"So I get the hell out of there," I continued, "and she's following after me, acting like I'd just done the wham-bam-thank-you-ma'am. And I see all these photographers."

"She set you up?" Chloe asked.

"Yeah. Did a good job of it too. Even hired these bouncers to keep me from leaving. She wanted a full spectacle."

"Boy, she sure got it," Chloe said. "How come you never told anyone?"

"I did. I said flat-out that none of it happened. You think *that* got any coverage? Besides, you think anyone gives a crap?"

"They might've," Chloe said, "if you had told the whole story."

"You think anyone wants the whole story?" I tried to laugh. "Besides, she did me a big favor, right? Right after that sex tape hit, I was signed to that reality show."

The show, *Hard World*, had changed everything, mostly because *I* had changed. By then, I'd become a different person, especially when it came to sex. As far as the female cast-members, I'd had them all, and had fun doing it, or at least that's what I told myself at the time.

Chloe was frowning. "About that show, was any of that true?"

"Which part?"

"You." She cleared her throat. "And all those girls?"

Chloe's question hung in the open air. And damn it, I didn't want to answer.

Basically, I'd screwed my way from one end of the house to the other, sometimes tapping two girls in a single night. They meant nothing to me. They were Brandy clones, each and every one of them, wanting quick fame and easy money.

I frowned. Or maybe it was too convenient for me to see them that way. The fun – if you could call it that – ended after some redhead named Macey threw another girl out a plate glass window.

The girl, an aspiring actress named Cookie of all things, needed fifteen stitches across her forehead and countless more on her arms and legs. The publicity was insane, but the show was over – cancelled, according to news reports.

Cancelled, my ass. I'd walked out and refused to return. As far as the producers? Rather than admit they'd lost the guy who had people tuning in, they'd quietly succumbed to "bad publicity", so they'd "cancelled for the safety of their amazing cast."

I could still remember that press release. What a joke.

Chloe was still waiting for my answer. Was any of it true?

I wasn't going to lie. "Yeah."

Disappointment darkened her features. "Oh."

"You've gotta understand," I said, "everywhere I looked, someone wanted something from me. I guess I was pissed off, maybe a little tired of fighting it." I squeezed her hand. "Until you."

"Why me?"

"What do you mean?"

"Why not Amber? Or Brittney?"

Was she kidding? I studied her face. "Is that a serious question?"

"Well, take Brittney," she said. "You obviously liked her well enough a few weeks ago. And Amber too. Why not them?"

I tried to find the words. "Girls like Brittney are easy."

"That's for sure," Chloe muttered.

"I don't mean that." I shook my head. "With girls like her, I know what I'm getting. And they know what they're getting, too."

"Girls like what?"

"You know the type," I said. "Girls from the wrong side of town who pretend to be something they're not."

Maybe that didn't describe Amber, but it described Brittney just fine, along with countless other girls along the way.

Chloe's hand grew stiff in mine. "What's she pretending to be?"

"I dunno. Some socialite, I guess. Take that sorority thing. Get this. She doesn't even go to college."

"Not now?" Chloe said. "Or not ever?"

"Not ever. And probably never will."

"You're kidding."

"Nope."

"How do you know?"

I gave Chloe the run-down of Brittney's drunken visit from a few weeks earlier, when she'd told me the truth. Her mom wasn't a banker, she wasn't in a sorority, and her life was a pathetic mess.

If Brittney were a nicer person, I might even feel sorry for her.

Chloe was shaking her head. "But she told that same lie tonight. About the sorority, I mean. Why would she do that if you knew the truth?"

I shrugged. "She probably forgot. Like I said, she was pretty trashed."

"But why didn't you call her on it?"

"Tonight? Because I didn't care. I figured you wouldn't either. I mean, c'mon, it's pathetic, right?"

And it *was* pathetic. I recalled Brittney's cheap-ass apartment in that shitty part of town. Brittney's bedroom, with its lacy bedspread and girly-girl pillows, had been the only clean room in the whole place. As for the rest of it, it was littered with garbage, including Brittney's roommate, who, as far as I could tell, turned tricks for drug-money.

I'd been in that apartment less than fifteen minutes, but it had made an impression.

Chloe's hand slipped from mine, and she started walking again. I fell in beside her and asked, "What's wrong?"

"Nothing." She kept on walking, looking not so much angry as overwhelmed.

I could see why. It was a lot to digest. But I didn't like the fact that we were moving again. Time was running out. Up ahead, I spotted Chloe's place, maybe five minutes away.

It might be now or never. "Chloe?" I said.

"Yeah?"

"Will you give me another chance?"

For a long time, she said nothing, and her silence grew heavier with every step.

Finally, I had to ask, "Is this your way of telling me no, that it's over?"

Still moving, I glanced over at her. She looked lost in thought, and part of me wondered if she'd heard my question at all.

Too soon, we were at the foot of her long driveway. She stopped and turned to face me. I stopped too and studied her face. I saw a flicker of warmth tinged with caution.

She was thinking about it. I could tell.

I pressed my luck. "Chloe, I do love you."

She looked down at her feet. "I love you too. But I'm not sure it's enough."

"It's enough for me," I said. "The first time I saw you, I just knew."

And I had. Funny, I'd always laughed at guys who fell too hard and too fast. But with Chloe, it was impossible to do anything else. Maybe it was because of how we met.

I'd been lying there half-dead, and she hadn't let *me* slip away. At the memory, I almost smiled. And now, five years later, here I was waiting for another chance.

She turned and looked toward the horizon. "It's really late."

I looked too. It was lighter now, almost sunrise. "No. It's early, remember?"

She turned and gave me a sad smile. "Lawton, I'm not sure you really know me. And if I'm being really honest, that's my fault not yours. But it is what it is."

"I do know you," I said. "At least all that matters."

She shook her head. "No. You don't. And honestly, I probably don't know you very well either."

Maybe. But somehow, I'd change that, even if it meant showing her things that I'd rather stay hidden. On impulse, I said, "You wanna know me? Come with me tomorrow."

"Where?"

"You'll see."

She bit her lip. "Tomorrow's not good."

"Then how about the next day?"

"Monday?" She gave a small smile. "I'm working that day, too."

"But you don't go in 'til late, right?"

"Yeah. But I can't afford to be late anymore."

I knew what she meant. Earlier tonight, she'd been at least a couple of hours late for work. My fault, not hers. "I won't make you late," I said. "I promise."

She hesitated, looking almost tempted.

I pressed the advantage. "C'mon. It's my last day in town this week. Say yes."

"You're taking a trip?"

"Not a vacation. Work. This event in Vegas." At a sudden thought, I smiled. "You wanna come?"

She gave a playful eye-roll. "Very funny."

"You think I'm joking?"

I wasn't joking. This trip, I wasn't looking forward to. But with Chloe, everything would be different. It could be a fresh start for both of us.

"I don't know what to think," she said, "but it doesn't matter. I'm working every day 'til Friday."

"Then c'mon, say yes for Monday." I looked into her eyes. "Please?"

Finally, I saw the hint of a real smile. "Maybe."

"I'm taking that as a yes." I glanced toward her house. "Can I walk you to the door?"

She shook her head. "Nah, that's alright." With a small wave, she turned and started walking down her long driveway. I waited, watching from the street, to make sure she got inside okay. And then, after I saw the lights flick on inside her house, I turned and headed back to my own place.

What I found there wasn't good.

CHAPTER 18

I heard them before I saw them. I was still on the sidewalk, walking toward my front gate when a female voice hollered out, "Let me in! I mean it!"

Damn it. The voice was Brittney's. With a muttered curse, I picked up the pace.

I was still moving when I heard Amber yell out, "Stop it! Or I'm telling!"

Striding through my open front gate, I spotted them in the turnaround. The way it looked, Amber was inside her car, and Brittney was crawling up on its front hood.

Amber's sunroof was open, and her head was poking out the top. Brittney lunged across the front windshield and made a grab for what? Amber's face? I never found out, because Amber ducked out of Brittney's reach just in time.

Brittney slid backward, down the front windshield. "Oh come on!" she yelled. "Just unlock the door, alright?"

Amber's head popped up long enough to yell, "No way! I'm not here to see *you*."

I looked toward the house and spotted Bishop, standing in the open doorway. He wore sweatpants and a white T-shirt. He had a coffee mug in his hand, and he casually took a sip.

I ignored him and strode toward the car. When Brittney spotted me, she froze, like a farmer caught fucking a sheep.

I stopped moving and gave her a good, long look. She looked

like a cartoon hobo in dark, masculine clothes that were twice her size and vaguely familiar.

I eyed her up and down, cataloguing her clothes – black slacks, a button-down dress-shirt, a suit-jacket, and men's dress-shoes that looked about five sizes too big.

Son-of-a-bitch.

I knew why the clothes were familiar. They looked exactly like the clothes the driver had been wearing maybe an hour earlier when he'd driven Brittney away. The only things missing were his cap and tie.

What the hell?

Brittney was still perched on the hood of Amber's car. "Oh, hey, Lawton." She gave me a nervous smile. "You're back."

"So are you," I muttered.

From inside the car, Amber popped up from the open sunroof long enough to yell, "She won't let me out!"

"Liar!" Brittney yelled before turning back to me. "She won't let me in!"

Again, I looked to Bishop. He was still drinking his coffee – or whatever. Come to think of it, he didn't drink coffee.

Did he?

Did it matter?

Cursing, I moved closer to Amber's car and peered through the glass. From the driver's seat, Amber yelled, "Tell her to go away!"

"Screw that!" Brittney yelled, crawling down from the hood. "Tell her to let me in!" A second later, she was at my side, saying, "I don't know what her problem is. She acts like I'm gonna kill her or something."

Brittney turned toward the car and hollered through the glass, "You see a chainsaw here? No! You don't! So open up already!"

"No way!" Amber yelled. "Not 'til you're gone!"

With a huff, Brittney turned to me and said, "Can you believe this?"

Yeah, I could.

"What the hell are you doing here?" I asked.

To think, I'd literally paid someone to take her away, and

somehow, she'd ended up right back on my doorstep.

She made a pouty face. "I forgot my purse."

From inside the car, Amber yelled, "I bet it's a fake!"

Brittney whirled toward her. "It is not!" She turned back to me. "You believe me, right?"

At this point, what I believed had nothing to do with anyone's purse. I turned my attention to Amber, who was still hunkered down in the car.

I spoke through the glass, "And what are *you* doing here?"

The nearest window slid down barely a crack. Amber lifted her face to the slim opening and said, "You said you wanted to talk."

I gave her a look. "And you couldn't have called?"

Here, I'd left a dozen messages, and none of them contained an invitation to stop by. In fact, I'd been pretty pissed off at the time and hadn't bothered to hide it. If Amber was smart, she would've stayed far away.

"I did call," Amber said. "You didn't answer. But you said it was important." She gave me a big, friendly smile. "So here I am."

Yes. Here she was.

"Big whoop," Brittney said. "I was here first."

"So what?" Amber said. "It doesn't count if they don't let you in."

I glanced toward the front door. Bishop was still there. Guarding the house? Or enjoying the show? Knowing him, it was probably both.

Next to me, Brittney gave a loud, dramatic sigh. "I've had the worst night, and nobody even cares."

Well, I sure as hell didn't care.

But she was still talking. "I just *know* I'm locked out of my apartment." She glanced toward Bishop. "And your stupid brother won't help." She cupped her hands and hollered out, "Thanks a lot!"

He lifted his mug in mock salute.

"It's called sarcasm!" Brittney called back. "Thanks for nothing, asshole!"

With a half shrug, Bishop took another drink of whatever.

Brittney turned back to me. "And Amber won't give me a ride

either."

Through clenched teeth, I said, "You had a ride."

"Yeah, but that one sucked."

From inside the car, Amber yelled, "You sucked *him*, you mean!"

"I did not!" Brittney said, and then muttered, "We did other stuff."

Well, I guess that explained the clothes. As for the driver, what was *he* wearing now? Just the cap and tie?

More importantly, where *was* he?

I pulled out my cell phone and found the contact. I hit the call button.

"If you're calling the driver," Brittney said, "don't bother. Something happened to his phone." She gave a little laugh. "The guy was a total idiot."

No. I was the idiot. I should've warned the guy. Just because a girl is naked, it doesn't mean she's harmless.

I knew *that* from experience. Too much experience.

I turned and called out to Bishop. "Get Brittney's purse, will ya?"

Brittney made a sound of annoyance. "Can't I come in?"

"No."

"But I don't have a ride!"

"You will," I told her. And I meant it, too. But this time, I wasn't taking any chances. This new driver was gonna be a lot smarter than the last one, even if he wouldn't be too happy about it.

CHAPTER 19

Ten minutes later, I was sitting in the passenger's seat of Amber's car with the engine running.

Amber glanced toward the house. "Can't we go inside?"

"Hell no."

"Why not?"

I gave her a look. "You gotta ask?"

For one thing, I wasn't in the mood for company. For another, there was no way in hell I was taking the chance of Chloe showing up and finding me in the house with yet another girl, especially if the girl happened to be Amber.

Amber's voice was quiet. "It's because of *her*, isn't it?"

Well, at least she didn't call Chloe "dog girl" again.

"Listen," I said, feeling that familiar edge creep into my voice, "her name is Chloe, and after what you did to her—"

"I didn't do anything to her."

"Cut the crap," I said. "I already got the story from Brittney."

"Brittney, the liar? You're gonna believe her over me?"

"She's *your* best friend," I reminded her.

"Not anymore." With a huff, Amber sank back against the driver's seat. "I'm totally done with her."

This wasn't a surprise. Amber went through best friends the way kids went through cookies. It always ended the same. After a few weeks, the friend would show their ass, and Amber would finally move on, only after getting hurt.

I felt my jaw tighten. But this time, the one getting hurt wasn't Amber. It was Chloe.

Amber and I had been friends for a long time now. I did business with her dad. My life would be a lot easier if I just let everything go and forgot what she did. But I'd never been one to take the easy route.

The only reason I was out here, talking to Amber at all, was to set things straight so she didn't show up on my doorstep later on. No matter what it took, I was going to win Chloe back. And when that happened, I sure as hell didn't need Amber in the middle, messing things up.

I turned to face her. "Amber, you need to know something. We're done. Our friendship, or whatever, it's over."

She blinked. "What? Why?"

"You know why."

She gave me a confused look. "No, I don't. Honest."

Did I really need to explain it? Just ten hours earlier, I'd seen Chloe lying on the ground with a knife to her throat. The knife might've been fake, but the scene was real enough. There was no way in hell I could let that slide.

From what I'd learned over the last few hours, Brittney and Amber had planned the whole thing. Maybe Amber hadn't been the mastermind — as ridiculous as that sounded — but she hadn't done anything to stop it either.

Whether she'd been too jealous or just too weak, it was the same result. Chloe had gotten hurt, thanks to Amber and her latest best friend.

But Amber was shaking her head. "But…what'd I do?"

Oh for fuck's sake. Amber wasn't the brightest bulb in the world, but even *she* couldn't be this stupid. Fine, if I needed to spell it out, whatever.

Through gritted teeth, I told Amber everything I knew, starting with the fact that Chloe had been jumped in her own front yard and ending with Brittney's lame excuse that it was all just a prank.

"But that wasn't supposed to happen!" Amber said. "At least not like that."

"Yeah?" I said, feeling my blood pressure rise. "How, exactly, was it supposed to happen?" I gave her a hard look. "Let me guess. I wasn't supposed to catch them in the middle of it? I wasn't supposed to force their sorry asses into their *own* trunk and make *them* jump out in *their* fucking underwear?"

When Amber said nothing, I went on. "So, it was supposed to be *Chloe* out there? Half-naked where she fucking works. Is that it?"

Amber drew back. "I don't know what you're talking about." She blinked back tears. "Honest."

"Oh yeah? So tell me. How was it supposed to happen?"

She was sniffling now. "It's hard to talk when you're so mad about it."

"Fine by me." I reached for the door-handle.

"You're leaving?"

"Yeah. And you should, too." I opened the car-door. "And Amber?"

"What?"

"Don't come back."

She paused. "Ever?"

"Ever." I got out of the car and slammed the door shut behind me, leaving Amber to drive off – or not. If she stayed too long, I'd call my usual security firm and have her hustled out like the trespasser she was.

Besides, I had something else to do, and it didn't involve being nice to a girl who didn't deserve it. I bypassed the house and went straight for the unattached garage out back.

A couple of minutes later, I was in the driver's seat of my basic dark sedan. I pulled out of the driveway, passing Amber's car, still sitting in the turnaround, with the engine still running.

If Amber was smart, she'd be gone by the time I got back.

But as it turned out, she wasn't.

CHAPTER 20

I'd been gone for two hours. Now, walking through my front gate, I wasn't happy with what I saw – Amber's car, parked in the same spot as before.

The car was empty, and the engine was no longer running. That could only mean one thing. She was somewhere inside my house.

What the hell?

Sure enough, I found her sitting with Bishop in the front living room. He was still holding that stupid mug and – damn it – now, Amber had a mug, too.

Well, this was just great. My brother – who'd been a dick to Chloe from day-one – had not only let Amber inside my house, but had actually served her coffee.

I stared at them. "What the hell's going on?"

Bishop lifted his mug, but said nothing.

I eyed the mug, some big ceramic thing that my decorator had picked out. "You know where you can shove that thing?"

"Nope." He took a sip. "And I don't wanna know."

I turned to Amber. "And what are *you* doing here?"

It was Bishop who answered. "She's my guest."

"*Your* guest?" I turned to give him a look. "It's *my* house."

Normally, I'd have said my house was his house, too. I trusted the guy. He might be the only guy I trusted. I wouldn't normally give a rat's ass who he invited over, or what they did. But why Amber? And why now?

Amber shifted in her seat. "Do you want me to leave?"

"Yeah," I said, "and this time, don't come back."

She'd barely budged when Bishop said, "Sit. You're not going anywhere."

I glared over at him. "The hell she isn't." After what she'd done to Chloe, she shouldn't even be here.

Bishop flicked his head toward a nearby chair. "Stick around," he told me. "You'll want to hear this."

I didn't move. "I've heard enough."

For hours, I'd been doing a slow burn about the thing with Brittney and Amber. Brittney had been Amber's friend, not mine. Amber had brought Brittney into my house, into my life, and into my relationship with Chloe.

The way I saw it, even if Amber didn't start the problems, she hadn't done a damn thing to stop them. It made her worse than an enemy. It made her a traitor, and I'd dealt with too many of those already.

"Just listen," Bishop said. "Consider it a favor, alright?"

"Yeah?" My jaw was tight. "To who?"

"Me," he said, "for getting blondie out of your hair."

My gaze shifted to Amber.

"Not that one," Bishop said. "The other one."

"So you gave Brittney a ride," I said. "Big deal."

Okay, yeah, it was a big deal. Brittney was a royal pain in the ass, and Bishop had taken her off my hands. But the idea was to get rid of these girls. Not invite them in for coffee.

"And," Bishop continued, "Brittney was locked out."

"So?" I knew Bishop. He could pop a lock in thirty seconds.

"*And*," he said again, "I had to toss out a couple of drunks who tried to block the door."

"What drunks?" I asked.

"Her roommate." He made a sound of disgust. "And some guy."

I recalled our last visit to Brittney's place. She'd been locked out that time, too. I recalled her frizzy-haired roommate, sleeping naked on the couch with some guy old enough to be her grandpa.

I had to ask. "The same guy as before?"

"Nah," Bishop said. "Different one. Huge guy with a nose-ring."

Amber spoke up. "Oh, I know who *that* was. It's one of her roommate's boyfriends. I think his name is John." She frowned. "Come to think of it, a bunch of them are named John. Pretty weird, huh?"

Bishop and I shared a look.

"Uh, yeah," Bishop said. "Weird." He cleared his throat. "Anyway…" He turned back to me. "Amber has something to tell you. So just sit and listen, alright?"

I glanced toward the nearest chair, but made no move to sit.

"You owe me," Bishop said. "Did I mention the guy smelled like cheese?"

Amber was nodding. "Yup, that was John, alright." She wrinkled her nose. "I hope you wore gloves. He has this really weird skin-condition."

Well, that did it.

I made for the chair and sat.

Bishop looked to Amber. "Go on. Tell him what you told me."

Amber gave me a nervous look. "Okay. I tried to tell you earlier, but you were so mad–"

"I'm still mad," I said. "So just spit it out, alright?"

"I will, honest. But first, I have to say something."

I waited.

Her voice grew very quiet. "I'm sorry."

"You should be."

"Hey!" Bishop said, "She's trying to tell you something. Don't be a dick, alright?"

"Me?" I gave him a what-the-hell look. "Now *I'm* the dick? What about *you*?"

"What about me?"

"Every single time you've seen Chloe, you've been a dick to her." I flicked my gaze to Amber. "And now, you're all nice to *her*, the girl who tried to have Chloe kidnapped?"

Amber spoke up. "But I didn't! That's what I'm trying to tell you!"

Yeah, whatever. I crossed my arms and waited.

She took a deep breath. "It wasn't supposed to happen like that."

"Right," I said, not bothering to hide my irritation. "So, how was it supposed to happen?"

"Let me start from the beginning, because *that's* the thing I'm sorry about." She looked down at her lap and said, "I was pretty mean to Chloe." She hesitated. "Brittney and I, well, we had her wait on us, you know, at that restaurant where she works."

When Amber looked up, her cheeks were flushed. "We were kind of awful."

In a careful voice, I asked, "How awful?"

"Well, the first time, we went in with Joey and Paul." She glanced away. "You know, the two guys who uh…"

"Attacked Chloe?" My voice was hard. "*Those* two guys?"

"Um, yeah," she said. "Well, it was the night of your birthday party, actually. Brittney thought it would be fun to go into that restaurant and—"

"Give Chloe a hard time?" I said. "Yeah, I got that."

After a long pause, Amber continued. "And then, we went in a few days after that. This time, it was just me and Brittney. We were pretty mad, you know, because you made us leave your birthday party…"

"Yeah, and you deserved it."

I'd been half-drunk at the time, but I remembered exactly why I'd kicked them out. That was the night I'd learned – from *them*, no less – that they'd been trying to get Chloe fired.

Amber's voice was almost a whisper. "I know."

"You know *what?*"

"That we deserved it. I knew it then, too. But…" She wiped at her eyes. "I just got so caught up in everything. You know what I mean?"

"No. I don't."

It was true. Chloe hadn't done a damn thing to deserve all the grief they'd given her. If they wanted to give *me* grief, fine. I could deal with it. But to gang up on a girl who'd done nothing wrong, especially a girl I loved, well, apology or not, I couldn't let that slide.

Amber was staring down at her hands. Other than the fact she was supposedly sorry, I hadn't learned anything new.

I stood. "Are we done?"

It was Bishop who answered. "Not yet." He turned to Amber. "Go on. Tell him the rest."

I didn't bother sitting back down. The way I saw it, we'd be done in a minute, maybe less.

Amber looked up and started talking again. "About the prank, it wasn't supposed to happen like that."

I made a sound of disgust. "It shouldn't have happened at all."

"But I was trying to be nice," she said. "You know, to make up for being *not* nice before." She gave me a shaky smile. "See?"

"No."

Bishop said, "Start at the beginning."

"Okay," Amber said. "You know at my sorority, we do these kidnapping things. Usually, it's just a mascot or something."

"Chloe's not a mascot," I reminded her.

"Yeah, but it was supposed to be fun. For her, I mean."

I stared at her. "Fun?"

"Yeah. You know, like we'd all show up and 'kidnap' her, like for a party or something." She smiled. "Or maybe a spa treatment. Like a girl's day out. Anyway, I was telling all of this to Brittney, and she said, 'Yeah, we should do that.'"

Amber's voice picked up steam. "And I said, 'Yeah, we totally should.' And I was totally planning something nice, but then before I knew it, Brittney set it up without me." Amber frowned. "Except she totally messed it up."

Amber looked to Bishop. "*You* see what I mean, right?"

He nodded. "Totally." He looked to me and said, "Eh, women. What are you gonna do?"

Amber slumped back in her chair. "I know what *I'm* going to do. I'm never talking to Brittney again." She glanced up. "You know, she's not even *in* my sorority. I just let her *say* that to be nice."

"Maybe that's your problem," I said, "you're too nice to the wrong people."

Even as I said it, I felt like a giant shit-heel. I was one of those people, and for years now, Amber had been nicer to me than I probably deserved.

Suddenly, I felt too drained to think about it. I'd been awake for how long now? At least twenty-four hours.

"So anyway," Amber said, "that's why I'm sorry, not just for being mean before, but because the prank got all messed up." She gave me a hopeful smile. "So, do you forgive me?"

Her question hung in the air. If it had been *me* who'd gotten hurt, it would easy to let this slide. I said, "It's not *me* you should be apologizing to."

"Oh, I'm gonna apologize to Chloe, too," Amber said.

I thought of Brittney's apology. "I'm not sure that's such a good idea."

Amber leaned forward. "Oh, but it is. I'm gonna wear clothes and everything." She glanced at Bishop. "I heard what Brittney did. God, what a slut."

An hour later, Amber was gone. From the open front doorway, I watched her car pull out of the driveway and turn onto the quiet street.

From somewhere behind me, Bishop spoke. "You'll be glad you did that."

I turned, and there he was, watching me with those sharp eyes of his. I didn't want anyone studying me, and I sure as hell didn't feel like talking.

"Glad?" I made a scoffing sound. "There's nothing to be glad about here."

Yeah, I'd given Amber another chance. But it was more for my own sake than for hers. Karma – I wasn't a big believer in that sort of thing. But desperately, I wanted another chance with Chloe. And maybe, just maybe, if I gave a chance to someone else, Chloe would do the same for me.

It was worth a shot, right?

I strode past Bishop and made for the stairway. I needed a shower, and to crash for a few hours. It was Sunday, and for once, I didn't have anything planned.

Over my shoulder I said, "When the tow-truck comes, open the garage, will ya?"

I didn't wait for his answer. Instead, I went upstairs and made for the master bathroom, where I turned on the shower and then stripped out of my clothes. Waiting for the water to warm, I stood naked, looking into the full-length mirror.

I didn't *look* like a monster. My face, my body, it all looked the same as yesterday. There was the same dark hair, the same dark eyes, the same body that was famous for more than fighting.

I recalled the words of some famous blogger. I had the face of an angel and a body for sin. I'd sinned, alright. Against Chloe.

In front of the mirror, I peeled off the wrist-bands and studied the raw skin underneath. I lifted my wrists for a closer look. The wounds went beyond simple rope burns. There was dried blood and damage so deep, it looked more like cuts than superficial scrapes from old-fashioned friction.

I thought of Chloe's wrists. My handcuffs. My fault.

I hadn't meant for her to get hurt. I hadn't even known. But I should have.

With a heavy sigh, I turned and headed into the shower, where I tried to scrub away the filth of the last twenty-four hours. But when the water ran cold however long later, I still felt dirty.

CHAPTER 21

Something was ringing. My cell phone. Instantly awake, I jerked upright in the bed. It was Chloe's ringtone. I grabbed the phone from the nearby nightstand and hit the button. "Chloe?"

Her voice, soft and sweet, was music to my ears. "So, I've got this mysterious car in the driveway."

I knew which car she meant. Hers, obviously. Last night, or more accurately, this morning, between my two conversations with Amber, I'd driven to the restaurant where Chloe worked.

Sure enough, I'd found her car parked in the same spot as before. And sure enough, just like she'd told me on my own doorstep, the thing didn't want to start.

"Yeah?" I said into the phone. "How mysterious?"

"Well, it *looks* like mine. But apparently, it can drive all by itself."

"Hmm."

"Even when it's broken down."

"Or maybe," I said, "it was just a dead battery."

One quick jump with my jumper cables, and the engine was up and running. I'd left my sedan in the restaurant parking lot, and then, I'd driven Chloe's little Fiesta back to her place.

I'd parked it in her driveway, and then I'd walked back home. A peace offering? Maybe. But I'd have done it regardless.

"Aha!" she said. "You went and got it, didn't you?"

The smile in her voice warmed me to the core. "It depends," I said. "If I did, is that a good thing? Or a bad thing?"

She hesitated. "What if it *is* a good thing?"

"Then it was all me."

"And if it's a *bad* thing?" she asked.

"In that case," I told her, "blame Bishop."

"Your brother?" she laughed. "Why him?"

"Because he's already on your list, so I figure, eh, what's the difference?"

"Heeeey," she said, "*you're* on my list too."

"I know. And I'm trying like hell to get *off* it."

"So, that's why you did it?"

"Nope. I'd have done it anyway."

"I've gotta ask," she said, "how'd you do it? It's not like you had my keys."

Who needed keys? Not me. "Long story," I said.

"Yeah, I just bet." Her voice warmed. "Still, thanks for the help. Seriously."

"Hey Chloe?"

"Yeah?"

"You might wanna get a new battery."

"Really?"

"Yeah. The car's starting okay now, but you know how these things go. Vintage cars. They're tricky, right?"

She was quiet a long time. When she finally spoke, the smile in her voice was gone. "How about your car? Is it, uh–"

"It's fine."

I'd seen my car on my way into the restaurant parking lot. It was dented and battered, with shattered headlights and missing mirrors. If the towing company had followed my instructions, it was now sitting in my bonus garage, waiting for me to fix it up again, or who knows, torch the thing and be done with it.

"Oh c'mon Lawton," Chloe said, "I know it's not fine. I was there. Remember?"

"Yeah. I remember."

"Why'd you do that?"

"Because it needed to be done."

"No, it didn't."

"Yes," I said. "It did."

"But why?"

"Because I meant what I said. For what I did to you, I deserved a good ass-beating. Still do. But *somebody* wouldn't take me up on it. So that car, it was the closest thing I had."

And it was. With the kind of money I had now, I could buy anything I wanted. They were just things – replaceable, interchangeable. But that car, it wasn't. I'd restored it with my own two hands. In a way, it was part of me, just like my wrists, just like my sanity, which had taken a serious beating over the last couple of days.

Chloe's voice grew softer. "You shouldn't have done it."

"You're right. I shouldn't have done it. But I'm not talking about the car."

She was quiet for a beat, and then said, "Speaking of cars, I've got to leave for work in a little bit, so I'll catch you later, alright?"

I didn't want her to go. But I forced myself to say. "Alright. We're still on for tomorrow, right?"

"Yup, it's a date."

At this, I had to smile. "A date, huh?"

"Um, well," she stammered, "I'll guess I'll see you this time tomorrow, huh? Okay, uh, goodbye then." And then she was gone.

Holding the phone, I was still smiling. There was hope. She might deny it, but I could hear it in her voice.

She still loved me. And, like the bastard I was, I was going to work that for everything I had.

I checked the time. It was mid-afternoon. I sank back onto my bed and looked up at the ceiling. Tomorrow – it felt like too damn long.

Later that night, I was in the bonus garage out back when I heard Amber calling out from somewhere outside. "Hey Lawton! Are you in there?"

Reluctantly, I opened the garage-door, and there she was, standing just outside the opening.

She was smiling. "I've got super-good news, and I wanted to tell you before anyone else did." Her smile widened. "I just saw Chloe."

"Where?"

"You know, the place where she works. That restaurant."

Damn it. So once again, Amber had been bothering Chloe on the job. I tried to keep my voice level. "Why'd you go *there*?"

"Because that's where she was. I mean, she wasn't *here*, at *your* place." Amber pointed toward Chloe's house. "And she wasn't *there*, at her place. So anyway, I found her where she was. See?"

What *I* saw was another reason for Chloe to hate me. "And you said this was *good* news?"

"Definitely." Amber was smiling again. "I stopped by, had some pancakes, and told her that I was really super-sorry."

Amber wasn't the only one who was sorry. Earlier today, when Amber had made noises about apologizing, this wasn't what I had in mind.

Amber was still talking. "And I explained about the other stuff too, so I think we're good."

"What other stuff?"

"Well, I explained how we *normally* kidnap mascots." She gave it some more thought. "And I told her about the car…"

"What car?"

"You know. Joey and Paul's car. You remember, right?"

Like I'd forget. It was the same car that they'd tried to drag Chloe into. It was also the same car that I'd left at the restaurant, with those guys locked in the trunk. "I remember."

"Anyway," Amber continued, "I think Chloe thought it was paint."

I shook my head. "*What* was paint?"

"You know, the stuff you wrote."

Finally, I got it. In the trunk of Joey and Paul's car, we'd found a bottle of white shoe polish, the kind with a built-in sponge. It didn't take a genius to figure out what it was for. They'd been planning to write something on Chloe's car.

Maybe it was a joke. Maybe it wasn't. Either way, I didn't like it. Sometimes, that stuff didn't come off.

So, I'd given them a taste of their own medicine. I'd taken their own shoe polish and wrote things of my own – profanity mostly. Recalling what I'd written across the hood, I said it out loud. "Asshole patrol."

"Yup, that was it," Amber said. "And you know, it's kind of true, about them being assholes, I mean."

Obviously, she didn't get it. "You think I was calling *them* assholes?"

"Weren't you?"

No. I wasn't. Simple name-calling wasn't my style. Those words were a warning. The asshole was *me*, and if they messed with Chloe in any way, they'd see that for themselves. I'd told them so, and I'd meant every word.

I had a lot of friends, in high places, in low places too. Those guys could run, but they couldn't hide. But Amber didn't need details, so I shrugged off the question by saying, "It doesn't matter."

Amber glanced down, and her body became very still. When she never looked up, I ducked my chin to see what she was staring at.

At what I saw, I stifled a curse. If I was lucky, she wouldn't ask. But luck, apparently, wasn't on my side.

CHAPTER 22

Amber was still staring at my wrists. "What happened?"

After showering, I hadn't replaced the bandages. I figured I didn't need to. I wasn't going anyplace, and there was no more dripping blood, just long dark scabs and raw skin around the edges.

It was ugly, but not as bad as it looked. Still, I didn't like anyone looking.

I crossed my arms to hide the damage. "It's nothing," I said.

When she looked up, her eyes were troubled. "You didn't try to kill yourself?" She hesitated. "Did you?"

"No."

She bit her lip. "You know, if you want to talk–"

"I don't." I looked toward my favorite car. The windshield was busted, and the side mirrors were missing. But the dents were my biggest problem. They'd be the hardest things to fix, assuming they were fixable at all.

The way it looked, my car had sustained a lot more damage than I had. Skin healed itself. Metal and glass, not so much.

I was still looking at the car when Amber spoke again. "You really love her, don't you?"

"Yeah." I turned to meet her gaze. "I do."

Her eyes were wet. "Lawton?"

Just great. More drama. When I spoke, my voice came out too fast and too sharp. "What?"

"I'm sorry." She blinked back tears. "About everything. Really.

This is all my fault."

"No." My voice softened as I realized that this time, it wasn't jealousy that had her upset. "It's not."

"But it is," she insisted. "If I hadn't become friends with Brittney—"

"That's not it." I paused, thinking of the bigger issue. "But there's something you need to hear."

"What?"

"It's not just who you *become* friends with, it's what happens after." I thought of my old friends. Some of them, I still had. But a lot more of them, I'd kicked to the curb after I'd gotten famous. And it wasn't because *I* had changed.

Well, okay, I *had* changed. But the bigger thing was how *they* had changed afterward. Guys I used to know suddenly became ass-kissers, or worse, users, who tried to cash in on my fame to make themselves rich and famous, too.

Even that sex tape, it wouldn't have happened if I'd surrounded myself with better people.

Amber blinked up at me. "What do you mean?"

"You *knew* how Brittney was," I said. "But you never called her on it. Whatever she wanted, you just went along, no matter how rotten it was." I shook my head. "If you do that too much, bad things happen."

And this, I knew from experience.

"But we're not even friends anymore," Amber said. "In your driveway, you saw us, right?"

"I'm talking before then." Feeling like some sort of amateur shrink, I went on to say, "You're a nice person, Amber. Maybe you should hang out with nicer people. That's all I'm saying."

"Oh." Her face brightened. "You mean like Chloe?"

I froze. "Uh…"

"She *does* seem nice." Amber was nodding now. "And she's a pretty good waitress, too. Like tonight, she remembered the extra syrup and everything."

I stared at her. "What?"

"You know, when I apologized, I asked her to bring extra syrup for my pancakes, and she was really nice about it, too."

What the hell? "You made her *wait* on you?"

"Well, yeah." Amber frowned. "That wasn't a bad thing, was it? I mean, I left her a really nice tip. And she totally earned it, too."

I closed my eyes, trying to block out the image of Amber sitting there at some table while Chloe waited on her – and the way it sounded, was sent to the kitchen for extra condiments.

Amber's voice broke into my thoughts. "Lawton? Are you okay?"

I opened my eyes. "You shouldn't have done that."

"But why not? I knew it was really super-important to you, and I didn't want to wait *too* long." Her gaze drifted to my crossed arms. "Especially now, with you all suicidal and stuff."

Through gritted teeth, I said, "I'm not suicidal."

"Are you sure?" she asked. "Because one of my sorority sisters, she works for a suicide hotline, you know, like a volunteer." Amber squinted up at me. "Do you want the number, just in case?"

My head was pounding now. "No."

"But I want to do *something* to help." She perked up. "I know. I could run to the store for bandages. Or maybe some ointment or something."

"No."

"But you need *something*." She winced. "Because those cuts looked pretty bad."

"They're not." Hell, they weren't even cuts, but I didn't want to get into it. Looking to shake her off, I glanced toward the house. "You really wanna do me a favor? Stop in and say 'hi' to Bishop."

She brightened. "You think he'd want me too?"

"He let you in the gate, didn't he?"

"Yeah, but only through the intercom. It's not like he came out in person or anything."

"Then at least stop by," I said, "you know, as a thanks for opening the gate."

Bishop wouldn't be thanking *me* afterwards, but at this point, it was better to have him dealing with her than me. And besides, I hadn't been the person who let Amber in.

When she finally turned and headed toward the house, I shut the garage door and threw on a dark jacket. A moment later, I was heading out the side door – and not only to escape Amber.

Maybe I couldn't see Chloe. But with a simple walk around the block, I *could* see her house, and I figured, hey, it was better than nothing.

But it wasn't. Because what I saw when I got there didn't exactly make me happy.

CHAPTER 23

I was standing on the sidewalk in front of Chloe's place. I'd just passed her driveway when I heard something that made me stop dead in my tracks. It was the sound of a garage door opening. I turned and saw a slick black Mercedes backing out of Chloe's bonus garage.

The car looked a lot like a certain dark sedan that I'd seen outside her place a few weeks earlier. The driver of *that* car had been a total douchebag.

And somehow, I just knew it was the same guy. Same car, same location – it had to be.

The night I'd seen him, he'd given his name as Leo. Other than that, I still didn't know who the guy was, but I had pretty good idea that he was her landlord or something.

The one and only time that we'd talked, he'd spent half the time griping about the electrical system and the other half offering me honeys – as he called them – for a price.

Chloe had never mentioned the guy, and after the whole basement fiasco, I sure as hell wasn't going to be grilling her about him now.

But standing there on the sidewalk, a new thought hit me. Maybe I couldn't grill *her*, but I could grill *him*. Hell, I wouldn't even have to be aggressive about it. From what I'd seen the last time, the guy loved to talk, especially about himself.

I stood where I was, betting on the fact that he'd stop the car when he spotted me. Sure enough, rather than backing out onto the street, he stopped the car at the end of the driveway and leaned his head out the open window.

"Hey neighbor," he said as I approached the car. He was an overly tanned man, maybe in his fifties or sixties. He had poufy blonde hair and big white teeth. He wore a shiny grey suit, but no tie. He was grinning. "You liking the hood?"

What hood? The neighborhood? I glanced around. If this was a hood, I was a housewife. I'd seen the real hood, and it looked nothing like this.

I shrugged. "It's alright. So, you're back in town, huh?"

The last time I'd seen him, he'd mentioned that he traveled a lot – for fun *and* business, or so he claimed.

"Eh, just for the day," he said. "Gotta check on my investments, you know?"

No. I didn't know. But this would be a good time to find out. "Yeah? What kind of investments?"

He flicked his gaze toward the house. "Well, like *this* place for one."

I nodded. "So you're the landlord, huh? Renting the place out?"

"You could say that." His smile widened. "I got people lined up like you wouldn't believe."

I looked again toward the house. It was a two-story Tudor – the house of a banker, a doctor, or maybe a nice, respectable family of five, assuming they had a decent chunk of money.

It hit me all over again that the house was an odd place to find a single girl like Chloe. Sure, I knew she came from money, but the house was still way too big for one person.

Yeah, I realized that my own house was three times the size, but my own situation wasn't exactly normal.

"What kind of people?" I said. "You mean like renters?"

He laughed like I'd just said something funny. "Sure, if you wanna call 'em that. As for me, I call 'em clients."

Clients? What the hell did *that* mean?

Before I could ask, he motioned me closer and said in a low voice, "You give any more thought to my business proposition?"

I had a pretty good idea what he meant, but I wanted to make him say it. I shook my head. "What business proposition?"

He gave an oily laugh. "You know…the girls."

I recalled his words from the last time. "If you call in the professionals, you get what you want – blond, brunette, bald, you name it. You pay for the stuff you want, and kick 'em to the curb when you're done. Easy-peasy."

Easy-peasy, my ass.

From the driver's seat, he grinned over at me. "I've got this one girl, she'll suck your dick like a fuckin' vacuum cleaner." He laughed. "I'm talking industrial strength. I call her Hoover. Swear to God, you'll be thinking, 'Man, is she gonna suck this thing clean off, or what?'"

At the sound of his laugh, I swear, I felt my own dick shrivel up inside my jeans. The guy had a messed-up vibe, and I hated the fact that he was here, where Chloe lived. Did she really know this guy? She must. This *was* where she lived, after all.

I stared down at him, wondering what the hell I should say to that. The plan had been to keep it civil. But the more he talked, the more I wanted to drag him out of his car and beat the answers out of him.

Right, because *that* would show Chloe that I wasn't a psycho.

I tried for a casual shrug and listened as he told me about this other girl who went by the nickname of Spanky.

I heard myself ask, "Giving or receiving?"

"That's up to you," he said. "So, you interested?"

I was a lot of things, but not interested. There was only one girl I wanted, and her name wasn't Spanky. Or Hoover, for that matter.

It was Chloe, the girl I loved. But standing there, my thoughts started churning with details that I didn't want to consider. Chloe wasn't just the girl I loved. She was a hot girl in a fancy neighborhood. She lived in a house that was off-limits for reasons that I still didn't get.

And now, looking at the guy in her driveway, a sick feeling grew in my gut. I tried to shove it aside. But I couldn't. Finally, I asked myself the question that I'd been avoiding for too long.

Is Chloe involved with this guy?

No. She wasn't. She couldn't be. Whether for business or pleasure, she wasn't like that.

The guy was an ass-wipe, plain and simple. Probably, he had a string of properties a mile long, all mortgaged to the hilt. I knew the type. I'd seen it before – guys getting in over their heads and trying all kinds of crazy schemes to claw their way out.

Fuck it. I was done listening to his bullshit. The way it looked, he wasn't going to tell me a damn thing that was useful – unless I went on the offense. And I couldn't. Thanks to my own stupidity, I was still on Chloe's shit-list, bigtime.

As of now, I wasn't even her boyfriend. I was a guy who'd already messed up once. If I were smart, I'd end this conversation now, before I dug myself a deeper hole. "I don't need any girls," I told him.

"Well, sure you don't *need* any girls," he said, giving me a look this side of creepy. "I mean, look at ya."

Yeah. Look at me. Standing on the side of the road talking to a scumbag.

"I'm just saying," he continued, "sometimes we want something special." He grinned. "Like extra-trashy. The dirty stuff, you know?"

Been there, done that. Those days were over, and if I stayed one more minute, I'd be going for the guy's throat. "I've gotta go," I said, turning away.

I'd gotten maybe two or three steps when he called out after me, "Hey! What about nice girls?"

Slowly, I turned to face him. "What?"

"I'm just saying, if you like 'em sweet, I got them, too."

Through gritted teeth, I said, "Sweet?"

"Hey, don't get me wrong. I'm not talking kids or nothing. I'm talking college girls, high-end stuff." He gave a laugh. "Tuition is crazy, right? You wouldn't believe the shit some chicks'll do for extra cash."

I gave him a long, cold look. "What chicks?"

"You know, regular girl-next-door types, the kind you could take home to mom." He was nodding now. "And hey, if your mom's into threesomes–"

"She's not."

But only because she was dead. Who knows the shit she'd do if she were alive. The way it sounded, she and this guy could've been best buddies.

"Hey, don't get all mad," the guy said. "I was just messin' with you." He laughed. "Not that the girls wouldn't do it. I'm just saying, most people's moms aren't into shit *that* freaky, you know?"

I glanced at Chloe's house – except it *wasn't* her house, was it? It was *this* guy's house. Who *was* he to her? Just a landlord? Or something different? Was *she* the "something sweet" he was offering me?

No. I refused to believe that. But he was up to something, and suddenly, I knew that I couldn't let it go without finding out. It wasn't just for me. It was for Chloe, whether she got pissed off or not. Because when it came down to it, I'd rather lose her forever than see anything bad happen to her.

I mean, what the hell? The guy was flat-out pimping where Chloe lived. Even if she wasn't involved, how long would it take before someone showed up here, looking for Spanky or whoever?

No. That wasn't going to fly. Not if I could help it.

CHAPTER 24

Deliberately, I moved toward the guy. "You conduct your business *here*?"

"Hell no," he said. "You think I'm stupid? I don't shit where I eat. Come on, man. Get real."

I didn't want the guy shitting *or* eating anywhere near Chloe. I leaned down until I was practically inside his car. "So then what's the deal with the house? You live here?"

He leaned back. "What?"

"You heard me." My jaw was tight, and my fingers were clenched. "Just what the fuck are you doing here?"

"Woah." He held up his hands, palms out. "No need to get all funny about it."

Funny? Like a head through the windshield? His head, his windshield, with some help from me. Right about now, it would be fucking hilarious.

Before I knew it, I'd reached in and grabbed the guy by the lapels of his shiny-ass suit. "Listen, asshole," I said. "You peddle that shit somewhere else."

"Hey!" He tried for another laugh. "We're just talking, right? No harm in that." He licked his lips like they'd suddenly gone dry. "Sorry man, I didn't take you for no choirboy, but hey, I got the message. Loud and clear. Alright?"

I stared at the guy, wondering if an elbow to the face would send a better message. I was still gripping his suit. "I've got a question," I said.

"Uh, sure," he stammered. "Anything."

I flicked my head toward the house. "The girl who lives here. You know her?"

"What?"

"It's a simple question, asshole."

"No," he said, trying to tug away from my grip. "Shit. I'm just the property manager."

"Yeah?" I gave him a hard look. "Just the property manager? I thought you owned the place."

"What? No? I mean, I'm gonna buy it. I'm just working to get the money together, you know?"

So much for Mister Bigshot. "So who the fuck are you?"

"Me?" He swallowed. "I'm just the guy who pays the light bill."

"Uh-huh."

He gave a shaky laugh. "Hard to keep a place rented when there's no juice, am I right?"

"And what about the girls?"

"What girls?"

Through gritted teeth, I said, "Hoover, Spanky, Whoever. Any of them live around here?"

"What? No." Again, he tried to pull away. "What the fuck is your problem?"

"*My* problem? *You're* the one selling pussy in my backyard." I gave another glance toward Chloe's house. "The girl who lives here? Is she for sale, too?"

"What? Her? No, never met her. Swear to God. My partner handles the rental stuff. You know, dealing with leases, credit checks, all that shit."

"So *he's* the property manager?"

"Well, uh, yeah. But I help. I collect and stuff." He gave another nervous laugh. "It's always something, right?"

Yeah, it was. I wasn't letting go. "And who's your partner?" I asked.

He blinked up at me. "What?"

"Your partner. Who the fuck is he?"

"He's a nice guy, totally legit." Again, the guy swallowed. "You got it all wrong. I don't know what you think, but I don't do my side-stuff around here." He made a show of looking insulted. "What kind of guy do you think I am?"

From the look on his face, he knew exactly what kind of guy I thought he was – the kind who peddled pussy in a nice neighborhood.

As I watched, his gaze shifted to something across the street. I looked to see some elderly lady walking out to her mailbox. Her steps faltered as she spotted us.

I knew exactly what she saw – some tattooed guy roughing up a man in a Mercedes.

Shit.

In a low voice, I told the guy, "If you're smart, you'll do your business someplace else."

With a push, I let him go. A split-second later, his car squealed out of the driveway and disappeared down the street, leaving me and the neighbor lady – whoever she was – staring after him.

Walking back to my own place, my thoughts were churning. I didn't regret running the guy off, but I wasn't blind to the downside. What would I say if Chloe found out?

And chances were pretty good that she would.

Screw it, I decided. I'd tell her the truth. That the guy was pimping pussy out of her driveway. If she blamed me for what I'd done, well, then we had bigger problems than I thought.

Back at my own house, I found Bishop in the kitchen, making a sandwich.

When he saw me, he said, "Thanks a lot, asshole."

"What?"

"Why'd you sic Amber on me?"

Like *he* was one to talk. "Why'd you sic her on *me*?" I said.

"Hey, all I did was open the gate."

"Yeah?" I crossed my arms. "And all *I* did was point to the house."

"You're still an asshole," he muttered, reaching for a loaf of whole-grain bread, uncut, straight from the bakery – or at least, that's what my housekeeper told me when she'd stocked the kitchen.

Bishop glanced around. "Hey, where'd you put the knives?"

I looked toward the usual spot and paused. Usually, I had a sixteen-piece knife set, right there on the counter. The block was still there. The knives were gone. I scanned the nearby countertops. No knives.

"Did you check the dishwasher?" I asked.

"Yeah. There's nothing in there."

Standing like a dumb-ass, I continued to look around. And then I spotted it – a handwritten note, taped to the fridge. It had two words, Suicide Hotline, along with a scribbled phone number and a smiley face at the bottom.

"Damn it," I muttered.

"What?" Bishop asked.

"You left Amber alone in here, didn't you?"

"Yeah. For maybe a minute." He laughed. "Why? You worried she'd make off with the silver?"

"Not the silver," I said. "The knives."

"The knives?" He gave me an odd look. "But why?"

I shook my head. "Don't ask." Besides, there was something else I wanted to talk about. I leaned back against the kitchen counter and told Bishop about the douchebag who'd just offered me pussy for pay. I didn't mention Chloe, or the fact that this happened right there in Chloe's driveway.

By the time I finished, Bishop was sawing into the bread with the switchblade he kept in his pocket. "Where was this?" he asked.

"Just down the street."

"Here?" He frowned. "In this neighborhood? What was he driving?"

"A black Mercedes."

"You get the plate number?" he asked.

I shook my head. At the time, I'd been so pissed off that I hadn't even thought of it. But next time, I would – except there'd better not be a next time.

CHAPTER 25

It was Monday, and I was happy as hell. After two long days, I was finally getting the chance to win Chloe back. No matter what, I wasn't going to mess this up.

It was two o'clock in the afternoon when I pulled into her driveway. I'd called her at noon to finalize our plans, but what those plans were, Chloe still didn't know.

All I'd told her was to dress in casual clothes and to be ready to see something that I'd never shown anyone. Other than that, I'd been secretive for a reason. I didn't want her to worry. And I sure as hell didn't want her to cancel.

She'd be safe. I'd make sure of it.

I was just getting out of my car when the front door opened, and there she was, heading toward me. She wore jeans and a dark V-necked shirt. Her eyes were bright, and she was smiling.

It was a good sign.

But when she saw my car, her smile faltered. Easy to see why. The car was a beat-up brown sedan with a rusty front bumper and a dented hood. It looked ancient and ugly, something that belonged in a junk yard, not on the road.

When I met her on the walkway, her eyes were still on the car. "What's that?" she asked.

"Our ride."

"Oh," she said, walking with me back to the car. When we reached its front bumper, she gave the car a long, worried look.

"You sure this thing runs?"

I grinned over at her. "It got me here, didn't it?" I flicked my head toward the passenger's side. "C'mon." I walked to the car-door and opened it. I waited.

Chloe didn't move. "How far are we going?"

"Not far."

She glanced back at her own car, parked in front of the garage. "Wanna take my car?"

I laughed. "Not a chance." For starters, she was my guest, not my chauffeur. But more importantly, there was no way in hell we'd be taking *her* car to the place we were going.

I owned a small fleet of cars. Every one of them looked a lot nicer than the one I was driving today. But I'd brought this car for a reason.

"Trust me," I told her. "It runs great."

She bit her lip. "I suppose you have a backup plan if we get stranded?"

"We won't," I assured her.

She gave me a shaky smile. "I must be insane," she said, finally climbing into the passenger's seat. I closed the door behind her, and walked around to get behind the wheel.

When I fired up the engine, she was studying the car's interior, as if unsure what to make of it. Her confusion was understandable. On the outside, the car was a heap. On the inside, it was vintage quality.

As for the engine, it was a nice, steady purr.

When I backed out onto the street, she turned sideways in the seat to face me. "Alright," she said. "You know I'm gonna ask, so let's just get it out of the way. Why this car?"

I put on my serious face. "What? You don't like it?"

"Am I supposed to?"

She looked so adorable that I had to laugh. Returning my attention to the road, I said, "Alright, as much as I'd like to mess with you, I don't want you to worry."

Her tone grew teasing. "Too late for that."

"So here's the thing," I said. "Where we're going, I'd never take any of my other cars."

"Why not?"

"Because they're not as safe." I gave her a quick glance. "And since I've got you here, I'm not taking any chances."

"Oh come on," she said. "Be serious."

"I am serious. My other cars, they draw too much attention."

It was true. I loved cars, the faster the better. Even my basic black sedan wasn't all that basic when you considered the engine and its corresponding price tag.

She gave me a worried look. "I don't want to be mean, but this car? It'll get plenty of attention."

"Yeah? Well don't let the exterior fool you. The engine, along with everything else under the hood, is in prime condition. And it's fast too. A lot faster than it looks." I reached up and tapped the driver's side window. "And see this glass? Bullet-proof."

She laughed. "Oh stop it."

"I'm not kidding."

"You serious?" she asked.

"Yup. And the wheels—"

"Don't tell me," she teased. "Also bullet-proof?"

"Not exactly. But close."

"Oh c'mon. How can something be sort of bullet-proof?"

"It's the way they're constructed," I explained. "Even if they're punctured, they'll keep going, at least long enough."

"How?"

"Polymer rings."

"What's that?" She paused. "Oh never mind. You're just messing with me."

No. I wasn't messing with her. And, once we got going, things would get a lot more serious. I glanced over at her and asked, "How good are you at keeping secrets?"

"Pretty good."

"Glad to hear it," I said. "Because I'm counting on that."

CHAPTER 26

We'd been driving for a few miles when she asked, "Is this where you tell me where we're going?"

We were going to Hell, or at least some version of it. But I didn't want her to worry, so all I said was "Call it a trip down memory lane."

"C'mon," she said, "give me a hint."

I'd give her more than a hint. I pulled onto I-75 and eased into the fast lane, heading South. There was a road-sign up ahead. *Detroit, 20 miles.*

I gestured toward the sign. "You haven't guessed?"

Her voice grew wary. "Detroit?"

"Yup."

She hesitated. "Which part?"

From the look on her face, she knew which part, so I kept on driving, letting the question slide into the background as traffic ebbed and flowed around us.

I was a car buff. Maybe it was the Motor City connection, or maybe it was the fact that growing up, decent transportation was hard to come by. During the whole reality show thing, I'd spent a lot of time in L.A., where foreign cars were the norm, not the exception.

Not so here. And not in my own garages, come to think of it.

In the shadow of Motor City, American cars still ruled the roads. But the roads were pitted, and too many of the cars riding on them were old, beat up, or covered in rust.

In a weird twist of fate, these old beaters were the cars that no one messed with, either because there was nothing on them worth stealing, or because their owners had nothing left to lose.

In my own beat-up sedan, I might be confused for one of those guys. But that was the whole point, wasn't it? I wanted to blend, not draw attention to myself, or even worse, to Chloe.

When I pulled off at the usual exit, I tried to see the city through a stranger's eyes. Some parts weren't so bad, but others, well, they weren't the kinds of places you wanted to be found after dark, or shit, during the day under the wrong circumstances.

From the corner of my eye, I saw Chloe taking it all in. Silently, she reached for the door lock and gave it a push. Funny, it was already locked. She pushed it again, probably not even realizing what she was doing.

It wasn't surprising. A rich girl like Chloe, what would *she* know about the deep parts of the city, where door locks wouldn't save you if your car broke down.

I had a loaded gun in the glove compartment and another one under the seat. But she didn't need to know that, because it would only get her thinking, and not in ways that would do me any favors.

We drove a few miles on Woodward, and then I turned off on a familiar side street, and then another, heading deeper into the guts of the city. Some streets were alright, but most of them weren't. I saw the usual boarded-up shops and burned-out buildings, along with houses that had been vacant for longer than I'd been alive.

I tried to make a joke of it. "Welcome to Zombieland."

Chloe gave a shaky laugh, but said nothing as the scenery changed with every block. We saw big, brick buildings with broken windows and vines creeping into the vacant spaces. We saw buildings that were gutted, and others that were still whole, but rotted with decay.

Silently, I drove past the spot where I'd stopped just a couple of nights earlier to have that not-so-friendly chat with the guys in that trunk.

The streets were quiet, with random, beat-up cars parked

crookedly along the curbs, and discarded garbage littering the shoulder.

On the next block up, we passed the old party store where one of my friends had been killed in a drive-by, except he wasn't *really* my friend, because at his funeral, I learned he'd been dealing drugs to my mom on the sly.

Then again, it wasn't exactly a rare thing. Maybe I couldn't blame the guy. He was a seller. She was a buyer. Maybe it all evened out.

In a low voice, Chloe finally spoke. "Zombieland. Or a war zone."

"Yeah. And we lost."

She looked around. "Where is everyone?"

"Moved, holed up inside, still asleep. Hard to say."

When I turned onto the street where I'd grown up, I tried to see it through Chloe's eyes. The homes were small, *really* small. Some were burnt. Some were boarded up. And some were missing patches of siding, porch rails, and even their front doorknobs.

Inside, I knew they were missing other stuff – copper pipes and plumbing fixtures, because that was the way it went around here. If it wasn't nailed down, it was gone by sunrise. And even if it *was* nailed down? Well, that was no guarantee.

From the passenger's seat, Chloe spoke in a quiet voice. "Is this where you grew up?"

"Almost. It's a few blocks up." I gave her a sideways glance. "We're gonna stop. But don't roll down the window, and don't open the door."

She tried to laugh, but didn't quite make it. "Trust me. I wasn't planning to."

A few minutes later, I stopped in front of the narrow two-story brick house that had once been my home. Even now, it hurt to look at the thing. Yeah, there had been some good times, but not as many as there should have been – and not only for me.

I flicked my head toward the place. "My grandma's house."

CHAPTER 27

Looking at that familiar house, I tried to laugh, but didn't quite make it. "Nicest one in the neighborhood."

It was an old joke between me and my sister. The neighborhood, like countless others in the city, was a festering boil on the ass of Detroit.

I looked around. As long as I'd been alive, the neighborhood had been this way. But I'd seen pictures – old pictures, where respectable-looking men drove respectable-looking cars to what had been a respectable working-class corner of a growing, industrial city.

I remembered Grandma's photo albums, filled with all those snapshots – the men coming and going, the women, watching their children play on the front lawns and ride tricycles up and down the smooth sidewalk.

Now, the sidewalk was cracked and pushed up at odd angles by trees that were long gone, just like the working men and their working-class families.

These days, nobody around here worked – some by choice, and others, because the factories were gone, and the schools were either shuttered or shit.

Growing up, I'd had a front row seat to all of its ugliness. And every year, it just got worse – the people, the streets, the houses, everything.

If something broke, no one fixed it. If shutters fell off, they'd lay in the mud or snow until someone walked off with them. For what?

Who knows?

Nobody painted. Nobody repaired anything. And nobody gave a rat's ass one way or another – I tried to smile – except for Grandma, who'd cared until the very end.

I took a long, hard look at the house that I'd grown up in. I tried to see it through Chloe's eyes. Construction-wise, it was the same as both houses on either side – narrow, with two-stories and a decent porch.

But if you looked hard enough, you could see the differences. Grandma's house was just a little nicer, a little fresher-looking, and a little more like a real home.

Sometime in the past couple of decades, the shutters had been painted, along with the porch. The shrubbery might be overgrown, but at least it was there – unlike the other houses that had no landscaping at all.

At one time, there had been flowers, too. In the spring, Grandma used to plant them – big orange Marigolds where it was sunny, and small white Impatiens for the shade.

Funny to think I remembered their names, just like I remembered standing by my grandma when she planted them year after year. While she planted, I'd hand her the flowers one-by-one, and then water them afterwards.

It wasn't because it was fun – although, if I were honest, it wasn't so bad. It was because of the other thing – the danger of letting my grandma kneel there without anyone watching her back. Around here, bad things could happen when you did stuff like that, as a neighbor lady the next block over had discovered the hard way.

And then, there'd been the hassle. I recalled this neighbor kid who lived three doors down – a kid named Duane who'd called me a pansy-ass, and worse, for touching the flowers at all. The grief hadn't stopped until I'd handed him his ass one night in July, and then threatened to take a shovel to his face if he bothered me or my Grandma, ever again.

That was how long ago? Maybe fifteen years?

I heard myself say, "She loved that house."

Chloe paused. "Is she, uh–"

"Still alive?" I shook my head. "No. She died a few years ago. I grew up here though."

"Just you and your grandma?"

"Sometimes my mom lived here too. But most of the time—" I shrugged. "She was off doing other things."

"Like what?" Chloe asked.

I heard myself laugh, a quiet, bitter sound. My mom had done a lot of things, and not many of them involved taking care of her kids. "Drugs, mostly. My grandma, she was a school teacher at St. Mary's. She always said she should've done better, especially with Mom being her only kid."

I looked ahead, feeling myself drift back in time. "But I dunno. Mom was just wild, I guess."

"Like mother like son?"

"No." I turned to look at her. "I'm *nothing* like her." My jaw tensed. "She *never* looked out for us, never gave a shit one way or another what happened to us when she was off doing fuck-knows-what."

Chloe shrank back in the seat, and I felt instantly ashamed. Chloe wasn't my mom. She didn't deserve this shit. With an effort, I softened my voice. "Sorry."

"It's alright," Chloe said. "You said 'us'? You mean you and Bishop, right?"

I shook my head. Back then, it would've been nice to have a brother, someone else to watch my back. But that came later. Some might say it came just in time.

"No," I said. "I didn't even know about Bishop 'til I was a teenager. We're half-brothers. Same dad, different cities."

"So how many kids did your mom have?"

"Two. Me and a sister."

"Where's your sister now?" she asked.

"College out East. Working on her master's in social work."

"And your mom?" she asked.

"Dead."

"Oh, I'm so sorry," she said.

That made *one* of us.

Into my silence, Chloe asked, "How?"

"Overdose. Finally. Best thing she ever did."

And it would've been even better if she hadn't chosen to do it right in front of my little sister.

I looked over at Chloe. Her look said it all. She was horrified, not only because of the way my mom had died, but also because of my attitude.

Nice people pretended. I wasn't that nice.

But I wanted Chloe to understand, so I said, "I know what you're thinking."

Obviously, she thought I was heartless. In some ways, I guess I was. But I'd brought Chloe here for a reason – to see the real me, where I'd come from – and maybe, show her why I wasn't always the most civilized guy on the planet.

In this neighborhood, too much civility could get you killed – or worse, get someone in your family killed.

Chloe's voice was carefully neutral. "I'm not thinking anything, just taking it all in."

"Let me ask you something," I said. "Your brother. He's thirteen, right?"

She nodded.

"Well, I'm the oldest," I said. "My sister, she's maybe three years younger than me." I couldn't help but smile. "Probably about your age, come to think of it." I felt my smile fade. "When she was thirteen, Mom tried to sell her."

Chloe grew very still, and her face froze in a carefully blank expression. "What do you mean?"

I gave her a serious look. "You know what I mean."

She blew out a long, unsteady breath, but said nothing.

So I went on. "That's when Grandma kicked her out for good, told Mom if she ever came back, she'd be dead before she hit the door. And Grandma meant it. She never said anything she didn't mean. She had this old Remington. She was a hell of a shot too. Took me deer hunting up north once."

Chloe gave me a faint smile. "She sounds like an amazing person."

"She was." At the memory, I felt some of my tension slide away. "She'd been a widow forever too. I never knew my grandpa. Neither did my mom, come to think of it. He died in some factory explosion a month after she was born. So I guess my mom didn't have it so good either."

I shook my head. "Anyway, even with Mom out of the house, I couldn't let the thing with Kara go. I mean, what kind of man does that? And why the hell should he get away with it? So I ask around, and I find out who the guy is."

"Then what?" Chloe asked.

This is where things got dicey. But I'd brought her out here to be honest. For better or worse, I needed to go through with it. "Then," I said, "I go after him."

"So were you what, about sixteen?"

"Yup."

"So what'd you do?"

I still remembered that night. It's not like I put a lot of thought into the plan, but I hadn't been completely stupid about it. "I showed up at his house, knocked on the door, all nice and polite. And then, when he answered, I beat the piss out of him. The guy was in I.C.U. for a week."

"Good," Chloe said.

"Oh c'mon," I said, trying to smile, "no warnings about vigilante justice?"

She shrugged, and something in her eyes made me wonder if she was thinking about her own brother. That night in the hospital, she'd talked about him a lot, sounding more like a mom than my own mom ever had. She looked out for the kid. I could tell.

Chloe glanced toward the street. "At least you didn't kill him."

"Yeah. But it didn't end there. The guy was a city councilman. Had a wife, a couple of grown kids." I heard the sarcasm in my own voice. "A regular pillar of the community."

"So he pressed charges?"

"Yup."

"What were they?" she asked.

"Attempted murder."

Her voice was quiet. "Wow."

"Yeah." I shrugged. "But hey, it was true, right?"

"You wanted to kill him?"

"Wouldn't you?"

She gave it some thought. "If you really wanted to kill him, you would've grabbed the gun. Right?"

"Maybe," I said. "Or maybe, shooting the guy seemed too easy."

"But with what happened to your sister, I mean, that had to count for something, right?"

I gave a bitter laugh. "Not when Mom wouldn't testify. And Kara, she didn't even know about it. And I was damned determined to keep it that way."

I looked over the street, littered with garbage, potholes and overgrown weeds. "And let's say the thing with Kara got out. She'd be the girl who almost got molested by some forty-year-old. School was hard enough already. She didn't need that."

"What do you mean?" Chloe asked.

"Our school? It was the worst in the district. But it was the only one we had. And Kara and me, we got enough shit already because of the way we talked."

Chloe shook her head. "I don't get it."

"Like I mentioned, Grandma was a teacher. English mostly. And she didn't put up with any sloppy talk."

"You mean swearing?"

"Or bad grammar."

"But that's a good thing," Chloe said.

"Yeah, well people didn't like it, especially other kids."

"Why not?" she asked.

I looked around, taking in the destruction around us. The streets were empty, but I'd be a dumb-ass to assume that no one was watching. I had to stay focused.

"Wherever you live," I said, "you gotta fit in, right?"

After a long moment, Chloe nodded.

"Well, we didn't fit in," I said. "It was a problem."

Funny, it was a different problem for me than it was for Kara. My problems, I could solve with my fists – or whatever else I might be carrying. With Kara, it was a different ballgame. There was only one way she might fit in – and it wasn't something I was willing to let happen.

I looked over to Chloe and added, "And the older we got, the bigger the problem."

"So what'd you do?" she asked.

I shrugged. "I learned to blend. Or when I couldn't, I learned to fight."

"Well, you sure learned that good. But what happened with that councilman?"

"Officially, I was a minor. But at first, the guy worked like hell to see me tried as an adult."

"At first?" she said. "So he changed his mind?"

"Yeah."

"Why?"

Now, that was complicated.

CHAPTER 28

It was just over ten years ago. I'd been sixteen-years-old and facing an attempted murder charge. And for what? Dishing out a justified ass-beating to some middle-aged perv who thought it would be fun to fuck my little sister.

If Bishop hadn't shown up looking for me when he did, where would I be right now? I glanced around, taking in the mostly abandoned neighborhood. I wouldn't be here, that's for sure. If I were lucky, I'd be in prison. If I were unlucky, I'd be dead.

As far as the attempted murder charge, the councilman *did* have a point. I *had* been trying to kill him. But I'd been stupid. If I'd been smarter, I'd have caught him in some dark alley instead of knocking on his front door and beating his ass while the next-door neighbors watched.

Chloe was still waiting for my answer. Why did the councilman change his mind? Why had he settled for sending me to juvie instead of fuck-me-in-the-ass prison?

"With that," I said, "I had a little help."

"From who?"

"Bishop." At the time, he'd been almost a stranger, a brother I didn't even know I had – until that one day he showed up at my front door and told me we had the same dad. I'd been out on bail, but headed for some serious hard-time.

Chloe said, "But he couldn't have been much older than you."

"He wasn't. But he was old enough."

"What'd you guys do?" she asked.

"That, I can't tell you."

I wanted to tell her. And I wanted to keep it to myself. It was ugly, *too* ugly for a girl like Chloe, who'd grown up in a different world.

"Why not?" she asked.

"Because, it wouldn't be right."

I thought of what we'd done. It had been Bishop's idea, and it had worked just like he said it would.

All we needed was video equipment, a baby-faced hooker willing to play along, and the guts to blackmail the guy afterward – not for money, but for a reduction in the charges and for a promise to stick with women his own age.

I turned to Chloe and added, "My secrets are one thing. But his?" I shook my head. "They're not mine to be giving out. Even to you."

"I can respect that," she said, looking like she meant it. "So tell me in general terms. What happened with the case?"

"Plea bargain. I spent a couple years in juvie, got out when I turned eighteen. And you pretty much know the rest."

Chloe gave me a dubious smile. "I seriously doubt that."

She was right. A couple years later, I was out of juvie and starting to make a name for myself on the underground fighting circuit. That's when the guy made his move, telling me he wanted the footage back.

The first time, he'd asked nicely. And then, he'd asked not-so-nicely, delivering his message through some rough friends of the paid variety.

But I didn't back down, and neither did Bishop. Looking to send a message of our own, we uploaded that X-rated footage to his work computer, thinking we'd put a good scare into him, remind him of what he could lose if he didn't lay off.

But he didn't lay off. Instead, what did he do? He'd put a hit out on me.

Dumb-ass.

It was one of the last things the guy did. So now, I didn't need the footage. And neither did he, because dead guys couldn't exactly bother under-age girls now, could they?

With an effort, I shoved away those memories and turned to Chloe. "Wanna know something funny?" I said.

"What?"

I glanced around. The street and houses were deadly quiet. A crumpled fast-food bag rolled like a tumbleweed along the pitted pavement. Other than that, I saw no movement. But that didn't mean no one was around.

The neighborhood was like that. You just never knew.

I heard myself say, "Juvie was a cakewalk compared to this."

"But why didn't you guys move?" Chloe asked.

"Because Grandma had a bad hip and a pension that barely paid for groceries. And besides, where would she go?"

Chloe's gaze drifted to my old house. "Anywhere but here."

I gave a bitter laugh. "Easy for you to say. When I was born, Grandma owned that house outright. But when I got in trouble, she mortgaged everything to pay for my legal team, sorry as they were."

"But what about a public defender?" Chloe asked.

"That's what I told her. But Grandma wouldn't hear of it. She said I deserved better."

"She was right," Chloe said.

Was she? Maybe. Maybe not. But it was nice that Chloe thought so. It was a good sign, right?

"By the time it was done," I continued, "she owed more than the house was worth."

"Oh wow," Chloe breathed. "That's awful."

"And what's worse," I said, "it wasn't all to the bank."

"Who else did she owe?"

Someone you didn't mess with. That's who. "This local guy," I said, "specialized in high-risk loans."

"You mean a loan shark?"

"More or less," I said. "Though he didn't like to be called that. Don't ask me how I know."

Chloe was looking at the house again. "So who owns the house now?"

"The bank, probably. When Grandma died, she still owed a lot of money."

"To the loan shark?"

"No. Him, I paid off."

"How'd you do that?"

"One day, he saw me mixing it up with a couple of guys in the neighborhood. Said he liked what he saw, offered me the chance to work off some of the loan."

"By fighting?" Chloe asked.

From the corner of my eye, I spotted movement up ahead. Casually, I turned forward for a better look. A few blocks up the street, some guy – a lean scruffy man with big, bushy hair – was weaving his way toward us.

As I watched, he stumbled from one side of the street to the other, heading toward a beat-up Chevy that was parked half on the street, half on the sidewalk. The guy stopped and peered into the Chevy's rear window, leaning his forehead against the glass.

He was still looking when I recalled Chloe's question. Had I worked off the loan by fighting?

With my gaze still on the stranger, I nodded. "It was the one thing I was actually good at. And for whatever reason, people liked to watch."

Chloe voice, warmer now, drifted over to me. "I can see why."

The warmth in her voice – warmth I hadn't heard in a while now – made me want to smile. Slowly, I turned to look at her. "Yeah?"

Her cheeks were flushed, and her eyes were bright. She was looking at me the way she used to, before everything had gone to hell.

"Yeah." Chloe said in a voice that was almost breathless. "Totally."

Her lips were parted, and she gave me that look – the one that made my pulse jump and my jeans grow tight. I wanted to kiss her. The way it looked, she wouldn't say no.

I shoved that thought aside. I wouldn't be kissing her, not here, as much as I wanted to – and not because of the guy heading toward us.

Him, I could keep an eye out for, and handle him just fine if it came to that. But who else was watching? I didn't know, and that was a problem.

It was time to get on with the story.

"So anyway," I continued, "one fight led to another. Every time, the money got a little better. And then there was that fight video that made the rounds." I shook my head. "I still don't know how that got out. The organizers weren't too happy about that."

"Because the fights were illegal?" she asked.

"That and taxes."

"Taxes?"

"Yeah. They didn't like to pay them."

"Oh." In the passenger's seat, Chloe gave a little jump as she spotted the guy weaving his way toward us. He stopped to peer in the window of a Buick – some rusty brown thing with a cracked front windshield.

"You know him?" Chloe asked.

I shook my head. "Not from before. And not from now either. I *never* come back here."

"So why today?" she said. "And why with me?"

"Because there's something I need to say." I turned sideways in the car to face her. "It's about what happened. What I did to you."

Her gaze was locked on mine. "What about it?"

I looked down and shook my head. "It wasn't right. I'm not stupid. I know that. Shit, I knew it at the time. And why I couldn't stop myself–" I looked up again, meeting Chloe's gaze head-on. "I am so fucking ashamed of myself, I can't even tell you."

Her breathing grew shallow, but she didn't move. Was that a good sign? Or bad?

I reached for her hand. "You're my dream girl, Chloe. You've got to believe that." I thought of all those years without her, even before I knew her name. "I wished for you, and here you are, everything I ever imagined. Yeah, I won't lie. I've been with a lot of girls. But there's been nobody like you."

The way it looked, she wanted to believe it. "Really?" she said.

I nodded, never breaking eye contact. "I mean it. I love you. I should've told you sooner. And I should've done a better job of showing it. But if you just give me one more chance, I swear to you, you won't regret it." □

CHAPTER 29

Her breath caught, and her eyes warmed. The way it looked, I definitely had her attention.

I went on. "I want to tell you something else. And I'm dead serious. The things I've told you today, I've never told anyone."

Her eyes filled with tears. "Ever?"

Slowly, I reached for her hand. It felt small and warm, and I fought the urge to pull her closer. "Ever," I said. "So when I thought you were just playing me, pretending to be something you weren't, well, I guess I went a little nuts. But I swear to God, it will never, ever happen again."

At this, she squeezed her eyes shut for a long moment. But she still wasn't pulling away. I held my breath and watched her in the quiet car.

When she opened her eyes, I saw something new, a look of resolve that caught me off guard. "You need to know something too," she said. "That house in your neighborhood? It's not mine. I'm just staying there, that's all." She looked down. "I don't really belong there."

She was wrong. She *did* belong there, because she belonged with me. The other stuff – it didn't matter, as long as we were together.

"Baby," I said. "I know it's not your house, remember?"

She gave a hesitant nod.

I squeezed her hand. "And you wanna know where you belong?"

"Where?" she asked.

"With me."

At this she smiled, a real smile, and that's when I knew. She'd be mine again before the night was over.

First things first. I needed to get us the hell out of here, so we could talk in peace – where I could keep both eyes on her, not on whoever might be watching.

"Now c'mon," I said. "No more serious talk. Whatever's going on, we'll work it out, alright?"

She nodded.

I leaned closer. "First, I just have a question."

"What?"

"Do you love me?"

Her voice was only a whisper, but somehow, the single word seemed to fill the entire car. "Yes."

I leaned a fraction closer. "Say it."

Her eyes met mine, and she finally said the words I was dying to hear. "I love you."

Over the last couple of days, the weight of everything – my epic screw-up, the stuff with Brittney, the thought of never holding Chloe again – all of it had been weighing on me, maybe even more than I knew. Because suddenly, all that weight was gone, and I felt like I was floating on air.

I grinned over at her. "Baby, I love you too. More than life itself. I mean it."

And then, I couldn't stop myself. I kissed her, long and hard, keeping my eyes open, and my senses on high alert. When she gave a breathless moan, it was half heaven, half hell, because this wasn't the place to be losing control.

I forced myself to pull away and take a good look around. "We'd better go," I said.

"What's wrong?" Chloe asked.

"Nothing yet. But it'll be dark soon." I settled back into my seat and turned the key in the ignition. "And trust me, the farther away we get, the better."

As we pulled away from the curb, Chloe asked, "So, this car? Is it really bullet-proof?"

"Pretty much."

"But why?"

I dodged the question. "Why not? Haven't you ever wanted a bullet-proof car?"

"No." She laughed. "Not particularly."

"Eh, you're not a guy. Besides, I'm glad I have it." I glanced over at Chloe. "Otherwise, I'd have never brought you down here."

"Yeah?"

I nodded. "I might take a lot of chances in life, but with your safety? No way I'm risking that. Not ever."

She was smiling again. Her tone was teasing when she said, "You couldn't have bullet-proofed one of your nicer cars?"

"Nope."

"Why not?"

"Let's say we drove the Lexus. We'd be taken for an easy mark." I shrugged. "Or a drug dealer. But in this thing, we're practically invisible." I glanced around. "It's perfect for stuff like this."

"Stuff like what?" she said.

"Seeing things without being seen, watching without being watched. A car like this in Rochester Hills, yeah, it sticks out like a sore thumb. But a place like this, it's just part of the landscape."

"But why the bullet-proofing?" Chloe took another look around. "It's practically a ghost town."

I turned to give her a serious look. "Just because you don't see people, it doesn't mean no one's around. Besides, I use it for a few other things."

"Like what?" she asked.

I grinned over at her. "It's a secret."

She gave a small shake of her head. "What?"

I laughed. "No more serious talk. Remember? You hungry?"

She nodded, and I turned left at the next corner, wanting to leave all the ugliness behind. It was funny in a way. Some might say that I'd ditched the ugliness years ago, when the money started rolling in.

But some things, you never left behind. Even when you moved away, parts of it stuck with you. And sometimes, they dirtied the new things, the pretty things, the things you wanted to protect from all that.

I gave Chloe a sideways glance. During the past couple of days, she'd seen the worst of what a guy like me had to offer.

From now on, it was my job to show her the best. I glanced at my watch, wishing we had more time. I recalled my original promise. No matter what, I wouldn't make her late for work.

But damn it, I really wanted to.

CHAPTER 30

A half-hour later, we were holding hands over dinner. I gazed at her across the table, wondering how I'd gotten so damn lucky. We hadn't made it official, but the way it looked, we were back together.

If I had my way, we were going to *stay* together.

"So," I said, "tell me about your brother. You said he's pretty smart, huh?"

She gave me a sheepish smile. "Oh come on, you don't want to hear about that."

She was wrong. I did. If I had my way, he'd be my brother too someday. Or brother-in-law. Whatever they called it. Either way, he was important to Chloe, so he was important to me.

But that wasn't the only reason I wanted to hear about him. On that night we'd first met, after she'd practically scraped me off the hospital sidewalk, she'd talked a lot about Josh. I might not have looked it, but I'd been listening.

Back then, family was a funny thing for me. My mom was a druggie, and my dad was a guy I barely knew. I loved my sister, and I loved my grandma, but even those relationships weren't always easy — because the more I loved them, the more I worried for their safety.

But Chloe, she'd grown up in a different world. I wanted to hear more about it.

I grinned over at her. "So, uh, you hiding something? Don't tell me he's flunking out?"

"Of what?" She laughed. "Seventh grade?"

I shrugged. "Hey, it happens."

"Oh stop it. He's in the gifted program." She gave a playful eye-roll. "And no, he's not flunking out."

"So tell me about him," I said.

And so she did. Some of the stuff I knew. Other things, I didn't. He played the oboe and was on the math team. He liked the Detroit Red Wings and was a picky eater.

"I can relate," I said.

"To which part?" she asked.

"Well, I sure as hell can't play the oboe." I smiled across the table. "I'm talking about the eating thing."

"You?" She was laughing again. "A picky eater? Oh, please."

"Well, I hate seafood."

She shuddered. "Don't we all?"

Not as far as I'd seen. Other than Chloe, almost everyone else I knew loved it. But me, I hated it for a good reason, and it wasn't one I liked to talk about.

I was a guy who'd been punched, kicked, and called just about every name in the book. Sure, I had some scars, but most of it just bounced off me. But when it came to shellfish, I was allergic as hell, as I'd found out the hard way a few years earlier.

The way the doctors talked, I'd almost died. But I liked to think of it differently. I hadn't died. And now I knew that I hated seafood for a damn good reason.

Superman had kryptonite. Me? I had seafood. Talk about embarrassing.

I changed the subject. "How about Erika?"

"What about her?" Chloe asked.

"The way you talk, she sounds kind of wild." I made a show of lowering my voice. "What's the worst thing she talked you into?"

"Hey," Chloe said in a teasing tone, "maybe *I* was the one talking *her* into stuff."

Now, *that* was interesting. "Were you?" I asked.

"I wish." Her tone grew more serious. "Nah, I was always focused on other stuff, you know?"

I didn't know. But I wanted to. "Like what?"

She waved away the question. "Okay, you wanna know the worst thing she talked me into?"

I leaned forward. "What?"

Chloe gave an embarrassed laugh. "Getting my belly-button pierced."

I felt my gaze drift downward. I couldn't see Chloe's belly-button, not through the table, but suddenly, I wanted to. Her skin was smooth, and she had the cutest belly-button. "Yeah?" I said, feeling the corners of my mouth lift. "Is it still pierced?"

She laughed. "You know the answer to that. No."

"You sure? I could check."

"You could," she said, "but we'd probably get kicked out of here."

It was a risk I was willing to take. Looking at her, I couldn't stop smiling.

Best of all, she was smiling back. She was still smiling when she asked, "What are you so happy about?"

I could've said a million things. I was happy because I loved her. I was happy because the look in her eyes told me she loved me too. I was happy to have a second chance. And hey, if that chance involved checking out her belly button, who was I to complain?

I leaned closer and said, "You didn't say I couldn't check, *ever*. You just said I couldn't check *now*."

Her cheeks were flushed, and her eyes were sparkling. She was leaning closer too. In a voice filled mischief, she said, "I'll show you mine if you show me yours."

Instantly, the blood went straight to my groin. I glanced down at the table. It looked pretty sturdy. I wanted to shove aside the dishes and show her lots of things, right here, right now.

But we weren't alone. So all I said was, "Promise?"

She gave a happy nod. "Promise."

Before we left, I leaned in close, ignoring the dirty plates and empty glasses. "Tell me something."

Her gaze was locked on mine, and when she answered, her voice was almost breathless. "What?"

"Are you still my girl?"

She was smiling again. When she nodded yes, I couldn't stop myself. I practically dove across the table and wrapped my arms tight around her. People were staring. I didn't care. I pulled her close and spoke into her ear. "Baby, I promise you. You're not gonna regret this."

As for me, I had two regrets. One, she had to work tonight. Two, I was flying to Vegas first thing tomorrow morning.

But those regrets were nothing. When I returned, things were going to be different. Chloe and I would have a new start, and this time, I'd make sure to do things right.

Driving back from the restaurant, I still couldn't stop smiling, and I didn't bother to hide it. But just before we pulled into Chloe's driveway, she told me something that didn't make me happy. ☐

CHAPTER 31

I pulled into her driveway and stopped the car. From the driver's seat, I turned to look at her. "What'd you just say?"

Chloe gave a weak laugh. "From the look on your face, I think you heard me just fine."

I *did* hear her. I just didn't want to believe it. "Are you serious?"

"Yup." Chloe sighed. "She starts tonight actually."

I leaned back in my seat and muttered, "I'm gonna kill her."

The *her* was Brittney. Somehow, she'd gotten herself hired as a waitress where Chloe worked.

I'd been to that restaurant. The waitresses were all insanely beautiful, and did more than simply deliver food and drinks. They had attitude and flaunted it by teasing the customers with mock bad service that somehow, managed to still be pretty good.

Supposedly, it was harder than hell to get hired there. How had Brittney done it so fast?

But then I recalled something Chloe had mentioned during Brittney's failed apology attempt – something about Brittney boning Chloe's boss in the parking lot.

Well, that was one way to get hired.

Chloe lowered her voice to a mock whisper. "When you kill her, can I help?"

Obviously, she was kidding. But I wasn't, not that I was planning to kill her or anything. But one way or another, I'd handle this – I hesitated – assuming that's what Chloe wanted.

Thanks to my other mistakes, I was walking on egg shells and didn't want to screw up anything else. So I did the polite thing and asked, "You want me to take care of it?"

Chloe gave me a doubtful look. "How?"

I shrugged. "However." If nothing else, I could always bribe her.

"Nah, that's alright," Chloe said. "It's not really a big deal."

But from the look on her face, I wasn't convinced.

"Sure you don't want me to talk to her?" I asked, wanting to insist, but trying to play it safe.

She gave me a smile that melted my heart. "I'm sure."

I loved that smile. I loved *her*. And now, I had to leave. I hated that. "I don't wanna let you go," I admitted.

"You mean to work?" she asked.

I leaned toward her. "I mean anywhere." I wrapped her in my arms and kissed her like I meant it, because I *did* mean it. I was going to be out of town almost a week, and I wanted like hell to drag her back to my place and do a whole lot more than kiss.

When our tongues met, she gave a muffled moan against my lips. My pulse throbbed, and my jeans grew tight.

Forget bribing Brittney. I should bribe Chloe to ditch work tonight, or better yet, ditch it forever. But I remembered my promise. No matter what, I wouldn't make her late.

Damn it. If I couldn't keep a small promise, how would she trust me with the big stuff? *Don't screw this up.*

When she pulled away, I didn't argue. She looked toward the house and suddenly smiled. I looked too, and saw Chucky peering out through the curtains.

I had to laugh. "Our chaperone."

"Yeah." Chloe sighed with obvious regret. "I've gotta go."

"I was afraid of that."

She leaned into me and asked, "When do you fly out?"

"Tomorrow morning. Six o'clock."

"So early?" she said.

I nodded. "Are you sure don't wanna come with me?" I leaned my forehead against hers. "Tell ya what, you don't even have to wake up. I'll carry you onto that plane myself."

She laughed. "I wish. But I've got Chucky. And work."

"When I get back, we'll have to talk about that." I lowered my voice. "And just so you know, I want to do a whole lot more than talk."

Her voice was all kinds of sexy when she said, "Me, too."

A few hours later, just before dawn, I was on the plane, heading for Vegas. The timing sucked. I didn't want to go anywhere, not without Chloe. But the Vegas thing – one of several mixed martial events in a global series – had been in the works for months, technically years, since it was an annual thing.

For these events, I delegated a lot, but there were some things – personal appearances mostly – that I couldn't farm out, not without damaging the brand. So I just had to suck it up and count the days until I returned.

While in Vegas, I called Chloe every night, taking advantage of the time-zone difference to catch her when she got off work.

Midnight in Vegas was three o'clock in the morning in Michigan. It was an obscene hour for most people, but not for Chloe. For her, three o'clock was early, thanks to her work schedule. In a way, I was lucking out. Usually, her shifts didn't end until nearly dawn.

Still, the phone calls weren't enough. By Friday morning, I was going crazy missing her, which is why late that afternoon, I was headed back to Michigan.

I couldn't stay long, but it would be long enough to see Chloe, and that's all that mattered. I was already on the plane when I called to tell her. There was only one problem. For some reason, she didn't sound happy to hear from me.

CHAPTER 32

Something was bothering her. I heard it in her voice from the moment she answered with a tense, "Hello?"

"What's wrong?" I asked.

"Nothing."

I paused. "Alright." *Something* was off. The way it sounded, she was driving. Maybe that was it. I pushed aside the distraction and asked, "Got any plans for tonight?"

"Not really. Why?"

"Because I've gotta be honest. I couldn't wait to see you."

At this, she perked up. "You came back early?"

"You might say that."

She laughed. "What does that mean?"

"It means that I'll be landing in a couple hours. I've got to be back in Vegas tomorrow morning, but I remembered you had tonight off, so—"

"So you want to get together?" She was smiling now. Even through the phone, I could tell.

It made me smile, too. "Yeah."

I wanted her in my arms and in my bed. I wanted to screw her silly and hear her moan my name as I did all kinds of obscene things to her. Last night, I'd actually masturbated in the shower to naked thoughts of her hot, tight body, and the things I'd be doing to it the next time we were together.

I wanted that to be tonight.

But there was something else I wanted – to tell the whole world she was mine. She wasn't my secret thing, to hide in my house until I wanted her in my bed. And she wasn't a groupie, a hanger-on, or a quick fuck for a night or two.

She was the girl I loved, and it was time to start acting like it. "But listen," I said, "no more hiding out in secret. You're my girl, and from now on, I'm doing things right. How about I'll pick you up at seven?"

"Sounds good. But hey, what should I wear?"

"What kind of night are you in the mood for?" I asked. "Casual, formal?"

"How about casual?"

"Casual, it is." I lowered my voice. "And Chloe?"

"Hmm?"

"I don't care what you wear. I'm dying to see you."

A few hours later, she was in my car – and not the rough-looking one that we'd taken the other day. I was driving one of my sports cars that *never* blended. It was fast. It was flaming orange. And so far, I hadn't seen another one like it in Rochester Hills.

The car got attention, and tonight, that was fine by me, because I wanted the whole world to take a good, long look and see that Chloe was mine. If I had my way, she'd be mine forever.

From the driver's seat, I gave her a sideways glance. Whatever had been bothering her earlier, I saw no sign of it. I chalked it up to traffic or whatever and focused on the fact that she was right here, within arm's reach.

She was dressed in jeans and a clingy white blouse that looked innocent and sexy all at the same time. She hit me with a smile that went straight to my groin. "You know," she said, "I just realized something."

"Yeah? What?"

"I've never seen anyone fly home just for one night. Especially to see *me*." She hesitated. "I mean, it's not like you came home *just* to see me. It's just that you came a long way for a short time." She cleared her throat. "You know?"

I turned off the road, and into a nearby parking lot. I pulled into a random spot and cut the engine. Chloe looked around. We were just outside some strip mall that had a bunch of offices and a takeout pizza place.

Her gaze landed on the pizza sign. "So, uh, is that where we're eating?"

I laughed. "Not a chance." I liked pizza as much as the next guy, but I hadn't flown across the country to take my girl to some cheap pizza joint.

"Then why'd we stop?" she asked.

"Because I've got to tell you something."

Her brow wrinkled. "What?"

I looked into her eyes and said, "I came home for just *one* reason, and her name is Chloe Malinski."

She gave me a slow, sultry smile. "Really?"

I leaned toward her and kept my voice very low. "Really."

Before I knew it, her lips were on mine. I pulled her close and kissed her like it was our last night on Earth. I was hard and ready, and the way it sounded, she was just as eager as I was. I felt her hands on the back of my neck, and her soft curves pressing up against my hard chest.

Clothes – we were wearing too damn many of them. I wanted to drag us both into the back seat for a pre-dinner appetizer of the naked kind. Trying like hell to behave myself, I ran a hand through her hair, loving how it felt as it sifted through my fingers while my tongue probed hers and our lips moved hungrily against each other.

This wasn't why I'd pulled over, but I sure as hell wasn't complaining. I had dinner reservations in a half-hour and some other plans after that. None of those plans involved screwing Chloe in some parking lot – as tempting as that sounded.

I'd learned a few lessons the hard way. One of those lessons was the fact that these days, cameras were everywhere. Shit, everyone had a cell phone, right? There was no way in hell *anyone* would be seeing Chloe's naked body on the internet.

Even when it came to looking, I wasn't going to share. She was mine. And only mine.

Just thinking of it made me smile against her lips. Tonight, I decided, I'd be smiling against her other lips. As soon as we got back, I was going to lick her all night long if that's what it took to make her totally lose it.

I was still kissing her when I heard a tap on the driver's side window. With a little jump, Chloe pulled back, and I turned to look. Standing just outside the window were a couple of teenagers, two guys, maybe fifteen or sixteen. They were grinning down at us. One of them was holding a pizza box.

The one who wasn't holding the box motioned for me to roll down the window.

I glanced over at Chloe.

"Be careful," she teased. "They look dangerous."

Yeah, right. We were still in Rochester Hills, and these guys looked about as dangerous as puppies. I rolled down the window and said, "Yeah?"

The nearest one said, "You're Lawton Rastor." He leaned around to look at Chloe. "Isn't he?"

Chloe turned to give me a long, speculative look. "Hmmmm…he definitely *looks* like him."

The kid's eyebrows furrowed. "You don't know?" He gave her a no-nonsense look. "Dude, it's *totally* him."

Chloe was smiling now. "Let's hope so. Otherwise the *real* Lawton Rastor's gonna be pretty mad at me."

I gave her a look. "Got that right." My gaze dipped to her lips. They looked so damn kissable, I wanted to taste them again. "The way I hear it, he's not big on sharing."

She laughed. "Well, there you have it." She turned back to the guys. "I'm pretty sure he's the real one."

"I knew it!" the guy said. He turned to his friend. "See? I told you." He turned back to us and said, "Ducky didn't believe me."

Chloe gave him a confused look. "Ducky?"

The kid with the box spoke up. "That's me." He shrugged. "Nickname."

"Anyway," the first kid said, turning back to me, "I told Ducky you lived around here. I recognized the car." He grinned. "You know, from the internet. Pretty sweet ride, huh?"

Yeah, the car *was* sweet. But it felt a lot sweeter when it was just me and Chloe. "Thanks," I said, trying to be a decent sport about it. It wasn't their fault I was dying to be alone with the girl in the passenger's seat.

But Chloe was smiling at the guys, looking amused as hell. "You come here often?" she asked.

"Yeah." The guy flicked his head toward the pizza place. "We're like regular customers." He glanced at the box in Ducky's hands. "You want some? It's pepperoni."

"Uh, thanks," Chloe said, "but we're on our way to dinner."

He was grinning at her now. "So, are you his girlfriend?"

Chloe looked toward me. "I don't know." She smiled. "He *is* Lawton Rastor, you know."

The kid was nodding like somehow this made sense. He turned back to me. "As long as you're here, can we have your autograph?"

I heard myself laugh. When I'd pulled into the parking lot, this wasn't what I had in mind. Still, I wasn't going to be a dick about it. I'd been a teenager once.

True, when I'd been their age, I'd been a lot less puppy-like. But the reason for that was obvious. My old neighborhood was more of a Doberman kind of place.

"Sure," I said.

"Except we don't have a pen," the guy said. "You got one?"

Next to him, Ducky spoke up. "If you don't, I could borrow one from the pizza place." He straightened. "On account of the fact we're regulars."

Chloe gave a small laugh. "Hang on, I think I've got a pen in my purse."

Ducky cleared his throat. "Um, we don't have anything to sign either." He gave me a hopeful look. "You got a picture? Or maybe a piece of paper or something?"

Chloe spoke up. "How about the pizza box?"

Now, they were both nodding. "Yeah," Ducky was saying. "Good idea." He thrust the box through the open car window. "But sign the *top* of the box, okay? Because the inside's all greasy." He paused. "Sure you don't want a piece?"

I looked down at the box. It was still warm, but not heavy enough to contain a whole pizza. Probably, they'd been scarfing it in the parking lot. "Thanks," I said, "maybe next time."

A couple of minutes later, the box was signed, and we were on our way.

From the passenger's seat, Chloe said, "That was really nice of you."

I shook my head. "What? Signing a box? It was nothing."

"It wasn't nothing," she said. "You let them take selfies with you."

I shrugged. The selfies happened so often, I barely noticed them anymore.

Chloe was still talking. "You were nice to them, too. I bet a lot of people wouldn't be."

"Nice?" I gave a dramatic groan. "Oh, no."

"What?" she asked.

"Nice," I repeated. "That's the kiss of death."

She gave me an amused smile. "What? You worried about ruining your reputation?"

"Baby," I said, "my reputation's *already* ruined."

I'd said it as a joke, but the funny thing was, it was true. I had a reputation alright, and it sure as hell wasn't for being nice.

The way the tabloids told it, I'd gotten my reputation by kicking asses, breaking hearts, and showing my dick on the internet. But if I were lucky, those days were over. This was a new start, and I was going to make the most of it.

It was a good thought, and I might have kept on thinking it, except just a few hours later, there was trouble. And like always, it wasn't the kind I could solve with niceness. ☐

CHAPTER 33

Up until now, the night had been going great. We'd had dinner at this Greek place that a friend of mine owned, and then we'd hit a comedy show at a downtown casino, where we'd laughed our asses off at jokes that we'd probably forget by tomorrow.

Everything – being with Chloe, listening to her laugh, having her look at me the way she used to – it had been worth the trip, even if it meant I'd need to hop back on the same plane in just a few short hours.

I liked being out with her. No. I *loved* being out with her, because no matter where we were, she brought something into my life that I hadn't realized I'd been missing.

All night, I'd been dying to get her alone. But I was determined to do things right, which is why at midnight, we were at some club off Six Mile, where the music was loud, and the bodies were packed. On the crowded dance floor, I'd held her in my arms, and felt our hips grinding against each other, moving in time with the music.

We'd been out there a while when Chloe glanced through the gyrating bodies toward our table. I followed her gaze and saw our drinks – the ones we'd ordered when we first came in.

With obvious reluctance, Chloe pulled away and pointed. "Look. Drinks."

I'd already seen the drinks, so I didn't bother looking. I was thirsty alright, but not for the beer that I'd ordered however long ago. "Yeah?" I said. "Ready to sit down?"

She nodded, looking flushed and happy, so I took her hand and led her back to our table, where I took a good, long pull of the beer, not caring that it wasn't really cold anymore. As for Chloe, she took one sip of her drink and practically choked.

"What's wrong?" I asked.

Now, she was half-coughing, half-laughing. "I think they made it a double. Wait." She glanced down and gave a small shudder. "Scratch that. Make that a triple."

I grinned over at her. "They probably thought they were doing you a favor." It happened to me almost everywhere I went, so I shouldn't have been surprised.

"A favor?" she said, still laughing. "Maybe. But it's not exactly thirst-quenching, if you know what I mean."

"Want me get you a new one?"

She looked around. Our cocktail waitress was nowhere in sight. "Nah, that's alright."

I grinned over at her. "You think so, huh?" I stood and reached for her drink. "Wait here. I'll be back in five minutes."

I left before she could argue, weaving my way to the far side of the club, where I had the bartender make Chloe a new drink. Not taking any chances, I watched personally as he added the right amount of alcohol, not too much, and not too little either.

Drink in-hand, I was halfway back to our table when I saw something that had me setting the drink wherever and pushing my way through the crowd, heading toward Chloe. She wasn't at our table, but I *did* see her, facing off against a guy who looked to damn familiar.

His name was Creed, and he wasn't exactly a friend of mine. The way it looked, Chloe was trying to move around him, but he wasn't letting her. She'd move, and then he'd move to block her path, and not only once.

That fucker was messing with her.

I was moving faster now, but the crowd was tight, and it was taking too damn long.

Creed – a big guy by any standards – was towering over Chloe and standing way too close. She craned her neck to glare up at him as they exchanged words that, even from this distance, were obviously unfriendly.

Chloe looked nervous, and maybe a little afraid, but she was standing her ground.

Damn it. She shouldn't *have* to stand her ground. I shouldn't have left her alone. I *wouldn't* have left her alone if I'd known that Creed was anywhere in the building.

I'd known the guy for maybe seven years now. Way back when I'd been just starting out, I'd kicked his ass in front of his girlfriend, or whoever the girl was. We'd been at this downtown dive, and she'd been coming on to me strong, right in front of him.

I hadn't been interested. But *she* was. It was a problem.

Creed's solution? Kick my ass to prove what a big man he was – except it hadn't worked out that way. I'd left him on the floor and made my escape a minute later – not from the cops, or even from Creed's friends, but from the girl, who the way it sounded, was looking to reward whoever won.

Classy. Just like Creed.

Like once a year, I had the bad luck to run into him. It always ended the same way.

He was such a dumb-ass.

Whatever he was saying now, Chloe didn't like it. She edged backward and bumped into a tall girl behind her. The music was still blaring, but even through the noise, I heard the shattering of glass as the girl's drink hit the floor.

The girl yelled something, but Chloe didn't even turn around. Her eyes were still glued on Creed, who was saying something that Chloe obviously didn't like. By now, I was shoving my way through the crowd, not caring whose drinks I spilled along the way.

Finally, I was there. Probably, it had taken less than thirty seconds, but it felt like a lifetime. I shoved my way between them, with my back to Chloe and my gaze on Creed.

He was smiling, showing off the gold grillwork that covered his front teeth.

I could feel Chloe behind me. Over my shoulder, I said to her, "Baby, go back to the table. I'll meet you there in a minute."

Behind me, I heard another drink hit the floor, followed the sound of a girl saying, "Oh my God. Is that Lawton Rastor?"

Shit.

In front of me, Creed glared at the crowd. "Hey, everyone!" he bellowed out. "It's fucking Lawton Rastor! And his fucking squeeze! Aren't we so fucking lucky?"

All of a sudden, the music stopped. At my back, I felt a distinct drop in temperature as if the crowd behind me was backing away. That was fine by me, as long as Chloe was part of that crowd.

From the corner of my eye, I caught sudden movement, a fist flying toward me. On instinct, I snapped my head back and watched that same fist fly past my face, missing by nose by just a couple of inches. Behind me, I heard a gasp. Chloe. Damn it.

Shoving aside the distraction, I looked to my side and spotted the guy who went with the fist. I'd seen him before, hanging out with Creed. He went by the name of Snake, and he was a big muscle-bound guy with complicated facial hair. Without turning toward him I reached out and slammed my fist into his ear.

"Motherfucker!" he yelled, staggering backward like I'd knocked his marbles loose. Behind me, I sensed that Chloe was still there. I don't know how, but I just knew.

"Chloe," I said, trying to keep my voice even, "you'd better not still be there."

I heard footsteps, like maybe she was backing up. She'd better be, because I'd be a dumb-ass to turn around and look.

Creed took a swing at me. I swatted his fist aside, and then jabbed him in the nose with my other fist.

He staggered backward, and his hands flew to his nose. A river of blood poured between his fingers. "My nose! You fuckin' broke it, you asshole!"

Funny that he felt the need to announce it. If someone broke *my* nose, I sure as hell wouldn't be telling everyone.

Again, I caught movement off to my right – Snake charging me. Without changing direction, I gave him an elbow to the neck. He dropped to the ground, wheezing. Looking to keep him down, I kicked him in the side, sending him rolling onto his back.

Already, Creed, with his face a bloody mess, was plowing toward me, head-first. I hit him in the gut and watched him double-over and drop to his knees.

About damn time.

Through the crowd, I spotted a couple of bouncers heading toward us. One was Terrell, a friend of mine who I'd introduced to Chloe on the way in. The other I didn't know. Terrell looked down at the Snake, who was still lying on his back. "Snake, you dumb-ass. Not again."

With something like a sigh, Terrell grabbed one of Snake's booted feet in each hand and started dragging him toward the exit.

Creed, now on his hands and knees, raised his head and muttered, "That son-of-a-bitch broke my nose!" He glared at me. "Third fuckin' time. You cock-sucker."

I took a step toward him and grabbed him by the collar of his shirt. In a low voice, meant for his ears only, I said, "You wanna fuck with me? Fine. Fuck with me all you want. But if you ever fuck with my girl again—"

I leaned closer to his ear and said, "I know where you live. The next time? It won't be your nose. It'll be your neck."

Creed glanced at Chloe but said nothing. With a shove, I let him go. The place was dead quiet. Creed looked around the crowd and muttered, "What the fuck are you lookin' at?" before getting to his feet and stumbling toward the exit.

And then, somewhere behind me, I heard a girl's voice, a different one from the first, say, "Holy shit, was that Lawton Rastor?"

CHAPTER 34

Chloe was laughing.

I wasn't.

I closed the passenger's side door and headed for the driver's side. I was pissed off and trying, for her sake, not to show it.

None of this shit was supposed to happen. Five minutes – that's how long I'd left her alone in that place. The way it turned out, it was five minutes too long.

I should've paid better attention to who was around. Creed was six-and-a-half feet tall. He had neck tattoos and gold teeth. How in the hell had I missed him?

And why had I left Chloe alone? I mean, the place was nice enough, but it was near some places that weren't so nice. A rough element – that's what some people might call it.

I made a sound of disgust. Rough element, huh? Money or not, that would describe me, too.

When I slid into the driver's seat, Chloe turned sideways in her seat to face me. "That was interesting," she said.

"That's one way to put it."

She paused. "Are you mad at me or something?"

I turned to stare out the front windshield. The parking lot was too dark, like someone forgot to pay the electric bill. You got that a lot out here, which was pretty damn stupid, considering all the bad things that could happen, especially in this town.

Chloe spoke again, her voice softer now. "Are you?"

Mad at her? "No," I said.

It was true. It wasn't *her* I was mad at. It was me.

"Are you sure?" she asked.

I couldn't look at her. I didn't know what to say.

She spoke again. "You *are*."

I gave a slow shake of my head.

I felt her hand on my thigh. "Then what is it?" she asked.

I turned to face her. Her smile was gone, and her eyes were worried. Great. Now, I had another reason to be pissed at myself.

I tried to explain. "You could've been hurt."

"But I wasn't."

"But you could've been."

"So *that's* why you're mad at me?"

I squeezed her hand. "No. Baby. Not you. *Me*."

"Why you?" Her tone grew teasing. "You rescued me. You're the hero of this story, not the villain."

"You sure about that?"

She smiled. "Definitely."

"Oh yeah?" I said. "Well, let me ask you something? You ever have that happen before?"

She shook her head. "What?"

"You ever have some stranger come up and give you crap for no good reason?"

"Well, I *am* a waitress," she said. "So, yeah. It happens to me all the time, actually."

"You know what I mean." I leaned toward her, over the center console. "I shouldn't have left you alone."

"Why not? I don't need a bodyguard."

"That place. I mean it's nice enough." I shook my head. "But the crowd. Shit." I reached out and brushed a stray lock of hair from her face. Thinking about what happened, I felt my fingers tense. "I wanted to kill him."

"Which one?"

"Both."

"Well, you did a pretty good job of *half*-killing them, so that's gotta count for something, right?"

Obviously, she didn't get it. This was no joke. I gave her a serious look. "I can laugh at a lot of things, Chloe. But seeing you hurt isn't one of them."

"Except I *wasn't* hurt." She grinned over at me. "I wasn't even touched. So there."

I recalled Creed's girlfriend – the one who'd been coming onto me way back when. I'd happened to see her a month later. She'd been sporting a black eye that she'd tried to hide with make-up. The work of Creed? Or someone else?

Either way, shit like that shouldn't happen. And with Chloe, what if I'd been ten minutes later? I closed my eyes, not wanting to think about it. I heard myself say, "But you could've been."

"Hey," she said, her tone growing serious, "I want to ask you something, and I hope you'll be honest with me."

At that point, I'd have answered her anything. I turned to look at her. And there she was, the sweetest thing I'd ever known. I loved her. And there was part of me that thought she'd be better off with someone else – maybe a nice accountant or something. That had been her college major, right?

What the hell was she doing with a guy like me?

If she wanted to ask me a question, *any* question, I was ready to answer it. Slowly, I nodded.

She leaned close and lowered her voice to just a whisper. "By any chance, are you Lawton Rastor?"

What the hell? Was she making fun of this? It was nothing to joke about. But damn it, I felt my lips twitch anyway. And then, I couldn't help it. I smiled over at her. "Me?" I said. "Nah. *I'm* the guy with Chloe Malinski."

"Oh her?" Chloe gave a dramatic sigh. "But she's just a nobody."

I gave her a good, long look. Chloe Malinski wasn't a nobody. She was the first thing I thought of every morning, and the last thing I thought of every night. She was the reason I'd come home, and the reason that returning to Vegas was the last thing I wanted to do.

I'd be flying out in six hours. She looked sexy as hell, sitting there in the passenger's seat. Her jeans hugged her hips, and the top of her blouse was unbuttoned just enough to make things interesting. I couldn't see much, but what I did see had me wanting to see more.

Chloe Malinski, a nobody? If she weren't driving me to distraction, I might have laughed.

I leaned closer. "Baby, she's somebody, alright." Slowly, I moved my lips close to hers. But I didn't kiss her. Not yet. "Matter of fact, she's everything to this guy I know."

She was breathless now. "Oh yeah?"

"Oh yeah."

I closed the distance, kissing her hard and hungry. She was here. And she was mine.

I felt her hands on my head, running her warm fingertips through my hair as our lips, our tongues, and our breaths combined.

She pulled away, flushed and trembling. "I want you," she breathed.

I wanted her, too. I always wanted her – physically, emotionally, and – I couldn't help but smile – legally.

Except, *some* things I wanted to do to her might not be legal in all states. I moved my lips lower. I kissed her cheek, her jaw, her neck. I moved aside the fabric of her blouse and kissed her shoulder. It was warm and smooth, and she smelled like spring after a long, brutal winter.

I moved my lips lower, trailing kisses until she gave a whimper that made my breath hitch and my hardness surge. I wanted to rip open that blouse and keep on kissing her until she begged me to take her, right here, right now.

But I'd made enough mistakes tonight. I wanted to get her alone, but someplace safe. I asked, "Ready to go home?"

"I feel like I'm home right now," she said, looking toward the rear of the car. "Hey, look a back seat."

I laughed into her shoulder. "No way."

"Aw c'mon," she said. "I know you want to."

She reached a hand to my knee and trailed her fingers upward across my jeans, working slowly and surely toward my cock, which was raging hard now. When her hand hit home, I groaned against her skin. "Baby, you're killin' me over here."

"Then you should just give in," she teased. "It'll be so much simpler."

I pulled back and looked into her eyes. They were bright with excitement and filled with hunger. Damn, I wanted her. Still, I made myself say, "Not gonna happen. Not here. As tempting as you are."

"Why not?"

Because I loved her. That's why. But more than that, there were practical reasons.

I made a point of looking around the darkened parking lot. "A place like this, bad things can happen. And if anything bad happened to you–" I shook my head "–I'd never forgive myself."

Already, I'd let too many bad things happen to Chloe. Some of those things, I'd done myself. No more.

Chloe leaned into me. "With you here? I'm not worried."

It was nice to hear, but there was no way in hell I'd be taking that kind of chance, not now. Sure, I'd had my share of back-seat action, mostly with girls I'd never take home. Shitty or not, that's just the way it was. But Chloe, she was something special.

Plus, Creed and Snake had to be around here somewhere. I didn't want to be distracted. I wanted to focus on one thing and one thing only – her naked body as I did all those things that she liked best.

I grinned over at her. "Here's the thing," I said. "Yeah, we could climb into that back seat, but I'd have to keep an eye out." I reached out and put a hand on *her* knee, just like she'd done to me a minute earlier. Taking my sweet time, I moved the hand higher, skimming it softly up her thigh and heading for the sweet spot where her thighs met.

When my hand hit home, her eyes drifted shut and she made a sound – a half-moan, half-sigh – that drove me crazy with wanting her. I watched her face, loving the flush of her cheeks and the fullness of her lips.

Through her jeans, I moved my thumb in a slow, deliberate circle, hitting her favorite spot in her favorite way. "Or," I said, rubbing more slowly now, "I could take you home, where the only thing I have to think about is you."

"Home," she said. "Now."

Home. I felt myself smile. Oh yeah, I'd take her home alright –
in more ways than one. ☐

CHAPTER 35

By the time I turned the car onto my street, I was ready to lose it, and the way it looked, I wasn't the only one. Chloe, with hungry eyes and parted lips, had been teasing me the whole way back and not in the joking way.

Both of us were still dressed, but that hadn't stopped our hands from roaming – Chloe's more than mine, since I was determined to get us back in one piece.

Inside the darkened car, I'd felt her hands skimming my chest and abs through my shirt, and then – holy fuck – caressing my cock through my jeans. Every so often, she'd lean close and whisper in my ear – sweet, dirty things that made me want to pull over and show her just how dirty I could be.

Finally, we roared through my gate and skidded to a stop in the turnaround. I cut the engine and jumped out of the car. Somehow, I'd made the thirty-minute drive in just under twenty, and the way things were going, it felt like too damn long.

I strode around to the passenger's side, flung open the door, and threw Chloe over my shoulder, barbarian style.

Laughing, she squealed out, "What you doing?"

"You'll see," I said, and kept on going.

She was giggling now, and I was loving the sounds of her. She was happy, and so was I. But I'd be a whole lot happier when I got her alone, *really* alone. I pushed through the front door and slammed it shut with a haphazard kick.

I headed up the stairway with Chloe still slung over my shoulder, laughing all the way. I heard a soft thud and looked down to see one of her shoes tumbling down the staircase. Forget the shoe. In two minutes, she'd be wearing nothing at all.

I turned down the long hall and headed straight to my bedroom. I strode through the open door and tossed Chloe onto my bed, where she landed in a fit of giggles that warmed the whole house. I'd been without her for how long now? A week?

Without Chloe, the house hadn't felt like a home. It felt cold and empty, and too damn big. But she was back. And this time, I wasn't going to mess it up.

I felt myself smile. No. When it came to Chloe, I was going to do other things – spoil her, love her and now, take that hot little body of hers and show her just how much I'd missed her.

I leaned over the bed. Her face was flushed, and her hair was wild. The giggles were gone, replaced by a breathless excitement that had me catching my breath too.

I leaned closer. With one hand, I unbuttoned her jeans and then went for the zipper, tugging it down until I saw the black lace of her panties. Soon, those panties would be off, lying wherever they happened to land.

But first things first. I straightened and took one of her pant legs in each hand. I tugged, slowly and surely, until her jeans slid down her thighs and past her toes. I tossed the jeans aside and looked down at her, feeling that same kind of crazy love I always felt when we were together like this.

She was my dream girl. When she was here, everything felt different. My house felt different. I felt different. Shit, even my body felt different, wired with anticipation. I could hardly breathe. The things I wanted to do to her – but where to start?

First, those panties? They were nice. But they had to go. I gripped them in my hands and started to tug them downward.

Chloe's eyes were bright, and her lips were parted. Her hips rose and fell, even as she breathed, "No fair. You're still dressed."

Fair? Fair was for pussies.

"Who said anything about fair?" I said, giving her panties a slow tug downward, past her hips, past her knees, past her toes. I was raging hard and wanted to take her right then and there. But I wanted something else too. I wanted her to be good and ready. I wanted her to want me like I wanted her. I wanted her to *need* me like I needed her.

I gazed down, devouring the sight of her lying there on my bed in just that white blouse and whatever she was wearing underneath. I ached for her, ached to be inside her, ached to feel her pressed up as close as we could get.

I looked into her eyes, those amazing eyes, and had to tell her, "Baby, you are so beautiful, it hurts to look at you."

Her breath caught. "So are you," she said, motioning me toward the bed. "But you're too far away."

Yeah? Let's see what I could do about that. I grabbed her ankles and pulled her toward me, until her pelvis rested at the edge of the bed. Slowly, I ran a hand up her naked thigh. "Better?" I asked.

She crooked her finger, motioning me closer. I leaned toward her, and she gripped the hem of my shirt. She tugged it upward until I lifted my arms, letting her yank the shirt over my head and toss it onto the floor.

I stood, shirtless, over the bed, looking down on the girl I loved. Her breathing was shallow, and her back was arched. I let my gaze travel slowly down the length of her, from her beautiful face, to her smooth neck, to the curves of her breasts, still hidden by her blouse. My gaze skimmed lower and stopped at her naked hips. They were still rising and falling in time with her breathing – subtle, but sexy as hell.

I recalled my plans from earlier, to lick her until she went as crazy for me as I was for her.

I moved back and knelt at the foot of the bed. I lowered my head and kissed the inside of her thigh, just above the knee. Her breath hitched, and she gave a warm shiver that made me smile against her skin.

Yeah. You'll be doing a lot more than shivering by the time I'm done with you.

I reached up and stroked the outsides of her thighs, loving the feel of her skin and the way she responded, arching her hips as if ready for more.

Oh, you'll get more, alright.

Before the night was over, those smooth thighs of hers would be wrapped around my back while I drove into her just the way she liked it.

But first things first.

With my hands still on the outside of her thighs, I moved my lips higher on the inside, teasing her with my tongue and leaving soft trails of kisses. Her hips were still in motion, maybe faster now, and her breathing was growing more unsteady with every second.

I loved feeling her like this, *seeing* her like this – naked and ready for all the things I wanted to do to her. And I knew just the thing I wanted to do first. I edged higher and brushed my lips against her opening. I ran a tongue over her center, brushing across her clit and I licked her with a long, steady stroke.

She was panting now, squirming against me, gripping the bed coverings with both fists.

She tasted like heaven, and sounded like an angel, a dirty angel with a knack for sin. My own breathing was getting ragged, but I had to tell her, "I love the way you taste." I moved a finger to her opening. "And feel." I saved the slickness of her growing excitement as I slipped the finger inside her. Her hips surged upward, grinding against my touch, as if she wanted more.

That made two of us. I slipped a second finger inside her and moved my mouth higher. I took her swollen clit into my warm mouth. She gave a soft moan and said my name. I loved the sound of it on her lips. And I loved the sensation of tonguing her and sucking her sensitive spot – lighter and then harder while I moved my fingers in and out.

She was so damn sexy that I was throbbing now. And from the feel of her, so was she, inside and out. Her body shifted, and I lifted my eyes, watching as she propped herself up on her elbows and met my gaze head-on.

Those eyes – they did the same thing to me that they always did. They pulled me in and made me want things that I'd never wanted before – a forever girl, a girl who drove me crazy and made me sane all at the same time. Impossible? Maybe. But here she was.

She was tight and slick around my fingers, and I knew she'd be tighter still around my cock. But I wanted her to be ready. No. *More* than ready.

I shifted my fingers, caressing her, playing her, teasing her. I sucked on her clit and flicked my tongue back and forth, again and again, just the way she liked it. I ran my free hand along her hip, nudging her closer and feeling her movements.

I loved feeling her like this, and I loved the taste of her, all sweetness and warmth against my tongue.

The next time I looked up, her head was thrown back, and her back was arched. Her blouse was half open and riding up on the bottom. With every stroke of my tongue, her chest rose and fell in time with her breathing. With a breathless moan, she sank back onto the bed, with her hips rising higher and faster.

I lowered my gaze and kept on going, loving the sounds of her, the scent of her, and the thoughts of what I'd want to do to her next.

She was trembling harder now, and I picked up the pace, twisting my fingers and flicking my tongue, slow, then fast, drawing every sensation out of her that I could think of, until she came against me, shuddering and moaning until I felt myself smile.

I looked up, and there she was, the girl I loved, quivering, hot and ready. She arched her hips and motioned me closer.

She didn't have to ask me twice. Hell, she didn't have to ask me at all, because I wanted her more than I'd wanted any other girl. I wanted to show her. And I wanted to tell her.

I stood and unzipped my jeans. "I love you so damn much, Chloe," I said. "I never wanna let you go."

She gave me a sexy smile. "Then don't, because I love you too."

She lifted her head, and made a motion to get up. To return the favor? Who knows? But that's not what I wanted. Not now. Now, I wanted to watch her as I drove deep inside her, claiming her back to me, right where she belonged.

"No," I told her. "Stay right there. I want you just like this.

You're so damn beautiful."

And it was true. She was the most beautiful thing I'd ever seen. Just a few days earlier, I'd thought that I'd never see her like this again. But now, here she was.

Mine.

All mine.

I shoved off my jeans, and then my briefs. She was gazing up at me, and what I saw in her eyes made all the other stuff fade into nothing.

Still standing, I pressed the head of my cock to her slick opening, and then, with one steady movement, I surged forward, loving how tight and hot she felt around me. I watched her face, loving the look of her as I moved in and out.

I gripped her thighs and plunged in deeper, loving the sounds she made as I kept on going. She was throbbing around me, and I was throbbing inside her.

I thrust forward and then back, sometimes fast, sometimes slow, watching her reaction with every movement. She was grinding against me now, begging me with her body for more and more.

And then, just like before, she was clutching the comforter, shuddering with me as we came together just like I'd planned. Still inside her, I fell onto the bed and gathered her in my arms, feeling her shuddering subside as I stroked her hair.

She was back. And I didn't want to let her go. Not now. And not ever.

CHAPTER 36

Around four o'clock in the morning, Chloe drifted off to sleep. Not me. I wasn't tired, and in less than two hours, I'd be leaving for the airport.

Until then, I sure as hell wasn't complaining. I had a hot, naked girl pressed up against me, with her head on my chest and her soft hand curled over my bare shoulder.

From this angle, I could just make out her face, cast in shadows from the moonlight that filtered in through the open blinds. Her lashes were long, and her lips were full, curved into a secret smile as she breathed evenly against my bare chest.

I stroked her naked back, loving the feel of her body pressed against mine. She was the perfect fit, and not just physically. She fit into my life, into my house, and into my dreams of a future that didn't revolve around celebrity status or one-night stands with girls whose faces and names were just a blur.

Chloe sighed in her sleep, and I felt myself smile. When she was here, everything felt right, almost normal, if there was such a thing.

I loved her. But that wasn't the only reason that things with her were different. Unlike all the other girls I'd met over the last few years, Chloe treated me like a regular guy. She teased me. She challenged me. She wasn't afraid to speak up or laugh at me when I had it coming.

There was something honest about it. Until now, I hadn't realized how hungry I'd been for something real in my life. Star-fuckers, fakers, publicity hounds, I'd had more than my share, and I was done with all of them.

But Chloe, she was real. I lowered my head and kissed her hair. It was soft and smelled almost like a day at the beach. Liking the scent, I inhaled again. Coconut shampoo? I didn't know. But it smelled nice. Exotic, too.

I thought of the first time we'd met, way back when, on the sidewalk outside that hospital. I'd been a beat-up, bloody mess without a pot to piss in. And she'd been this beautiful girl who, from what I learned afterwards, happened to drive a Porsche and wear jewelry that cost more money than I'd been worth at the time.

Funny how things changed. About us meeting before, Chloe still hadn't made the connection, and I still hadn't mentioned it.

Maybe I should've.

There was just one problem. I didn't know how she'd take it, not now, after everything I'd done. God, I'd been such an asshole. After everything I'd put her through, it was a miracle she was here at all.

And if I told her about the hospital thing now, how would I explain not telling her sooner? Originally, my plan involved an engagement ring – the same one that was still tucked away in my safe downstairs. I still wanted her to wear it, but I wasn't dumb enough to believe she'd say yes *now*. Not yet, anyway.

Funny what happens when you handcuff a girl in your basement.

At the memory of what I'd done, I frowned into the darkness. It would take more than a night of fun and sex before she saw me as a guy she could trust, a guy she could count on, a guy who'd die before hurting her again, ever.

As if hearing my thoughts, she shifted in my arms, and her eyelids fluttered open. She gave me a sleepy smile and mumbled, "You're still awake?"

"Nah," I said.

She snuggled deeper into my arms. "Liar," she whispered before drifting back to sleep.

I *was* a liar. Because even now, I didn't want to tell her a damn thing that would make her doubt me. No, I decided. I'd wait until I returned from Vegas. Then, there'd be plenty of time, and I'd make it count.

Besides, I reminded myself, I wasn't the only one with a story to tell. Chloe was still acting funny about her house. Yeah, I knew it wasn't hers. She'd told me that much. But I still didn't get why it was so completely off-limits.

When I'd picked her up tonight, she'd met me on the walkway rather than letting me anywhere near her front door. Was she just eager to see me? Or hiding something inside?

Damn it. I was doing it again.

Just stop.

But for some reason, I thought of the douchebag. Property manager or not, I didn't like him hanging around. When I got back, I'd be looking into that, too.

Again, Chloe stirred in my arms. "What's wrong?" she asked in that same sleepy voice.

"Nothing."

She lifted her head and squinted through the darkness. "You sure? I thought you called someone a douchebag."

Had I? Shit. I loosened my fingers and kissed her hair. "Nah. Go back to sleep."

She laid her cheek against my chest and mumbled, "You too."

I glanced at the clock on the nightstand. Not a chance. Soon, I'd have to get out of bed, and there was no way in hell I'd be wasting it with sleep. So I pulled her close and reminded myself that she was mine, and whatever else was going on, we'd work it out.

An hour later, I slipped out of bed, leaving Chloe tucked under the covers. I padded to the master bath, where I took a quick shower and got dressed. When I was done, it was still dark, and Chloe was still sleeping, now curled up on her side with a bare breast peeking out from under the covers.

One look was enough to make me want to take off my clothes and crawl back into bed. I wanted her. I always wanted her. But damn it, I was already running late, and when it came to Chloe, a quickie wasn't gonna cut it.

I knelt by the bed. "Baby?"

"Hmmmm…."

"I've gotta head out. Stay, alright?" I smiled. "Keep the bed warm for me."

Slowly, she sat up and squinted through the darkness. "But you're gonna be gone a few days."

"I know." I leaned down and kissed her forehead. "Tell me you'll be here when I get back."

She looked around. "What about Chucky?"

Probably, he was in his favorite basket downstairs. We'd picked him up from Chloe's place a few hours earlier. Well, Chloe had picked him up. I'd just waited in the car, because she didn't want me going inside her house. Again, I wondered, why was that?

I tried not to think about it. "Him too," I said.

With a sleepy sigh, she pushed aside the covers. "I'd better not."

"Why not?" I asked.

"Because." She smiled up at me. "If I don't leave now, you're never gonna get rid of me."

Didn't she know? That was the whole idea.

But in the end, I dropped her and Chucky back to her place on my way to the airport, wishing like hell that she was coming with me. Chucky too. Why not? It's not like I was flying commercial.

Next time, I told myself.

But a few nights later, after one weird phone call, I started to wonder if there'd *be* a next time.

CHAPTER 37

It was Sunday night, the last night of my trip. I'd be flying home the next morning, and I couldn't wait. I'd been missing Chloe like crazy, and was dying to see her.

Yeah, we'd talked on the phone whenever we had the chance. And some of those talks were hot and heavy. But no way could it compare to the real thing.

I'd just returned to my suite and pulled out my cell phone, glad that Chloe wasn't working tonight. I smiled as I brought up her number and hit the call button.

She answered right away with a quick, "Hello?"

I sank into a nearby armchair and started shoving off my shoes. "Hey."

"Oh." She paused. "It's you."

I froze in mid-motion. Who else would it be? I glanced at my watch. Here in Vegas, it was just before nine. In Michigan, it was almost midnight. Other than me, who'd be calling her this late on a Sunday?

I heard myself ask, "Is this a bad time?"

"No." She hesitated. "Not at all. Just waiting for a phone call."

Oh yeah? From who?

I waited, thinking she'd tell me something more. She didn't. And for some reason, I didn't like it.

Trying not to be a dick about it, I asked, "You need to go?"

"Nah," she said, sounding distracted, "I have call-waiting."

"So…" I tried to keep my tone casual. "Who'd be calling you so late?"

"No one. It's just a business thing."

I felt the muscles in my shoulders ease. Now *that* made sense. Chloe *did* work nights, after all, and her boss was a real asshole. I'd seen that for myself. "You mean from the restaurant?"

She hesitated. "No. Something else."

What kind of something else? A business thing? At midnight? If she was running some kind of business, this was the first *I'd* heard of it.

The tension was back, and I suddenly felt too wired to sit. I pushed myself up from the chair and asked in what I hoped was a normal voice, "Anything you wanna talk about?"

"Nah, it's nothing." She sounded tense and maybe a little worried. Whatever it was, it wasn't "nothing." In an obvious bid to change the subject, she asked, "Are you still coming home tomorrow?"

Yeah. I was. And if that hadn't been the plan before, it sure as hell was the plan now. What wasn't she telling me?

A lot. That's what. But I'd already known that, hadn't I? What was it? Problems at work? Problems at home? I felt my jaw clench. Problems with another guy?

Just stop. She's not like that, and you damn well know it.

I recalled the last time I'd jumped to some stupid conclusions about Chloe. It hadn't worked out so great, had it? Not for me and not for her either.

Tomorrow, I'd find out more. For now, my options were limited. With an effort, I forced myself to sit back down. Trying to keep my tone easy, I managed to say, "Yup. Tomorrow morning. You still have the day off?"

"Oh yeah," she said, sounding happier now.

And why *was* that, exactly? Because I'd stopped asking all those hard questions?

Damn it. What the hell was wrong with me? I reached up to rub the back of my neck. "You still want to get together?" I asked.

"Definitely," she said, with a smile in her voice. The smile was real. Even through the phone, I could hear it loud and clear. And suddenly, I was glad that I hadn't made an ass of myself.

Whatever was bothering her, it obviously wasn't about us. Or at least, it sure as hell didn't sound like it.

I shoved aside the distractions and focused on the upside. Tomorrow, I'd be seeing her. There was a lot to say, and too much of it couldn't be said over the phone. Over the next couple of minutes, we finalized our plans to meet the next day.

The plan – Chloe's idea – was for her and Chucky to swing by my place around noon. "We can all go for a walk," she said. Her tone grew teasing. "For old time's sake."

"Don't forget new time's sake," I reminded her. "And Chloe?"

Her response was soft and breathless. "Yeah?"

Screw the doubts. They were just noise, messing with my head. Chloe was the girl I loved, and I wasn't about to let some random phone call come between us. I lowered my voice. "I've gotta tell you, I'm missing you like crazy. The other night, I was thinking…"

I heard a beep. I tensed. What was that? Another call?

Chloe cut me off. "I'm really sorry, Lawton, I've gotta go. See ya tomorrow, alright?"

And then she was gone. No goodbye. No "I love you." No "I'll call you back." No nothing.

What the hell was going on?

☐

CHAPTER 38

Early the next morning, I stood motionless on the sidewalk, telling myself that I wasn't seeing what I thought I was seeing. It was almost eight o'clock, and I'd just returned from Vegas.

Unable to sleep and eager to get home, I'd bumped up my flight to get home faster.

And where was I now? Standing like a dumb-ass in front of Chloe's place. Her driveway was long and lined with trees, so I wasn't exactly lurking outside her front door. But I had eyes, and I didn't like what they were seeing.

Who *was* that guy? I shook my head. And who was he to Chloe?

I wasn't spying on her – or at least that's what I told myself. I'd come here for a reason. It was because of our conversation last night. The way she'd been acting, it had me on edge. Something was off, and I wanted to know what.

The idea had been to walk by, check things out, make sure everything was okay. Yeah, I knew she'd be asleep, so I didn't plan on ringing the bell or anything. But I could still check for busted windows or a broken-down car – because the more I'd been thinking about it, the more I decided that Chloe was in some sort of trouble.

Nothing else made sense – not unless I was willing to think the worst of her. And I hadn't been. I'd learned my lesson the hard way. Chloe wasn't like that.

Or so I thought.

From the far edge of the sidewalk, I took a good, long look at the guy leaving her front porch. He was some slick-looking guy around forty, maybe fifty years old. He wore dark sunglasses, dark slacks, and a tailored sports coat that screamed old money.

Asshole.

I'd rounded the corner just in time to see Chloe give him a little wave before shutting the front door behind him.

She'd been wearing tiny black shorts and that lacy yellow tank top, the one that was so thin, you could practically see her nipples. I felt my muscles bunch into tight, angry knots. She didn't dress like that in public. She dressed like that for bed – when she wasn't naked, that is.

My jaw clenched. Naked.

I felt my fingers tighten into fists. Had she been naked with that guy? It sure as hell looked like it.

Fuck.

Standing there like a dumb-ass, I tried to tell myself it was something different. Maybe he'd just stopped by. Maybe he was selling something. Maybe he hadn't been inside the house at all.

Yeah, and maybe she just happened to answer the front door in not much more than her underpants.

I watched as the guy strolled back to his vehicle. Even his car pissed me off. It was some flashy red sports car. A mid-life crisis car. A car for picking up girls half his age.

The guy climbed inside, smiling like he'd just gotten a nice taste of something sweet. I knew that look. When Chloe stayed over, I'd seen that same look in the damn mirror.

Shit.

It took everything I had not to stride down that long driveway and yank that fucker out of his flashy-ass car and ask him what the hell he was doing. At the thought, I felt my fingers flex. And if the guy didn't want to tell me? Not a problem. I'd persuade him. It wouldn't take long.

Who knows, it might be fun.

I took a deep breath. Shit. Or, it might fuck everything up.

Damn it. Remember the basement thing.

My jaw was tight, and my breathing was unsteady. If I took one step toward him, it wouldn't end there. And it wouldn't end pretty. With a muttered curse, I held my ground.

Lucky for him? Or lucky for me? When his car backed out of the driveway a minute later, I was standing in the same spot. Trying to get a grip, I watched silently as his car disappeared down the quiet street.

With him gone, I turned to stare at Chloe's front door. It was closed. But was it locked? And if it was, so what? If I wanted in, no lock on Earth could keep *me* out.

Or hey, let's make it simple. I could just ring the fucking doorbell. And then what? Show my ass a second time when I learned it was just some cousin from California or a guy selling Amway?

I heard a scoffing sound – my own. The car had Michigan plates, and as far as I knew, Chloe didn't *have* any cousins from California, not that I knew of, anyway. And Amway, was that even a thing anymore?

I tried to think. But my thoughts were a jumbled, fucked-up mess. It didn't help that hadn't slept.

From the sidewalk, I was still staring at Chloe's front door. If I walked up to it now, the odds of me pulling off the "I'm-just-stopping-by-to-say-hi" act weren't looking so good.

I was too wound up, and worse, I was spoiling for a fight. Even if I *tried* to play it cool, she'd know something was up, and as soon as I opened my mouth, she'd know exactly what I'd been thinking.

I took a long, deep breath. Maybe I *wasn't* thinking. Or at least, maybe I wasn't thinking straight. It wasn't that long ago that I'd found out the hard way that with Chloe, things weren't always the way they looked.

Still, I couldn't stop thinking about that guy. A salesman? Yeah, right. What kind of salesman shows up at eight o'clock in the morning? And what kind of girl answers the front door in those skimpy-ass, fuck-me clothes?

I shoved a hand through my hair. I'd been standing here how long now? Five, ten minutes? It was time to shit or get off the pot.

Trying to be smart about it, I turned and started walking – not toward Chloe's house, but back toward my own.

In four hours, I'd be seeing her.

For different reasons than usual, it felt like too damn long. Or maybe it wasn't long enough, because I had some serious cooling off to do. If the whole thing was innocent, I was like five seconds away making an ass of myself.

Again.

CHAPTER 39

I spent the next few hours pumping iron and obsessing over Chloe. But before all that, I'd made a phone call. It was almost noon when Bishop finally called me back, telling me, "I've got that thing you wanted."

I'd showered a half-hour earlier and was now pacing my study. I'd been wired to work and too distracted to do anything else.

"About time," I muttered. I'd left the message almost four hours ago. What the hell had taken so long? Chloe would be here any minute, and I still didn't know how I'd handle it.

Bishop ignored my comment and said, "Do I need to ask?"

"Ask what?"

"Who's the guy?"

"If I knew," I said, "I wouldn't be needing your help, now would I?"

After returning from Chloe's, I'd called Bishop with the guy's license plate number, along with the make and model of his car. Since Bishop hadn't answered, I'd left the info in a voicemail and told him that I needed an answer like yesterday.

All I wanted was a name. And an address. I frowned. And anything else that might tell me who the guy was and what the hell he was doing at Chloe's place.

"You *know* what I'm asking," Bishop said. "Who's the guy to you?"

In the message, I hadn't said where I'd seen the guy's car, and I sure as hell hadn't said anything about Chloe.

When it came to her and me, Bishop had been a royal pain in my ass. It was like the guy couldn't even say her name without being a dick about it. In fact, he could hardly say her name at all.

"He's no one," I said, glancing at my watch. "Just tell me what you learned, alright?"

"Lemme guess," Bishop said. "It's about that neighbor of yours. Isn't it?"

She wasn't just my neighbor. She was the girl I loved, the girl I'd been wanting to marry – I felt my jaw clench – the girl who let *other* guys into her house, but not me. What the hell was that about?

When I didn't answer, Bishop said, "Or should I call her 'dog girl'?"

Great. My brother was turning into Brittney.

Fuck that.

"For the last fucking time," I said, "her name is Chloe. And if you've got some problem with that, you can just fuck off, alright? Because I'm in no mood for your bullshit."

He was quiet a beat before saying, "You're losing it. You know that, right?"

Hell yeah, I knew it. But I needed information, not grief from someone whose relationship track record was worse than my own. Through gritted teeth, I said, "You gonna give it to me, or should I call someone else?"

"In your mood?" he said. "I wouldn't recommend it."

I wasn't in a "mood." I just wanted the information without all the bullshit. Looking to move this along, I kept my mouth shut and waited.

Finally, Bishop told me what I needed to know. The guy's name was Chad Flemming. He was forty-nine years old, married, and lived in Bloomfield Hills, maybe a half-hour away. From the guy's address, I knew the general area. The head of my legal team had a place on the next street over. Homes in that neck of the woods ran a million dollars, give or take.

So the guy had money. Big deal. I had money too. A lot more than *he* did.

"What else?" I asked.

Bishop sounded annoyed. "What do you mean, what else?"

Before I could answer, the doorbell rang. I glanced toward the front entryway, but didn't move. Into the phone, I said, "Well?"

"Well what?" he said. "You want *me* to get the door?"

Did he have to be such a dick? "No," I said.

"Good. Because I'm two hours away."

"What I need," I said, "is to hear the rest of it."

"There is no 'rest of it.'"

"Why not?"

"Because that's all you asked for. If you wanted more, you should've said so. Now, you gonna tell me why you wanna know?"

The doorbell rang a second time. It was Chloe. It *had* to be. "I've gotta go," I said and ended the call before he could ask any more questions.

But I still didn't move. Not yet. A minute – that's all I needed, or so I told myself. I was still trying to fit the pieces together. The guy was married. Was that good? Or bad? Maybe it meant nothing. Maybe the guy *was* nothing, just a random door-knocker who had nothing to do with me or Chloe.

I frowned. Or maybe, he was the reason that Chloe had practically hung up on me last night.

Stalling, I headed for the kitchen and shoved a bag of doggie treats into the front pocket of my jeans. I'd have done it anyway, but it was good to buy myself a few more seconds.

My head was full of ugly images. They all starred Chloe, except she wasn't alone.

And it wasn't just the guy from this morning. Not too long ago, I'd seen another guy at Chloe's place. The douchebag. He'd offered me girls for a price. High-end girls. Girl-next-door types. Nice and sweet.

Like Chloe.

I shook my head. No. I wasn't going to believe that. Not about Chloe. There was another explanation. There had to be. I just had to figure out what it was. And this time, I'd do it without making an ass of myself.

I took a deep breath and strode toward the door.

Don't mess this up.

But I did.

Bad.

CHAPTER 40

I opened the front door, and there she was, dressed in jeans and a basic blue sweater. I gave the sweater a quick glance. No lacy tank-top for me, huh?

Damn it. Stop being a dick. She looks great, and you damn well know it. Shit, she could be wearing a dirty sweatshirt, and you'd still be all over her.

Dumb-ass.

At her feet, Chucky was spazzing out, just like he always did. He lunged toward me, whining and pawing at my legs. For some stupid reason, it made me feel better. Because it was distraction? Or because it was nice to know that *someone* was dying to see me?

I crouched beside him. "Hey Buddy," I said, ruffling his fur. "I know what *you* want." I stood and pulled out the bag of doggie treats. When I shook it, Chucky went so nuts that I almost smiled in spite of my shitty mood. I pulled some treats from the bag and crouched down to give him some.

I glanced up and saw Chloe watching me. When our eyes met, I managed to say, "I'm glad you're here."

She gave me an odd look. "Is something wrong?"

Now, that was a funny question. Maybe I should ask *her* the same thing – except she wasn't a big fan of questions, was she? I stood and brushed Chucky's crumbs off my jeans. "Nope."

She glanced toward the street and said, "Still up for a walk?" She hesitated. "Or maybe you wanna do it another day? I mean, if this is a bad time for you–"

"It's not. Wanna come in?"

She glanced down at Chucky, who was still spazzing. "I'd like to come in, but do you care if we walk first?"

"Nope." I held out my hand, palm up.

She eyed the palm, and her eyebrows furrowed.

What now? She didn't *want* me to walk her dog? I felt my jaw clench. Why? Had the other guy done it already?

Yeah, right. A guy like that? He wouldn't be walking her dog. He'd be pounding her pussy.

At the image, I felt a murderous rage sweep over me. Trying to shove it down, I said, "Leash?" When she still didn't hand it over, I made a sound of impatience. "Unless *you* want to take him."

"Oh," she stammered. "Sorry." She handed me the leash, and as she did, our fingers brushed. I sucked in a quiet breath, wondering where those fingers had been.

Damn it. Bishop was right. I *was* losing it. I reminded myself that I didn't know anything, not for sure, and if I didn't get a grip now, I'd be blurting out accusations that I couldn't take back.

I strode forward, shutting the door behind me. "Let's go," I said, walking past her. When she joined me on the walkway, I kept on going, striding through the open front gate and onto the sidewalk, with Chloe walking beside me.

The day was cool, but sunny, with a light breeze. Some might call it a beautiful day. Not me. Not now. Chloe and I headed out on the usual route, following Chucky, who lunged forward like he always did.

For a long, awkward time, Chloe said nothing, and neither did I. We did that sometimes, just walked without talking. Normally, it was alright, nice even. Not today. With every step, things got more tense.

Or maybe that was just me.

On the next block over, I couldn't stop myself from saying, "So, you got your call last night, huh?"

She gave me a sideways glance. "What call?"

Great. So now she was playing dumb? Screw that. "Never

mind," I told her. "Forget it."

Her steps faltered. "Oh," she said, before picking up the pace again. "You mean that business call?"

"Yeah." I heard the sarcasm in my own voice. "The business call."

"You don't believe me?"

"I never said that."

"But you're not saying you *do*, either." She sounded insulted.

Hey, she should put herself in *my* place. See how insulted she'd feel then.

I shrugged. "What do you want me to say?"

"I don't want you to say anything." She stomped forward, not looking at me. "Not if you're gonna be like that."

Oh, so *she* was the victim now? Yeah, whatever.

"Alright," I said, like I didn't give a shit either way. "If that's what you want." I kept moving, but said nothing else. Hey, at least I tried. It was more than I could say for her.

We plowed on like that for maybe five or ten more minutes. I kept my mouth shut and eyes straight ahead, wondering what would happen when the walk ended. We'd been planning to spend the day at my place. Now, I just couldn't see it.

There was no way I could pretend that nothing was wrong. And worse, there was no way to ask her what I needed to know – not without insulting the hell out of her. And if I was wrong…?

Shit, I'd better be. Hey, I'd been wrong before, right?

Something squeezed at my heart. Yeah. I had. But I'd lost her, anyway.

The best thing now, I decided, was to keep my mouth shut and see what played out. Who knows? After some sleep or something, I might see things differently. Maybe I was just missing something.

Yeah, I was. My sanity.

Chloe's voice, softer now, broke into my thoughts. "You're mad about that call last night, aren't you?"

When it came to things I was "mad" about, yeah, that was part of it. But overall, it was pretty low on the list. I shrugged, but said nothing.

"Okay." Chloe blew out a shaky breath. "You know I'm just staying in that house, right?"

Yeah, but that's *all* I knew. I nodded and kept on moving.

"Well," she continued, "that call last night. It was from the home-owner, just some financial thing that couldn't wait."

Sure it was.

"At midnight," I said, not bothering to hide my doubts.

"It wasn't *quite* midnight," she said in that teasing tone of hers, the one that normally made me smile no matter what.

But this time, it didn't. I kept on moving. "Uh-huh. And how about this morning?"

"What about this morning?"

"Forget it," I muttered.

I felt a tug on my wrist and looked to see Chucky straining against his leash. In front of us, a chipmunk made a break for it, running just out of Chucky's range. Chucky went nuts, lunging toward it for like five whole seconds, until he spotted a big gray housecat sitting on the other side of the street.

Chucky froze, and then started barking his head off, acting like he'd chew the cat up and spit it out, if only the leash weren't holding him back. The cat looked at him like, "Yeah, sure you would."

Out of habit, I looked to Chloe. We were still walking, and she was smiling down at her dog. I loved that smile, but today, all it did was piss me off – because everything was pissing me off.

When she looked to me again, she was still smiling. I didn't smile back. I couldn't. Not today. Not today.

And then I saw something else – something that made me stop dead in my tracks. Already, we'd circled back to Chloe's place. Until this moment, I hadn't really noticed. But now, I did. And I didn't like what I saw.

In Chloe's driveway was a familiar black Mercedes.

The douchebag – he was back. And he was standing on Chloe's front porch.

CHAPTER 41

The guy wore the same sort of flashy business suit that he'd been wearing the last time I'd seen him. In one hand, he held a briefcase. In the other was a large manila envelope.

As for Chucky, he'd given up on the cat, and was now lunging toward a group of senior citizens who were power-walking toward us. I held Chucky firm and turned my attention back to the douchebag.

He was just standing there on Chloe's porch, looking around like he was expecting someone. Who? Chloe?

Funny, this was the third time I'd seen him, but it was the first time I'd actually seen him when Chloe was around. I glanced toward her, wondering what she'd say now.

"Hey, that's my uncle. Wanna meet him?"

"Look, my landlord's here."

Or maybe I'd get really lucky, and she'd say, "Who the hell is that creep? Can you run him off for me?"

But she didn't say any of those things. Instead, she said, "I'll be right back." Without waiting for a response, she turned and started jogging down the long driveway.

Watching her go, I felt my blood begin to boil. I didn't know who the guy was, exactly. But I knew *what* he was. His words from earlier rang in my memories.

"What about nice girls? If you like 'em sweet, I got them, too."

Chloe was a nice girl.

Supposedly.

I stood, watching as she hurried up to the front porch and started talking with the guy. I couldn't hear a damn thing they were saying, but the conversation looked friendly enough. They talked for maybe a minute before I saw Chloe glance in my direction.

Following her gaze, the guy turned to look, and I knew the exact moment he spotted me, because he practically jumped out of his skin.

It almost made me smile. So, he wasn't happy to see me? Yeah, that made two of us, except in my case, I wanted to kill him.

Slowly.

He turned and exchanged a few more words with Chloe before giving me another quick glance. I glared over at him, not bothering to hide my hostility.

A minute later, they were still talking, and I was still standing there like a dumb-ass, baby-sitting Chloe's dog. How the hell had it come to this?

I glanced down at Chucky. He'd given up on the power-walkers and was now lying across my tennis shoes, staring up at the clouds. Talk about a contradiction. The dog was cute, and my life was fucked.

When I looked up again, the douchebag was handing Chloe that big envelope. She took it and peered inside, sneaking a nervous glance in my direction. The way it looked, she wasn't happy I was watching.

Too fucking bad.

She reached into the envelope and pulled out its contents. I froze. It was cash. A big wad of it. She rifled through it, as if counting the bills. When she finished, she looked up and gave the guy a big, friendly smile.

Just what the hell was the money for?

I had some ideas, but none I wanted to think about. What the hell was I doing here? What the hell was *she* doing there? I took a good, long look at the house – a house that was way too pricey for a waitress in her twenties. I took a good, long look at Chloe – a girl with the perfect mix of sweetness and sex.

I took a good, long look at her dog, still flopped across my shoes. Was he just a prop for whatever was going on here?

No. She loved the dog. That much was obvious. But did she love me? And even if she did, what did that mean? I knew she had secrets, but somehow, I'd convinced myself they were simple things, like an embarrassing parent or some weird food allergy.

Hell, I was hiding something like that myself.

On her porch, she was still talking to the douchebag. As I watched, she rolled up the cash and stuffed it into the front pocket of her jeans.

Well, at least she didn't stuff it into her bra.

This time.

She was still smiling when she handed the guy back his envelope, now empty. He pulled out a shiny gold pen and handed it to her. She signed some slip of paper and handed it back.

And then, Chloe laughed. As I watched, she turned and pointed straight at me. For some reason, I didn't like it. I looked at the douchebag. The way it looked, he wasn't liking it either.

Why? Because I was still standing here?

What a dumb-ass. Didn't the guy know? He was lucky I was standing in the same spot, because I'm pretty sure that if I took one single step, I wouldn't stop until I was on Chloe's front porch, beating his sleazy ass until he stopped moving.

Finally, the guy turned and hurried back to his car. As I watched, he got inside, backed out of the long driveway, and drove off at probably double the speed limit. From my spot on the sidewalk, I turned and watched him until he disappeared from sight. On his car, I saw no license plate.

How convenient.

A moment later, Chloe was back, looking happy and a lot more relaxed than before.

Well, that made one of us.

She gave me a smile. "Sorry about that."

I didn't smile back. I turned and gave her house a good, long look. What exactly was the house for? Business? Or pleasure? Or a sick combination of both?

Chloe's voice broke into my thoughts. "Ready to finish our walk?"

Fuck that. I was ready for something, alright. For starters, I'd be getting some answers. I turned to face her. "First, tell me something. What's the money for?"

CHAPTER 42

She stared up at me, like she didn't understand the question. When I said nothing else, she looked down at Chucky, who was still flopped over my feet, looking ready for a nap.

After a long moment, Chloe lifted her chin and said, "I don't really like the tone of your question."

Fine by me. I had plenty more where that came from. "Alright," I said. "Then how about this one? Who do you live with?"

She shook her head. "What?"

"It's a simple question, Chloe."

"I already told you, I don't live with anyone."

I pointed toward the place she called home. "So that's *your* house."

"No," she said through gritted teeth. "And I've already told you that."

"Uh-huh." I made a forwarding motion with my hand. "Go on."

"With what?"

"Your explanation."

"What's gotten into you?" she said. "It's a job. That's what the money's for. There. You happy?"

I was a lot of things right now, but happy wasn't one of them.

Chloe threw up her hands. "What do you want me to say? That this house is beyond my price range?" Her voice rose. "Well, obviously it is. Is that what you wanted to hear?"

Her skin was flushed, and her breathing was unsteady. I looked down and eyed the wad of money, bulging out of her front pocket. How much was in there? Hundreds? Thousands?

I tried to keep my voice level. "All I want to hear is the truth."

She reached up to rub the back of her neck. She glanced toward the house and said in a quieter voice, "Can we talk about this somewhere else?"

Where? Her place? I gave it a quick glance. There it was, just an easy walk down the driveway. But no. She couldn't mean that, because for some reason, *her* house was off limits. For the millionth time, I wondered, why was that?

I gave something like a shrug. "If that's what you want." I turned away, and Chucky jumped up, as if ready to get moving again. I knew the feeling. I started walking, and Chloe joined me.

She didn't say anything, and neither did I. We passed at least a dozen houses without speaking. The silence felt like a powder-keg, ready to explode any second. Or maybe that was just me. I kept telling myself to stop thinking the worst. But Chloe was making it so damn hard.

All I wanted was the truth. Maybe the douchebag *was* her uncle. And maybe what's-his-name from this morning was just a salesman. And maybe the house was off-limits because why? She had a dozen horny roommates who'd jump me if they had the chance?

Yeah, it was that ridiculous. But it was better than the other stuff rattling around in my head.

Up ahead, I spotted my own house. When we got there, would Chloe come inside, like we'd planned? Shit, did I even want her to?

Damn it. I did. How messed up was that?

I gripped Chucky's leash and tried like hell to sort everything out. It did no good. My thoughts were still raging when we reached my front door.

I opened it up, but made no move to go inside. She'd promised me an explanation. So far, I'd gotten nothing. Yeah, it was about what I'd expected.

I turned toward her and held out the leash. If she wanted to leave, I wasn't going to stop her. Not this time. Silently, she took it from my hand, but made no move to turn away.

Instead, she put her hands on her hips and said, "Lawton, what the hell is your problem?"

Well, that was rich. "*My* problem?"

Just then, Chucky made a break for it, bolting into my house, dragging the leash behind him. I didn't bother to look. I was still looking at Chloe.

She made a sound of frustration. "Chucky!" she yelled. "Damn it."

Looking at her, watching her, thinking of her with someone else, it was making me crazy – so crazy that I couldn't stop myself from saying exactly what was on my mind.

"Wanna know what my problem is?" I said. "Alright, here it is. When I think of someone else holding you, touching you–" my voice caught. "–being with you in the ways I'm with you, it makes me want to tear their fuckin' throat out."

CHAPTER 43

She looked at me like I'd lost my mind. "What someone?" she asked. "Who the hell are you talking about?"

"You tell me."

"I can't. Because he doesn't exist."

"Alright. Then who was that guy?"

"Which one?"

I shrugged.

She stared up at me. "You mean the guy on the porch?"

"That'd be a good start."

She made a sound of disbelief. "You've *got* to be kidding me. That guy? You seriously think he's my boyfriend or something?"

No. I didn't think he was her boyfriend. I thought he was something worse. But I didn't want to say it, so I just shook my head. "That's not what I said."

"Then what *are* you saying?"

"I'm saying that I don't get it."

"Get what?" she asked.

"Alright," I said. "I'll spell it out. I don't *get* why some guy in a fancy car would be showing up on your doorstep and handing you a pile of cash. I don't *get* who you live with, or why you've never asked me inside."

I was talking louder now, probably too loud. But I couldn't seem to make myself stop. "I don't *get* why you're getting 'business calls' at midnight on a Sunday night or why I'd happen to go by early this morning and see some guy in a sports car leaving your house."

My heart was pounding, and my muscles were tight. I stared down at her, waiting for her to tell I was seeing things. Hell, at this point, I'd be relieved to hear it.

She was glaring up at me. "You're twisting everything around, making it sound worse than it is."

"Is that so?" I crossed my arms and waited. "Then go ahead. Tell me how *you'd* say it."

"I already told you." She gestured vaguely toward the place she called home. "I get paid to stay there. What don't you get?"

An image of the cash flashed in my brain. What, exactly, had she been paid for?

She lifted her hands. "Yeah. I do it for money. Big fucking deal. And the reason I didn't tell you right from the start is because that's part of the deal. I'm supposed to look like I actually belong here."

The douchebag's words echoed in my brain. "What about nice girls? I got them, too."

I stared down at her, wondering what, exactly, she did for that money. Straight stuff? Kinky stuff? The kind of stuff she did with me?

I felt sick. All the secrets, all the shit she didn't want to talk about. No wonder.

Her eyes were filling with tears. "Yeah." She made a scoffing sound. "I've got the dog, I've got the plants. Hell, I've even got some stupid lawn guy coming once a week to trim shit that doesn't need trimming." Her voice cracked. "But it's all about the money, because I don't have any of my own."

No. That wasn't true. I *knew* it wasn't true. The Porsche, the jewelry, the house…what the fuck?

She looked down at her front pocket, still bulging with all that cash. Her shoulders started to shake, and she swallowed a sob. "I'm broke. There, you happy?"

I felt my eyebrows furrow. "What?"

"Yeah. You want the whole story?" In a choked voice, she kept on talking. "Well, here it is. I've got a grandma who gets all her rent money from this fake job I had to make up. I've got a kid brother who thinks our mom gives some sort of a crap, even though she doesn't. I've got student loans from a degree that as far as I can tell, probably cost me a lot more than the damn thing's worth."

Her voice rose. "And now, I've got you ragging on me like I'm some kind of horrible person!"

I stared at her, not knowing what to say, or hell, what to think. All this time, she'd been broke? And I'd had no idea?

It couldn't be true. But what if it was? Why hadn't I known? I claimed to love her. I *should* have known.

I swallowed a lump in my throat. "Chloe–"

"Don't 'Chloe' me," she said. "What the hell? Have you been rich so long that you've forgotten what it's like to live in the real world?"

The real world – yeah, I'd seen it, alright. But for some reason, all this time, I'd pictured Chloe as this rich girl who never knew what it was like to need anything.

On raw instinct, I moved toward her. "Chloe, you need money? I mean, shit, why didn't you say something?" I reached toward my wallet, thinking to offer give her whatever was in there, anything to make things better.

She lifted her chin. "I don't want your charity. As you so aptly observed, I just got paid. So I'm practically rich, right?"

"But you just said–"

"I *know* what I said. Quit rubbing my nose in it, alright?"

None of this was making sense. I stared down at her. "But what about your waitressing job?"

"What about it?"

"So you do *that* for the money too, not–?"

"For the ego trip?" She gave a bark of laughter. "You ever work as a waitress? It's fucking hard work. I take shit all night long from people who act like they're better than me just because they're sitting down, and I'm standing up. I dress like some bimbo and act like I'm stupid, for God's sake."

She tugged her hair. "You know how many times I've got to wash this to get the hairspray out? You think I'm doing this for some sort of ego trip." She made a sound of disgust. "That's rich. At least with this job, I get to dress how I want. And I get to live in a nice place where people treat me half-way decent."

The way she was talking, it ate me up inside. Half-way decent? What did *that* mean? That the guys didn't beat her?

How had this happened? It's not like I hadn't seen this sort of thing before. I knew girls in my old neighborhood. Some of them weren't too bad. And the things *they* did for money…

But this was Chloe. How the hell had I missed that?

In a quiet voice, I said, "And that's good enough for you?"

"It's gotta be." She squared her shoulders. "I've just got to keep doing what I'm doing, that's all."

My thoughts were churning, and I didn't know what to say. All this time, she'd been so broke, so hurting for money, so desperate, that she'd been selling herself. And I hadn't seen it. What kind of asshole doesn't even know that his girlfriend has no money?

"But Chloe…" I shook my head. "You don't need to. Not anymore."

"Oh yeah? Why not?"

"You just don't." I shoved a hand through my hair. "So, you want a loan or something? I mean, if you won't take money…" I blew out a long, unsteady breath. "All I'm saying is, you don't have to do this. Don't go back there, alright?"

The pain in her eyes was a knife to my heart. All this time, she'd been desperate, and I'd been blind to everything. There was nothing that could make me feel shittier – or so I thought, until she started crying.

CHAPTER 44

Unable to stop myself, I moved forward and wrapped her in my arms. She felt small and fragile against my chest. I wanted to protect her. I *should* have protected her. She shook against me, her muffled sobs going straight to my heart as I held her close and whispered soothing sounds into her hair.

"Baby, don't cry," I said. "I'm sorry. We'll work it out. You can move in with me, alright?"

She leaned closer, and I felt like a giant shit-heel, listening to her cry. *I'd* made her cry – not the guy from this morning, and not the douchebag who'd paid her.

A hypocrite – that's what I was. The things *I'd* done for money. I'd beaten men bloody. I'd partnered with violent people. In a way, I'd let *my* body be used, too. And why? Because desperate people did desperate things.

I wasn't desperate anymore. And I didn't want Chloe to be either.

I held her for a long time, telling her it was going to be okay. And it *was* going to be okay. I'd make damned sure of it. When she finally stopped crying, I vowed to do anything in my power to make sure she never cried again.

She pulled back and gazed up at me. Her face was flushed, and she tried to smile. "I've been such an idiot." She wiped at her eyes. "I should've told you sooner." She gave a little laugh. "Like it's such a big deal, right?"

I tensed. I didn't want to judge her. Hell, after the things I'd done, how could I? But in my book, it *was* a big deal. And the fact she couldn't see that, well, it made me feel funny, like I might not know her as well as I thought.

But this was Chloe, the girl I loved. I clutched her tighter and said, "Baby, I don't want you to do this with anyone else. Not ever."

I heard a smile in her voice when she said, "Yeah?"

I nodded. "I mean it. Move in with me. Right now, today. This'll be our home. Together, alright?"

She clung to me, and I tried not to think about everything else – the guys, the money, the things she'd probably done to earn it. I loved her, and somehow, I told myself, we'd work it out.

I felt her smile against my chest. "I'll think about it."

"Don't think." Sudden panic clawed at my heart. "Just do it." She *couldn't* go back there, to that house, where guys would show up expecting something special, and leave smiling in the morning. She couldn't. I wouldn't let her.

I pulled away and gave her a pleading look. "You don't want to take money from me. I get that. And I respect the hell out of that, honest. But baby, please. Come on. Stay with me. Or shit, I'll buy you a house of your own if that's what you want. Just no more other guys anymore, alright?"

Her eyebrows furrowed. "What do you mean?"

"I mean I love you."

She hesitated. "I love you too."

I reached out, gathering her against me. Desperate now, I tightened my grip and whispered an urgent plea into her ear. "You don't have to sell yourself anymore. From now on, let *me* take care of you, alright?"

At this, she grew utterly still. For a long moment, she didn't say or do anything. And then, she pulled back and gave me an odd look. "Sell myself?"

I leaned in close, trying to pull her back into my arms. I wasn't judging her. Or at least, I was trying like hell not to.

She yanked herself back and looked up at me. "Just what are you implying?"

I met her gaze. "Baby, I don't want to judge you. I mean, the things I've done for money…" I tried to find the words. "In a way, I guess I sold my body too, right?"

She stared up at me for a long, tense moment. For some reason, the look on her face was making me nervous as hell. I didn't get it. I mean, I knew she had to be embarrassed, ashamed even. And I couldn't blame her. Whatever she'd been doing, it couldn't have come easy.

In front of me, she was looking unsteady now, and maybe a little shell-shocked. I reached out, wanting to wipe the look of horror from her eyes. But she took another step backward, as if desperate for some space.

In a choked voice, she said, "Oh my God."

I hated to see her like this. "Hey," I said in a low, soothing tone. "Like I said, I don't wanna judge you for doing what you had to do, but–" I shook my head. "It stops now, alright? You've gotta promise me."

She closed her eyes, and all the remaining color drained from her face. I wanted to reach out for her, but something made me stop. Obviously, I was missing something. But what?

She didn't feel dirty, did she? Who knows? Maybe she did. After that whole sex tape, I hadn't felt exactly right either.

When she opened her eyes, she looked at me like I was the biggest asshole on the planet. "Let me get this straight." Her body was trembling now. Her voice rose. "You think–" She swallowed. "You think I'm some kind of *hooker*?"

"Chloe." I kept my voice soft. "I didn't call it that."

I mean, shit, I'd *seen* hookers, not that I'd used their services. But I knew the difference between a hooker and a high-end call girl. It was pretty obvious that a girl like Chloe didn't walk the streets.

She was breathing too fast and too shallow. "But that's what you think?"

"Baby," I said. "What is it? You okay?"

She glared up at me. "Okay?" She shook her head. "Nope. Definitely not okay here."

She cupped her hands around her mouth and hollered toward

the interior of the house. "Chucky! C'mon! We're leaving!"

"What?" I reached for her hand. "Why?"

She slapped my hand away. "Don't touch me."

"Why not?"

"Because, you idiot, I'm not a hooker." She spoke very slowly and clearly, enunciating every word. "I'm a house-sitter!"

CHAPTER 45

Her words echoed in the silent space. I stood, utterly still, wondering if I'd heard her right. The house-sitter?

I shook my head. "What?"

"Oh yeah." She made a sound that might've been a laugh, except there was no trace of humor in it. "Big difference there, huh?" She turned away and called out again, "Chucky, where are you?"

For a long moment, I couldn't move. My thoughts were coming too hard and too fast. What about the guy this morning? What about the douchebag? What about the house? I couldn't be wrong.

But – a sick feeling settled in my stomach – what if I was?

Fuck.

Chloe turned and stalked toward the kitchen.

With growing panic, I followed after her. "Chloe." When she ignored me, I reached for her elbow. "Baby…"

She shook off my hand and whirled to face me. "I already told you, stay away from me!"

The look in her eyes sliced through my heart. But I *had* to know. "So those guys—"

"Who?" she said. "The property manager who stopped by this morning?"

I swallowed. "Property manager?"

"Or maybe," Chloe continued, "you meant the financial guy?"

"Financial guy?"

The douchebag – was *that* who she meant? I recalled something he'd told me earlier. *"I'm just the guy who pays the light bill."* Shit. In a twisted way, it made sense.

"Yeah," Chloe said. "The guy on the porch." She gave me a cold smile. "And just so you know, when I say financial guy, I mean someone who manages the home-owner's accounts, not for example, some fucking pimp!"

I felt the color drain from my face. I *knew* what I knew. The guy *had* offered me girls for money. But he hadn't offered me Chloe, had he? In fact, he'd flat-out denied knowing her. Was today the first time she'd actually seen the guy? The way it sounded, it was.

As for the rest of it, it made no sense. Turns out, I didn't know as much as I thought I did. But I knew enough to realize I was in some very deep shit. I heard myself ask, "And the call last night?"

"It was just what I said. And in case you're wondering, she's a woman. And she called me last night because their accounts are all screwed up, which, in case it hasn't escaped your attention, is a whole lot different than screwing for money!"

Accounts screwed up? That would explain the cash, wouldn't it? Houses in this neighborhood weren't cheap to maintain. Hell, my own landscaping service cost more than any waitress made in a month.

Had Chloe been fronting those bills?

I was finding it hard to think. "So she's the home-owner?" I said.

"Renter, owner, hell, at this point, I have no idea. But she definitely lives there." Chloe crossed her arms. "Except, I guess, when she's off in Costa Rica with her husband."

I shook my head. "But the guy who lives in that house, he's not married."

"Oh yeah? How do *you* know?"

I tried to remember. It was something Bishop had said, maybe on the night of my birthday party. Right now, I was finding it hard to remember anything. Still, I managed to say, "Bishop told me."

"Yeah? Well, maybe he's wrong."

"No. He's never wrong."

She gave me an icy smile. "Then maybe you should ask *Bishop* whether or not I'm a hooker. I mean, he knows everything, right?"

She threw up her arms. "Why am I even discussing this with you?" She turned to call over her shoulder. "Chucky!"

My heart was pounding. This was happening too fast. Somehow, I could make it right. I *had* to make it right. I reached out for her. "Baby, c'mon, don't go. Not like this."

She slapped my arms aside. "Look, let me make this really clear. Whatever we had, it's over."

No.

It wasn't over. It couldn't be over. I shook my head. "Don't say that. C'mon. I'm sorry, alright?"

"No, it's *not* alright." She glared at me. "What is it with you? Why do always assume the worst about me?"

"I don't."

"You do." She turned and stalked through the house, calling out for Chucky.

I followed after her. "C'mon, Chloe." My voice broke. "Don't go like this."

She whirled to face me. "You've got to promise me something."

"Anything."

"Don't call me. Don't talk to me. Don't–"

"Baby, c'mon–"

"Don't write me. Don't email me. Don't text me. And, if you see me on the street, don't fucking wave to me." She choked down a sob. "Just leave me alone, alright?"

Desperately, I reached out, wanting to gather her in my arms. Again, she slapped my hands aside, yelling out, "What part of 'leave me alone' don't you understand?"

I hated to see her like this. And I hated the fact that I'd caused it. "But Baby, you're upset."

"Of course I'm upset! My boyfriend–" She raised her hand. "No. Make that my ex-boyfriend, thinks I'm a damn hooker!"

"Chloe, c'mon, don't say that. That's not the way I thought of it."

"Yeah, right." She took a deep breath and wiped at her eyes. "Now, promise me."

"To leave you alone?" My insides were churning. The thought of life without her, what kind of life was that? I gave her a pleading look. "I can't."

"If you ever loved me, you can."

"Don't ask me to." Shit, there had to be another way. I'd pay. If not with money, then with something else, anything. But not this. I gave her a desperate look. "Beat me, yell at me, whatever, but don't make me do this. Please."

She made a scoffing sound. "Look, all the time I've known you, I've never asked you for one fucking thing. And I know damn well that other girls have. So now, this is it, the first thing I've ever asked, and you can't even say 'yes'."

"Baby–"

"Promise me. I mean it."

I couldn't.

At that point, I'd have done anything for her – anything but that. My mind was frantically searching for another way, a shred of hope, anything. I couldn't lose her. I just couldn't. Not forever.

Seizing on the only hope I had, I made myself ask, "And if I do promise you? What then?"

She looked away. "I don't know."

I could hardly talk, but somehow I managed to choke out, "Are you saying there's a chance?"

"Yeah. Slim to none."

She was hurting. And once again, it was all my fault. "I am so fucking sorry," I said.

"You already said that."

Just then, Chucky skidded around the corner, with one of my socks dangling from his teeth.

Chloe looked at her dog and said, "C'mon Chucky, time to go."

My voice dropped to a whisper. "Don't go. Please?"

She gave me a hard look. "Where's my promise?"

"I can't."

"Alright, fine. Whatever. I guess it's all about you, huh? Heaven forbid *you* do anything you don't want to."

What could I say to that? Not a fucking thing.

Because she was right.

CHAPTER 46

Standing there, the cold, hard reality slammed into me. All this time, she'd been hurting for money. But she hadn't asked me for a dime.

Her "vintage" car wasn't vintage. It was just old.

I thought of the dead battery that had kept Chloe from driving home the other night. I'd been such a dumb-ass. Yeah, I'd given the battery a jump. And I'd driven the car back to her place. And then, what had I done? I told her in a half-assed way that the battery needed replacing.

A new car battery – it would've cost me almost nothing. What? A hundred bucks? To me, that was pocket change. But I'd been poor once. A hundred bucks was a fortune when you didn't have it.

And then, there was the house. Chloe lived on just the other side of my fence. But she wasn't really *living* there, was she? She was working there.

No wonder she hadn't wanted me inside. It wasn't a home. It was a place of employment. I thought of all the money that I'd pissed away on stupid shit that didn't matter. It wasn't a fortune. But to someone who didn't have any, it might as well be millions.

All this time, I'd been blind and stupid. What the fuck was wrong with me? Here, I claimed to love her. But all I'd seen was a rich girl in a rich neighborhood. And then, when I'd figured out that she wasn't exactly what she seemed, what had I assumed?

That she was a fucking prostitute.

If she left me now, it would rip out my heart. But I deserved that. So, somehow, I made myself say what needed saying. "Okay."

She was still glaring at me. "Say it."

I could hardly choke out the words. "I promise."

She gave me a slow nod, and turned away, walking toward the door.

I should've let her go. It was the decent thing to do. But even now, I was a selfish bastard at heart, because I couldn't stop myself from saying, "Wait."

She turned around. The look in her eyes said it all. Even now, I was living down to her lowest expectations.

And she was right.

But I had to tell her something. "I'm not giving up."

Her gaze narrowed. "Well so much for your promises." She made a sound of disgust. "What'd that last? Two seconds?"

She didn't get it. I wouldn't be bothering her. But I *would* be waiting. And by some miracle, she walked back into my life, I'd consider myself the luckiest guy on Earth.

I met her gaze. "I'll keep it, even if it kills me."

"I mean it," she said. "Even if you see me in the supermarket, just keep on going. Alright?"

I thought of the places I might see her – my own back yard, the restaurant where she worked, the sidewalk in front of my house. The thought of seeing her, but not speaking to her, not holding her, not knowing she was mine, it was a nightmare I didn't want to face.

But it was a nightmare I'd brought on myself.

Somehow, I made myself nod.

But I couldn't leave it at that. I looked into her eyes and tried one last time. When I spoke, my voice came out in a strangled whisper. "You call me. I'll be waiting."

Her voice was quiet, too. "Then you'll be waiting a long time."

"I don't care," I told her. "Call me anytime. Day, night, middle of the night. I don't care. Just call me. Okay?

"Don't count on it," she said. And then, with Chucky in her arms, she turned away, heading toward the front door. I didn't try to stop her, but I couldn't just stand there like I didn't give a shit. So like a dead man walking, I followed after her, haunting her steps and silently begging for her to turn around.

She didn't.

Instead, she opened the door and walked out, taking her little dog with her. I stood in the open doorway and watched, wondering how I'd managed to fuck this up yet again.

I'd already done this once – watched her walk away because of something stupid I'd done, something that had hurt her, something that showed I didn't deserve a girl like that.

When she reached the front walkway, she set Chucky down. But he didn't move. Instead, he flopped down on the concrete and refused to budge.

In his own way, he was saying the thing I couldn't. *"Don't leave."*

If someday, I ever won Chloe back, I wasn't going to forget this. In fact, I decided, I'd carry his favorite doggie treats with me wherever I went, on the off chance I ever got near him again.

It was stupid, I know. But everything was stupid.

I'd been stupid.

When Chucky refused to cooperate, Chloe picked him up and started walking toward the front gate, with Chucky wriggling in her arms. As for me, I still hadn't moved. I couldn't, even though I desperately wanted to.

What if this the last time I saw her?

A horrible thought occurred to me. That wasn't even her house. For all I knew, she'd be moving tomorrow. To think, I'd spent all those years wanting her, searching for her, and then, I'd lost her, not only once, but twice, because I'd been too blind to see through the bullshit.

From where I stood, I could still see her. She was almost to my front gate. If I wanted, I could be at her side in ten seconds, maybe less. But I had promised. And breaking that promise now would just prove that she'd been right. It *was* all about me.

So I stood there, knowing that I had to let her go. Not for my sake. But for hers.

Even if it killed me.

When she passed through the gate, Chucky gave a long, plaintive whine that cut me to the bone. This was all my fault. I was losing the girl. I was losing the dog. I was losing my mind.

I watched until she disappeared from sight, and then I trudged back inside the house and tried to figure out how in the hell I'd live without her.

CHAPTER 47

Bishop's voice cut into my consciousness. "What the hell are you doing?"

It was dark. It had been dark for a while now. How long? I had no idea. I'd gone straight from the front doorway to the nearest chair. Hours later, I was still sitting there.

Bishop switched on a nearby lamp and stared down at me. "What's wrong?"

I shrugged. "Nothing I want to talk about."

He was quiet a long moment. "Where's Chloe? I thought you two were hanging out today."

Great. So *now* he remembers her name? Screw it. What did it matter? What did anything matter?

My voice was a monotone. "She's gone."

"To work?"

"No. Just gone."

His eyebrows furrowed. "For good?"

"Yeah." I almost choked on the words. "For good."

"What happened?"

"What do you care?" I said. "You never liked her, anyway." It was true. He'd been giving me grief from day-one. Probably, this was *good* news to him.

His voice was quiet. "I never said that."

"Yeah, whatever." It wasn't Bishop's fault that she was gone. And it wasn't Chloe's fault either. It was *my* fault. And me getting mad at Bishop wasn't going to solve a damn thing. Or maybe, I just didn't have the energy to fight with him.

The last couple of weeks had been a roller-coaster of ups and downs. But this last down – it had knocked me on my ass.

I stood. "I'm going to bed."

"But it's only seven o'clock."

Was it? Did it matter? It was November. This time of year, the nights were long, and darkness came early. Just yesterday, I had been looking forward to long, winter nights curled up with Chloe. Now, they'd just be long and cold.

No Chloe. No little dog. No one to blame but myself.

Without another word, I turned away, feeling Bishop's eyes on my back as I left the sitting area and trudged up the stairway. He knew the way out. Or shit, maybe he was planning to stay a while.

Either way, I didn't care. I didn't care about a lot of things.

That night, I couldn't sleep. And I didn't sleep all that great the following night either, or the night after that.

Over the next couple of weeks, I spent an obscene amount of time at the office and too many hours hitting the weights. And, no matter where I was or what I was doing, I spent every waking moment, thinking of Chloe.

Like a dumb-ass, I was still carrying around those doggie-treats in the pocket of whatever I was wearing, even to places where I knew Chloe wouldn't be – at the office downtown, on the basketball courts at the gym, to some anti-poverty thing, where I was supposed to be the keynote speaker. I'd done a piss-poor job of it. They wouldn't be asking me back.

About the treats, maybe they were just part of the punishment. Sometimes, as I moved, I'd hear the package crinkling in my pocket, and it would remind me all over again how stupid I'd been.

For whatever reason, Bishop was sticking around. We didn't have any side-ventures planned, so I couldn't see the point, unless it was to keep me from slitting my wrists – hard to do with no knives in the house.

I hadn't bothered to replace them, and Bishop didn't seem inclined either.

But I wasn't going to kill myself. For one thing, it was too easy. I didn't deserve easy. So I kept on going, cursing myself for the promise that I'd made to stay away, and cursing myself even louder for the things I'd done to make that promise necessary.

What a cluster.

A couple of weeks after Chloe had walked out my front door, I found myself standing in the same doorway, staring at different girl, Brittney.

Damn it.

CHAPTER 48

I stared down at her, wondering what the hell she wanted, because let's face it, Brittney was the last girl I wanted to see on my doorstep.

Like too many others things, this was probably my own fault. These days, the front gate was always open, because stupid or not, I still had this crazy hope that one day, Chloe might walk back through it.

So far, she hadn't. And the way it looked, she wasn't going to.

Instead, here I was, looking at someone who annoyed the piss out of me. I didn't bother to hide it. "What do you want?"

She frowned. "Aren't you gonna invite me in?"

"Hell no."

She made a sound of frustration. "Well, this is special. First *her*, and now you. I'm starting to think you *both* have issues."

Just a couple of hours earlier, it was Amber on my doorstep, complaining about Brittney. Supposedly, Brittney had been spreading some rumor about Amber getting a boob job. Was it true? I didn't know, and I didn't care. Why they chose to put me in the middle, I had no idea.

From what Amber had told me earlier, she'd retaliated by spreading a rumor of her own – that Brittney couldn't tell the difference between a *real* designer purse and a *fake* designer purse. The same with shoes.

Just shoot me, now.

I looked to Brittney. "Not my problem. If you're unhappy, take it up with Amber."

"Amber?" She shook her head. "Why her?"

My head was pounding. Last night, I'd had about six beers too many, and I was still feeling it.

Shit, who was I kidding? I felt this lousy every day, whether I'd been drinking or not. I reached up to rub the back of my neck, wondering if I should grab another beer now, just to take the edge off.

"Well?" Brittney was saying.

I was still rubbing my neck. "Well what?"

Did I even *have* beer? Damn it. That's right. I'd gone through the last of it last night. Maybe I should give my house-keeper a call, have her put it on the list. Was *today* grocery-shopping day? I had no idea. It's not like I'd been eating a lot lately.

Brittney gave me an annoyed look. "I wasn't talking about Amber. I was talking about your girlfriend."

My girlfriend? Now *that* got my attention. She must mean Chloe. At the thought of her, I felt that familiar ache in my heart. She wasn't my girlfriend. She was the girl I'd driven away.

But Brittney would know that. Right? After all, she and Chloe worked together. But then again, they weren't exactly best buddies, were they?

For all I knew, they didn't even talk at work. If *I* worked with Brittney, I sure as hell wouldn't be talking to her. Hell, I didn't want to be talking to her, now.

But suddenly, I was curious. "Why are you here?"

"Because I've got a message for Chloe, and I didn't want to give it to her at work."

A nicer guy would've told Brittney that she was in the wrong place. A nicer guy would've confessed that I couldn't give Chloe anything, no matter how much I might want to. A nicer guy would've admitted that Chloe wasn't here, and probably never *would* be here.

But I *wasn't* nice. And I was dying for news of the girl I'd lost.

For too many nights, I'd walked along my fence, desperate for the smallest glimpse of her. I never spotted Chloe, but I did see other things – the trashcan by the curb on garbage day, lights glimmering through the bare branches of the trees, Chloe's car in the driveway, sometimes in one spot, sometimes in another.

From what I could tell, she'd been going about her business like nothing had changed. Well, that made one of us. As for me, I was letting everything go to shit.

I heard myself ask, "What's the message?"

At this, Brittney smiled. "Tell her that when the flu is over, she's outta there."

I shook my head. "Out of where?"

"Work. You know, her waitressing job." Brittney went on to explain that the only reason that Chloe hadn't been fired so far was because too many other employees were down with the flu.

Brittney gave a mean little laugh. "But once they're all better, Chloe's totally fired."

God, what a bitch.

That aside, I didn't get it. Why would Chloe be fired? From what I'd seen, she was amazing at her job. But then I recalled something else. A couple weeks earlier, I'd caused a scene at that restaurant, beating up my own fucking car. At the time, her boss hadn't looked too happy.

Shit. As if I hadn't done enough damage already.

Brittney finished by saying, "So if Chloe wanted to save herself some humiliation, she'd just go ahead and quit already."

With a pang, I recalled Chloe crying in my arms. She had no money. She had no home. All she had was her job. And she was about to lose it, thanks to me.

I looked to Brittney. "Where'd you hear this?'

Brittney was still smiling. "From the manager." She gave a toss of her hair. "He tells me everything."

The manager had to be Chloe's boss – the guy Brittney had been, as Chloe put it, "boning in the back seat" of that Lincoln Town car. What was the guy's name? Keith?

Maybe it was time to pay Keith a visit.

CHAPTER 49

Later that night, I was parked behind the restaurant where Chloe worked. Looking to keep a low profile, I was hunkered down in my basic black sedan, hoping like hell that Chloe didn't see me.

In spite of the risk, I was liking my odds. Her car was nowhere in sight, and unless her schedule had drastically changed, I still had a couple more hours before her normal shift began.

For once, that was a good thing. I wasn't waiting to see *her*.

I'd been sitting in my car for maybe a half-hour when my cell phone rang. I pulled it out and glanced at the display. It was Amber.

Bracing myself for another round of "Guess what Brittney's saying about me *now*," I answered with a half-hearted, "Yeah?"

"Fun news," she said. "We're having this thing for Thanksgiving."

"A thing?"

"You know. A big get-together."

"Huh." I was still scanning the parking lot. "Sounds like fun."

"Oh, it *will* be," she said. "You know how we normally go to the Hamptons? Well *this* year, we're going in December, so anyway, you wanna come?"

I was only half-listening. "To the Hamptons?"

"No. I mean, yeah, you could totally come there too. But I meant for Thanksgiving. I figured that maybe, you'd want to join us."

She figured wrong. I mean, it's not like I didn't appreciate the offer. But I'd been in a shitty mood for weeks now. And it wouldn't be improved by yucking it up over turkey with a bunch of people who weren't Chloe.

"Thanks for the offer," I said, "but I'd better pass."

"But why?" she asked. "You already told me you don't have plans."

That much was true. My sister was spending the holiday with her new boyfriend's family, and my brothers weren't exactly the turkey-baking types.

When I made no response, Amber said in a voice filled with concern, "You're still bummed about Chloe, aren't you?"

Bummed. It was a funny word for how I felt.

I had a hard time getting up in the morning, and an even harder time falling asleep. I spent my waking hours replaying all the stuff I should've said or done differently. And then, when I *did* fall asleep, I woke up, cold and empty, hours before my alarm, only to lie in bed, wondering what the hell I should do now.

I wasn't bummed. I was a fucking mess.

But all I said was, "I dunno."

"How about this?" Amber perked up. "Invite Chloe, too. Like a reunion thing. She likes turkey, right?"

If only it were that simple. "Thanks, but I'm pretty sure she has plans."

What those plans were, I had no idea. I just knew they didn't involve me.

Her voice grew softer. "Just think about it. Okay?"

From inside my car, I saw a pair of headlights turning into the lot. Under the headlight's glare, I couldn't tell the car's make or model, so I waited, keeping an eye out while Amber switched gears by saying, "Hey, you wanna hear the *latest* thing Brittney's saying?"

"Sure. Hit me."

"Check this out." Her voice rose. "She's running around telling people that I screwed her boyfriend."

"She has a boyfriend?"

"No. And that's my whole point. It's a total lie, unless you count her new boss. And there's no way I'd hook up with *him*. Seriously.

Ick."

Brittney's new boss happened to be Chloe's boss, too. It confirmed everything I'd been thinking. Not only had I caused that scene outside the restaurant, I'd also been the person who'd brought Brittney into Chloe's life, and as a result, into her workplace, too.

Now, because of all this, Chloe was about to get fired – except she wasn't. Not if I had anything to say about it.

I watched as the car pulled into a nearby spot and cut the lights, giving me a nice, clear view of the front end. I felt myself smile. Sure enough, it was a Lincoln Town Car, the same one that Brittney had crawled out of the other night, in this same parking lot.

"Sorry," I told Amber. "I've gotta run. Catch you later, alright?"

I disconnected the call and got out of my car. I strolled, nice and easy, taking the long way, toward the back of the Lincoln. When the driver's side door opened, there I was, waiting just a couple of feet away.

When the driver spotted me, he almost jumped out of his skin. Sure enough, it was Keith, Chloe's manager. And he looked scared shitless.

God, what a pussy.

"I'm not gonna hurt you," I said.

He straightened. "I know that." But then, he ruined the effect by glancing at his car, looking like he was about to make a break for it.

I stepped closer. "You wanna take off? Fine by me. I'll just come back tomorrow." I smiled. "Or, I could visit you at home."

He stuck out his chin. "You don't even know where I live."

As an answer, I rattled off his street address and waited.

After a long, tense moment, he said, "What do you want?"

I kept my tone friendly. "I want to make you an offer."

"Oh yeah?" He crossed his arms. "Like what?"

"Let's call it a carrot and a stick."

The carrot would be something nice. The stick, not so much.

His gaze narrowed. "What kind of carrot?"

Funny he wasn't asking about the stick. But eh, that would come later. "The carrot," I explained, "is this. I'm gonna give you a nice little bonus for something you should be doing anyway."

"Yeah? What's that?"

"Not firing Chloe."

"Who says she's gonna be fired? I've got half the girls out with the flu. I can't be firing anyone." Under his breath, he added, "Not yet, anyway."

"Uh-huh," I said. "How about *after* they get better, and there's no more flu?"

He glanced away. "I dunno. I haven't thought that far."

Like I believed that. "Uh-huh," I said again.

"And Chloe," he said, "she's got a mouth on her."

Yeah, she did. A nice one. Her lips were soft and full. And she knew how to use that mouth, too. But what did that matter? The way it was looking now, I wouldn't be getting anywhere near Chloe, or that mouth of hers.

God, I was a losing it.

The way it looked, so was Keith, but not in the same way as me. Apparently, he'd gotten over his initial fear and was working himself up into a nice little hissy-fit. "Get this," he was saying. "One time, she comes into *my* office and tells me to fuck off." He snorted. "Me! And I'm her boss."

I knew Chloe. If she told him to fuck off, he probably deserved it. What had the guy done to her? And who'd put him up to it? Brittney?

Remembering why I was here, I pulled out my wallet and started peeling off some bills.

He eyed the money. "You're serious?" He licked his lips. "I thought you were just saying that."

"You thought wrong."

He shook his head. "I don't get it. If it's a money thing, why don't you just pay *her* instead?"

Because Chloe wanted nothing to do with me. That's why.

If I could, I'd make all her problems go away. I'd buy her a house. I'd buy her a car. I'd pay off her student loans and anything else she might owe. But I couldn't. Because she'd know who did it. And she'd think I was buying her, like the prostitute I'd accused her of being.

But I wasn't here to explain myself to this idiot. So all I said was, "If I were paying *her*, I wouldn't be paying *you*. Now would I?"

He was practically salivating now. "Good point," he said, reaching for the cash. A thousand bucks, all in hundreds. When he tried to tug the bills away, I didn't let go.

"First," I said, "let me tell you about the stick." I leaned closer. "If Chloe hears one word about this, and I mean one single word, whether from you or anyone else, I'm going to pay you a little visit." I smiled. "And your medical bills? Well, let's just say they'll cost a lot more than a thousand bucks."

In the end, he took the money. Then again, I hadn't expected anything else. And if he was smarter than he looked, he'd keep his mouth shut.

I was liking my odds. And not because of the carrot.

I spent the next few days trying like hell to push Chloe out of my mind. But no matter what I did, I couldn't, because everywhere I looked, I saw her face – not for real, but in my mind.

On the home front, Bishop was starting to drive me crazy. He wasn't leaving. And instead of the annoying hard-ass, he was turning into some kind of nursemaid, giving me worried looks when I wasn't looking.

And the knives were still missing.

I didn't bother to replace them. Whatever. I wasn't spending a lot of time in the kitchen anyway. Without Chloe, even steak had lost its flavor.

Sometimes, I thought I was losing my mind. Who knows, maybe I was. But a couple days before Thanksgiving, I tried to shake it off by going for a run someplace different.

In the end, I didn't shake off anything, because I'd just rounded a bend in the nature trail when I stopped short at the sight of something that knocked the wind right out of me.

It was Chloe.

For real.

CHAPTER 50

I stood, frozen in my tracks, as I drank in the sight of her. The way it looked, she hadn't yet spotted me. I took advantage of that fact, staring at her with a hunger that gnawed deep into my heart and made it hard to breathe.

Her eyes were on Chucky, and her mouth was upturned in a faint smile that looked more sad than happy. Or maybe that was just wishful thinking on my part, as shitty as it was.

As for Chucky, he was doing what he did best, spazzing out at something in a nearby cluster of evergreens. Any other time, I might have smiled.

I loved that dog.

I loved the girl.

I recalled what she'd told me the last time we spoke, on that awful day when I'd accused her of having sex for money. In my mind, I could still hear her words.

"Don't write me. Don't email me. Don't text me. And, if you see me on the street, don't wave to me. Just leave me alone, alright?"

She'd been crying. *I'd* made her cry.

Standing on the path, I was still watching her. This wasn't the street, but did it matter? I recalled something else she'd told me that day. As long as I'd known her, she'd never asked me for a damn thing – except for that one promise, the promise to leave her alone.

And like an idiot, I'd given it. So now, in what felt like a giant kick to the teeth, I'd have to stand here and pretend this wasn't killing me. I'd have to stop myself from flat-out begging for another chance. I'd have to act like she didn't exist at all, as if she *weren't* the only thing that mattered in my whole fucked-up world.

Standing there, I knew the exact moment she spotted me. I could see it in her eyes and feel it across the distance, and not only from her. From Chucky, too.

What now? Should I leave? Stay? Finish my run like I hadn't seen her? In the end, it didn't matter, because I was powerless to move.

Chloe glanced over her shoulder toward the nearby parking area. From this angle, I couldn't see her car, but the way it looked, she could. I held my breath, wondering if she'd hurry to her car and drive away.

But she didn't. Instead, as if facing a demon that had been tormenting her for too damn long, she squared her shoulders and continued on her original path.

In front of her, Chucky was going nuts, straining at his leash and whining like he always did when he wanted some attention. Watching him, I tried to smile. But I couldn't quite pull it off, not even for him.

When he barreled into me a moment later, I wondered if Chloe would pull him away. But she didn't. Instead, she stood silently off to the side while I crouched down and ruffled Chucky's fur, feeling my heart melt as he welcomed me like I was his second-favorite person in the entire world.

Funny, I still carried treats in my pocket. Suddenly, glad to have them, I pulled out the package and tore it open. I shook some onto my hand and let Chucky have as many as he wanted, which turned out to be all of them.

Smart dog.

Through all of this, I was obscenely aware that Chloe was standing within arm's reach. I could talk to her. I could wrap her in my arms and wipe the worry from those suddenly sad eyes of hers.

No. I couldn't.

Because I'd promised. And I was going to keep that promise if it killed me. Funny, it felt like it just might.

Gently, Chloe picked up her dog and cradled him tight against her body. She met my gaze one last time before continuing down the trail with Chucky whining in her arms and his leash dragging behind them.

I watched until she was out of sight. I said her name, so soft she would never hear it. And then, I drove home and got so fucking drunk that I forget my own name.

But I never forgot Chloe.

CHAPTER 51

A couple days later, it was Thanksgiving, and I was alone – not that I cared. There was only one person who I wanted to spend any holiday with, and she wasn't talking to me.

It was nearly noon, and I was in the garage out back, working on the vintage car that I'd beaten with a crowbar in front of Chloe.

The car was still a mess, but not as bad as before. I'd replaced both headlights and the side-view mirrors. As for the rest of it, I had to be honest. It looked like shit. The windshield was still cracked, and the hood was still covered in big, ugly dents.

Funny to think I could write a check and have the car looking exactly like it had before. Or even easier, I could have a dealer find me a replacement car, already restored. With enough money, anything was possible, right? And I had plenty.

But for all kinds of crazy reasons, I was attached to *this* car. I'd restored it once, and so I'd be doing it again – *without* help. This time, it wasn't for fun. It was because it sucked, and I deserved to suffer. Writing a check would be too easy, and I didn't deserve to take the easy way out.

I stood back and studied the car with a critical eye. It was painful to look at, but not for the obvious reasons. It was because every dent, every chipped piece of paint, every spider-webbed pattern in the cracked windshield, it all reminded me of Chloe and how I'd lost her like a dumb-ass.

What was she doing today? Spending Thanksgiving with her

family? I blew out a long breath and pictured us together, not just today, but every day. If things had turned out differently, Chloe would've *been* my family. At the thought, I tried to smile, but my face felt frozen, and my heart wasn't in it.

Stalling, I popped the hood of the car and was just checking the oil when something made me stop in mid-motion. My cell phone was ringing – and it wasn't just any ringtone.

It was Chloe's ringtone.

My hands were slick with motor oil. Frantically, I wiped the grease onto my jeans and white T-shirt, and looked around, wondering where the hell my phone was. I could hear it, but I couldn't see it.

I circled the car and finally spotted it in the driver's seat. I yanked open the car-door, grabbed the cell, and answered with an urgent, "Chloe?"

"Yeah." She hesitated. "Listen, I've got a question."

I was clutching the phone with both hands. "Yeah?"

"You still want that beating?"

I paused. "What?"

"Sorry," she said with a shaky laugh. "Bad joke."

Finally, I got what she meant. When she'd been walking out on me, I'd practically begged for a beating instead of the alternative. The reason had been simple. And selfish. A good beat-down would've hurt a lot less than losing her.

I still felt that way. The dull ache of life without her was grinding me down like nothing else. Maybe she *was* joking, but that didn't change the facts.

"I remember," I said. "And for what it's worth, the offer still stands."

I meant it, too. I'd welcome that kind of pain, because the other kind was killing me. Even now, listening to her voice and knowing that she wasn't mine, it was salt in a wound that had been festering for weeks.

She hesitated. "Well, that's the thing, I really hate to ask, but I need a favor, and it's kind of awful."

"Whatever it is, the answer's yes."

"Really?" Her voice caught. "Because I know that I shouldn't be asking. And I wouldn't, except I'm kind of desperate, and I don't know what else to do."

The hitch in her voice hurt to hear. "Hey," I said, my own voice growing softer, "just tell me what you need. No matter what it is, the answer's still yes."

"Alright." She paused. "I need a ride."

Just a ride? That didn't seem so awful to me. "Great," I said. "Just say when."

"Well, um, now actually."

I didn't ask where, and I didn't ask why. All I said, "Alright, give me five minutes to change."

"Actually," she said, "we don't have the time. I'm *really* sorry. But can you come now? I mean, like *right* now?"

I froze as a horrible thought slammed into me. "Are you hurt?"

"No," she assured me. "It's nothing like that. It's just that I've got to get to my dad's for Thanksgiving, and I can't be late. I mean, I *really* can't be late. It's *so* messed up. But if I don't make it on time, I'm worried that Josh will be in trouble."

I didn't get what she meant, but I wasn't going to waste time asking questions now. "I'll be right there," I said.

"I'm sorry to be pushy, but can you hurry?" Her voice grew more urgent. "It's probably already too late. It's just that I've got to try. I mean, seriously, if you could just grab the nearest car and leave right now, it would be *such* a huge help. My dad's place is like twenty minutes away, but I've *got* to be there in—" she paused as if checking the time "—fourteen minutes."

I glanced down. My clothes were greasy, and my jeans were ripped. I was out in the garage with only one set of keys – the keys to the car I was working on.

"I'm on the way," I said.

CHAPTER 52

When I squealed into Chloe's driveway a minute later, she was standing near the trunk of her own car, waiting for me. At the sight of her, my breath caught. She wore a formal-looking green dress that was sweet and sexy as hell, with long, lacy sleeves and a scooped neckline that only hinted at the cleavage it was hiding.

She was holding a giant bowl of something leafy, probably a salad. On the concrete near her feet were two white bakery boxes.

Without cutting the engine, I jumped out of the car and joined her in the driveway. I looked down at the boxes. "We taking those?"

When she nodded, I picked them up and strode toward the passenger's side of my car. I shifted the boxes to one arm and opened the car door with my free hand. I set the boxes on the floor behind the seat and stepped aside, holding the door open for Chloe.

Moving quickly, she got into the car and settled the big bowl of salad onto her lap. She crossed her ankles, and I felt myself swallow, catching the curve of her thigh as she shifted in the seat.

The sight of her was heaven. And hell. Because I still loved her, I still wanted her, and yeah, I was wishing like crazy that this wasn't just a one-time thing.

She looked up, meeting my gaze, and that was all it took. Her eyes grew warm, and I saw a flicker of something that gave me hope.

Wishing? Screw that. Wishing wouldn't do a damn bit of good. I wasn't going to wish. Sometime, before I dropped her back off, I was going to act. How, I didn't yet know. But I'd figure it out.

She gave me a nervous smile. "Boy, are *you* gonna be sorry."

I grinned down at her. "Not a chance." I shut her door and circled back to the driver's side. I was still smiling. I couldn't help it. She might try to hide it, but that look in her eyes told me all I needed to know. She still loved me, and before the end of the day, I was going to hear her say it.

My smile was still there when I climbed into the driver's seat and shifted into reverse. Backing out of the long driveway, I gave Chloe a sideways glance. Her smile was gone, and she was biting her lip.

When she saw me looking, she let out a long, shaky breath. "I wasn't kidding," she warned. "This is gonna suck." She gave my clothes the once-over and winced. "Especially for you."

I knew what she meant. Just seeing the way *she* was dressed told me this wasn't exactly a casual thing. The way it looked, her family was the kind that got dressed up for holiday dinners.

I sure as hell wasn't dressed up. My shirt was stained, and my jeans were ripped. I'd be outclassed and then some.

I didn't care. I was with Chloe, and nothing else mattered. I shrugged. "I think I can handle it."

She gave a weak laugh. "That's what *you* think."

At the end of the driveway, I stopped and asked, "Which way?"

She gave me general directions to her dad's place, and I backed out onto the street. And then, remembering she was in a hurry, I floored it.

The car was fast, and I wasn't afraid to push it to the limit. I still didn't get why she was so nervous about the time, but for whatever reason, she was. And that was good enough for me.

Sitting there within arm's reach, I wanted to turn and give her a good, long look. I wanted to see if she'd smile in that special way that drove me crazy. And yeah, I wanted to see that flicker of interest grow into a spark. And then, who knows? Whatever happened, I wasn't going to mess this up.

But first, I had to get Chloe there safely, which meant I needed to keep my eyes on the road. The streets were nearly empty, which was a good thing, because I was going almost double the speed limit. If we got stopped by the cops, it wouldn't be just a speeding ticket. It would be reckless driving.

Totally worth it.

On the next straightaway, I gave Chloe a sideways glance. She looked nervous as hell, and for some reason, I didn't think it was because of my driving.

Looking to lighten her mood, I said, "So, this wasn't exactly the beating I expected."

She gave me a look that was almost sympathetic. "Trust me, by the end of the day, you'll be wishing for the other kind."

"I don't care," I told her. "I'm just glad you called."

She tried to smile. "Oh, that's what you say *now*."

"Ask me later," I said, turning my gaze back to the road. "I'll say the same thing."

She hesitated. "You didn't have plans today?"

I shrugged. "I had invitations. None I wanted."

"Yeah." She sighed. "I know the feeling."

I was still watching the road, but something in her voice – sadness, maybe – made me risk another glance. She was leaned back in the seat with her eyes shut and her hands fisted around the salad bowl, like she was holding onto it for comfort.

What was wrong?

In spite of the fancy dress, she didn't *look* like someone heading to a holiday dinner. She looked like someone heading to the gallows.

But who was the hangman? Me? I didn't think so.

Over the roar of the engine, I said, "For someone who's about to put me through the ringer, you don't look too happy."

"That's because I can't just send you in my place." She opened her eyes and reached for her cell phone. She checked the time and frowned. "We've got ten minutes."

"Oh c'mon," I said. "What are they gonna do? Lock the doors?"

"You don't think they wouldn't?" She made a scoffing sound. "You poor, misguided fool."

From the corner of my eye, I watched as she leaned down to shove the cell phone back into her purse. As she did, the salad toppled off her lap. The clear wrapping came loose, and half of the lettuce spilled onto her shoes.

She gasped. "Oh my God. Stop the car! No. Wait. Keep going." With desperate motions, she righted the bowl and looked down at the salad, which was now half the size as before. Her face grew pale, and she sucked in a breath.

She looked terrified. What the hell?

She gave me a quick glance. "Oh jeez, sorry about your floor mat." She pushed a trembling hand through her hair. "I guess I should've apologized first, huh?"

"Don't worry about it," I said. "It's just lettuce. No big deal."

"Yeah, I guess," she said in a distracted tone. "Good thing it wasn't soup, huh?"

"Salad, soup, whatever, it all cleans up." We were on a long straightaway. I turned to give her a better look. "Baby, what's wrong?"

She glanced down at the salad and shook her head. "It's too small." She reached up to rub her forehead. "This is bad. What am I gonna do?"

"Chloe," I said in a low, soothing voice, "it's just a salad."

"No," she snapped. "It's not just a salad. You don't get it. This? It's a big deal. Because everything's a big deal."

Still driving, I reached for her hand. "C'mon, what is it?"

"Nothing. It's fine." As if seeking comfort, her hand closed around mine, and I felt her fingers tremble. "Watch the road, alright?"

She had a point. We were going way too fast for me to be careless. Still, it didn't take much to see that something was very wrong.

And before we got there, I was going to find out.

CHAPTER 53

Chloe took a long, deep breath, as if trying to get a grip. I risked another glance and didn't like what I saw. She was leaned back in the seat again. Her eyes were shut, and her face was pale as death.

"Aw c'mon," I said, giving her hand a reassuring squeeze, "it can't be that bad."

"I hope you're right." Her eyes were still shut. "And this time, you'll be there, so–" She shrugged and let the sentence trail off.

"So? Go on."

"Well, normally they're a lot nicer in front of strangers." After a long pause, she opened her eyes to look at me. "And you're a stranger to them, so–" She shook her head. "Crap, I don't know. What if it backfires?"

"Chloe?" I kept my voice low. "Are you scared?"

She turned to look out the window. "No."

She was lying. I'd seen plenty of fear in my life, but whatever this was, it hurt to watch. For the life of me, I couldn't see what was so scary about a Thanksgiving dinner.

"Baby, what is it?"

"Okay, here's the thing." She blew out a long, shaky breath. "I almost never go there, and when I do, it's always awful."

"What's so awful about it?"

"Like my dad," she said. "Whenever he has company over, he starts talking funny."

"How so?"

"Well, he's a commercial real estate broker–"

"A salesman?"

"Basically," she said. "So he's always trying to bond with whoever he's talking to, but he never gets it quite right."

"What do you mean?"

"Well, one time, Loretta had this Australian couple over for dinner, and by the time we hit dessert, my dad's talking in this weird accent, more English than anything."

I wasn't following. "But you said they were Australian, right?"

"Yeah, and the harder my dad tries to show that he's exactly like them, the worse everything gets. They start talking less. He starts talking more." Chloe was shaking her head again. "I'm pretty sure they thought my dad was making fun of them."

I had to laugh. "Aw c'mon, that's not so bad."

"I guess," she said. "And actually, it's a lot better than how he acts when it's just family."

"How so?"

"Well, when no one's there except us and Loretta, he's either giving me and Josh a hard time or kissing Loretta's butt."

"Who's Loretta?"

"My stepmother, who totally hates me, by the way."

"Oh yeah? Why?" I made a mental note. Loretta. I'd never met the woman, but she was already on my shit list.

"Mostly, she hates everyone, well, except for her own daughter." Chloe paused. "And my dad. Sometimes."

"What about your brother?"

"That's the worst part," Choe said. "She doesn't loathe him quite as much as she does me, but she still has this way of tormenting him, even when she's pretending to be nice."

In the road ahead of us, I spotted an oversized pickup, going a whole lot slower than we were. Reluctantly, I pulled my hand from Chloe's and downshifted to pass it. We flew past the thing like it was standing still.

By the time I shifted again, Chloe's hand was back on the salad. Probably, it was a smart move, all things considered. About everything else, I didn't know what to think.

If Chloe were any other girl, I'd say she was blowing things out of proportion, like her dad talking funny. Shit, in my old neighborhood, that would've been nothing. I gave her another sideways glance and reminded myself that she hadn't grown up in my old neighborhood. She'd grown up someplace nicer, where people were a lot more civilized.

And that wasn't a bad thing. I mean, that was one reason I loved her, wasn't it? Because she'd come from a better place. But then I remembered something else. All along, I'd been assuming that she'd come from money. And she hadn't. For all I knew, she'd grown up in a neighborhood as rough as mine.

But if that were the case, how had she turned out so sweet? I thought of my own sister. By some miracle, and a whole lot of male ass-beating on my part, she'd turned out sweet, too. But who had been looking out for Chloe?

A sick feeling was growing in my gut. Maybe no one had been looking out for her, not even her dad. And that royally pissed me off.

Her voice broke into my thoughts. "I know what you're thinking. You think I'm exaggerating, right?"

"I never said that."

"Uh-huh." She sounded sick with worry. "You'll see. It doesn't take anything to set her off."

"Like what?" I asked. "Gimme an example."

"Well, a couple of Easters ago, it was oyster gravy."

At the thought, that sick feeling grew and twisted. Oyster *anything* was enough to send me running in the opposite direction, and not only because of the taste. It was because of the fact that I was deathly allergic to shellfish, not that I'd admit it in a thousand years. It was fucking embarrassing.

But aside from that, who the hell made gravy out of oysters? I shook my head. "That's just wrong."

When Chloe said nothing, I looked over at her. "So…" I prompted. "The gravy?"

"Oh." She sounded distracted. "Supposedly, it's a delicacy. Or at least, that's what Loretta keeping telling us."

I wanted to look at her, but I kept my eyes on the road as we squealed around the next turn. "I've got this friend from Texas," I said. "Know what he'd say to that?"

"What?"

I said it the way my friend used to say it, in that Western drawl of his. "You can call it Nancy and put a dress on it. But I'm still not gonna eat it."

Finally, I heard the hint of a smile in Chloe's voice. "Say that to Loretta, and you're a dead man." She paused. "As much as I'd totally love to see that."

"So about Easter?" I said. "What happened?"

"Anyway, Loretta made this special batch of oyster gravy, and then flipped out when we didn't want any."

"You and your brother?"

"Yeah. And Lauren Jane too, except she didn't get in trouble for it."

"Who's Lauren Jane?"

"Loretta's daughter."

"Ah."

"And then there was my dad, no help as usual." Chloe deepened her voice in a decent imitation of a pissed-off older guy. "Loretta spent all morning in the kitchen making this for us, and the least you kids can do is have some."

"So did you?" I asked, risking another glance.

She nodded.

I had to ask. "How was it?"

She shuddered. "Awful. Like fish barf."

"But your dad likes it?"

"Nope."

"So he doesn't eat it."

"Nope."

I was shaking my head. "I don't get it."

"Don't get me wrong," she said. "He'd probably eat a smoking turd if Loretta asked him to."

"Better than fish barf," I muttered.

"On second thought, you know what? He wouldn't eat it. He'd

make *us* do it. That way, he gets the credit, and we get the shaft."

The more she talked, the more I wanted to kick her dad's ass. I was tempted to tell her so, but figured that some things were better left unsaid. Trying for a neutral tone, I said, "So *Loretta* likes the gravy?"

"I dunno," Chloe said. "Couldn't tell you either way. She's always on a diet. So it's not like she actually eats the stuff herself. Mostly, she just picks at a salad or something and goes straight for dessert."

What the fuck? "So this gravy," I said, "who exactly was supposed to eat it?"

Chloe shrugged. "Me and Josh, I guess."

Listening to this, I felt a cold anger settle over me. Trying not to show it, I said in the calmest voice I could muster, "Go on."

"So like I said, there's no getting out of it. At least not for me. So I put some on my potatoes, and take a bite."

"And?"

"Like I said, it's awful." Chloe shuddered. "Worse than awful actually. But I know what I've got to do, so I smile and tell her it's delicious."

"Was she happy?"

"Loretta?" Chloe said. "Never. But at least she's not throwing plates. So I keep shoveling it down, figuring that once it's gone, the whole thing's over, right?"

"It wasn't?"

"No," she said, glancing out the window. "It was just beginning."

CHAPTER 54

We were getting closer to her dad's place, but I *had* to know what the hell was going on. I eased off the accelerator, not a lot, but enough to save us maybe another minute or two. If we were late, and they tried to lock us out, well, let's just say good luck with that.

Going for a casual tone, I asked, "What happened next?"

"So Josh," Chloe said, "he's a picky eater. Always has been. And no matter how many times my dad tells him that something's a delicacy, he still doesn't want anything to do with it."

"Smart kid."

"You have no idea," Chloe said with obvious pride in her little brother. "So anyway, Josh keeps saying 'no thanks' to the gravy, but Loretta won't take no for an answer. So she shoves at this vase, and it tips over. Flowers spill, the vase cracks, and my dad gets mad."

"At Loretta?"

Chloe snorted. "Dream on. No. At Josh. So my dad grabs a ladle and starting slopping all this gravy onto Josh's plate, one scoop after another. And this crap gets on everything, not just the potatoes either." Chloe shook her head, and her voice trailed off. "The chicken, the corn, even the salad."

She blinked long and hard before glancing over at me. Seeing the worry on her face, I tried not to think about beating Loretta's ass the moment she opened the door. I reminded myself that Loretta was a woman, and it would be wrong on so many levels. But Chloe's dad, he deserved an ass-beating and then some.

Trying not to show what I was thinking, I said, "Keep going."

"So," Chloe continued, "my dad tells Josh that he's not getting another thing to eat 'til he finishes what's on his plate, even though it looks like some fish threw up on it."

I could practically see it, and I didn't like the way it looked. I wasn't liking a lot of things that I was hearing. "What happened?" I asked. "Did he eat it?"

Chloe shook her head. "No. Josh just sits there, looking down at his plate, and my dad keeps hassling him, saying what a great cook Loretta is, and how lucky Josh is to be living under her roof. And the whole time, Loretta's just sitting there with this half-smile on her face, like everything is turning out exactly like she planned. And Josh, he doesn't eat anything else. Not one bite. And I can tell he wants to cry."

Chloe blew out a shaky breath and continued. "But he's in fourth grade. Or at least he was back then, so he's too big to cry. And he's too little to take on my dad, obviously, or Loretta for that matter. So he doesn't do anything but stare at his plate until everyone else is done."

"But what'd *you* do?" I asked. "You were there, so—"

"Yeah. I was there. And I *knew* I'd be smart to stay out of it."

Somehow, that didn't sound like Chloe. I knew her. Or at least, I thought I did. Trying to get a handle on everything, I asked, "Because you didn't need the trouble?"

She turned sideways in the seat to face me. Still holding the salad in a death grip, she said "No. Because I know better, or at least I should've. Because every time I try to help, I just make it worse."

"Is that what happened this time?"

"Oh yeah. Because stupid me, I couldn't just let it go. But doing the thing I *want* to do is completely out of the question."

"What was that?" I asked.

"Breaking that damn vase over her head."

I liked that thought. I liked it a lot. "Sounds good to me," I said.

"Yeah, but I don't want to make everything worse. So as nice as I could, I suggest letting Josh get a new plate. I say stuff like, 'I think we've all learned a good lesson here.'" She shook her head. "What a load of crap. Anyway, I get Josh to say he'll try some gravy on his potatoes if we can just start over."

"So *that's* what happened?"

"Hell no. Because by now, my dad's all worked up. He gives us this big lecture on how we don't appreciate how much Loretta's done for us. Then one thing leads to another, and I'm so stupid that I actually give an honest opinion on why Loretta made that stupid gravy in the first place."

"And what happened then?" I asked.

"Well, before I know it, Loretta takes Josh's plate and crashes it onto the floor, food and all. Then she goes after the serving dishes, the gravy boat, the chicken platter, a couple of wine glasses. It totally sucks, because everyone's freaking out. But part of me's thinking 'So what? At least Josh won't have to eat a bunch of fish barf.'"

She pushed a trembling hand through her hair. "And in the end, Loretta storms off to her room, and my dad gives us yet another lecture, this one about how we ruined Loretta's favorite holiday."

"Easter?"

"Supposedly. But they say that about every holiday, so I dunno. Talk-Like-a-Pirate-Day could be her favorite for all I know. Anyway, after my dad tells me to get the hell out, Josh is stuck dealing with the fallout."

Chloe looked down at her lap. "And as far as that gravy? Loretta made another batch, special just for him. And they wouldn't give him anything else to eat until the whole thing was gone. And they wouldn't let him eat anyplace else either."

Chloe swallowed, hard. "And I *knew* it was all my fault." Her voice was trembling now. "Because if I hadn't said something, it would've ended at dinner, one way or another. Swear to God, I'd have eaten that whole bowl myself if I could, but after I was kicked out, I wasn't allowed inside at all for at least a year."

What the fuck? All this time, I'd had Chloe pegged for a girl who grew up easy. Obviously, I'd been wrong – so wrong, in fact, that I added my *own* ass to the list of things that needed kicking. She deserved so much better, and not only from her shitty parents.

Thinking of parents, it suddenly hit me that Chloe hadn't said a damn thing about her mom. Where the hell was *she* in all this? I thought of my own mom, and knew the answer without asking. Obviously, she was off doing her own thing, leaving Chloe and Josh to fend for themselves.

"When you left," I said, "you couldn't take Josh with you?"

Chloe shook her head. "I didn't have my own place, still don't. Besides, he's a minor. My dad has full custody, so, well, you know how that goes."

I *did* know how that went. Maybe in some ways, I'd been luckier. My dad was a no-show, and my mom had the decency to drop dead soon enough to keep from fucking things up further. I couldn't help but wonder…if Chloe's dad happened to meet with some 'unfortunate accident,' would Chloe be able to get custody?

Thinking *further* ahead, if we were together, would *we* be able to get custody? Yes. We would. With my legal team, I was sure of it. Shit, we'd probably be able to get custody now, as long as we were married. I still had that ring, and there was still only one girl I wanted.

Damn it. I was getting off track. This wasn't about me. This was about Chloe, and the way it sounded, she'd been on her own almost as long as I'd been. And no one – not even me – had been looking out for her.

Chloe shifted in her seat. "It's not like we were abused or anything," she assured me. "Lots of kids have it worse, right?" With an obvious effort, she brightened her tone. "And at least Grandma lives next door. So Josh spends a lot of time at her place."

The positive spin, as brave as it was, was enough to break my heart, and I felt a growing darkness settle over my soul. Trying not to show it, I asked, "How much time is that?"

"Well, pretty much all of it actually, except for when he's sleeping, or when Grandma's out of town."

"On that Easter," I said, "was your grandma there, too?"

"No. She's my mom's mom, which puts her way down on Loretta's guest list."

"But they're neighbors?"

"Sort of. Grandma rents Loretta's guest cottage."

"So renting the cottage is okay, but coming to dinner isn't?"

"It's complicated," Chloe said. "The cottage is nice, but it's not a real rental. It's got no driveway of its own, and besides, their neighborhood isn't zoned for that sort of thing."

"So it's all done on the sly? That's what you're saying?"

"Yeah. Grandma can't drive anyway, so there's no car. And since she's a relative, the neighbors think she's just a guest."

"But she's paying?"

"Yeah. All cash, so there's no zoning trouble."

"You ever think of renting the cottage for yourself?" I asked.

"I tried. But Loretta wouldn't let me. She still won't let me stay overnight there, even as Grandma's guest."

"Why not?"

"Because," Chloe said in a mocking tone, "I need to learn real responsibility." She let out a long sigh. "Just as well. I work most nights anyway. But Grandma, she works from home, so—"

"Are we talking about that job that isn't real?"

Obviously, Chloe had forgotten. She wasn't talking to some stranger here. I recalled her words from a few weeks earlier. *"I've got a grandma who gets all her rent money from this fake job I had to make up."*

Chloe paused. "Oh. Yeah. I guess I did mention that huh?" She nodded. "Yup. That's the one."

We were turning onto her dad's street. Chloe reached out, putting a hand on my arm. "Lawton," she said, "no matter what she does, don't set her off, alright? She'll probably be pissy about what you're wearing. But that's okay, because it'll keep the focus off Josh."

She looked scared to death. It hurt to see. Didn't she know? I'd let Loretta beat me senseless with a gravy bowl before I'd let anything bad happen to Chloe or her little brother. I was trying to put that into words when Chloe spoke again. "I'm sorry." She hesitated. "You don't mind, do you?"

Mind? Hell no. I was looking forward to it. "Nope," I said. "This'll be fun."

"I'm serious." Chloe gave me a worried look. "She's a total

psycho."

    "Yeah?" For her sake, I smiled. "Haven't you heard? I am too." □

CHAPTER 55

Less than a minute later, we squealed into the driveway of a nice two-story brick house. Actually, it was more than nice, with a manicured lawn, a four-car garage, and a partial view of the cottage out back.

It wasn't the hood, that was for damn sure.

In fact, the place was just as nice as the house where Chloe had been house-sitting. I eyed the whole setup with disgust. I knew the prices of homes in my neighborhood. They didn't come cheap. And neither had this one, obviously.

What the hell? So Chloe's dad was living high on the hog while his daughter was practically homeless? That whole ass-beating idea was sounding better every minute.

In the front window, I caught movement. I cut the engine and looked to Chloe, letting her set the pace. As pissed off as I was, I had to remind myself of everything else she had told me. If I created a scene, I wouldn't be doing Chloe or her little brother any favors.

And beating her dad's ass definitely qualified as a scene. Unfortunately. So I waited, trying to fake a civility that I wasn't feeling.

Chloe blew out a nervous breath. "C'mon," she said, shoving open the passenger's side door. Salad in hand, she jumped out of the car and waited as I circled around to grab the two desserts from the back.

By the time we reached the front door, it was already open. A skinny kid, Josh, obviously, was standing in the open doorway. He was dressed in dark slacks, a white dress shirt, and damn, even a tie. Boy, they really *did* dress up, didn't they? Shit, when I'd been twelve, I didn't even *own* a tie.

Josh was giving Chloe a worried look. With a quick glance over his shoulder, he stepped out of the house and shut the door behind him. "You made it," he said.

Chloe gave him a smile that looked a little too nervous for my liking. "Told you I would."

Josh lowered his voice. "She was just about to lock you out."

He didn't say who *she* was, but I had a pretty good guess.

Chloe's smile was still plastered in place. "Good thing I found myself a fast driver then." She cleared her throat. "Speaking of which, this is Lawton, my, uh, friend." She turned to me and said, "This is Josh."

I held out my free hand. "So you're the genius Chloe's always talking about."

"Aw, I don't know about that," Josh said, looking down at his shoes.

Chloe leaned closer to Josh and said, "You look good."

Josh looked up. "Thanks. So do you." He reached up to tug at his tie. "I wanted to wear jeans." He shrugged. "But you know."

Chloe nodded like she knew exactly what he meant. And then, as if she and her brother were thinking the same thing, they both turned to look at me. They paused, like they didn't know what to say.

I was still holding the dessert boxes. They were a decent size, but not nearly big enough to hide the obvious. Unlike Chloe and her brother, I sure as hell wasn't dressed up.

My clothes were trash, and my sleeves were short. I glanced down, taking in my tattoos, the grease stains on my white T-shirt, and the rips in my ancient jeans. If I were meeting Chloe's dad under any other circumstance, I'd be embarrassed as hell.

But the way I saw it, the guy had a lot more to be ashamed of than I did. And besides, if my ratty-ass appearance took the negative attention off Josh, that was fine by me.

Josh was staring down at my bare knees, visible through the shredded denim. He blew out a low whistle. "She's gonna totally chew you up."

Loretta? Eh, she could try. Looking to make the point, I grinned over at him. "Who?"

Behind Josh, the door swung open fast and hard, hitting the doorstopper with a loud clang.

"Her," Chloe muttered under her breath.

Standing in the open doorway was a thin, middle-aged woman with short brown hair, Loretta, obviously. She gave Chloe a cold look. "You think I can't hear you?"

Chloe froze like a deer in headlights. She didn't say it, but I could tell what she was thinking. *Busted.*

Looking to take the attention off Chloe, I shifted the boxes in my hands. Instantly, Loretta's head swiveled in my direction. She gave me a long, disgusted look, starting at the top of my head and finishing at the tattered edges of my grease-stained jeans.

When she finally looked up, her lips were pursed, and her eyes were narrowed to cold, hard slits. She leaned around me and made a show of looking at the driveway. "Who are you?" she said. "The tow truck driver?"

Right, because that busted-up hot-rod was really a tow-truck in disguise.

Next to me, Chloe cleared her throat. "Loretta, I'd like you to meet Lawton. My friend, and uh, my ride."

"I see." Loretta was pursing her lips again. "Lorton, is it?"

Nice try, I thought. I'd played that game myself, and there was no way in hell I was going to give her the reaction she wanted. "Close enough," I said, holding out my hand.

Loretta looked down at the hand, but didn't take it. "Are you some kind of mechanic?"

"You could say that." With a shrug, I lowered my hand. "Just part-time though. You know how it is."

"No," she said with a sniff. "I'm afraid I don't." She glanced again toward the driveway. "I assume you're also providing our Chloe with a ride home?"

I grinned. "Definitely."

And in the meantime, I'd be staying for dinner, because there was no way in hell I was leaving Chloe to fend for herself. One way or another, I was getting inside that house. If possible, I'd do it the nice way. If that didn't pan out, well, I guess we'd see.

Loretta glanced at her watch. "Fine. But don't be later than two o'clock." She turned to Chloe and said, "Will you be waiting for him in the driveway? Or shall he knock on the door?"

"Actually," Chloe said, "he's my guest. You said I could bring one?"

Loretta opened her mouth, but before any words came out, a different female voice squealed out, "Oh my God!" A brunette, maybe around Chloe's age, appeared just past Loretta's shoulder. Based on the resemblance, this had to be Lauren Jane, Loretta's natural daughter, as Chloe had called her.

Lauren Jane was staring me. "Is that–? Are you?" She looked to Chloe and asked, "Is that Lawton Rastor?"

Loretta whirled around to face her daughter. In a hushed voice, she asked, "Who's Lawton Rastor?"

"Oh my God, Mom, he's only like a zillionaire," Lauren Jane said, not bothering to lower her voice. "I can't believe you didn't know that. I mean, jeez, have you been living under a rock or something?"

Loretta turned to give me a quick glance before turning back to Lauren Jane. "Him?" Loretta hissed. "You can't be serious."

Lauren Jane snorted. "I am, too. God, you are *so* embarrassing." She looked over to me and said, "Sorry, she doesn't get out much." She turned back to her mom and said, "For God's sake, Mom, there's this thing called the internet. Use it sometimes, okay?"

Loretta's mouth tightened. "Lauren, I don't appreciate—"

"Mom!" Lauren Jane rolled her eyes. "It's Lauren *Jane* now. Remember?"

"Of course I remember," Loretta said. "I was the one who named you."

"You were not," Lauren Jane said. "It was dad who named me. Remember him? The guy you left for some salesman?"

"He's not a salesman," Loretta said through gritted teeth. "He's a commercial real estate broker."

"Whatever," Lauren Jane said. She turned back to me and smiled. "Hey, I heard you just bought a killer mansion around here. Does it have a hot tub?" She elbowed her way forward, past Loretta. "Because I just bought a new bikini. You wanna see it?"

I shrugged. "Maybe after dinner."

It was a load of bull. I had no interest in Lauren Jane's bikini or anything else that she might wear. From what Chloe had told me in the car, combined with what I'd seen with my own eyes, this girl wasn't someone I wanted to see more of.

Besides, there was only one girl I wanted to see in a bikini, and she was standing next to me, holding a salad. I gave it a quick look. Correction, half a salad. The rest was still on the floor of the passenger's seat. It was too bad, in a way. I'd have liked to see Loretta eating the grubby lettuce off my dirty floor mat.

In fact, I'd like to see that woman eating a lot of things. The gravy story was still pissing me off. I glanced over at Josh. He seemed like a nice kid, *too* nice to live with a woman like that.

Loretta cleared her throat. "Chloe," she said, "Don't just stand there. Show our guest inside, will you?" Loretta gave me a thin smile. "You try to teach them manners, but..." She let out a long-suffering sigh. "What's a person to do?"

I knew what Loretta could do. But it would be a mistake to spell it out, so I let Chloe lead me inside. The way it looked, it was meet-the-parent time.

CHAPTER 56

Ten minutes later, we were seated around a long, oval table in their formal dining room. Chloe's dad was at one end, and Loretta was at the other. As for me, I was seated between Josh and Lauren Jane, who had dragged her chair so close that our elbows were touching.

I looked up, catching Chloe's eye across the table. She gave me a shaky smile that went straight to my heart. She looked nervous. I wasn't. Whatever might happen today, I knew I was in the right place, because it meant that Chloe wasn't here alone, and neither was her brother.

At the foot of the table, Loretta shook out a cloth napkin and settled it over her lap. She gave Chloe a stiff smile and said, "We're all *so* glad you could make it, Chloe."

Right. Because nothing says "welcome," like locking someone out.

With a little laugh, Loretta glanced around the table and added, "We were just about to send out the cavalry." She looked to Chloe's dad and said, "Weren't we, Dick?"

Dick. Yeah, the name fit.

Within five minutes of walking in the door, I had Chloe's dad pegged for the loser that he was. From what I'd seen so far, he was a pompous blowhard who liked to pretend he was someone important. Too bad he wasn't. The way I saw it, any guy who treated his daughter like garbage was a nobody, no matter where he lived or how much money he made.

As for Loretta, she'd apparently decided that I was the real deal and worth sucking up to. Already, my ass had been kissed so many times, it was a miracle I could sit at all.

At the head of the table, Chloe's dad was nodding like his wife had just said something brilliant. In a big, booming voice, he said, "Anything for our little Chloe." He gave me a man-to-man smile and said, "It sure wouldn't be a family dinner without her."

What an asshole.

Just ten minutes earlier, he'd been willing to lock out his daughter for being one minute late. And now, he was acting like dad-of-the-year? I wasn't buying it. But I couldn't exactly call him on it, so I kept my thoughts to myself and hoped like hell that the look on my face didn't match what I was thinking.

Next to me, Lauren Jane reached out and ran a finger along my forearm. "I like your tattoos," she said. "Do you have more?"

Yeah. But she wasn't gonna see them.

I was spared the trouble of answering when Chloe jumped up and blurted out, "Who's ready for salad?"

The table was packed with plates, bowls and silverware, but no actual food. Apparently, we were eating the meal in courses. What those courses were, I had no idea, because everything edible was laid out on a sideboard against the dining room wall.

Each dish was covered with a big silver lid. It was like hotel room service, without the wheeled cart. I glanced over at Loretta, wondering if she'd be expecting a tip for this.

I had a tip for her. Stop being shitty to your step-kids.

Chloe hurried to the sideboard and snagged the salad. She carried the bowl over to Loretta and held it out, as if waiting for Loretta to serve herself some.

Loretta was frowning. "Where's the rest of it?"

Chloe bit her lip. "Well, you see, on the way here—"

"I ate it," I said.

Loretta turned toward me and said, "Pardon?"

"I thought it was a snack." I shrugged. "Sorry."

Loretta's gaze narrowed. Chloe was still holding the bowl.

Loretta looked up and asked Chloe, "Is that true?"

But it wasn't Chloe who answered. It was Lauren Jane who said, "Oh Mom, of course it's true." When I turned to look, Lauren Jane was licking her lips. "I mean," she continued, "just look at this guy."

She gave me a long, lingering look that started at my pecs and ended at my abs. Probably, it would've gone lower if it weren't for the tablecloth that hid most of my lap. She licked her lips again and said, "You don't get a body like that on cheeseburgers."

Chloe choked back a laugh. I knew why. As far as I was concerned, cheeseburgers were one of the three basic food groups, right between steak and French fries.

Loretta gave Chloe an annoyed look. "Is something funny?"

Chloe shook her head. "Nope. Sorry."

With a little sniff, Loretta finally took the bowl from Chloe's hands and started serving herself some salad. She nodded toward Chloe's chair and said, "Sit. Please." With a stiff smile, Loretta added, "We'll just pass the courses around, family style." She looked around and said, "Now, isn't this nice?"

I felt a warm hand on my bicep. "Mmm…it sure is," Lauren Jane said in a low, husky voice. I'd been taking a drink of my wine, and had to stop in mid-motion to keep from spilling it. Lauren Jane tightened her grip. "You must work out like crazy. Just how much *can* you lift, anyway?"

On the other side of me, Josh spoke up. "Wait, I know this. Three-hundred pounds."

Everyone turned to look.

Josh shrugged. "I read it on the internet."

Chloe was still standing in the same spot as before. She glanced from me to Lauren Jane, whose hand was still squeezing my bicep.

Well, at least it wasn't my cock. Yet.

"Chloe dear," Loretta said, "will you be taking your seat any time soon?"

Chloe looked around the table. As if shaking off a distraction, she returned to her seat and watched the salad making its rounds. When the bowl got to Lauren Jane, she finally let go of my arm and grabbed the salad bowl with both hands.

She dumped most of the remaining lettuce onto her salad plate, leaving almost nothing for anyone else. That was fine by me. It's not like I was a huge fan of the stuff. When she passed the nearly empty bowl to me, I passed it to Josh without taking any.

"You don't want any?" Josh asked.

"Nah. I'm good," I told him. "Since I already ate half on the way." I lowered my voice. "Don't tell anyone, but there was also this chocolate cake."

Josh's eyes widened. "Seriously?"

"Yeah," I said. "And a side of beef, couple of hams." I shrugged. "A pie. A dozen donuts. After that, I lost track."

"Oh, you," Lauren Jane said with a playful swat to my arm. "Stop teasing that boy. He'll believe anything."

"No I won't," Josh said.

"Josh," Loretta said, "don't sass your sister. It's not polite."

Josh looked to his plate. "Sorry."

I felt my blood pressure rise. Polite? What would Loretta know about it? Looking to make Josh smile again, I leaned toward him and spoke so low that only he could hear, "Don't tell, but there was a slab of bacon, too. But eh, your sister snagged it first."

Josh was looking happier until his step-mother's voice cut across the table. "Lawton? Care to share with the rest of us?"

Nope. I sure as hell didn't.

I put on my clueless face and said, "You mean salad?" I looked down at my empty salad plate. "Sorry, I didn't take any." I turned to Lauren Jane, whose plate was overflowing. "How about you? Got any spare salad for your mom?"

She gave her plate a worried look. "There's not that much here."

Hey, there's more on my floor mat. Want me to get it, so you can really make an ass of yourself?

Loretta spoke up, sounding irritated as hell. "That's not necessary. I wasn't referring to—" She made a little huffing sound. "Oh, never mind."

When the salad reached Chloe, she took two small pieces of lettuce and stood to return the bowl to the sideboard. Now *that* was the girl I loved. I leaned closer to Josh and said, "You know, your sister's pretty awesome."

On the other side of me, Lauren Jane spoke up. "Thanks. I think *you're* awesome, too." She pressed her knee closer to mine and whispered, "And just so you know, my bikini's *really* skimpy."

What bikini? Oh yeah, the one she mentioned when we first showed up. Like I cared.

"Bummer," I said. "You should get that looked at."

She gave me a confused look. "Huh?"

It wasn't *supposed* to make sense. It was supposed to distract her so I could focus on the sister who *was* awesome. I watched as Chloe returned to her seat. She looked good in that dress. When she leaned forward to retrieve her napkin, I saw a hint of cleavage that made me swallow.

I couldn't help but wonder, what kind of bra was she wearing today? She had great taste in bras, sweet and sexy, just like everything else about her. Undressing her was like unwrapping a present. And back when she'd been mine, it was like every day was my birthday.

Somehow, by the end of the day, I'd win her back. She loved me. And I loved her. The other stuff was just bullshit, and whatever it took, we'd work it out. Watching her across the table, I wanted to smile.

Now *Chloe* in a bikini, that was something I *did* care about. She had this yellow one that drove me crazy when it got wet. It wasn't even that skimpy, but the way it hugged her curves when it was weighted down with water, well, it was something that I liked a lot.

I wanted to smile. The last time she'd worn it, I'd taken it off with my teeth and kissed her in all the spots it had been covering. At the memory, I felt an embarrassing tightness in my jeans.

Great. Because nothing says Happy Thanksgiving like a good old-fashioned boner.

Suddenly, I felt a hand grip my thigh. I looked across the table. Unless Chloe's arms had tripled in length, the hand *wasn't* hers.

I looked over at Lauren Jane, who was attacking her salad with one hand, and yup, sure enough, attacking my thigh with the other.

I pretended not to notice. If nothing else, she'd solved my boner problem.

Thanks Lauren Jane, you lettuce-loving psycho.

I looked up, and caught Chloe watching me. Thanks to the long tablecloth, she'd have no idea what Lauren Jane was doing. And I didn't *want* her to know, because she sure as hell didn't need one more thing to worry about.

Looking to make her smile, I grinned over at her. When she smiled back, I wanted to lean across the table and kiss away all the bullshit, including her sorry excuse for a family – well, except for Josh. And as far as him, he deserved better, too.

I was just thinking of what I could do to help when Chloe's dad boomed across the table. "So I hear you're some kind of fighter."

Shit. Unless he was referring to Lauren Jane and her epic battle with the salad, he must be talking to me. Slowly, I turned to look at him. He was giving me another man-to-man smile.

I didn't smile back. "Yup."

His smile faltered. "You're not gonna try any of those fancy punches on me now, are you?"

"Nope." And then, I *did* smile, but not in a friendly way. "At least not 'til dessert."

His eyebrows furrowed, and then he laughed, a big booming sound that sounded fake as hell. "Hah!" He shot me with both index fingers. "You got me there."

Next to me, Lauren Jane giggled. She leaned her head close to mine and said, "You're so funny." She turned to Chloe's dad and called out, "You'd better watch it, Daddy, or he's gonna get you."

Yeah. Maybe I would.

CHAPTER 57

Lauren Jane turned her attention back to me. "Speaking of funny things," she said, leaning closer, "did you notice that *your* name begins with an 'L' and *my* name begins with an 'L'?"

Yeah. Just like lettuce begins with an "L". Big deal.

Lauren Jane glanced across the table and said in a snotty voice, "Sorry, Chloe. I guess you're not in the club."

From the look on Chloe's face, she'd like a club alright, but not the kind you joined.

Chloe's dad spoke up. "Uh-oh. *My* gal's name begins with an 'L', too." With a big chuckle, he shook his index finger at me. "But you don't be stealing my Loretta."

Reluctantly, I shifted my gaze to Loretta. Shit. The way it looked, she was giving it some thought. Nice. More boner-prevention.

Across from me, Chloe jumped up from her seat and blurted out, "Want me to get the turkey?"

Loretta's mouth tightened. She gave Chloe a cold look. "Are *you* the hostess?"

Chloe froze. "No. But I'm happy to help." She hesitated. "Unless you'd rather do it?"

With a sigh, Loretta pushed back her chair and stood. "So much for a relaxing dinner. Chloe, will you please sit? You're making everyone nervous."

When Chloe sat back down, Loretta – with all the dignity of an English butler – started delivering the covered platters to the table.

One by one, she lifted each silver lid and told us what we were looking at. There was turkey, mashed potatoes, corn, stuffing, and more platters to come.

As for everyone else, they were busy too, telling Loretta how great everything looked, or smelled, or whatever.

For Chloe's sake, I played along with the rest of them. Funny, if this were someplace else, I might be having a great time. But there was something about this whole scene that just wasn't right.

I started wondering if we could invite Josh over to spend the night at my place, and conveniently forget to return him.

I might not look it, but I was good with kids. And I liked Chloe's brother. More to the point, I loved his sister, and I could tell she was worried about him. It would be nice to change that.

Loretta was still delivering platters. Across from me, Chloe's gaze kept drifting to the mashed potatoes. She was biting her lip again, and I knew why. With mashed potatoes, there was usually gravy. But today was Thanksgiving, and there was a turkey right there in front of us. That meant we'd be having *turkey* gravy.

Not oyster gravy. Not shit-in-a bowl gravy. And no other weird-ass gravy that Loretta might dream up.

Next to me, Josh had grown still and quiet. I didn't want to look, because I didn't want to make the kid uncomfortable. But with every dish, the tension around the table was growing. I could feel it in the air in spite of all the compliments that were still flowing Loretta's way.

The only one who seemed oblivious was Lauren Jane who started blathering on about a recent trip to Cancun. I pretended to listen while I watched Loretta bring out the final platter, a small one with a tall silver lid. She lifted the lid, and there it was, a small gravy boat filled to the rim.

But what kind of gravy was it? I couldn't tell. And from the look on Chloe's face, neither could she.

"And then," Lauren Jane said with a giggle, "we got totally drunk and stole his sombrero."

Screw the sombrero. I looked to Loretta, waiting to see what she'd say next. What kind of gravy was it?

For fuck's sake, just tell us already.

"And finally," Loretta said, "my very own holiday specialty." She gave Chloe a thin smile. "Oyster gravy."

Fuck.

And this is when Lauren Jane went for my cock.

CHAPTER 58

I froze. Her hand was pressed tight against my crotch, looking for an erection that wasn't there – and wasn't *going* to be there, not for her.

Now normally, a hand on your privates is a hard thing to ignore. But that's exactly what I did, because something even more disturbing was going on.

I gave Chloe a quick glance. She looked pale as death as she stared at that fucking gravy. Next to me, Josh was silent, staring down at his empty plate – probably hoping it would *stay* empty, at least of fish barf.

As for Lauren Jane, she was surprisingly good at multi-tasking, because she was still yammering on about her trip to Cancun, even as her hand ground tighter against the crotch of my jeans.

Whatever. She could root around all she wanted, she wasn't going to find anything interesting. And soon, she'd be needing that hand to pass the dishes. Thank God.

I gave Chloe's stepmother a sideways glance. She'd returned to her seat and was giving Chloe a smug look, almost like, "Yeah. It's oyster gravy. What are *you* gonna do about it?"

Didn't she know? Chloe wasn't going to do anything, because *I* would. Silently, I ran through my options. I recalled what Chloe had said about the last time, that she'd put up a fight, only to see Josh pay the price afterwards.

So, that ruled out beating someone's ass. Unfortunately.

We could take Josh and get the hell out of here. But then what? Some judge would make us return him, and he'd be eating oyster gravy every day until he was eighteen. That meant we had to stay, and we had to keep it friendly.

I studied Loretta from the corner of my eye. The way it looked, she was spoiling for a scene, maybe even a fight.

A fight – that didn't scare me. I'd welcome it. But there'd be collateral damage, and it wouldn't fall on me. It would fall on the girl I loved and a kid who didn't deserve this kind of treatment.

As far as the gravy, that left only one option. I had to get rid of it the old-fashioned way. And then, I'd need to get the hell out of here fast, but not so fast that it would piss anyone off.

"So," Lauren Jane was saying, "we're wearing these matching bikinis, and some guy staggers up to us, and says, 'Hey, are there two of you? Or am I seeing double?'"

Her hand was still there, pressed up against my crotch. Nothing was happening, and it wasn't *going* to happen. It especially wasn't going to happen while I eyeballed fish barf in a fancy bowl.

While Lauren Jane blathered on, I did the math in my head. Fifteen minutes to eat, ten minutes to visit afterward, fifteen minutes to get to the hospital, and then what? An hour for stomach-pumping or whatever?

Hey, I'd survived worse. In a few hours, I'd be as good as new, or at least that was the idea. I'd just need to hit the hospital in time. Not a problem. I was a fast driver with a fast car. Whatever it took, I'd make it happen.

I had to. Because I couldn't stand the idea of seeing Chloe – or her little brother – being abused like that.

I loved her. And I *owed* her. Twice, I'd accused her of horrible things that weren't true. I'd doubted her. I'd made her feel like trash. If it came down to it, I'd take a bullet for her – not because of our fights, but because I loved her more than life itself.

I glanced at the gravy. Yeah, it was a bullet, alright.

Next to me, Lauren Jane giggled. "And I told the guy, if you think *this* one's skimpy, you should see the Brazilian. And *he* thought I meant a Brazilian girl, so he's looking around, like 'Where?' And so

I point to my bikini bottom and say, 'Right here.' But the guy's *still* looking around, and we're totally laughing at him, but he *still* doesn't get it." She rolled her eyes. "God, he was *so* dense."

I was only half listening. I gave Chloe another quick glance. She was staring at Josh with such concern that it tugged at my heart. All this time, I'd had Chloe pegged as something different, a rich girl with no worries. Come to find out, her life was more complicated than I ever imagined.

And I loved her all the more for it.

Next to me, Lauren Jane made a sound of impatience. "Lawton? Are you listening?"

To her? Not if I could help it.

Still, I made myself say, "Sorry, what was that?'

"I *asked* if you wanna see it."

"See what?"

She gave a sigh of irritation. "My bikini."

"Why?" I gave her a look. "You wearing it now?"

"No. But I have a picture. It's right here on my phone." She lowered her voice. "We're not supposed to have phones at the table, but they don't need to know *everything*, right?" As she said this, she gave my crotch an extra squeeze – for all the good it did.

If I was lucky, she'd need *both* hands to work that phone of hers, because the longer this went on, the more I was thinking that oyster gravy might be just the thing to put me out of my misery.

"Sure," I said. "Let's see it."

Finally, her hand left my crotch. She looked down at her lap and started doing something under the tablecloth. Whatever it was, I was just glad my privates weren't involved.

She was still looking down when Chloe's dad spoke up. "Lauren Jane? Potatoes?"

With a sigh, Lauren Jane stopped doing whatever and took the bowl from his outstretched hands. She spooned some potatoes onto her plate, and then, as she passed the bowl to me, she whispered, "I'll show you after dessert."

Yeah, right. That's what *she* thought.

The other dishes were still making their way around the table –

except for one. The gravy. It was just sitting there, like a stinking turd in the punchbowl of this family freak-show.

I knew exactly how this was supposed to play out. The gravy was supposed to sit there, making Chloe and Josh uncomfortable until it was time for Loretta to make a scene. And then, her two step-kids would have to eat it, whether they wanted to or not.

Fuck that.

I reached over and picked up the gravy boat. Ignoring the smell of rotten fish, I gave its contents a good, long look. I saw chunks of something that could only be oysters – a type of shellfish, unfortunately. For me, anyway.

As I looked at the stuff, a new thought hit me. If I played my cards right, Loretta wouldn't be thinking this was so fancy after all. And maybe, just maybe, she'd be too embarrassed to make it again. Liking that thought, I felt a real smile spread across my face.

Showtime.

CHAPTER 59

I looked over at Loretta. "You said oyster gravy, right?" I took a big whiff of it and grinned. "My favorite. Did you know, my great-grandma, she was a fishwife on the Detroit river, this was her specialty too?"

Loretta froze. From the look on her face, she wasn't flattered by the comparison.

Good. It's not like it was true, anyway.

Loretta bared her teeth. "How nice."

I shrugged. "Not really. She stunk like fish something awful. But man, she made the best gravy." As I spoke, I ladled a heaping helping of it onto my mashed potatoes, and then kept on going, one ladle after another.

There wasn't a whole lot of it, and I knew why. Only two people were expected to eat it, Chloe and Josh. But I wasn't going to give them the chance. I kept ladling until the bowl was empty. I looked to Loretta and tried like hell to look disappointed. "This wasn't all of it, was it?"

Her mouth tightened. "I'm afraid it was."

I looked down at my plate. "Oh jeez. I'm sorry." I lifted my plate and held it out toward Loretta. "You want mine?"

My plate wasn't even close to her face. Still, she leaned her head back like the stuff was pure poison.

Yeah, I knew the feeling.

I was still holding out the plate. I nudged it closer. "Or, we could share?"

"No," she stammered. "That won't be necessary. But thank you."

"Oh well. More for me." And then, I dug in.

Fish barf. Yup, that was pretty good description. There was no way in fuck this shit was considered a delicacy – at least not the way Loretta made it. But that was probably the point, wasn't it?

As I shoveled it in, I gave Chloe a quick glance. From the look on her face, she didn't know whether to argue or cheer. I gave her my best cocky grin and kept on going.

I didn't want her to worry. And I knew she would, especially if she knew exactly why I avoided seafood. Looking for a distraction, I glanced around the table. No one was moving. They were just sitting there, watching me eat.

Between bites, I said, "You guys are eating too, right?"

Chloe, looking suddenly embarrassed, grabbed her fork and started eating. Soon, everyone except for Loretta joined in.

Chloe's dad looked over at me and said, "Boy, you sure have a good appetite."

"Can't help it," I said. "I never eat this good at home." I made myself smile. "And if the tabloids are true, I have two French chefs."

It wasn't true. Yeah, I could afford a whole houseful of French chefs, but why would I bother? The way I heard it, they couldn't make a decent cheeseburger to save their lives.

A cheeseburger – too bad I wasn't eating one of those now. The gravy was chunky – and worse, slimy in a way that just wasn't natural. As I ate, I tried to imagine it was something else. *Anything* else.

But I couldn't. It was that bad, not that it mattered in the long run. It wasn't the taste that would kill me. Choking down my disgust, I shoveled in the last few bites and made myself swallow – all without hurling it back up again.

I was actually pretty proud of myself.

I looked to Chloe's dad and his heaping plate of gravy-free food. That fucker. What kind of guy doesn't look out for his own kids?

He was digging into his mashed potatoes, looking happy as hell. "Two chefs, you say? Lucky me, all I need is Loretta."

I looked to Loretta. So did everyone else. She hadn't even touched her food.

"Gee Mom," Lauren Jane said, "aren't you gonna eat anything? You're not on another diet, are you?"

"No," Loretta said through clenched teeth. "I'm not on a diet."

Chloe's dad spoke up. "Then dig in, honey. This is some darn good eatin'."

What the hell was that? His cowboy voice? I recalled what Chloe had told me in the car, that he tried to mimic his guests in some sort of bonding ritual.

Across the table, Chloe was looking more embarrassed with every minute. I didn't want her to be. I wanted her to smile.

I grinned over at her. I leaned back and rubbed my stomach. "It shore is, ma'am," I said, looking to Loretta. "Mighty thanks."

Loretta pursed her lips, but said nothing.

"Gee Mom," Lauren Jane said, "aren't you gonna say 'you're welcome?'" Lauren Jane leaned her head close to mine and said in a loud whisper. "Parents can be so rude."

Loretta glared across the table. "So can daughters."

"Well," Lauren Jane said in a snotty tone, "at least I say you're welcome when someone thanks me."

After a long, tense silence, Loretta cleared her throat. "Lawton, I apologize. Of course, you are quite welcome.'"

"See?" Chloe's dad said. "Now honey-bun, was that so hard?" He pounded his fist on the table. "Now what do you say we rustle up some dessert?"

Shit. That's right. Dessert. The clock was ticking. How long had it been since I'd choked down that godawful gravy? Five, ten minutes? I glanced at my watch. In fifteen minutes, we'd need to get the hell out of here no matter what.

Chloe stood. "Dessert? I'll get it." She looked toward Loretta. "Unless you'd rather?"

Loretta waved a loose hand toward the desserts. "Go ahead. Whatever." She reached up to rub her temples with both index fingers. "I give up."

Chloe picked up the dessert dishes and started serving up cheesecake and cobbler to everyone at the table. When she got to me, I waved it away. I wasn't feeling so good, and there was no way I could choke down anything else, no matter how great it might've tasted otherwise. "None for me, thanks."

She gave me a worried look. "You sure?"

My tongue was feeling too dry and a little too thick. I nodded and reached for my water-glass. It was nearly full, but I downed the whole thing in one long, gulp. Chloe reached for the water-pitcher and filled my glass.

When I looked up, her eyes were troubled. I forced out a smile and said, "Thanks, dumplin'."

She snickered and then caught herself, turning it into a poor imitation of throat-clearing.

Lauren Jane stuck her head between us and smiled over at me. "Oh you," she said, giving me another swat on my arm.

Hey, it was better than a grab to the crotch.

Lauren Jane made a pouty face at me. "How come you never call *me* dumpling?"

Suddenly, Loretta blurted out, "Stop it! I don't know what's gotten in to all of you, but I've just about had it."

Chloe's dad eyed her with concern. "What's wrong, Sugar Cube?"

Loretta glared at him. "I. Am. Not. Your. Sugar. Cube." And then, as if realizing she was making an ass of herself, she gave him a tight smile. "Alright?"

He held up his hands, surrender-style. "Woah. Hear ya loud and clear, chief. No more sugar cubes." He looked around the table. "Got that, everyone?"

"Oh for Heaven's sake," Loretta muttered, reaching for her wine glass.

Lauren Jane ignored her mom and turned back to me. "So, you and my sister are just friends, right?"

I glanced around the table. They were still eating dessert. The way it looked, we couldn't leave yet, so I might as well make it count. I grinned across the table. "Chloe? You wanna answer that one?"

She smiled back. "Not particularly."

Ignoring Chloe, Lauren Jane turned back to me and said, "So how'd you two meet? Was she your waitress or something?"

I leaned back in my chair. "Nope."

Chloe's dad gave another slap to the table. "Don't be shy, son. Go on. Tell us how you two met."

I looked to Chloe. "Chloe, you wanna tell the story?"

Her mouth opened, but no words came out. From the look on her face, she didn't know what story to tell. But *I* did, and it wasn't a story that Chloe had heard before.

But it was still the truth.

"Never mind," I said. Going for a casual move, I leaned forward, trying to ease the cramping in my stomach. "Lemme tell it."

CHAPTER 60

I looked around the table. Chloe downed the rest of her wine, and Josh was grinning like he was actually having a good time. And in that moment, I knew that whatever happened, it would be totally worth it.

As for the rest of them – Chloe's dipshit of a dad, her stepmother from hell, and her grabby, lettuce-loving step-sister – I didn't care what they thought, as long they weren't giving Chloe or Josh grief.

With another glance around the table, I started talking. "It was right after this underground fight in downtown Detroit. I'd just had the worst beating of my life. Total massacre. And I'm lying there in a pool of my own blood–"

"Oh for the love of God," Loretta muttered.

"Mom!" Lauren Jane said. "Don't interrupt." She gripped my arm. "It's just getting good." She squeezed my arm tighter and said, "Go on. We're all dying to hear the rest of it."

I smiled over at Chloe. "And I look up, and I saw this girl, and she was the most beautiful thing I'd ever seen."

Next to me, Lauren Jane asked, "Who was she?"

On my other side, Josh spoke up. "It was Chloe. Wasn't it?"

I nodded. "Yup." I turned to Josh. "And you know what?"

"What?" he asked.

"She probably saved my life."

"I knew it!" Josh said.

Loretta was frowning at us. "That's some story."

Yeah. And it was all true. When I glanced at Chloe, she was smiling like she knew I was full of it, but was too polite to say so.

I held up a hand, palm out. "All true, I swear."

Lauren Jane snorted. "But you've never lost a fight in your life." She turned and announced to the whole table, "I know everything about him, probably even more than Chloe."

Yeah. Because random groping, along with whatever she read on the internet, made her some kind of expert. What a dumb-ass.

Across the table, Chloe choked back a laugh. The sound of it warmed me to the bone and made me almost forget how shitty I was feeling in every other way.

Lauren Jane gave Chloe a dirty look. "What's so funny?"

Chloe blinked. "Nothing." She patted her throat. "Chicken bone."

"But we had turkey," Lauren Jane said.

"Oh," Chloe said. "Turkey bone then."

Under the table, I felt that fucking hand grip my thigh again. I stiffened, and not in the way she wanted. It was one thing to ignore it earlier when I felt okay. But now, I was feeling less okay with every minute.

It was too damn hot in here, and a hand anywhere wasn't going to cool off anything. When the hand inched higher, I reached under the table and shoved the hand aside. I turned and gave her a warning look.

"What?" Lauren Jane whispered.

Across the table, Chloe was gathering up the dessert dishes. Glad for the noisy distraction, I leaned closer to Lauren Jane and said under my breath. "Grab me again, and you'll be wearing that gravy I just ate."

She froze, looking surprised and more than a little insulted. Yeah, whatever. *She* was the skank groping her step-sister's date.

After a long moment, she whispered, "How about the picture? Still wanna see it?"

Fuck no. I didn't want to see it. I turned away without

answering.

With a sound of irritation, Lauren Jane announced, "I'm bored."

Loretta spoke up. "Then maybe you can do the dishes."

"But I don't wanna do the dishes," Lauren Jane whined. "I know. Make Chloe do it." She turned to Chloe. "I mean, you're used to it, right?"

What the hell? No. That wasn't going to happen. And besides, the clock wasn't just ticking. It had run out. If we didn't leave now, it would be Chloe driving *me*, and not the other way around.

I pushed back my chair and said, "Sorry, but Chloe and I have to get going."

Loretta frowned. "Why?"

"Prior engagement," I said. "A thing at the hospital. You understand, right?"

I knew exactly what she'd make of it. She'd assume it was some charity thing and then use that assumption to make herself feel important. I knew the type.

Sure enough, Loretta said, "Oh. Of course."

Chloe's dad pushed back his chair and stood. "I guess we'll let you two cowpokes head on down the trail, then."

Loretta slammed down her wine glass. "Oh for Heaven's sake, Dick. Enough already!"

He gave her a blank look. "What?"

I looked to Chloe. "You ready?"

She glanced at Josh, who was still smiling. She glanced at Loretta, who was glaring at her dad. She glanced at her dad, who had sat back down and was reaching for more dessert. She glanced at Lauren Jane, who was scrolling through her phone, probably looking for that stupid bikini picture.

Shit, for all I knew, it was a full beaver shot, minus the bikini.

"Lauren Jane!" Loretta said. "For the last time, no phones at the table."

Lauren Jane mimicked her mother. "No phones at the table."

"Young lady," Loretta said. "Are you mocking me?"

Chloe, looking amused as hell, turned to me and said, "Yup, I'm ready." Looking to Josh, she asked, "Wanna walk us out to the car?"

At the table, the argument between Loretta and her daughter was heating up. We heard words like "old bag" and "ungrateful snot," followed by a threat to cut Lauren Jane's allowance.

It should've been funny, but it mostly pissed me off. All this time, Chloe had been hurting for money. Where was *her* allowance?

I had to ask. "She *still* gets an allowance?"

Chloe shrugged. "Maybe not for long."

By the time we reached the front door, the argument had turned into a wrestling match, with Lauren Jane gripping the phone with both hands while Loretta tried to pry it away. If there was any justice, the phone *did* have a beaver shot, and Loretta was about to get a good eyeful.

As sick as I felt, I had to smile. It would serve both of them right. As I opened the door, I turned to see Chloe's dad shoveling more cobbler into his face, not bothering to say goodbye to the daughter who brought it.

What a tool.

When we reached the driveway, Chloe hugged Josh goodbye, and I shook his hand, man-to-man.

He grinned over at us. "Best Thanksgiving, ever."

I glanced toward the house. If I had anything to do with it, it would be the last Thanksgiving dinner either Chloe *or* Josh ate at *that* place. But now, I had to get the hell out of here, and fast. My skin felt funny, and my tongue was getting that thick feeling again. Somehow, I knew that water wouldn't be solving anything this time around.

When we pulled out of the driveway a minute later, Chloe was smiling in the way I loved best. "You know what?" she said. "You're right. That *was* fun."

I hit the accelerator. "Told ya."

She laughed. "Oh my God. That whole story about how we met—" She shook her head. "Where'd you come up with that? I can't decide if I should kiss you or scold you for lying."

"Baby," I said, "I'm a lot of things, but a liar isn't one of them."

"Yeah, right," she teased.

In that moment, I wanted to tell her everything – how we met, how I'd been thinking about her for years, and how, if she just gave us another chance, I wouldn't screw it up this time. But I couldn't tell her, because my lips felt funny, and I knew that if I tried to tell her anything now, it would come out all wrong.

So instead, I pushed down on the accelerator. The sooner I got to the hospital, the sooner we could sort everything out. And oh yeah, I was pretty sure I'd be needing my stomach pumped.

She turned to look out the window. "Hey Lawton. We're not running late anymore. Wanna slow it down?"

"Sorry. Can't."

"Why not?"

I didn't want to lie, especially because she'd be finding out soon enough. I tried to sound as normal as possible as I said, "Because, I figure we got about fifteen minutes to make it to the hospital."

"You weren't kidding?" she said. "You really do have plans there? Oh jeez, I'm so sorry. Why didn't you say something when I first called?"

"Because when you called, I didn't know we'd be going."

"Huh?" She turned to face me and paused. "Lawton," she said, speaking too slow for everything to be okay. "What's wrong with your face?"

Oh, shit.

I leaned over to glance in the rear-view mirror. My face was swollen so bad I could hardly recognize myself. Trying not to scare Chloe, all I said was, "Huh. That's not good."

I hit the brakes and skidded to a stop on the side of the road.

"What is it?" Chloe asked.

Things were getting fuzzy around the edges. On the steering wheel, my hands looked too big, too swollen, too strange. And my tongue felt like ten times too big for my mouth.

Staring ahead, I tried to shake my away my confusion.

Chloe's voice was panicked. "Are you alright?"

My hands slipped off the steering wheel. I tried to talk, but was having a hard time of it.

"Oh my God," Chloe said. "What's wrong?"

I leaned my head against the back of the driver's seat. Slowly, I turned to face her. She looked blurry, just like everything else around us. I struggled to get out the words. "Baby, can you drive a stick?"

CHAPTER 61

We were in a private hospital room, surrounded by machines, IV stands, and the usual stuff.

From a chair beside the bed, Chloe was holding my hand. She'd been holding it for a while now, and I loved the feel of it, having her so close to me after all this time.

If I weren't so groggy, I'd be asking her to get even closer, in spite of the nurse hovering over the chart at the foot of my bed. Through the grogginess, I told Chloe, "Tell me again."

Her voice was soothing. "Tell you what?"

"You know."

"This?" She leaned close and whispered in my ear. "I love you." She paused. "But you're still in big trouble."

I focused on the first part, and forgot the second. "I love you, too. You know that, right?"

She nodded, and her eyes filled with tears. "But damn it, you are *such* an idiot."

"Please," the nurse told her yet again, "no yelling at the patient."

"I wasn't yelling," Chloe said. "Much."

I wanted to smile. Chloe had called me worse names than that over the last couple of hours. I'd been mostly out of it, but not so far gone that I hadn't heard.

Screw all the other stuff. She loved me.

I was still too damn groggy, but awake enough to realize that I was feeling almost human again. The reason for that was obvious. Over the last couple of hours, I'd gotten a bunch of shots, an IV, and yeah, unfortunately, had to have my stomach pumped.

It's not like I hadn't seen *that* coming.

The nurse checked off something on my chart and hung the clipboard at the foot of the bed. With a final warning look at Chloe, she adjusted my IV drip and left the room.

Blinking away the tears, Chloe looked down at me. "You're looking a lot better."

Better than what? How I'd looked in the rear-view mirror? If so, that wasn't saying much. Even so, I felt myself smile. "Yeah?"

"Yeah." She squeezed my hand, and the tears kept coming. "But you're still an idiot."

"Not this time," I told her. The last couple of hours were a foggy blur, and I tried to recall exactly what had happened after leaving her dad's place. The last thing I remembered was asking her to drive. "So, you know how to drive a stick, huh?"

"No. But I know how to call an ambulance." She bit her lip. "I think I forgot to lock your car."

The car was the last thing on my mind. "Eh, no biggie."

"And, uh, I might've left your keys in the ignition." She winced. "I'm sorry. Your car's probably long-gone by now."

"Don't worry," I told her. "It'll turn up. Or not."

She scooted her chair closer and leaned down so our faces were just inches apart. "You shouldn't have done that." Her voice caught. "The doctor told me you could've died."

I tried to shrug. "They always say that. Hasn't happened yet."

"Seriously," she said. "Why on Earth would you do that? It was *really* stupid." She gave me a desperate look. "And don't try to tell me you didn't know."

"I would, but like I told you, I'm not a liar."

"So why'd you do it?"

I told her the truth. "Because I couldn't stand to see you hurt."

"You think I like seeing *you* hurt?"

"This? It's nothing."

She rolled her eyes. "Okay, *now* you're a liar."

I shook my head. "Baby, I'm not lying. Seeing you cry? Hurts way more than this."

She reached up to wipe at her eyes. And then, she gave a weak laugh. "Oh so, *now*, you tell me." She closed her eyes as if wanting to block out the memories. And for some reason, it made me close my eyes too. But then, I forgot to open them and must've drifted off again.

The next time I woke, it was dark outside. I heard a new voice – Bishop's. Silently, I turned my head and spotted him a few feet away, talking to Chloe in a quiet voice.

Trying to clear the cobwebs, I let my eyelids drift shut as I listened to the soothing sounds of their voices. The way it sounded, they were actually getting along. Now, *that* was a first.

Chloe was asking, "So how about you? Haven't *you* ever been in love before?"

I knew the answer to *that* question. Yeah, he had. And it hadn't ended so good. He almost never talked about it, but it was always there, eating him from the inside out.

Chloe's question hung in the air until Bishop said, "Yeah. Once."

"What happened?" she asked.

When he didn't answer, I opened my eyes and saw him reach into his back pocket. He pulled out his wallet. From somewhere inside, he pulled out something that I'd only seen once. It was a folded square that looked almost like a playing card.

"What's that?" Chloe asked.

Silently, he handed it over. She unfolded the card and studied the image. "Is this a tarot card?"

He nodded.

"The Fool?" she said. "Is this supposed to be you?"

He gave a humorless laugh. "No. Not if I can help it."

He was wrong. He *could* help it, and it was time for me to tell him so. Again.

For too damn long, he'd been a miserable bastard. I'd found *my* girl. It was time for him to do the same. I spoke up, hearing the grogginess in my own voice as I told him, "Damn it. For the last time, just go find her already, will ya?"

Together, Bishop and Chloe turned to look. Chloe gave me a smile that melted my heart. "Oh yeah? You're one to talk."

I wasn't following. "What do you mean?"

Moving closer, she reached out to stroke my hand. And then, she trailed her fingers higher, past my wrist and up my arm, tracing the lines and shapes of my tattoos. Suddenly, her fingers paused, stopping at a spot I knew all too well.

The spot was a circular scar, the site of an old cigarette burn, now covered in ink. I'd gotten that burn, along with a few others, on the night that Chloe and I had first met.

She looked up, meeting my gaze. Her voice was quiet. "That was you." Her fingers moved higher, tracing the outlines of another scar, almost exactly like the first. "The guy on the sidewalk."

I stared up at her, not quite sure what to say.

She knew.

CHAPTER 62

The guy on the sidewalk – yeah, that was me. I knew exactly which sidewalk she meant. It was the one outside a different hospital five years earlier.

Earlier that night, I'd gotten those burns, along with the worst beating of my life, not from my opponent, but from two guys who were just doing their jobs, "rewarding" me for my epic failure to throw a fight.

One stupid punch.

Now, five years later, I was in a different hospital under different circumstances. I felt a slow smile warm my face. But the girl was the same. And now, she was mine.

It made everything worth it.

Chloe eyes were still trained on mine. Her voice grew softer. "It was. Wasn't it?"

What could I say? I'd been planning to tell her. Just not like this.

It was Bishop who spoke next, sounding surprised as hell. "You've got to be kidding." He looked from me to Chloe. "*You're* the girl who scraped him off the sidewalk?"

She'd done more than that. She'd given me a glimpse of something different. She'd been the voice in the darkness and the reason that for years afterward, no other girl could hold my attention, not for more than a few days, anyway.

Right from the start, Chloe had been *the one*. She was still the one.

Chloe looked from Bishop to me. "I knew it!" she said. "So I was right. It *was* you."

"That depends," I said. "Would that be good news, or bad news?"

She was still smiling. "I don't care."

Bishop was shaking his head. "Well that's nice."

She gave him a dirty look. "What I *mean* to say," she continued, looking back at me, "is that, well, I love you either way."

"Yeah?" I said, reaching for her hand. "You wanna prove it?"

Bishop cleared his throat. "Do I *have* to listen to this?"

Chloe turned to him and said, "Yes. You do, in fact."

"Oh yeah? Why?"

She smiled at him. "Because you have it coming, that's why."

To my surprise, he actually smiled back. "Eh, you might have a point there."

Bishop pulled up a chair next to Chloe's, and we spent the next half-hour reliving the Thanksgiving dinner from hell.

For Chloe's sake, I didn't mention what Lauren Jane had been doing under the table. Later, when we were alone, I'd be mentioning it, along with a few other things, like my ideas for having Josh move in with us, *after* Chloe moved in with me, that is.

By the time Bishop stood to leave, I was feeling as good as new, and eager to get the hell out of that bed. My grandma used to say that I had an iron stomach. I didn't know about that, but I did know that I didn't want to waste my night in some hospital bed, when the girl I loved was back in my life.

Bishop gave Chloe one final look. "So *you're* Hospital Girl," he said, as if the shock hadn't quite worn off. He glanced back at me. "You could've mentioned that."

"Why?" I said. "So you could spend another five years giving me a hard time? No thanks."

Chloe turned to smile at me. "Hospital Girl?"

I smiled back. "I didn't know your real name."

"Well, you could've mentioned it to *me*," she said. "I never gave you a hard time."

Bishop made a scoffing sound.

"Hey," she told him. "I didn't. Much." She turned back to me and said, "So why didn't you tell me?"

There were so many reasons, but I stuck with the simplest. "Maybe I wanted you to love *me*, not that guy on the sidewalk."

"Because the guy on the sidewalk lost a fight?" She squeezed my hand. "Lawton, don't you get it? Win, lose, it doesn't matter. I don't love you because of what you do or what you have. I love you because of who you are."

I grinned over at her. "You wanna say that again?"

"That's it," Bishop said. "I'm gonna go get your car. See ya in a few days."

"Um, actually," Chloe said, "I think I lost his keys."

"Not a problem," Bishop said.

"So you've got a spare?" she asked.

He headed toward the door. "Something like that."

"Hey," I called after him. "Have 'em drop a car in visitor's parking, will ya? Something low-key."

Nodding, Bishop walked silently out, leaving Chloe staring after him. "He's kind of scary," she said.

"Baby, you don't know the half of it."

"Speaking of which." She turned to face me. "Since you're incapacitated…"

"Incapacitated? That's what you think, huh?" Was that a challenge? If so, I knew exactly how to prove her wrong. But first, I needed to get the hell out of here.

CHAPTER 63

A couple of hours later, we were back at my place. On our way back from the hospital, we'd swung by Chloe's to pick up Chucky, along with some of Chloe's overnight stuff.

I still couldn't believe my luck. She was back, and she was going to *stay* back, because I was done screwing up.

Before leaving the hospital, I'd told her almost everything – starting with the real reason that I'd gotten my ass beat that one night, and ending with a pretty strong hint that I was looking to make our relationship a forever thing.

The best thing was, something about the look in her eyes told me that when I popped the question, she'd be saying yes.

Talking with her, I'd also gotten something that I hadn't been looking for – an apology for being so secretive about the house-sitting gig. But looking back, it all made sense. She'd had an agreement with the owners, and she'd been determined to keep it.

In my book, that was a plus, not a minus. Over the last few years, privacy had been a hard thing for me to come by. And to have a girl who knew how to keep a secret, well, that was a big deal for me.

Now, we were both in the master bathroom, washing up after the whole hospital thing. I glanced over at Chloe, who was brushing her teeth in the nearby sink. As for me, I'd already brushed mine – twice – the moment we'd gotten home five minutes earlier.

Home. With Chloe. I felt myself smile. When she was here, that's exactly what it felt like, a real home. And the way it sounded, the feeling was mutual. She belonged here, and from what I could tell, she finally got that.

Chloe finished up and set her toothbrush in the spot where she used to keep it, before the whole basement thing and all the other stupid stuff that had torn us apart.

If I had my way, her toothbrush would never be leaving. And neither would she. Or her dog. Or anything else that was important to her.

Chloe turned to me and smiled. "I still can't believe you left the hospital like that."

"Why not?"

"Because you weren't supposed to."

"Oh yeah?" I wasn't worried. I was fine. And as far as the administrative stuff, I'd have someone take care of that tomorrow. But tonight, I had other things in mind.

Slowly, I moved toward Chloe and said, "Maybe I like doing stuff I'm not supposed to."

Back at her place, she'd practically dragged me out the front door, joking that she – and not the house – was on fire. But so far, she'd been taking things slow, and I wondered if the events of the day had finally caught up with her.

She was still wearing that green dress, and as nice as it was, I wanted to see her out of it. As for me, I was back to wearing the same clothes that I'd been wearing at her dad's place. They felt dirty, and so did I.

I glanced toward the shower. It was a nice one, with fancy tile on the bottom and glass on three sides. Chloe would look good in that shower. In fact, I'd seen her there before, all soaped up and sexy. It had been way too long since I'd seen her that way.

"You wanna shower?" I asked.

"Uh, sure." She hesitated. "Do you wanna go first, or….?"

"Yeah." I laughed. "And I want you to come with me."

She bit her lip. "Can I confess something?"

I moved closer. "Anything."

"I'm feeling kind of guilty."

"Why? Because of the gravy thing? Forget it."

"Well, that's part of it," she said. "But…" She blew out a shaky breath. "The truth is, I know you should probably be resting, and…" She glanced toward the shower. "The things I want to do, well, they're not exactly restful."

I felt a slow smile spread across my face. I closed the distance and wrapped her in my arms. "Yeah?"

She nodded against me. "Except, I know we probably shouldn't."

I gripped her hips and pulled her close, letting my hardness surge against her pelvis. "That's what *you* think."

The hell with resting. I didn't need it. I didn't want it. And thirty seconds later, I was in that shower, proving it.

CHAPTER 64

She was wet and naked, pressed tight against me as the steaming water fell over us. I was rock hard and ready, and if I wasn't careful, this would go way too fast. Here she was, my dream girl, the girl I'd lost, the girl I'd found – and the girl I was never, *ever* going to let go.

We stood there for a long moment, lost in everything but each other. There were so many things I wanted to do with her, and yeah, *to* her. Her tight body fit perfectly against mine, and I savored the feel of it, loving the roundness of her breasts and the softness of her wet cheek pressed against my bare chest.

I loved her. And I'd love her always if she gave me half the chance.

As if reading my thoughts, she lifted her head and gazed up at me. Her eyes were bright, and her lips were full. I lowered my head and kissed her long and hard, caressing the back of her neck, and loving the feel of her long, silky hair falling over my wet fingers.

She was rubbing against me now, as if desperate to be closer. Yeah, I knew the feeling. My hardness was surging, and her skin was warm and slippery. I stifled a groan as she pressed herself tighter, making my erection slide, wet and slick, against the warmth of her naked stomach.

She pulled back and reached for the soap. With that familiar look in her eye, she started rubbing it between her hands.

I watched, hypnotized by the sight of her, the girl I loved, and the girl I wanted. I saw her naked breasts rising and falling with every movement. I saw the water falling off her shoulders and dripping down her bare stomach and naked hips. I saw her hands, the ones I loved to feel everywhere, lathering the soap in a way that might've been innocent if she were alone, and if I didn't have some nice ideas about where those hands might be going soon.

She lifted her hands, soap and all, to my chest, rubbing my skin in slow, steady circles. Like always, her touch was pure magic, and I let myself get lost in it, watching her every move with a hunger that grew with every motion.

When she looked up, I could hardly breathe. What I saw in her eyes – the love, the passion, the sweet sexiness that drove me crazy – was everything I'd been missing over the last few weeks.

No. Not weeks. I'd been missing this for years, from the first moment I'd met her, way back when.

With a secret smile, she lowered her eyes and watched as her smooth hands moved, slow and sexy, across my pecs and then, lower toward my mid-section. Loving the sight of her hands *anywhere* on me, I watched, too, as the lather gathered between her fingers and slid downward, falling in soapy waves past my hips and down my legs.

Her hands drifted lower again, sliding and teasing their way onto my hips. She moved closer and ran her soft hands over my bare ass, making me surge even harder when she squeezed me tight and pulled me close.

I wanted her. I wanted her so bad, I could hardly wait. But I didn't want to rush it. If I had my way, there'd be thousands of nights just like tonight, with just her and me, doing this and a whole lot more.

She pulled back and worked up more lather between her fingers. And then, setting aside the soap, she eased forward and gripped my hardness in her soft hands. I closed my eyes and savored the feel of it, the feel of *her*, so close, finally, after all this time.

I felt her slippery hands slide up and down my shaft, driving me crazy in the best possible way. When she tightened her grip, I moaned her name and tried not to lose it. No matter what, I *had* to make this last. But she was making it so damn hard, literally.

Desperate to see her, I opened my eyes and saw her looking up at me. She was smiling in that special way, like a girl who knows exactly what she's doing and is loving every minute of it. I was loving it, too. And I loved *her*.

I smiled back. But that didn't mean I'd let things finish the way they were going.

"Turn around," I said.

"Why?"

Because I wanted this to last. Because I wanted to run my hands over her tight, little body and make *her* want *me* like I wanted her. Because she was my girl, and I wanted her to know it. Because I loved her, and if she wasn't ready and then some, I wasn't doing things right.

But all I said was, "Do I need a reason?"

She smiled. "But I'm not done yet."

"Me neither. And I don't want to be. Not yet." I took her shoulders and gently turned her away from me. I wrapped an arm around her stomach and pressed my front against her back, loving how she fit perfectly against me, like she always did.

I lowered my face to kiss her neck. "Baby, I love you so much it hurts."

With a happy sound, she let her head fall back against my chest. "I love you, too. And God, I've missed you. I've missed this. I've missed everything."

She wasn't the only one. I heard myself whisper, "You're mine. And I'm never letting you go."

Whether she heard me or not, her body responded. Her hips were moving, making her hot, wet ass, grind seductively against my pelvis. She reached up and wrapped her fingers around the back of my neck. I lowered my gaze, liking what I saw. Her back was arched, and her breaths were coming fast and shallow. Her nipples were hard, and her breasts were glistening.

I slid my hands upward and cupped them in my palms, loving the feel of her body and the weight of her breasts as I squeezed them gently together and then cupped higher, into the cascading water. I pressed my lips to her neck, and felt my erection surge against her back as she gave a sweet little moan that drove me half-insane.

I caressed her curves, loving how her softness fit perfectly in my hands. She was trembling and breathing harder now, and I was loving every minute of it, loving that she was liking this, and more than anything, loving that this wouldn't be a one-time thing.

When my fingers brushed the tips of her nipples, she arched into me, as if silently begging for more. So I gave it to her, toying with her nipples in just the way she liked, stroking them, and gently tugging at them until they were hard little knobs in my wet fingers.

She was grinding against me, harder now, pressing against my length and driving me to distraction. I moved a hand lower, sliding it over her wet stomach and then lower again. As I moved, I took my sweet time, letting her savor the knowledge of where I was going.

I slid my hands past her pelvis and reached between her thighs. I slid my wet fingers back and forth on either side of her hot center, loving the sound she made as she ground desperately into my touch. Liking the way she moved, I rubbed my thumb along her clit and ran a finger across her opening, loving the slick, hot feel of her against my teasing touch.

With a desperate moan, she twisted around and coiled her hot body tight against mine. When she reached between us and grabbed my cock, I was too lost to fight it.

"Lawton," she breathed, "I need you so bad."

I needed her, too. And I started with a long, slow kiss that had me remembering just how good this felt. With a sexy sound, she reached up, wrapping her arms around my neck and pressing herself tighter against my naked body.

I couldn't wait another second. I cupped her ass and lifted her hips high against me, loving it when she wrapped her wet legs around my hips as if desperate for me to take her.

And so I did. I slid into her slick warmth, liking the sound she made as she wrapped her legs tighter and ground her pelvis close against mine.

I thrust into her, loving everything about this – the hot tightness of her, the feel of her wet skin pressed up against mine, the curves of her sweet ass in my steady hands. But mostly, I loved the fact she was here, with me, after all this time.

She was mine.

Desperate to make myself believe it, I said her name over and over as we moved together under the steaming water. When she convulsed against me, I held her tighter, feeling my hardness pulse as she trembled and moaned, and said my name too many times for me to count.

And then, I couldn't hold back any longer. I surged into her, savoring the sweet release and the way she clutched me tighter with every stroke.

When it was finished, we sank down together into a trembling heap, letting the steaming water wash over us as we gazed into each other's eyes, oblivious of everything except each other.

I reached out, running the back of my index finger across her lower hip. "If I wake up, and you're not here, if this is all a dream, I don't want to wake up at all."

She gave me a slow, sleepy smile and leaned her head on my shoulder. "Me neither," she murmured as she held me tighter.

After the shower, we collapsed, naked and warm, onto my king-size bed. We were still naked when I drifted off with the girl of my dreams wrapped in my arms. It would've been a perfect night, except for one thing.

When I woke an hour later, Chloe was gone.

And I couldn't find her anywhere.

CHAPTER 65

I stood in my kitchen, trying to figure out where she'd gone. I'd already checked every room in the house, along with the basement and back patio. I looked around. Her stuff was still upstairs, and as for Chucky, he was right here. That was a good sign. Right?

She *was* coming back.

But for some reason, I was feeling on edge. I looked to Chucky, who was sitting on the kitchen floor, staring up at me with his head cocked to the side.

"Where'd she go?" I asked.

He didn't answer. No surprise there.

It was just after nine o'clock, early by my standards, and even earlier by Chloe's. She *did* work nights, after all. But the restaurant wasn't open today, and I hadn't seen a note or anything. That left only one possibility. She'd returned to her own place for some reason or other.

Earlier, we'd left her house in a hurry. Maybe she'd forgotten something. It shouldn't have been a big deal, but with every passing second, I was liking it less and less.

I considered everything else that had been going on with that house. We still hadn't talked much about it, but I remembered the douchebag who'd been hanging around far too often. I recalled the other stuff – details that Chloe had mentioned in passing, like financial problems with the owners and confusion as to who actually owned the place.

Standing there, I tried to convince myself to stay put. We'd been back together for only a few hours, and muscling my way over there wouldn't earn me any points. Besides, I told myself, she'd been staying at that house for weeks now without needing me as a babysitter.

But I didn't like it. I liked it even less when something else hit me. If she walked there alone, she'd be walking *back* alone, too.

No, I decided. She wouldn't. Not if I could help it. If she got mad, well, it wouldn't be the first time. And if she got *too* mad? Eh, there were ways I could make her forget all that. Some of those ways were sounding pretty nice.

I was already dressed, so I pulled on a dark hoodie and some sneakers, and then headed out the back patio door, figuring I'd take the shortcut through the narrow gate that led to a neighboring sidewalk.

I was halfway across my back yard when I saw something that made me pick up the pace. Her house was dark, but in her bonus garage out back, there was a light glimmering from the attic window. That light *hadn't* been on earlier. I was sure of it. And I knew for a fact that Chloe never used that garage.

So, who was up there?

I moved faster, sticking to the shadows. I glanced at the gate that I'd been planning to use. Not anymore. It was too visible, especially from that upper attic window, so I skipped the gate and headed toward the part of my back fence that was cast in the deepest shadows.

I hoisted myself over the thing and landed in Chloe's darkened backyard with hardly a sound. I'd taken only a couple of steps forward when something sent my heart straight into my stomach. It was the sound of something shattering, like dishes or who-knows-what.

I swallowed, hard. The sound had come from *inside* the house.

Fuck.

Silently, I moved toward her back patio, trying like hell not to run. I *wanted* to run. I wanted to bust through that patio door and face whatever it was, head-on. But from the things I'd seen in my old neighborhood, I knew better. That approach was risky, not so much for me as for Chloe.

She was inside that house. She *had* to be. And if something happened to her...

No. I wasn't even going to think about it. I couldn't. And I wouldn't.

So I moved faster through the shadows, conscious of the fact that somebody might also be inside the bonus garage, just a few paces away. But if that was true, odds were pretty good that person *wasn't* Chloe. So with quiet precision, I made for the back door and silently tried the knob.

By some miracle – or more likely, by the work of someone else – the door was already unlocked. Silently, I pushed it open, not liking what I saw.

Through the shadows, I spotted upended furniture, broken pottery, and a couple of paintings lying near the remnants of busted-up frames. With my back hugging the wall, I moved deeper into the house, listening for any sign of where Chloe might be.

And then, I heard a voice – *not* Chloe's. It was deep, masculine sound, coming from somewhere near the front of the house. "Where's our money?"

I froze in my tracks. And when I heard the response, raw panic clawed at my heart. It was Chloe, sounding scared as hell. "What money?"

I was on the move again, listening as I went, planning to take the guy by surprise.

The guy spoke again, louder now. "The money you owe us, bitch."

Bitch? He'd pay for that.

"I don't owe you any money," Chloe stammered.

And then I heard something else, a new sound that had me moving faster now, opting for speed over silence. Because the way it sounded, time was running out. And if something bad was going to happen, I'd rather have the guy's attention focused on me, not Chloe.

Never Chloe.

Because the sound I heard was the cocking of a gun.

CHAPTER 66

I rounded the nearest corner, heading into the kitchen, and slammed into someone I hadn't seen coming – a heavy-set guy, dressed all in black. Whatever he was carrying crashed to the floor and shattered on impact.

I lunged forward, wrapping an arm around his thick neck and squeezing it hard. Whatever else he'd been holding thudded to the floor as he struggled uselessly to claw my arm away from his windpipe. I reached up and clamped my free hand over his mouth, choking off whatever other sounds he was trying to make.

From the other room, the first guy called out, "Hey! You break anything good, and it's coming out of your ass!"

Under the cover of his yelling, I twisted the guy's neck and lowered him slowly onto the kitchen floor. Dead, not dead. I didn't know. I didn't care. And I sure as hell wasn't going to take the time to check.

In the other room, Chloe was pleading with the guy. "Whoever you are, you've got the wrong house."

Yes. He did.

Conscious now that I had no idea how many people were here, I silently crept forward, through the kitchen and into the short hallway that led the main living area. They were still talking.

"Well, Louise," he was saying, "that's where you're wrong."

Louise? Who the hell was Louise?

"Because," he continued, "we have *exactly* the right house. And you have *exactly* one minute to start talking, or we're gonna break more than some vase or whatever the fuck that was."

"But I'm not Louise," Chloe insisted. "She's not here."

"Sure." His tone grew sarcastic. "I believe you."

"It's true," she stammered. "I can give her a message if–"

"Shut the fuck up," the guy said.

"But I'm not Louise. I don't even–"

"I said shut up!"

Forcing myself to move slowly, I finally spotted him, a dark silhouette, facing the front windows. Sure enough, he was holding a gun.

Fuck.

Near the front door, I spotted Chloe, a few paces away from the guy. She was facing me. *He* wasn't.

Thank God.

Slivers of moonlight streamed in through the partially open blinds, giving me a distorted view of Chloe's face. She looked scared to death. Easy to see why.

I was scared, too. But not for me – for Chloe. Because the gun was pointed straight at her, which meant that if I fucked this up… No. I wasn't going to. I was going to play it smart, even if it killed me, or better yet, the other guy.

Slowly, the guy started prowling toward her, like the sick fuck was getting his jollies, toying with a girl half his size.

Big mistake.

I was moving too, looking to catching him quietly, before he could even think of pulling that trigger. I was just a couple paces behind him when Chloe's expression changed.

She'd spotted me. I could see it on her face, even if the guy couldn't. But she didn't give me away.

Smart girl.

As if sensing someone behind him, the guy hesitated. He started to look around.

But then, Chloe started talking. "Please…" Her voice sounded small and weak, and maybe a little breathless. "Don't hurt me."

At this, he laughed, low and deep, making me want to rip out his throat and strangle him with it. The way it sounded, the gun wasn't the only thing he was thinking of using.

I was almost on him now. Almost, but not quite.

Chloe spoke again. "I'll do anything you want. And I mean–" She choked on the last word. "Anything."

"Oh yeah?" Slowly, the guy lowered his gun. "You bet your ass you will."

That's when I barreled into him, slamming him sideways and going for the gun. But the gun wasn't there. Not anymore. His hands were empty. I knew, because his fists were flying, trying to fight me off, even as I slammed him into a marble-top table and knocked over a lamp.

I grabbed his fist and gave it a squeeze. And then I kept on squeezing. It was the same hand that had been holding the gun on Chloe. If I had *my* way, he wouldn't be doing that to her – or anyone else – ever again. The guy was cursing now, and struggling like a madman to get away.

Yeah, good luck with that.

I slammed his face into the fallen table and twisted his hand until I heard a crunch. Other than that, he made no sound at all, which told me that one way or another, the fight was over.

A split-second later, the room was flooded with light. I turned to see Chloe standing near the light-switch, eyeing the scene with wide, anxious eyes.

The guy was lying in a fallen heap. His hand was twisted, and his face was covered in blood. Was he still alive? Probably.

For now.

I glanced around and spotted the gun, lying a few feet away. Chloe rushed forward to pick it up.

"Wait," I said. "Don't touch it."

She stopped and gave me a questioning look.

"Hang on," I told her, getting to my feet. I looked down at the guy still lying on the floor. That son-of-a-bitch. What the hell was he planning for Chloe? I didn't want to think about it. But whatever it was, it couldn't have been good.

Unable to stop myself, I turned and gave his lifeless body a vicious kick. The guy didn't even budge. I didn't care. If he eventually woke up, a couple broken ribs would slow him down nicely.

I rushed toward Chloe, and she fell into my arms. I squeezed her tight. Too tight? Maybe. But it's not like she was complaining.

She looked up and whispered. "There's someone else here." She looked toward the back of the house and said, "Toward the kitchen."

I wasn't letting her go. Not yet. I gripped her tighter and said in a low, quiet voice, "There was, but not anymore."

My mind was still churning. Were there only the two guys? Probably. Because if anyone else were here, they'd have come running already.

But I didn't want to take any chances, and I still didn't know about the garage. I had to get Chloe out of here, like *now*.

I glanced toward the back of the house. As far as the other guy, I didn't know his condition, and I didn't want to be finding out while Chloe was around.

For all I knew, the guy was dead. If he was, she didn't need to see that. And if he wasn't? Well, then I'd have to see, wouldn't I? Either way, the clock was ticking.

"Now c'mon," I told her, "we're leaving."

I pulled the sleeve of my hoodie over my hand and stooped down to pick up the gun. I thrust it into my front pocket and reached for Chloe's hand.

"Wait," she said. "My purse."

"Screw the purse," I said, hustling her toward the back of the house, making sure to take a different route than the one I'd taken just a few minutes earlier.

I led her out the back door and kept on going until we reached the tall iron fence that divided our properties. I made a foothold with my hands. "Over the fence," I said. "And don't stop 'til you're inside the house."

She looked down at my hands. "But how will you get over?"

"I'll jump it," I said. "But not right now."

Her voice grew panicked. "Why not?"

"Because I've got to take care of something."

"What?"

The sad thing was, I didn't know. But I'd find out, and then I'd deal with it. But only *after* Chloe was safely back at my place.

I *had* to make her leave. *Now.*

"Chloe," I said, trying to keep the edge out of my voice, "I don't want to boss you around, but if you don't get your ass over that fence right now, I'll have to toss you over. And you could get hurt. I don't want that. So just listen to me, alright?" I gave her a pleading look. "Please, baby. Just go. You need to do this, alright?"

She gave me a pleading look. "But I want you to come too."

"I'll be there in a few minutes, a half hour tops. You know how to close the gate, right?"

She nodded.

"Good. Get in the house. Lock the doors, and hit the control for the gate. I'll see you in a little bit."

"Wait," she said. "I should call the police, right?"

"No."

She blinked. "What?"

"Trust me." I flicked my head toward my hands, still waiting to give her a boost. "Now c'mon. You've gotta go, alright?"

After a small hesitation, she stepped cautiously into the foothold. Before she could even *think* about backing out, I launched her safely over the fence, hating it when she landed ass-first, on the mulch-covered ground. She glanced back, and our eyes met.

She looked okay, and I breathed a sigh of relief. "Go," I told her.

With obvious reluctance, she stood and started walking toward my house. Halfway there, she turned around and saw me watching.

Yeah, I was still here. Because I wasn't going anywhere until I knew was she safe. As if realizing that fact, she finally turned and disappeared from sight.

Good.

Already, I was reaching for my phone. When Bishop answered, I said in a hushed tone. "You still in town?"

"Why?" he asked. "You planning a party?"

"Cut the crap," I said. "Are you still here or not? Because if you are, you need to get over here now."

Instantly, he was on alert. "Where?"

"Chloe's place. Meet me out back. Okay?"

"I'll be there in fifteen minutes." And then, he was gone.

As for me, I couldn't afford to wait.

CHAPTER 67

By the time fifteen minutes passed, I was in the attic above the bonus garage, wondering what the hell I was looking at.

Through the open attic window, I spotted Bishop, making his way across the backyard. Quietly, I called down to him. "Up here."

A minute later, we were both staring at the thing.

"What is it?" I asked.

If anyone would know, it was Bishop. Electronic security was his specialty, and as far as I could tell, the system I was staring at fell into that general category. Either that, or it was just a weird-looking computer that I was too stupid to figure out.

He reached for the compact keyboard and hit a few buttons. Sure enough, the system lit up. A few keystrokes after that, and I felt my whole body tense. Near as I could tell, I was watching footage from inside the house.

Bedrooms only.

And fuck, the master bathroom, too.

That son-of-a-bitch had been filming her.

I turned to Bishop. "What the fuck?"

"Hey, don't look at me," he said. "I didn't set this up."

I gave him an annoyed look. "I *know* you didn't put this here, but what is it? I mean, where does it go?"

He glanced at the thing. "You mean the footage?"

"Yeah, the footage." I had visions of somebody watching Chloe's bedroom, even now. Yeah, I knew she wasn't currently in there, but she *had* been. For weeks. No. Months. And tonight, *I'd* been in that bedroom, too – *all* of the bedrooms, in fact.

Had someone been watching me remotely? If so, that wasn't good. I'd gone through every closet. I'd looked under every bed. I'd grabbed everything of Chloe's that I could possibly find, and I'd stuffed it into a couple of garbage bags, not caring if anything got wrinkled or wrecked.

And then, I'd gotten the hell out of there, ignoring the two guys – now tied up – who happened to be half-dead, courtesy of me. Well, they'd been half-dead the last time I'd checked. Hard to know their status now.

Bishop was still working the keyboard. When he finished, he circled around the thing, tugging on wires and seeing where they led. Finally, he said, "It's just here."

"What do you mean 'just here'?"

"It's local only. No wireless. No other connections, except for the line that ties into the house. The way it's set up, the footage downloads to a hard-drive, probably retrieved every few weeks or so."

Every few weeks, huh? Well, that explained a lot, didn't it?

I recalled the douchebag and all those so-called electrical problems. I recalled the other stuff he'd offered me – freaky pussy with bald chicks and what-not.

The guy wasn't a pimp. He was movie producer, of the secret variety.

I felt my blood pressure rise, thinking of the footage he probably already had. Chloe naked on her bed. Chloe taking a shower. Damn it. Chloe on the toilet.

I felt my hands tighten into fists. The next time I saw him, I was going to kill him.

"So that's why you called me?" Bishop asked.

I shook my head. "No. It's something else."

His eyebrows furrowed. "Something else?"

I gave him a brief rundown of everything that had happened inside the house and finished by saying, "So, what do you think? Should I just burn it down?"

"You serious?"

Hell yes, I was serious. But as an answer, I only shrugged.

"And about the two guys?" he asked.

I gave another shrug. "I haven't decided."

He lowered his face and rubbed his eyes with the tips of his fingers. "You're nuts. You know that?"

When I said nothing, he added, "You're not a killer. And trust me, you don't wanna start now."

So I wasn't a killer, huh? Well, that made one of us.

But I didn't say it, because if there was blood on Bishop's hands, there was blood on mine too. The guy he killed? Well, it was because of me. When push came to shove, *he'd* been the one who'd taken out that councilman, the one who'd been after my little sister.

I hadn't asked him to do it. But he had. And he'd done it while I'd been fighting in front of a hundred people – the perfect alibi, not that I'd realized what was happening at the time.

I didn't regret what happened to the guy, but I *did* regret not doing it myself.

When I said nothing, Bishop spoke again. "Those guys in the house, were they after Chloe? Or was she just in the wrong place at the wrong time?"

I recalled what the guy had been saying. He'd been calling Chloe by another name. What was it? Louise? He'd been demanding some sort of loan-repayment.

And one thing was for damn sure. He wasn't from the bank.

"He was a loan shark," I finally said. "Or more likely, they worked for one." From old experience, I was painfully familiar with that sort of thing. Shit, for all I knew, they worked for the same guy who'd loaned money to my grandma all those years ago.

It seemed unlikely, but then again, it wasn't exactly a popular business.

Bishop's voice broke into my thoughts. "So Chloe owed them money?"

"No. Not Chloe. Someone else owed them, probably whoever was *supposed* to be there, the owners, I'm guessing."

He nodded. "Yeah, that makes sense."

And five minutes later, we had our plan, which, as it turned out, didn't involve gasoline and a pack of matches. But it would take some creativity. And I'd need Chloe to do me a favor.

Lie.

CHAPTER 68

When I walked through the back door of my own house, Chloe threw herself into my arms. "I was so worried," she said. "What were you doing?"

I'd been doing a lot of things, and some of them weren't exactly legal. But the *last* thing I'd done? I'd used a burner phone to leave an anonymous tip for the police.

"Well, that's complicated," I said, stepping back to take her hands in mine. "Do you trust me?"

She nodded.

I gave her a serious look. "Say it."

"I trust you."

"Good." I was still gripping her hands. "Because in about an hour, you're gonna have to lie like a rug."

"Why?" Her hands tensed against mine, and she gave a little tug. "I didn't do anything wrong."

I glanced down. "Was I hurting you?" Deliberately, I loosened my grip. "Shit, I'm sorry."

"Forget that," she said. "Tell me why I have to lie. I didn't do anything."

That's where she was wrong. She *had* done something. She'd been in the wrong place at the wrong time. And the way it looked, she'd been working for the wrong people.

On top of that, there was her *real* job description. Half porn-star, half patsy. As far as tonight, she'd witnessed way too much for her own good, and way too little to have a decent idea of what, exactly, was going on.

Even *I* didn't know everything, but sooner or later, I was determined to find out.

At the moment, I didn't want to get into all that. By telling her now, I wouldn't be doing her any favors, especially when the cops showed up. And they *would* show up. Hopefully, I'd made sure of it.

I looked into her eyes. "Baby, I know. But these people, they don't think like you and I do."

"What people?" she asked. "Who are you talking about?"

"People I used to know. That's who." I pulled her close and wrapped her tight in my arms. "And I won't let 'em hurt you, but you've gotta help."

In the end, I had to give her credit. When the cops showed up, she played her role perfectly. Funny, it looked a lot like the role she played at work – sexy as hell, but not too bright.

She was even dressed for the part, in a red bikini and some sort of flimsy cover-up that hid next to nothing. As for me, I was still damp from the hot tub, but wore jeans and a white, unbuttoned shirt over my wet torso. The way it looked, we'd been hanging out, having a good time, oblivious to whatever was happening on just the other side of my fence.

The cops were taking notes as Chloe told her story. "So then," she was saying, "they stopped paying me, so I said, 'Screw this. I'm outta here.'"

"When was this?" the taller of the two cops asked.

"A while ago." She paused, as if thinking. "Maybe a couple of weeks?" She glanced briefly in my direction. "Besides, I found a better deal." She lowered her voice and said, "Do you know, he even has a hot tub?"

"Um, yeah," the cop said, "you mentioned that." His gaze shifted to her dripping wet hair. "When we showed up, in fact."

"Oh yeah." She gave something like a giggle. "That's right. Sorry, I guess I was distracted."

Her story boiled down to a few basic facts. She'd been hired to watch the house, but when the owners' checks started bouncing, she'd stopped going there, except for a few trips here and there to check the mailbox, just in case the missing payments showed up.

Supposedly, she'd left her car in the driveway because, "I think it's dead. And besides, Lawton has cars that are a ton nicer."

As for the dog, she claimed she hadn't seen him in a week, not since "the little sucker escaped" through no fault of her own. She finished by saying, "I'm still looking though, so he'll probably turn up. Right?"

"Uh, sure," the guy said.

What we *didn't* mention was the fact that right now, Chucky was with Bishop, who'd taken the terrier for a drive and wasn't returning until we gave him the all clear.

Looking to change the subject, I said, "Just curious, how'd you know she was staying here?"

In a bored tone, he answered, "From some papers we found at the house."

I let it go. There were no papers. But there *was* a brand-new semi-crumpled note that I'd left taped to the fridge. The note was a scribbled message from me to Chloe. All it said was, "Saw you walk by. You're smoking hot. Bring your bikini, and stop by sometime." It was signed with my name and included my street address. Nice and convenient.

The cops stayed less than ten minutes, but mentioned they might be calling us later with further questions. That was fine by me. Who knows? By then, we might have some answers, assuming my suspicions were correct.

Already, I knew a lot more than Chloe did. Some of it, she might not *want* to know, like the thing with the hidden cameras, or about the GPS tracking device that I'd found hidden underneath the passenger's seat of her car.

After the police left, I pulled Chloe into my arms and said, "You're amazing. You know that?"

"Me? Hardly." She lifted her head to look at me. "And I still don't get it."

"Get what?" I asked.

"Why I had to lie. I mean, I didn't *do* anything."

"Yeah, but that story wasn't for *them*."

Her brow wrinkled. "Then who was it for?"

"The grapevine."

"What grapevine?"

From experience, I knew how this worked. But apparently, Chloe didn't, so I spelled it out. "They'll file a report. Someone with connections will get ahold of it. And one important thing will be spelled out for anyone who looks."

"What?

"That you weren't there."

"But why does it matter?" she asked. "I wasn't the one who trashed the house."

"It matters," I explained, "because whoever sent those two guys isn't gonna give up. And trust me, there'll be hell to pay for what happened to them."

"You still haven't told me. What *did* happen to them?" From the look on her face, she wasn't completely sure she wanted to know.

"They'll be fine," I told her.

She gave me a skeptical look, but said nothing.

I shrugged. "I left them in the living room."

"Alive?"

"Last time I checked." I gave her a reassuring smile. "Hey, if the cops had found a couple of dead bodies, we'd have heard about it by now. Now c'mon." I led her to a nearby sofa. Once we were seated, I turned to her and said, "I've gotta ask you something."

"What?"

"When you were staying there, did you sleep naked?"

CHAPTER 69

"What?" She blinked over at me. "When I was house-sitting? No. I wore shorts and stuff. Why?"

"How about in the bathroom?" I asked. "Were you ever naked there?"

She gave me an odd look. "Well, I *do* shower naked, in case you haven't noticed."

Oh, I noticed, alright. I just didn't want anyone else to notice. "In which bathroom?" I asked.

"Over there?" she said. "I used the guest bath. Why?"

Again, I dodged the question. "Not the master bath?"

She shook her head. "No. Never."

That house had four bathrooms. By far, the master bathroom was the nicest. "Never?" I persisted. "Not even once?"

"No. Not even once."

I didn't get it. "Why not?"

"Because, it was part of their master bedroom," she explained. "I considered it off-limits."

"They told you that?" I didn't see their logic. I mean, why would anyone put a spy-camera in a bathroom that was off-limits?

But Chloe was shaking her head. "They didn't *say* that I couldn't. It just seemed disrespectful, you know?"

I did know. She took that job seriously, *so* seriously that until today, she'd refused to let me inside the place. Funny to think, it was that same quality that kept her from being filmed on the toilet.

Chloe was studying my face. "Why are you asking?"

I didn't want to tell her, but she deserved to know. "Because I found a camera."

"What?" She sat up straighter. "You're kidding. In the bathroom?"

"In the *master* bathroom," I clarified. "No other ones."

"You sure?"

I nodded. "A hundred percent."

And I was. That's part of what took me so long. Bishop and I had gone through that house inch-by-inch, looking for anything else that might cause trouble for Chloe.

Next to me, Chloe blew out a sigh. "That's a relief."

I was relieved, too. But the camera in the bathroom wasn't the only one.

Trying not to alarm her, I asked, "So, when you got dressed over there, where'd you do that? In the bedroom?"

"Not usually," she said. "I kept most of my stuff in the bathroom, so I normally got changed there." She gave a nervous laugh. "Good thing it wasn't the other bathroom, huh?"

Yeah. Good thing. But there was more I needed to know, as much as I hated to ask it. I tried to keep my tone easy. "Baby, I've gotta ask something else, and don't get insulted, okay?"

Her tone grew cautious. "Okay?"

"I know you said you didn't *sleep* naked, but is there anything…" I hesitated, trying to find the words. "…X-rated you wanna tell me about? Like at that house?"

"Are you serious?" She gave me a what-the-hell look. "No. Of course not. I'm not a cheater."

"I know that." I softened my tone. "But we weren't together the whole time."

"So what?" she said. "Cheating aside, if I wouldn't let *you* inside the house, why would I let someone else in? That doesn't make any sense."

"I know."

"Then why'd you ask?"

"Because I had to know for sure. For your sake."

"For *my* sake?" She frowned. "Why?"

"Because…" I met her gaze. "We found cameras in the bedrooms, too."

Her mouth fell open. "*Every* bedroom?"

I nodded.

"Wow." She said nothing else for a long moment, and I could see it all over her face. She was horrified.

Yeah, that made two of us.

"You okay?" I asked.

"I guess. Maybe." Suddenly, she froze. "Oh, crap."

I tensed. "What?"

She shifted on the sofa. She was blushing now. When she didn't answer my question, I tried again, making a lame joke out of it. "You didn't star in your own sex tape, did you?"

"Well…" She glanced away. "Oh, God, this is so embarrassing. I guess you say, um, yes?"

I froze. Yes? What the hell? Trying to keep the edge out of my voice, I said, "Who was he?"

"Well, uh, you, actually." She winced. "Except you weren't really there."

I felt a slow smile spread across my face. "Yeah? So you were…"

"Yeah." Her face grew a couple shades redder. "I was."

"And you were thinking of me?"

The way it looked, she didn't know whether to laugh or cry. "Stop looking so happy about it," she said.

"I'm sorry." I pulled her close and whispered in her hair. "You're right." And she *was* right. I might love the thought of her pleasuring herself to thoughts of us together, but that didn't change the thing I hated – someone might have copy of that footage.

After a long moment, Chloe asked, "So someone was watching? *While* I was doing that?"

I shook my head. "No. It was local only." I paused, hating what I had to say next. "But they might have a copy of it."

The blush disappeared, replaced by skin so pale, I was almost worried.

"You okay?" I asked.

She nodded, and figuring I might as well get it everything out there, I went on to tell her the other thing we found, the GPS tracking device on her car.

I finished by saying, "Best we can tell, he used the GPS to make sure he only showed up when you were gone."

She gave me a confused look. "Who?"

"The guy you were house-sitting for."

"Mister Parker? But I never met him."

"Not true," I told her, thinking of the douchebag. "Remember the property manager? Best I can tell, that was him."

"How do you know?"

"I met the guy." I went on to tell her about the times I'd talked to him, and how he'd offered me girls of the paid variety.

"Oh my God," she said. "So *that's* why you thought I was some kind of hooker?"

I shook my head. "No. I thought that because I was stupid. I should've known better."

"Oh stop it," she said. "Knowing that, I can see why." She bit her lip. "And now, he has footage of me? In bed?"

"We don't know that for sure," I told her. "We ripped everything out. Bishop's gonna check out the system, see what he can learn. If there's something there, he'll find it."

She closed her eyes. "Oh my God," she groaned, before opening her eyes again. "So Bishop might see it?"

"Hey." I squeezed her hand. "He's just looking at the technical side, for connections, download history, stuff like that."

"You sure?" She paused. "I guess I shouldn't complain about it." She gave a humorless laugh. "Cripes, for all I know, everyone will be seeing it."

"We don't know that," I told her. "For all we know, the guy never downloaded the footage. And if that's the case, we'll just delete the files, trash the system. End of story."

"When will we know?" she asked.

"A couple days."

And if I was lucky, it would be even sooner.

CHAPTER 70

A couple mornings later, I opened the front door to see Amber, dressed in a long, formal evening gown. She was holding a bouquet of flowers and smiling up at me.

I glanced toward the front gate. Sure enough, it was open. Damn it. I needed to keep a better eye on that thing. I looked back to Amber and waited.

Her smile widened. "Well?"

"Well what?" I asked.

"Who am I?"

I gave her a look. "You don't know?"

She made a sound of impatience. "*I* know. I just need to know if *you* know." She struck a pose. "So go ahead. Guess."

Screw it. "You're Amber," I said.

"Well, yeah." She rolled her eyes. "Obviously. But what else am I?" When I said nothing, she lifted the flowers higher and started humming something that sounded vaguely like the wedding march.

The way it looked, she was either a bridesmaid or a bride. Either way, I decided to keep my mouth shut.

She sighed. "I'm a bridesmaid. If you were a girl, you would've totally known that." She peered around me and asked, "So, is Chloe here?"

She wasn't, actually. Thank God.

I shook my head. "She's at her grandma's."

"Oh." Amber frowned. "You got the address?"

I looked at her for a long moment. In a careful voice, I asked, "Why?"

"So I can audition."

I wasn't following. "For what?"

"To be her maid of honor. Duh."

I froze. Amber knew? How? Chloe didn't even know, not for sure, anyway.

I still had the engagement ring, and was planning to pop the question on Chloe's favorite holiday, Christmas Eve. It was less than a month away, and I could hardly wait.

The last day or so, I'd started carrying around the ring in my front pocket. Stupid or not, I couldn't stop looking at it. Already, I could practically see it on Chloe's finger, telling the whole world that she was mine, and was going to *stay* mine.

Always.

But things weren't official yet, so all I told Amber was, "I think you're getting ahead of yourself."

She nodded. "Exactly."

I wasn't following. "What?"

"I wanna be first in line. You know, before all the good slots get taken."

That actually made sense in an Amber sort of way. Scary.

"Just what have you heard?" I asked.

"Well, you know, my parents are really good friends with this super-exclusive jeweler guy. And he was over for Thanksgiving. We had a ton of people there." She poked me in the shoulder. "You should've come. There were like five kinds of pie, too. And I know how you love *that*."

Why deny it? "Well, I do like pie," I said.

"Anyway," she continued, "he mentioned that last month, he sold the biggest rock he'd *ever* seen to some super-famous guy who lives right here in Rochester Hills."

What could I say to that? Not a whole lot. I tried to play it off by saying, "Eh, it could be anyone."

But Amber was shaking her head. "Nope. Because I asked him, 'Is it a super-famous hot guy with tattoos?' And *he* said, 'Sorry, that's confidential.' So of course, I *knew* that if it *weren't* some super-famous hot guy with tattoos, he would've just said, 'No. It was a regular guy.' So I *knew* it had to be you." She smiled. "See?"

"Uh…" I looked past her. "Look who's here. Bishop." And he really was, too. Thank God. He'd just pulled into the driveway and was getting out of his car.

Amber whirled around and called out to him. "Hey Bishop! Guess who *I* am?"

Taking his time, he strolled up to us and gave Amber a good, long look. "You don't know?" he said.

She made a sound of frustration. "Guys – they don't know anything." She turned back to me. "You never answered my question."

"There was a question?"

"Yeah. The address where Chloe's at. Do you have it?"

I shook my head. "Nope."

It was actually true. From Thanksgiving, I knew where Chloe's grandma lived, but as far as the exact street-address, I didn't have it on me, and I sure as hell wasn't going to track it down for Amber, especially considering her big audition plans.

Amber frowned. "Oh, poo. If I don't catch her now, I'll have to wait like two whole weeks."

The way I saw it, this was *good* news. "Why?" I asked. "You going somewhere?"

"Yeah." She smiled over at Bishop. "Hey, Bish, you wanna come?"

He hated being called Bish. And for some reason, that made me smile.

"That depends," he told her. "You going to a gun show?"

"No." Her brow wrinkled. "We're going to the Hamptons."

He shrugged. "Eh, I'd better pass. But thanks for the invite."

"You sure?" she said. "Because they *might* sell guns there."

I spoke up. "You know what? You should discuss it over lunch."

Bishop's jaw tightened. "I already ate."

"But *I* haven't," Amber said. She glanced down. "And look, I'm already dressed up."

He glanced down at her dress. "Yup. You sure are."

She grabbed his elbow. "We should probably go someplace fancy." She gave his jeans a quick glance. "I know *you're* not dressed up. But I'm super-dressed up, so it evens out." She looked to me and said, "Right?"

I nodded. "Right."

As I watched, Amber practically dragged him back to his own car. I felt myself smile. Over the last couple of months, he'd given Chloe so much grief that he deserved at least *some* back. Before getting into the driver's seat, he turned in my direction and mouthed, "You dick."

Yes. I was. Just like my brother. Go figure.

CHAPTER 71

Later that night, Chloe and I had something to celebrate. Whatever footage those cameras had picked up, it was gone now, destroyed for good, electronically *and* physically, thanks to my favorite sledgehammer.

Best of all, Bishop had confirmed that none of the footage had been downloaded, which meant that when we destroyed the system, we destroyed everything. No one – except for me – was going to see Chloe pleasuring herself any time soon.

We were sitting in the hot tub when I turned to her and said, "I wish I could've seen it."

"Seen what?" she asked.

"That bedroom scene." I gave her a nice, long look. "I was liking how that sounded."

She probably would've blushed, except her skin was already pink from the steaming water. The corners of her mouth lifted. "Oh stop it."

"I'm serious." I reached over to stroke her thigh. "Maybe you'll act it out for me sometime?"

She smiled. "Maybe."

It wasn't a maybe. It was a yes. I could see it in her eyes, which made me a very happy guy. Then again, I was always happy these days. Funny what could happen when you found the girl of your dreams.

About that other house, Chloe never returned, not even once, in spite of the fact that it was located on just the other side of our fence. At the thought, I had to smile. *Our* fence. *Our* house. *Our* life together. I was liking the sounds of all that, too.

About Chloe's car, I got it up and running again, and moved it to my place, and then tried like hell to keep her from driving it. What I *really* wanted was to get her something new, but she wouldn't hear of it, telling me it was too much.

That's what *she* thought.

For now, I let it slide, because the way I saw it, soon, stuff like that wouldn't matter. My money would be her money, too. And from what I'd seen so far, it would be in very good hands.

In the last couple of days, we'd also confirmed that my initial hunch was right. Chloe wasn't just the house-sitter. She was the sucker-in-waiting.

Apparently, the couple – going by the name of Mister and Mrs. Parker – didn't even own the place. They'd been renting it the whole time and owed a shit-load of money to the wrong people, including some shark in Detroit who specialized in high-interest loans.

We were still in the hot tub discussing it when Chloe wondered out loud why the "Parkers" had paid her anything at all.

"They needed you to stick around," I explained. "You were the fall girl, the one who'd pay the price when the bills came due."

"But I didn't have any money."

"I'm not talking about money," I said. "Think about it. The Parkers give you this wad of cash, which they're probably planning to steal right back anyway. Then later, when someone comes looking for the *big* money, they're long gone. But you're not."

"But that night, I told that guy I wasn't Mrs. Parker."

"Yeah," I said. "Because nobody lies when they're about to get their legs broken."

"But they would've found out eventually," Chloe pointed out. "I mean, let's consider the worst-case scenario. Let's say they killed me–"

My heart clenched. "No. We're not saying that, even as a what-if."

"But the point is," she continued, "those guys would've found out pretty quick that I was just someone staying there."

"Yeah. But so what if it's the wrong person? You were living there, taking care of the dog, handling all their stuff. It would be easy for someone to get the idea the Parkers wouldn't want to see anything bad happen to you."

See, that's where I was different from the Parkers. Because if something bad ever happened to Chloe... I shook my head. I wasn't even going to think about it.

Instead, I focused on keeping her safe while things settled down. For me, that included driving her back and forth from work. If I had my way, soon, she wouldn't be working at all, unless it meant she was working for me.

I didn't trust a lot of people, but I trusted her. And I liked the idea of her keeping an eye on the numbers. One thing I knew for sure, if she had an agreement, she'd sure as hell stick to it.

Things were rocking along pretty good until maybe a week later when I pulled into the restaurant parking lot to pick up Chloe, and saw something that made me pause, and not in a good way.

It was Amber's car.

The way it looked, she'd cut her vacation short.

Damn it.

CHAPTER 72

I walked into the restaurant and stopped short at the spectacle in front of me. Near the waitress stand, Amber and Brittney were wrestling around on the restaurant floor. Their clothes were stained. Their hair was wild. A crowd of guys were cheering them on.

On the sidelines, I spotted Chloe, along with that Shaggy guy who, a few weeks earlier, had tried to video me as I beat the shit out of my own car. Now, just like before, he was holding out his phone, capturing the action.

I looked to Brittney and Amber. There was some action alright. I saw shoes and arms – and yeah, a lot of blonde hair, flailing all over the place.

As I watched, Amber grabbed a squirt-bottle of ketchup and aimed it at Brittney's face. Just in time, Brittney shoved aside Amber's hands, and a geyser of ketchup streamed upward, raining down on both of them and splattering the nearest spectators.

Some guy near the front said, "Somehow, I thought this would be sexier."

"Got that right," another guy said.

I had to agree. The whole thing was surprisingly unsexy. What *was* that in Brittney's hair? Blueberry syrup?

Suddenly, another guy bellowed out, "What the hell is going on here?" I looked to see Chloe's boss wade into the action. The crowd booed as he separated Brittney from Amber and positioned himself direction between them.

I wasn't booing. The way I saw it, better him than me.

I made my way toward Chloe and placed a hand on her elbow. She turned and gave me a smile, looking amused as hell.

Like always, I couldn't help but smile back. "So," I said, "How was *your* day, honey?"

She glanced toward Brittney and Amber, who'd been hustled to opposite sides of a long booth a few feet away. "Eh, same ol', same ol'," Chloe said.

Suddenly, Amber called out, "Lawton! Yoohoo! Over here!"

I turned to look.

"Have you heard?" Amber said. "I'm gonna be a bridesmaid!"

I froze. I shouldn't have been surprised, but that didn't mean I was happy about it. I glanced at Chloe. The way it looked, she didn't know what to say.

I knew what I wanted her to say – yes.

But it wasn't supposed to be here. It was supposed to be someplace nice, like under the mistletoe or in front of our very first Christmas tree. I wanted it to be special, something that Chloe would never forget.

I turned back to Amber, and felt my gaze narrow. It suddenly hit me that she was wearing the same formal dress that she'd been wearing on my doorstep for her "bridesmaid audition."

Until now, I hadn't noticed, with all the food-goo and what-not.

"Oh c'mon," Amber said. "It's not like it's a big secret or anything."

I looked down to the floor and gave a slow shake of my head. It was *supposed* to be a secret, or at the very least, it was supposed to be a surprise. But you know what? It *would* be a surprise, because I had the ring, and I had my girl.

And screw it, I wanted the whole world to know it.

I turned to face Chloe. I reached out, taking both of her hands in mine. Slowly, I sank to my knees.

Around us, the restaurant had gone completely silent. I looked up, looking deep into the amazing eyes of the girl I loved.

"Chloe," I said, "this isn't exactly the way I had it planned, but it doesn't change the way I feel. I love you more than life itself…"

A different female voice cut through the crowd. It was Brittney yelling out, horror-movie style, "Lawton, noooo!"

I ignored her and focused on the only girl who mattered. "Chloe," I said, "will you marry me?"

Her cheeks were flushed, and her lips were parted. The way it looked, she was having a hard time catching her breath.

And then, she smiled that wonderful smile of hers. And even before she said it, I knew exactly what her answer would be. Still, it was music to my ears when spoke in a voice that was almost too breathless to be heard. "Yes."

And then, she threw herself into my arms and kept on saying it. We tumbled together onto the floor, not caring where we were, or who was watching, or for that matter, whether we were covered in ketchup or blueberry syrup.

She was mine. Really mine.

Finally.

EPILOGUE

Three months later, I was standing in a very different place, waiting for the girl I loved. Next to me, stood Bishop, dressed in a tux that wasn't much different from my own. He looked surprisingly happy, and not only for me.

It was because he'd finally done it. He'd finally taken my advice and tracked down the one girl he'd lost all those years ago. And if I wasn't mistaken, I'd be serving as *his* best man in the not-too-distant future.

I looked out, scanning the crowd, wondering how it had gotten so big, not that I was complaining. As long as I had Chloe, everything and everyone else here was just a bonus.

In the front row, I spotted Chloe's grandma, who was now working for me, even if she didn't realize it. Within the last few months, I'd replaced her old envelope-stuffing job with something better, a *new* envelope-stuffing job for ten times the money and products she got a real kick out of.

In truth, I'd have paid her a hundred times her salary, without any work required, but just like her granddaughter, Grandma Malinski had a real independent streak, which meant that charity of any type was off the table.

She was still living in the same guest cottage, but things were looking up all-around. Loretta, the stepmother from hell, was also working for me, not that she knew that.

These days, Loretta is the official taster for a brand-new food magazine that reviews all kinds of crazy stuff – like fried rat and fish sperm, to name just a couple.

Loretta might not realize it, but I pick the foods personally and keep her travelling all the time, which means, surprise, surprise, she couldn't make it to our wedding, and more importantly, she's not around to hassle Josh.

I glanced over at Josh, standing a few feet away in a smaller tux of his own. He looked good. And best of all, he looked happy. I was glad to see it.

We'd invited him to live with us, but to our surprise, he turned us down, even after we offered to move across town, so he didn't have to change schools.

I still remember what he told us. "With Loretta gone, things are actually pretty nice. And besides, Grandma really likes it there."

Well, I couldn't argue with that. And neither did Chloe. So instead, we made it a standing offer. If Josh ever said the word, we'd be there in fifteen minutes to pick him up, no matter what anyone else might say about it.

I took another look around. There were lots of people, but only one I was dying to see.

From the back of the church, I heard music, not the same tune Amber had been humming, but one that was leading up to the main event.

A moment later, Amber started walking slowly up the aisle in a bridesmaid dress that didn't look that much different from the one she auditioned in. As it turned out, Chloe couldn't quite bring herself to say no, especially when Amber started chasing Bishop around like a kitten chasing a wounded wildebeest.

Amber was smiling like this was the most fun she'd had in a while. Or maybe she was just glad to see the end of Brittney, who'd moved to L.A. to pursue a film career after the whole catfight video went viral, thanks to footage from that Shaggy guy.

And then, there was the footage of me proposing. That went viral on steroids, which meant that if I wanted the whole world to know that Chloe was mine, well, I definitely got my wish.

About the restaurant, Chloe didn't work there anymore, and neither did her boss, who'd gotten fired for a whole slew of things, including screwing Brittney in the back office while a post-football game riot broke out in the main seating area.

As far as Chloe's non-waitressing career, it was really taking off. Turns out, she'd found a great use for her accounting degree – keeping an eye on all our money, professionally and personally. And as much as we have, it's a full-time job.

As my sister, looking happier than I'd ever seen her, started walking slowly up the aisle, I snuck a quick glance at Lauren Jane, who was slouched near the back of the church. She was scowling down at her cell phone, looking sulky as hell.

I knew why. Chloe had flat-out refused to make Lauren Jane a bridesmaid, no matter how much begging or threatening went on, from Lauren Jane *or* Loretta.

I could be wrong, but I had sneaking suspicion it was the crotch-grabbing that got Lauren Jane booted, especially after she tried to pull those moves one more time *after* Chloe and I were engaged.

After the final bridesmaid reached the front, the music changed to the melody that I'd been dying to hear for months.

A moment later, there she was, on the arm of her dad, who at last night's rehearsal dinner had the misfortune to sit across from the wedding planner, a lady named Daisy who happened to be from Georgia. As of this morning, Chloe's dad was still saying "y'all."

As for Chloe's mom, she was a no-show. But the way it sounded, that's about what Chloe expected. And if it made her sad, I wasn't seeing any signs of it.

I watched, utterly hypnotized as Chloe practically floated down the aisle, looking almost as happy as I felt. There were hundreds of people here, but I only had eyes for one. And the way it looked, the feeling was mutual.

Her gown was white and hugged her tight curves in all the right places, while somehow managing to look almost innocent – a regular girl-next-door, which of course, had a ring of truth to it.

By the end of the night, I vowed, she wouldn't be feeling so innocent after all, because I was going to rock her world in every possible way.

Always.

THE END

ABOUT THE AUTHOR

Sabrina Stark writes edgy romances featuring plucky girls and the bad boys who capture their hearts.

She's worked as a fortune-teller, barista, and media writer in the aerospace industry. She has a journalism degree from Central Michigan University and is married with one son and two kittens. She currently makes her home in Northern Alabama.

ON THE WEB

Learn About New Releases & Exclusive Offers
www.SabrinaStark.com

Follow Sabrina Stark on Twitter at
http://twitter.com/StarkWrites

47238980R00214

Made in the USA
Middletown, DE
21 August 2017